B2 4/29/88 17.95

FIC
MIL
W

D0116949

$17.95

DATE			

THREE
RIVERS

THREE RIVERS

Carla J. Mills

ST. MARTIN'S PRESS • NEW YORK

Design by Jeremiah B. Lighter

Library of Congress Cataloging-in-Publication Data

Mills, Carla J.
  Three Rivers / by Carla J. Mills.
    p. cm.
  ISBN 0–312–01522–4
  I. Title.
PS3563.I42295T5 1988
813'.54—dc19   87–27110

First Edition

10 9 8 7 6 5 4 3 2 1

To Mom and Dad with love and gratitude

Three Rivers

CHAPTER

1

THE TRAIN LEFT the snow behind and chuffed across the dry brown plain, trailing sparks and black smoke. Doreen Anderson, absently pushing a straggling lock of hair under a pin in the knot at the back of her head, looked thoughtfully out her soot-grimed window. A large tan ball of weed rolled away from the track in the wind of the train's passing. Ahead, in the distance, a church steeple, made small by the backdrop of mountains, marked the town of Jamesville, Wyoming Territory. Doreen glanced at her aunt, who was dozing, then rubbed a small clean circle on the glass so she could see better. The soot felt gritty against her fingertips.

Beyond the glass, dun-colored antelope with sharp black horns lifted their heads from grazing for a moment. A tart scent began seeping into the car. Doreen's thoughts sped ahead of the train. A new life lay ahead, just beyond Jamesville. The past month had been so busy, what with selling the rooming house and packing and saying good-byes, that she had had no time

1

to wonder about that life. Now questions crowded her mind. What did Three Rivers Ranch, Wyoming Territory, look like? What kind of people lived in this God-forsaken land? Were they as wild and dangerous as the country? Did Indians attack often? Did Three Rivers have many neighbors? Were there any young women nearby? What was Bill Haycox like, the neighbor who had written he would meet them at the station? Would she recognize him from the description in his letter? Would he even be waiting? Snow in the pass had delayed the train almost a full day.

Doreen shook herself. It was too late to wonder; she had committed herself to this new life. Anyway, no place could be as savage as the newspapers and penny-dreadfuls said Wyoming was. This was 1878, after all. But life in Wyoming Territory would be very different from life in Chicago. She was so tired of scrubbing walls and floors, of evading improper proposals, of much-patched dresses and too little to eat. Almost anything would be an improvement. She ran her hand caressingly along the sleeve of her new camel's hair traveling dress, her first new dress in six years. Indirectly, Uncle Jacob had made that, too, possible. She owned a ranch now. Doreen looked affectionately at her sleeping aunt. Cary had willingly agreed to come live with Doreen in the Wyoming wilderness, but she had refused to take a share of the property in no uncertain terms.

Doreen remembered the day the letter from Jacob Anderson's lawyer arrived, informing her of her inheritance. She had immediately offered her aunt a home on the ranch and a share of the property. Cary had taken the letter from her and read it carefully, then walked to the rooming-house window. She had looked out at the street for a long, silent moment. "Jacob Anderson was a tight-fisted old buzzard I never could abide," she had said finally, turning. Her tone had shown her dislike even more than her words. "I'll be pleased to live with you, Doreen, but I won't touch a share of Jacob's property. It would be hypocrisy." Her mouth had thinned into a hard line and she had turned back to the view of the narrow muddy street outside the window. "I still don't see how he could leave you, his only relative, in dire straits just because you're female." She had sighed. "Still, though he wouldn't help you when he was alive, he's helped you now. Apparently he considered leaving his life's work outside the family a worse crime than leaving it to a female." She had given Doreen a tentative half smile then. "Now you can have the nice things I couldn't afford to give you."

The train slowed. Cary stirred in the seat, breaking into Doreen's thoughts. She shook her aunt's shoulder.

"It's not far now, Aunt Cary. I see the church. Time to wake up and start getting ready." Doreen smoothed her hand over her red-brown hair and felt the silky braided knot at the nape of her neck to be sure every hair was now in place. First impressions were very important, and they would need Bill Haycox's help. They would need it badly. She settled her bonnet, tied it, and stood to get her portmanteau, only to have someone coming down the aisle run into her from behind. She whirled, blazing with indignation, and snapped, "Why don't you look where you're going!" She looked up, and up, to meet light-gray eyes crinkled with laughter.

One of the other passengers smothered a chuckle. The gray-eyed cowboy swept off his battered hat and made a small bow.

"Beggin' to differ, ma'am, but it was you got up sort of sudden-like." His voice was a soft drawl. He lifted a lock of sandy hair away from his forehead. "I won't hold it against such a pretty lady, though, and if you'll just point out your bag, I'd be tickled to get it down for you. Bags get mighty dirty up in that rack, with the soot and dust and all comin' in."

Doreen seethed. Not only would he contradict a lady, but she sensed that, inside, he was still laughing at her. She looked him up and down coolly, the kind of stare that always stopped boarders in their tracks. Red-blond hair and tanned face, blue flannel shirt and faded denims, square-toed brown boots, a dark-handled gun in a worn holster, a sheepskin jacket slung carelessly over one shoulder, and an impudent grin. The cowboy stood still for her inspection and she sensed he refrained from laughing out loud only from courtesy. She looked up at the baggage rack, a good stretch for her five feet two, then at the cowboy, who must be nearly a foot taller. The conductor had put her bag up there and it was going to be difficult to get down, unless she exposed her limbs and climbed onto the seat. On the other hand, she hated to ask anything of this impertinent, laughing man. However, if she didn't let him help, he would surely stand right there and watch her struggle. She just knew he would! And if she slipped and fell, she could just see that cowboy arranging to be underneath. She swallowed her pride and looked up into the tanned face. "If you would be so kind, sir," she said finally, as coldly

4

as anger and embarrassment permitted. She thought the corner of his mouth twitched.

Laughing at me, is he? she raged inside. Frontier barbarian! Cow poker! Her thoughts snapped and crackled like lightning, but she kept her fury from her face.

The cowboy set her bag on the worn red carpet, made another small bow, and continued on his way toward the next car. In spite of herself, Doreen watched him, intensely aware of the controlled power in every movement of his lean body. At the door, the man turned, gave her a jaunty salute, and left the car.

Doreen's cheeks burned. He knows! He knows I watched him! And Doreen grew even more embarrassed, because staring at a man as she had done was most improper. She had never done such a brazen thing before. She looked anxiously at the passengers sitting between her place and the door just closing. They had returned to their newspapers, or knitting, or child-tending, or to the view outside the window.

"That one didn't fall at your feet," Cary Williams said dryly.

Her remark was very irritating. Doreen had not had much chance to have men "fall at her feet" since her parents died and she had had to leave the big house on Lake Michigan. Her life since then had been full of work and strictly ineligible men who had either dubious ethics or no visible means of support. Now she was twenty-five and too old to have men "falling at her feet," as Cary knew very well.

Doreen bent to pull the portmanteau closer to the side of their seat. Well, at least I have the ranch to keep me busy in my spinsterhood, she thought with some asperity.

The train's bell clanged, the clickety-clacks from the wheels came farther and farther apart as the train approached the station. Doreen smoothed her skirts, sat down in the window seat again, and leaned toward the glass. A small cluster of clapboard buildings bordered a narrow, rutted dirt street not far ahead. At the near end of the street, a gray building with open barn doors might be the livery stable. Across the ruts from it stood the tiny, very white, very new church, almost over-balanced by its proud steeple. Beside the church, and conveniently near the station platform, sat the freight office. As the train slid up to the platform, the backs of the buildings beside the track blocked the far side of the street from view. Early morning sun glared down on the little town, a harsher light here than in the East, mercilessly picking out the weathered wood, the worn platform steps, the cracked window in the crude passenger shelter, the barren limbs of a single cottonwood beside the track. Doreen sighed and straightened.

Cary Williams briskly pulled on her gloves and smoothed them along each finger. "Don't make snap judgments, Doreen. Jamesville's not what we're used to, but we're not used to much. It's just different. The ranch is yours, free and clear. Whatever it's like now, we can make it home." Cary stood and brushed dust from the folds of her serviceable serge traveling dress. "You'll have experienced help. Mr. Haycox's letter told you that. You may even be well off." She met Doreen's eyes. "Remember what Clarence Dinnig said before we left about the price of beef continuing on up? And if the worst happens, and the price drops like a stone, there's still land to grow our own food. We won't have to go hungry anymore."

Doreen's mouth tightened as she remembered the hungry times.

Cary squeezed her hand. "I'll always be deeply grateful that you wanted to share your good fortune with me, Doreen," she said very quietly.

The train had come to a full stop. Doreen let her face show her love, which was all propriety allowed, though she ached to give her aunt a powerful hug. Cary scooped up the small suitcase and moved toward the door. Doreen followed, struggling to carry the portmanteau and at the same time hold her wide skirts discreetly down as they brushed against the seats in the car. No one else seemed to be getting off.

The women stepped down onto the platform just as a gust of wind with the bite of winter still in it whipped across the bare wood, forcing them to draw their capes closer around their necks. Doreen half-closed her eyes against the sun's powerful brightness. Cary set the suitcase down.

"It looks pretty bare, doesn't it?" She sounded less confident than she had just minutes before. She sighed, then brightened with effort. "Just think what it will be like not having to worry where our next dollar's coming from!"

A boxcar door slammed toward the back of the train and a horse whinnied. A dog poked around in the litter beside the saloon's back door, making small rustling noises. One horse of a team hitched to the rail in front of the general store lifted its head and looked toward the sound. The other horse nosed a puddle still hard with morning ice.

"It's so cold!" Doreen pulled her cape tight around her already-stinging ears. "Where's Mr. Haycox? Maybe he's gone home. Should we ask someone?"

But there was no one around to ask. The town looked like it was still asleep. Doreen tucked her neck even deeper into her collar. Her fingertips tingled with the cold, in spite of her new kid gloves.

She saw a man in a sheepskin vest and leather leggings leave the general store and stride toward the platform. He put a hand on the weathered wood and sprang up. He was middle-aged, lanky, with graying hair and a weathered brown face. He took off his hat and approached the women hesitantly. "Beg pardon, ladies, are you Miss Williams and Miss Anderson?"

"Who asks, sir?" Cary responded with a proud lift of her head.

Doreen admired her aunt's tone, cool enough to discourage forwardness, yet not so cool as to be rude. That tone had served Cary well in years of dealing with rowdy, uncouth boarders. Doreen wished she had met that sassy cowboy's impertinence with the same kind of dignity.

The man's weathered face broke into a welcoming grin. "I'm Bill Haycox, Miss Anderson. Blue Mountain Ranch. Jacob's executor."

Cary turned to Doreen. "*This* is Miss Anderson. I'm her aunt, Cary Williams." Cary's smile lit her face. "I'm so glad you waited, Mr. Haycox. The train is so very late . . ."

Haycox extended a large, work-roughened hand to each of the women. "We expect delays in the spring, Miss Anderson."

The horse they had heard earlier screamed and

hooves banged into the wooden side of its boxcar. They looked toward the noise. A regal black nose poked out of the boxcar door, then the head. The horse examined the scene, then backed out of sight. A man's voice, cursing, followed the retreat. The horse turned inside the car, making a great clatter. The man with it managed to drag it to the top of the unloading ramp, but the horse would go no farther. All the spectators could see was the horse's plunging head and shoulders, denim-clad legs, and, once or twice, a blue shirt-sleeve.

Haycox watched the action intently for two or three minutes, then took a step toward the rear of the train. "Sorry I mixed you two ladies up. I expected Jacob's niece to be older, Miss Anderson." He began walking sideways toward the boxcar, still keeping his eyes courteously on the women he was speaking to. "Please excuse me for a few minutes. I'm not meanin' to be rude, but I've been expectin' a friend for quite some time and that has to be his horse. There's only one horse like Tennessee." Haycox turned and trotted toward the battle, calling back over his shoulder, "I'll be back. Tennessee never did like ramps."

The horse in the doorway jerked at its reins and tried to back into the car again. Haycox grabbed its halter and the legs of the horse's owner disappeared into the boxcar. Haycox pulled at the horse's head. The women heard a sharp crack inside the boxcar. The horse jerked forward and walked down the ramp, looking indignant. The owner followed, tugging his hat brim down against the sun. He greeted Haycox with a mighty slap on the back, which Haycox returned, with interest. There was much shoulder pounding and laughter, then Haycox's companion saddled the black horse, tied a bedroll and slicker behind the saddle and a satchel on top of them, slipped a rifle into the saddle sheath, and dropped the horse's reins to the ground.

"They say a horse will stay still that way out here," Doreen ventured.

"We'll see," Cary answered dryly. "The men are both coming this way."

Haycox's companion followed him onto the platform, his head bent to converse with the shorter Haycox, sheepskin jacket snug across his shoulders, his face completely hidden by his hat. When Haycox stopped, his friend looked up, saw the women, swept off the hat, and bowed. Doreen had not needed to see the sandy hair and tanned face to know who Haycox's companion was. The cowboy's eyes met Doreen's, and crinkled at the corners.

Haycox drew his friend farther forward. "Ladies, meet Laramie Smith, a top rider and owner of Tennessee over there."

Mr. Laramie Smith held his hat in mock humility against his chest. "Your servant, ladies. Bill was tellin' me 'bout y'all takin' over Three Rivers Ranch. I knew Jacob, years ago, when I was foreman at Bill's place." His eyes flicked over their fashionable traveling dresses and feathered bonnets. The laugh-wrinkles deepened at the corners of his dancing gray eyes.

Doreen knew he was laughing inside at the tenderfeet in their city clothes, and women at that, who thought they were going to make a go of a ranch in the wilds of Wyoming. They had seen a lot of that attitude already. Doreen prepared to look haughty and aloof, but the corners of Mr. Smith's mouth twitched, making her decide against it. She turned away and studied the soft gray surface of the platform. She heard a low chuckle, then Smith began talking quietly to Haycox and Cary. Doreen resolutely shut out the slow, drawling voice.

A short time later, Smith said good-bye, swung into his saddle, and rode away. His horse walked fast, with a peculiar, rolling gait, its head nodding, its ears swinging in rhythm. Haycox caught Doreen's glance and the quirk of her mouth.

"Tennessee looks a little strange, I'll admit, but don't let Larry see you laugh. Tennessee covers miles better'n any other horse I've ever seen. Just the thing for a fiddle-foot like Larry."

Doreen knew "fiddle-foot" was not a complimentary description, yet when Haycox said it, his voice was warm and affectionate. A long, uncomfortable pause followed.

Cary pulled her cape closer and tucked her gloved hands into the warmth of her bent elbows. "Kind of brisk for late April, isn't it?"

A smile lit Haycox's otherwise homely face. "This is the high country, ma'am. We can get snow as late as June." He picked up the women's bags and started toward the platform stair, then set the bags down again and turned around, his face sobering. He stared intently at the worn wood ahead of his boots for a time, then looked Doreen in the eye. "Miss Anderson, there really ain't any point in you drivin' all the way out to Jacob's place. You aren't gonna want to stay when you hear what I have to tell you. Three Rivers Ranch is in bad trouble, rustler trouble. All the ranches are, but Three R gets the worst of it because it's lacked an owner's hand for more'n a year now, ever since Jacob got so sick." Haycox looked Doreen up and down as if assessing her.

"Sell the ranch and go back East, Miss Anderson. It's going to be tough sleddin' around here for people who know the ropes. For a tenderfoot, a young, female tenderfoot—" He grimaced and shook his head. "Asa Johnson of the Circle X and I'll pay you a fair price for the land and what stock we estimate is left, if you're willin' to take it in installments. The bank'll vouch for us." And he mentioned a sum.

Doreen shut her eyes tight for a moment to keep from crying, her dreams of a secure future shattered. She had no idea if the price he offered was fair, but clearly Haycox had no idea how much things cost back East. The amount he named would not even buy a house like the one Cary had sold, let alone furnish it. They would not even have enough for train fare back. They would be safe from rustlers, but they would starve. Doreen felt Cary's hand fleetingly caress her clenched one, then Cary began to gabble to Haycox about the weather and the town, giving Doreen the time she desperately needed to collect herself. Doreen licked suddenly dry lips and stared at the gray planks beyond the edge of her skirt, already regretting the euphoria that had prompted her to talk Cary into buying new wardrobes for them both. If she sold Three Rivers now, they'd have to hire out as servants, waiting on and cleaning up after strangers. It would be worse than the rooming house, but neither of them had the training for any other sort of work. With the ranch, they'd at least have a place to grow their own food. Doreen straightened, as much to stiffen her own resolve as to convince Haycox she could not be persuaded to leave.

"I have no home to go back to, Mr. Haycox," she

said firmly. "We sold everything before we came. I intend to make Three Rivers pay, sir."

Doreen thought she saw a glimmer of admiration in Haycox's eye, but his gruff words gave no encouragement. "Life is rough here, Miss Anderson, rougher than you can imagine."

Doreen shook her head. "I doubt it, sir. I've survived running a boardinghouse in Chicago for eight years and if there's a low life I haven't met, I'd be surprised. I wasn't trained for that life either, Mr. Haycox."

Haycox hesitated, as if reluctant to say what came next. He cleared his throat and met Doreen's eyes frankly. "I didn't tell you the worst, Miss Anderson. There would've been no need if you'd decided to go back. One of your riders was murdered two days ago, shot in cold blood while he was out checking waterholes."

Doreen felt the bottom fall out of her stomach. "Murdered?" she repeated in a shaking voice.

Cary's face went white.

"Murdered. I was blunt, Miss Anderson, but I have to make you see the danger you'll be in. Keepin' the ranch out of rustler hands is going to be a life-and-death contest." His sharp eyes pinned her. "Could you send men out to work every day, knowin' some of them may die?"

Cary shut her eyes, took a deep sobbing breath, and pressed her fingers against her lips. Haycox turned to her sympathetically.

"I'm sorry, Miss Williams. You've come a long way to hear such bad news. I'd've written you not to come, but I didn't get through the books to see how bad things were till after you were on your way. And, as I said, the murder happened only two days ago, too late to tell you." He took a deep breath, then continued briskly. "The train'll be here an hour or more, loadin' wood and freight. Have some breakfast, think about what I've told you. Three Rivers is no place for beginners."

Doreen glanced at her aunt's white face. Cary had spent too many hard and bitter years caring for invalid parents, then struggling with their debts; when those were finally settled and a life of her own seemed possible, Cary's sister had died, leaving Doreen in Cary's care. Doreen, a suddenly penniless seventeen-year-old, at first could not believe her moneyed life was over forever. But it was most definitely over. Cary had had to turn her home into a boardinghouse so the two of them could eat. Doreen smiled tenderly, remembering those years. Money had been scarce, but love had been plentiful.

Doreen licked her lips nervously. The ranch offered them a chance to be warm and dry and to eat regularly. Perhaps it would eventually make enough money to let them return to Chicago and the life and friends of days when her parents were alive, but that could no longer be counted on, and Doreen suddenly realized how much she had been counting on it. She swallowed her fear. There must be sheriffs or some sort of law out here to protect women and the innocent from murderers and outlaws. She tried to make her voice sound firm. "I think you've misinterpreted my aunt's reaction, Mr. Haycox. We won't give up, not before we even start."

"You don't seem to realize the danger."

Doreen lifted her head proudly. "You've warned us.

We'll take the risks and trust we can learn 'the ropes,' as you put it, faster than we go bankrupt."

Haycox was not convinced. He scuffed his boot across the dusty platform. "Take your hour to think about it anyway." He hesitated a moment. "If we don't break that gang, most of us ranchers will be on our way to the poorhouse by fall. There won't be any money left to buy you out."

Doreen put all the conviction she could summon into her voice. "Thank you for your concern, Mr. Haycox, but we're staying."

"We have nothing to go back to," Cary added. "We've burned our bridges."

Haycox stared at the women for a moment, then grinned and shook hands with both of them. "I don't know right now whether that's courage or foolhardiness, ladies, but I'm bettin' you'll make good neighbors." He paused and his grin widened. "And since we're gonna be neighbors, please call me Bill. Every time you say 'Mr. Haycox' I have to stop and think who you mean."

A little of Cary's anxious stiffness eased away. She smiled. "All right, Bill."

Haycox turned and motioned down the street. "There's a boardinghouse beside the livery stable. Sarah serves a good breakfast. While you eat, I'll see to your trunks. You did bring more than just that?" He nodded toward the two bags sitting on the platform.

"Two trunks," Cary replied.

Haycox escorted the women to the boardinghouse and introduced them to Sarah James, then went back for the trunks. Mrs. James led them to a long, narrow

15

room at the back of her house, next to a huge kitchen. The dining room held one very long table with a bench on either side and a battered sideboard.

Mrs. James waved at the recently scrubbed table. "The men ate more'n an hour ago, so you'll have the dining room to yourselves. Just as well, too. They're a rough lot for ladies such as you." And Mrs. James disappeared into the kitchen to cook them her standard breakfast.

Cary and Doreen exchanged amused looks. "Too rough for ladies such as us," Cary whispered.

Doreen giggled, then sobered. "We *are* still ladies, Aunt Cary. Aren't we?"

"Ladies?" Cary frowned. "I don't know anymore. Your mother's friends wouldn't think so. 'Ladies' have money and blooded horses, jewels, and handsome men dancing attendance. We don't. We've washed laundry and cooked for strangers. Male strangers. Here we'll have half-broken wild horses, violence from what Bill says, and no time to be danced attendance upon. But we've always kept the proprieties. That's what makes a 'lady' by *my* definition."

Doreen smiled affectionately. "That's what I needed to hear, Aunt Cary." She slid onto the bench and tucked her handbag securely between her feet by habit. "Mr. Haycox is quite a surprise, isn't he? He's far more a gentleman than I expected a Westerner to be."

"People are people wherever they are, honey. My sister filled your head with too many silly notions about 'class' and 'status.' She took too well to your father's moneyed life."

"Well, at least that life taught me one useful skill for our life here: how to ride."

Cary snorted. "Sidesaddle. How much use is that on a half-wild horse? What good are the lessons in elocution, or deportment, or how to play the spinet, for that matter? What you needed was cooking and cleaning lessons, not some East Coast finishing school."

Doreen bridled. "I've done plenty of cooking and cleaning."

Cary reached quickly across the long dining table and laid her hand affectionately over Doreen's. "You have. You learn quickly."

The train was still loading when the women and Haycox were ready to leave town. Haycox handed them both up onto the high wagon seat and motioned toward the buffalo robes atop the load in the wagon.

"Wrap up, ladies. Mountain mornings are a lot colder than mornings back East. You'll freeze sitting here. There's a lunch under the seat and quilts, too, for keeping warm tonight, after the sun goes down." Haycox climbed into the wagon, took up the reins, and released the brake.

A few yards away, a man outside the saloon descended carefully onto the packed dirt of the road and peered at the slow-moving wagon. He waved an arm vaguely after it. "Haycox! Stop. I wanna talk to you 'bout water—"

Haycox looked over his shoulder. "Some other time, Whitly." He did not stop.

The blond man clamped a slender, elegant hand on the sideboard and stumbled alongside, trying to keep up. "Introduce me to the ladiesss, Bill." Slurred with drink though it was, the voice was unmistakably British.

Bill looked pointedly at the unwelcome hand, but

17

the Englishman did not remove it. Haycox stopped the wagon. "They *are* ladies, Sir Adrian. Not your sort at all. They're your new neighbors at Three Rivers. Introduce yourself some other day, when you're sober."

"Introdush me now. Must be prop—erly introduced. Beautiful ladiesss." The Englishman stepped closer and peered owlishly at the women. "Had a bad night, ladiesss. Lost a lot. Comfort myself with Scotch, you know?"

Haycox took advantage of the Englishman's preoccupation with staying on his feet to flick the horses into motion. Doreen looked back. Sir Adrian stood swaying in the center of the dusty street, looking after the wagon. A short dark man with a red brocade vest hopped down onto the street, gripped the Englishman's arm, and propelled him back toward the saloon. Bill cracked his whip above the horses' backs and muttered darkly under his breath. The horses picked up their pace.

Jamesville was soon hidden by folds and creases in the land. The silence in the wagon stretched tight.

Doreen broke the silence hesitantly. "You said we wouldn't reach the ranch until after the sun goes down, Mr. H— Bill?"

"Later than that, Miss Anderson. It's forty miles and we'll have to change horses at a road ranch halfway there. I usually stay overnight there, but they don't have provisions for ladies. I reckon it'll be nearly dawn before we get to Three Rivers."

"Dawn? It takes that long?"

"That long. You'll have to get used to bein' alone, Miss Anderson. Most people out here get to town maybe once every month or two in good weather, not at all in the winter."

Doreen swallowed. Stores, church, mail, people, would be very far away then. But perhaps that would be easier than her life the last eight years—here there would be no theater, no music, no balls to long for and be unable to attend. Doreen glanced at her aunt's thoughtful face. It's a good thing Cary and I are such good friends, she thought. She turned again to Haycox. "Tell me about the ranch, Bill."

Haycox shrugged. "I've told you all the important things. It's laid out and run pretty much like everyone else's. You'll have to see the land yourself, and the books, well, I hope one of you can keep accounts."

Doreen hated telling a stranger so much about their need, but she saw no other course. She had to have expert advice and Jacob had trusted Bill enough to make him executor. "I *have* to make that ranch pay, Bill," she finally forced out. "I can plan better the more I know. Besides," she added, "it sounds like we'll be all alone out there. Aren't there any other women?" Her voice cracked a little in spite of her resolve to get used to the idea.

Haycox shifted in his seat. "A few. There really aren't that many women in the whole territory. Maggie Johnson's probably the closest. She and Asa have five kids. Johnson's foreman, Carson Brown, has a wife, too. That's Circle X. Conrad French, of the Fishhook spread, is married, has two girls in their teens, but Fishhook's almost as far as Jamesville, even if you could go as the crow flies. Frank Wentworth of the Lazy R lost his wife just last winter. Has five boys, too. My wife, Ann, died six years ago, and we had only one boy, who's back East learnin' to be a lawyer. Your neighbor to the northwest, at the Rolling W— What women he has around you

19

ladies wouldn't want to know." Haycox's mouth twisted and he said nothing for quite some time, just tipped his hat back on his head and stared at the team's nodding heads.

"Sir Adrian Granscomb-Whitly." He let the name hang in the air for a while. "His English family sent him here to recoup embarrassingly huge gamblin' losses over there by makin' a fortune on the risin' price of beef. Another tenderfoot, ladies, though he's been here two years. He's unlikely to survive as a rancher through the summer. Too much gamblin' and too few waterholes." He cleared his throat. "You'll meet all your neighbors at the party before spring roundup. Party's at my place this year."

Conversation ceased after that. The tired women braced themselves against the jolting of the wagon and learned what they could of their new land by watching the frost-silvered landscape pass. The sun climbed, the horses' hooves no longer sounded like they were striking rock every time they touched the dirt track. The air warmed and the women put aside the buffalo robes. When the sun was high, Haycox stopped the wagon on the sunny side of a box elder grove so they could all stretch their legs and eat the cold lunch Sarah James had provided.

Early in the afternoon, the wagon's clatter startled a small group of antelope, which bounded away across the sage flats, white rump-patches flashing their alarm. Later Doreen saw a large, dark shadow drift across the face of the sun, turn lazily, and drift back.

"Eagle," Haycox said, noticing her interest in the bird.

Just before sunset they stopped at the road ranch

for fresh horses, then went on. The sun sank behind the bank of thin clouds that topped the mountains to the west and, one by one, then by twos, fours, and hundreds, the stars blinked on, dimmed only a little by the brilliance of the full moon. Doreen's sitting bones ached, her muscles burned from the effort of resisting the bruising rhythm of the wagon, her body cried for rest, yet the squeaking, jolting wagon allowed no rest. The night became agony. She wanted to cry with exhaustion and pain, but would not in front of a stranger.

As the sky grayed toward dawn, Haycox broke the long silence. "Look."

They had just crossed through a low pass in the mountains and were looking down on a wide basin ringed by more mountains and cut by three rivers. Several hundred yards from the nearest of the rivers, ranch buildings, sheltered from the wind by a wide band of cottonwoods and willow, spread red roofs in the gray light. Beyond the buildings, flats just turning green stretched from the trees to the foothills and the snow-covered mountains.

"On the bright side," Haycox said, as if continuing the discussion begun in Jamesville, "Three Rivers was a top ranch before Jacob got sick, and it can be again. The pass is low, the ranch house itself rarely gets snowed in like some on the higher spreads do, the grass is good, and you have a fortune in water rights. Three Rivers always has water, and water is like gold in the Territory." Haycox shook the reins and the horses started down into the basin. "Be another hour before we get there," he added.

The wagon track followed the bank of a river down to the basin floor. The willows at the water's edge showed the bright-yellow stems of spring and were beginning to show tips of green. The little river burbled under its thin shield of ice, a few birds twittered sleepily, disturbed by the passing wagon and the coming dawn. The horses crossed the river, the ice crunching under their hooves, the wagon wheels splintering the pieces they left. They plunged up the low bank on the other side and trotted through a grove of cottonwoods and box elder. The barn, and haystacks, and the rest of the buildings came into sight, and the horses made low eager sounds.

The wagon passed a fenced, empty pasture, a cluster of small, drooping buildings which Doreen's small experience of farms suggested might be chicken coops, and a smokehouse or wash-house. A long, low, gray barn sprawled across the dirt yard beyond. The first rays of sunlight shot over the mountain peaks and touched the paintless trim along the edge of the house roof with a pinkish glow. Then a raucous noise, like someone banging on sheet iron, shattered the dawn quiet. A door banged several times and a string of men, some still tucking shirttails into their denims, appeared at the east end of the ranch house, stepped up onto the porch, and lined up to use a basin and roll towel set out by the door. Doreen smelled bacon and sausage and coffee. Her stomach rumbled.

Haycox stopped the horses, set the brake, eased himself out of the wagon, and wrapped the reins around the hitching bar beside the porch. He looked up at the two women. "I know you're bone-weary, ladies, but it'd be best to meet your riders now. No point in delay, and the sooner they know you, the more useful they'll be to you. No one expected you to come." He grinned. "Some men are gonna lose their shirts. The odds of you comin' were reeeeal long." He stood patiently, waiting.

Indignation burned off some of Doreen's weariness. *They were* betting *we wouldn't come!* "Let's go settle the bets," she snapped, her voice far brisker than her movements. She climbed stiffly from the wagon before Haycox could give her a hand and stalked toward the kitchen door.

Cary sighed, her eyes following her niece. "Her temper's up. I'd better stay awake long enough to say hello, too, I guess."

Doreen was not sure afterward if there had been any benefit to the brief introduction. She remembered only the amazed looks the moment the riders saw her and the most unusual of their names—Tinker, Stinky, Diego, and Speck. Of these, only Diego's face stuck to a name. She had been too tired to eat. Haycox had carried their bags to the doors of their rooms in the west end of the house and had gone to the bunkhouse to get some sleep himself. Doreen fell asleep the moment her head touched the pillow.

CHAPTER

2

DOREEN STRETCHED herself awake and opened her eyes slowly. Sunlight poured through her window, brightening the rather shabby room. Dust motes danced in the light. Doreen sat up slowly and looked around. The bed posts were gritty with dust. The rug on the floor, though it must have been beautiful when new, was so worn that the pegged floor showed through the backing in places. The walls had not been papered but painted and had not been washed in years. Someone had made a gallant attempt to clean the windows, but they had apparently used a greasy rag, for the windows gleamed with oily swirls and were still fly-specked in many places. The bedding, however, looked and smelled clean and the pitcher and basin on the commode glistened.

"Men," Doreen said.

She rose, poured water from the pitcher into the basin, and splashed her face. She gasped with reaction to the cold. She removed a dress from her portmanteau, shook out the worst of the wrinkles, and hurried into it, then brushed her hair with the customary hundred strokes, wound it quickly and deftly into a bun on the back of her neck, and drew on a shawl. She gave herself a quick inspection in the spotted shaving mirror hanging on the bedroom door. Her hair glistened. Her eyes were bright. Her cheeks glowed pink from the effect of the cold room and the icy water. She was rested, clean, and in clean clothes, and she could take on the world.

Doreen hurried from her room toward the center of the house, glancing into four rooms as she passed, all bedrooms. Apparently Three Rivers had had children once. She reached the center of the house and a large parlor with doors opening out to the front and back porches. Through the open back door came shouting, cursing, the squeals of angry horses, and the thin acrid smell of dust. Cary stood in the opened front door, looking out at the mountains.

She turned back to the parlor and examined her niece, but her mind was elsewhere, for her eyes were troubled. "If you're still planning to get back to the kind of life your parents led . . ."

Doreen slipped an arm around her aunt's shoulders. "I'm not planning on it." She looked away, biting her lip. "I've put that away, beside my girlish dream of marrying a good man and raising a houseful of children."

"Doreen dear, you're not so old as that."

"Yes, I am. I'm twenty-five, Aunt Cary. It doesn't hurt as much as it used to." But it did still hurt. Doreen forced the sadness away and hugged Cary vigorously. "I'm truly glad you came along to help me."

Cary smiled, then sobered. "I'll do what I can. After all, you've helped me for eight years. But can we survive

25

in this lonely place?" Cary looked away and ran a fingertip along a nearby windowsill. She wrinkled her nose at the gray tip that resulted. She sighed and looked back at Doreen. "Two tenderfeet, and women at that, against powerful rustlers . . ." She shook her head rapidly, as if clearing her mind. "Bill has all the papers and accounts laid out in the office, waiting for you. Cookie allowed us to bring some biscuits and a pot of coffee out of the kitchen for you. And I mean 'allowed.' He was like a king dispensing favors."

The women turned from the mountains and crossed the parlor to the east hall. They paused a moment to look out the back parlor window. Horses were milling in the corral. Men on horseback forced the press of bodies away from a target horse. A moment later, a rope sailed out and settled over the tossing head. The captured horse squealed in indignation and jerked away from the rope. Then a large man seized the horse's halter and led it out of the corral to the farrier, who began his work. A rider in a sweat-soaked shirt sprang over the top rail of the corral and dipped himself a drink from the bucket standing near the side of the corral, then drank greedily.

"Shoeing time."

The women both started at the sound of Haycox's deep voice right behind them.

"Didn't mean to frighten you," Haycox said. "The horses get new shoes just before roundup. They've been barefoot all winter and don't take to being messed with. It's usually quite a show, the shoeing. You ladies should watch some after you've seen the books and heard how things are here."

He motioned toward the hall, then led them to the office, where he presented Doreen with the ranch books and the legal papers he had examined in his role as executor. The ranch had no debts, but it had slid far from good management during Jacob's long illness. Haycox made rough estimates of wages and maintenance, talked about the prices of beef and staples, pointed out some of the most common mistakes in ranch management, commented on the likelihood that Three Rivers and the Rolling W would come to blows over water, then leaned back in his chair and poured himself a fresh cup of coffee. He let the information sink in for several minutes before he leaned forward again and addressed Doreen earnestly. "You can see life's going to be tough around here, real tough. Even for people who've lived in the Territories a long time. We can hold our offer to buy open until after your spring roundup tallies are in. You may decide then that you're going to have to live too close to the bone if you stay on."

Doreen shook her head. "Thank you, Mr.— Bill, but no."

"I can't emphasize enough how tough things may get, Miss Anderson."

"We're staying," Doreen countered firmly.

Haycox studied his work-worn hands for a long moment before he spoke again. "In Wyoming, the climate is dry, the animals are fierce, and many of the human residents are fiercer. Though even the wildest of men only rarely raises a hand against a woman. The law is weak, and some places there isn't any law at all. Around here, the law belongs to the Englishmen. Your womanhood may keep you physically safe, but it won't protect your property. You'll see very few people other than your own riders except at roundups and dances. Those you do see will be very different from the people you've known before; Westerners don't talk the same, dress the same, or even think the same as people do back East. My son's shown me that. He's all Easterner now. You won't get to church much, because the nearest is the Methodist church in Jamesville. A Methodist circuit rider comes to the ranches sometimes, but he has a lot of ground to cover every year. A mail rider comes once a week when the pass is open, which means you may get no mail at all in the winter. Also, in winter, there will be just you two and the few riders who stay on all year. That's a very lonely time. If you don't plan well, you may even be very hungry before thawtime. If you need a doctor out here, you'd better have someone on the ranch that knows something about healin', because anyone who needs a doctor is gonna be dead before Doc Patterson could be found. You think you can handle all that?"

The recital only stiffened Doreen's resolve. "We're staying."

Haycox shrugged, and set his coffee mug on the document-littered desk. He cleared his throat. "McTaggert, your foreman, needs a strong hand and Jacob wasn't able to give that to him for quite a while. In addition, McTaggert's a woman-hater of the first water. But he has great respect for The Boss. If you let me and some of the other old-timers advise you and you tread carefully around his prejudice, McTaggert will probably work well for you. If not, you'll have to replace him." Haycox stared down at his hands again. "Sir Adrian, your neighbor on the northwest, will be a real problem. He bought the Rolling W while he was still in England. The ranch has little open water and in a bad year like this last, its wells go dry. He doesn't know what he's doing and he doesn't like advice from 'colonials.' He had an agreement with Jacob to water cattle from the Pinto summers, which you may as well continue, to avoid worse trouble. He's supposed to pay for the privilege, but you'll have to keep an eye on him. As I said, he has huge debts to pay off and he's piling up more with his gamblin'." Haycox paused to let the information sink in, then looked up and held Doreen's eyes with his own.

"I know this may be hard for you to swallow, Miss Anderson, but you're going to have to trust somebody to help you through the first year or two. It may sound pushy to say I'm the one to trust, because you've probably already guessed I wouldn't mind havin' this place and its water. For all you know, I might be one of the rustlers. But Jacob trusted me to manage the place after he died. And, if you want to take the time and trouble, you can check up on me with neighbors and with businessmen in town. I keep my word and I pay my debts."

"My uncle's trust is enough for me," Doreen said.

Bill's face crinkled into the huge grin all his wrinkles had promised. "Great! The roundup's scheduled to begin on my spread next week. In a roundup, we gather the cattle from each ranch in the district, sort them, brand them, and drive them back to their own range. We'll do the same in the fall, only in fall we drive a lot of four-year-old beef to the railhead. The roundup oughta begin here in two, three weeks. McTaggert's prepared well. You have a good bunch of regular riders, Miss Anderson, honest, good-natured, hard-working, and Mc-Taggert's already begun hiring for the season."

Someone knocked at the doorway. A swarthy man in a sombrero banded with silver came into the room.

"The wagon ees unloaded, Beel. California and I are going back to the bunkhouse."

"Thanks, Diego." Bill turned to Doreen. "I took the liberty as executor to stock up for you. When the roundup gets here, Three Rivers is gonna need a lot of extra food and supplies. And while I'm thinkin' of it, if some emergency comes up before then, like McTaggert actin' pig-headed, you can ask California for advice. Not publicly, of course. That's bad politics. But he's level-headed, smart, and quick. He won't lead you wrong."

Doreen swallowed, hesitated. Her hands twisted together. "Are there likely to be emergencies, Mr. Haycox?"

"Very likely, I'm afraid. Men get thrown, dragged, crushed under a falling horse, just in the normal run of things. But you'll also have to fight for the cattle and water that're yours, Miss Doreen. If you don't, someone else'll take them. Either way, men'll get hurt. Men will die, like I told you. Until the rustler gang's stopped, no one's safe. Not even women. I've just heard the rustlers ran a squatter and his family off their land at Fishhook. They hurt the woman and killed the man, just to use the squatter's shack for a while. The cattlemen's association is trying to identify the rustlers and get enough evidence to hang them, enough evidence to convince Territory officials, since the local law's no good. We've just hired a man to find that evidence. But until he can, you're on your own."

On our own. On our own. Against cattle thieves and killers. The thought beat in Doreen's head. She thought about the row of gray clapboard houses back in Chicago, the skinny trees, dusty flowerbeds, flaking paint. And the friends, friends who shared firewood or food,

30

knowing Cary and Doreen would do the same when they could; neighbors who lived so close she could hear them when they shouted at each other. Had a shabby rooming house really been worse than what Haycox promised? Doreen licked dry lips and watched her aunt. Cary, too, was involved in this decision. Was she also looking back at the rooming house and wishing they had not so lightly disposed of it?

Cary was plucking nervously at tired folds of skirt falling over her knees. "Will the rustlers attack us or just the cattle, Mr.— Bill?"

"Just the cattle, Miss Cary, unless you happen to surprise them herding off some beef or running brands."

Cary stood abruptly and took a brisk turn around the tiny office. She stopped for a long moment behind Doreen's chair, resting one hand on Doreen's shoulder. "It's your choice, hon."

Doreen straightened. The new life was worth the danger. "We've burned our bridges. Will you help us?"

Haycox nodded. "Just ask. Let's shake on it." He extended his hand.

But the gesture was never completed. A horseman galloped into the yard, thudded onto the back porch, and stumbled through the parlor. He burst into the office, pale, clutching his left shoulder, and panting. Haycox sprang to his feet.

"Speck and Tinker's been shot," the rider gasped. He noticed the two women for the first time and stopped in confusion. Bright blood seeped out between his fingers and ran slowly down the left side of his shirt.

Haycox had sprung to his feet. "The new owner and her aunt, Shadow," he snapped. "What happened?"

The rider sagged against the nearest wall. "Speck

31

said he and Tinker caught Rolling W riders pasturin' a big herd on our grass and got shot for tryin' to run 'em off. Tinker's dead."

Doreen gripped the edges of her chair and willed herself not to faint. A rider dead and two wounded, one of these right in the same room! They had been at the ranch only hours and already violence had come right to them. Doreen opened her eyes and got to her feet. The rider needed bandaging. Doreen scurried out of the office to find something, anything to bind the wound and stop the awful bleeding. Bill hurried outside, drawing Cary with him, to alert the riders in the corral and send them to bring Speck and Tinker in. Unable to find any medical supplies, Doreen finally tore up a clean sheet for bandaging, then hurried to the kitchen to tell Cookie to heat water. She cringed at the thought of looking at and tending a gunshot, but when the water was hot, she could delay no longer. For mercy's sake she had to take care of Shadow's wound. She returned to the office, carrying the bandage, the teakettle, and a basin. She found Shadow sprawled in the leather desk chair, looking very white. He had somehow struggled out of his double-breasted flannel shirt and had dropped into the chair, unclothed from his belt up.

Doreen froze in the doorway. She had never before seen a man who was not completely dressed. She felt weak and embarrassed. Shadow, already on the edge of unconsciousness, noticed her embarrassment and blushed red himself. Doreen felt ashamed. She must do something! Her mother had, after all, nursed many such wounds and worse during the late War, and she had sometimes spoken to Doreen about how it was done.

Doreen squared her shoulders, gritted her teeth, and marched across the room to the wounded rider.

Tinker and Speck were brought in as quickly as possible. Tinker was laid out in one of the spare bedrooms, and Diego and Stinky set to work at once on a rough coffin. Haycox motioned the riders who had carried Tinker in to leave. He stood for a time looking down at the dead man, then closed Tinker's eyes and gently laid a penny on each lid. His face hardened. "You're gonna have to get used to this. Tinker won't be the only man to die here this summer."

Doreen had no time to adjust to the shock. Diego washed the dead rider's body and dressed him in clean clothes from the saddle bundle Bill called a war bag. Only hours later six riders carried Tinker to the tiny cemetery beyond the garden. Haycox said a few words over the grave. Afterward, he walked with the women back to the porch, unwound the reins of his horse, and stood with one hand on the hitching rail. He scuffed the dry dirt underfoot with one toe. He spoke to Doreen, but he watched Cary.

"You're just gonna have to swallow that little incident, Miss Anderson. Without more witnesses, and a willing sheriff, the Rolling W goes free. You won't find the Englishman apologizing, either. He's an arrogant, half-soused, unmentionable word. He doesn't deal with us 'colonials' except across a card table."

Bill looked up and pointed toward the northeast. "My spread lies there. Your riders know how to reach me. If you need to send word, a man on a strong horse can make it in under two hours. This particular fight's

33

over. I have to get back to my own place now. I'll see you next week when the roundup starts. Don't forget to come to the party." He swung into the saddle and turned his mount toward the pass. He stopped and looked back at the women. "Don't think we're callous. Death is close all the time out here. If we took time out to mourn, nothin' would get done. There'd be no ranches. We care that Tinker's dead, we just don't stop livin' for it." He spurred his mount toward the banks of the Yellow River, just beyond the trees.

Three days later, a visitor in jodhpurs, riding a long-legged Thoroughbred, came down the road. Doreen was tossing scrub water off the front porch when he rode up. It was the Englishman, looking slenderer and blonder than he had in Jamesville. In addition to the jodhpurs, he wore tall shiny boots and an impeccably tailored riding coat. For a moment, Doreen felt again the pain of her parents' loss.

The man swung gracefully down and swept his hat from hair glistening with pomade. With a bow and a flourish, as if she were wearing a ball gown instead of an old skirt and damp shirtwaist with its sleeves rolled up above her elbows, he presented Doreen a bundle of hothouse roses. "In honor of your arrival in our country, miss." His voice was mellow, his words clipped. "I'm Sir Adrian Granscomb-Whitly, your neighbor to the northwest. Sir Adrian, if you please. I cannot accustom myself to your American informality of address." He watched Doreen touch the velvety rose petals appreciatively and his blue eyes twinkled. "Hothouse flowers are my hobby, miss, one of my few civilized pleasures in this abandoned land." Without invitation, Sir Adrian stepped up onto the porch. "I hear you ladies are from

Chicago. Have you started missing the music and theater and polite company of the city?"

"Yes, I miss them." Doreen thought with a pang of her parting from Amelia Webber that last evening in Chicago. Amelia, with her elegant carriage, standing outside Cary's shabby house, her freckled, laughing face framed by the rich dark fur of her cape. Amelia, whose friendship had survived Doreen's fall from wealth without damage. Doreen looked at the Englishman's cool patrician face and felt a strange reluctance to alter this polished Englishman's view of her by telling him she had been without that "music and theater" for nearly eight years.

"May I come in?" Sir Adrian asked.

Doreen remembered her manners and motioned him into the house. She and Cary had cleaned vigorously for three days; she had no reason to be ashamed to show even so polished a gentleman as Sir Adrian Granscomb-Whitly into the parlor. The parlor smelled of lye soap and lemon oil and floor polish. Wood furniture surfaces gleamed. The new wrangler, Luke, had beaten the scatter rug until its blues and reds lay clear. The upholstery on the parlor chairs had lost its layers of dust and grime. A vase of silk daffodils that had once stood on Doreen's mother's dressing table now brightened the table beside the door to the west wing.

Sir Adrian turned slowly, admiringly. His eyes slid politely past the mop that leaned against the doorjamb in the east hall and the bucket and pile of rags beside it. "Hmmm. Much improved. Jacob didn't spend any time on spit and polish himself."

"Doreen—" Cary entered from the east wing and stopped. She flushed pink, pushed her damp sleeves down to her wrists, and brushed perfunctorily at a smudge on her skirt. "I didn't know we had company."

The Englishman bowed with consummate grace. "Sir Adrian Granscomb-Whitly, Miss Anderson. I've come to introduce myself to you and to your charming niece."

Cary's manner chilled somewhat. "We met in town, sir. I'm Cary Williams. Doreen is the one you want to talk to." Cary nodded her head in Doreen's direction.

The Englishman looked nonplussed for a moment. "In town?"

"In town. You hung onto our wagon, insisting we be introduced immediately."

The Englishman flushed at the ice in Cary's voice, then relaxed. "Ah. I must have been in my cups. Had a big loss that night, a very big loss. I was comforting myself. Forgive me?"

How often has that boyish pleading worked for him before? Doreen asked herself. He certainly has the tone exactly right. She studied his face, but found no clue to whether his technique was natural or studied. "We aren't on any terms that would make that necessary, sir," she responded coolly.

The Englishman looked annoyed for an instant, then he smiled. "I see. Well, we soon will be. We are neighbors, after all. And it would be a pity for—three—cultured people such as ourselves to pass up opportunities for mental stimulation." He turned to Cary again. "You've come with Miss Anderson as a sort of chaperone?"

"You might say that," Cary said dryly. She glanced at Doreen. There was no reason to explain anything to this stranger. "It would hardly be proper for a well-bred young woman to live here alone."

Sir Adrian leered engagingly. "I know what you mean." He looked toward Doreen. "I came to apologize for that unfortunate incident along the Pinto the other day and tell you how it came about. I want us to be friends."

"Friends, sir?" Doreen flared. "Friends? When your riders kill mine? An explanation was due the moment you learned what had happened!"

For a moment Sir Adrian looked taken aback. He swallowed and his face took on a contrite expression. "A serious mistake was made, Miss Anderson," he soothed. "The men responsible for it have been sacked. I'll explain what happened if you're willing to take a little time from your labors to listen."

Doreen nodded and sank into a nearby chair. It felt good to get off her knees for a while. Sir Adrian sat next to her and waved a languid hand toward Cary. "If there's something you'd rather be doing, Miss Williams . . ."

Doreen's temper rose again. The arrogance of the man! "My aunt and I work together, Mr. Granscomb-Whitly," she told him in icy tones.

Sir Adrian's eyes narrowed for a second, then he smiled at them both. "I seem to be getting off on the wrong foot with you ladies. I don't mean to. It's a pleasure, as I have already said, to have as neighbors two lovely women who know and appreciate the finer things in life. Especially after a winter of seeing no women at all. There are only about a thousand adult women in the entire Territory, you know. But I'm sure you knew that before you decided to leave Chicago to come to a frontier outpost such as Three Rivers Ranch."

So he thinks the two spinsters from the city are husband-hunting, does he? Doreen's temper rose another two notches. She sat even more erect than usual. Cary's lips drew tight.

Sir Adrian rose and walked to the front window, holding his classically beautiful profile in just the right light to be best admired, apparently oblivious to the insult he had just delivered. When he returned his cool blue eyes to the women, Doreen thought his face smug.

Perhaps he relies on the beauty of his patrician profile to compensate female listeners for his insulting remarks, she fumed.

Sir Adrian continued. "Matters in the Territory have gone from bad to worse just in the two years I've been here. Rough and uncouth men have come into the area, bent on making a fortune from other people's cattle. In a word, outlaws are stealing mightily from our herds and killing the riders who try so valiantly to protect them. It's a very hard country for anyone, especially women used to the safety and comforts of city life."

Cary snorted, but she did not enlighten the Englishman about the "safety and comfort" of their life in Chicago.

Sir Adrian looked startled at her rude noise. He continued, but with less confidence in his tone. "I, myself, know of two young women like yourself, Miss Anderson, who married cowboys but returned to their parents in the city, unable to bear the danger, loneliness, and privation of life on a ranch so far from stores and churches and other aspects of the cultured life. And as I said earlier, outlaws are stealing and killing with impunity. Such savage criminality is far from a gently bred woman's understanding, nor should she have to deal with such things."

Doreen studied the Englishman's face. What *is* he leading to at such length? she wondered. Offering his protection? Or is he really saying that if we are "gently bred" we'll go and leave Three Rivers Ranch to a man's care? Her hands clenched in her lap. I know just what man he has in mind, too! He's also saying if we stay and fight the rustlers, we're not "gently bred" or ladies.

Doreen glanced at her aunt. Cary, as an outsider in this "business" discussion, was restraining her tart comments and turning pink in the process.

She's going to let him hang himself, Doreen thought with an entirely improper glee. This may be fun to watch.

Sir Adrian took a quick turn around the parlor and stopped before the women, feet apart, hands behind his back. "This last is very difficult to say, but now that I've explained about the rustlers, perhaps the facts will be clearer to you."

So we're dim-witted, too, are we! Doreen had all she could do to stifle a furious and very unladylike retort. I'll watch this performance to its end without any of the interruptions it so richly deserves, she promised herself. I *will!*

Sir Adrian picked an imaginary piece of lint from his jodhpurs. "We've come to the incident between my men and yours."

An incident! Doreen bit her tongue to keep it silent. An "incident" he says, as if he'd broken a window or injured one of our horses! If I were a man I'd— But she could not think of a punishment appropriate to the crime. I must keep silent until he's through. I *must* keep silent or he'll know we're not as stupid as he thinks and he won't tell us as much.

Sir Adrian noticed her inattention and cleared his throat discreetly and pointedly. Doreen focused widened eyes on him again, fluttering her lashes coquettishly. Sir Adrian continued. "I'm deeply sorry that a man of yours died. You see, ladies, Jacob sold me the land where the incident occurred just two weeks before he died. The land was to be mine upon payment of the agreed-upon price to his heir." Sir Adrian looked at Doreen, his blue eyes liquid with sympathy. He paused for a moment to let the liquid look take full effect, then went on. "I grazed my cattle on that land on the basis of that agreement. Your hands apparently didn't know of the agreement and rightfully attempted to chase my men away. My men, rightfully, protected my herd. This tragic misunderstanding is a direct result of rustler activity in the district." Sir Adrian, looking appropriately regretful, licked his lips, steepled his long, elegant fingers before his long, elegant nose, and stared down thoughtfully at the shining floor.

"You see, ladies, so much theft makes every rancher suspect every other rancher. Many of them have hired marksmen to ride with the other cowboys and guard the herds. I understand Blue Mountain has just brought in a hired gun from Arizona Territory, a man named Smith. They say he has eight notches on his gun." Sir Adrian glanced at Cary. "You do know what that means?"

Doreen could hear his eagerness to enlighten the "gently bred" ladies on the meaning of a gun with "notches."

"I know," Cary answered curtly.

Sir Adrian returned his attention to Doreen. "I have, myself, been compelled to hire several marksmen—not gunfighters like Smith, you understand—to defend my cowboys and my herds." Sir Adrian paused to observe the women's reactions.

Cary's mouth tightened still more, but she remained silent. Doreen remembered Smith's laughing eyes, his teasing voice, his gentle mockery and sharp sense of humor, and looked at the Englishman with a new distrust and anger. Surely someone who had killed eight men, as Sir Adrian claimed Smith had, would be quite different. The laughter, the mockery, the gay impertinence could not belong to a man who killed easily and for hire. She looked at Sir Adrian with new eyes. She had thought him merely a pompous ass, but he had to be lying about Smith. She rose with all the dignity she could summon and walked to the front door. She looked back at the Englishman. "My aunt and I will discuss what you've told us and talk to you again later. It's too soon to talk of selling ranch land. Good day, Mr. Granscomb-Whitly."

"Sir Adrian," he corrected automatically. He stood, as a gentleman must when a lady does, but he made no move to leave. "We still have a contract to discuss, Miss Anderson."

"You have mentioned no contract till now, sir!" Doreen snapped, no longer pretending politeness. "You had a contract with my uncle, to water your stock in the Pinto for a fee, sir! No other contract was among his papers."

"Miss Anderson," Sir Adrian protested, "I mentioned no *written* contract. Here in the West, thousands of acres or hundreds of cattle are sold on merely a handshake. That was the sort of contract I meant."

Doreen stared at him through narrowed eyes. "You have water, for which you owe me last month's payment."

"But—"

"Please leave. I find your insistence distressing."

Sir Adrian's face drew tight, but he had been well bred. Distressing a gentlewoman, at least very much, was just not done. He bowed gracefully to each woman and strode out, the heels of his tall shiny boots clicking on the polished floor.

Doreen watched through the window as he mounted his Thoroughbred, gave it a quick blow with his quirt, and rode swiftly away. She turned back to her aunt. "Do you think Uncle Jacob actually sold him any land?"

"No, Jacob would never have let the ranch go out of the family. He left it to a *female*, didn't he?" Cary stood abruptly and brushed the wrinkles from her damp skirt. "Your father's brother was no fool. If he'd made a deal to take place after his death, he would've written a contract. Even if a handshake is usually good enough out here. You should check with Bill to see if that's even true. You remember what Bill told us—rich Englishman, ripe for the plucking, and plucked with a vengeance. Bill says the local banks are ready to foreclose and that Granscomb-Whitly needs water, or water rights, just to hold off the banks until fall, when he might, with water, make enough profit to meet his payments. You have lots of water. Sir Adrian has strong reasons to shade the truth or even to lie. He'll be back. He has to be."

"Bill seems to have told you a lot in a short time."
Doreen's tone was dry.

Cary began rolling her sleeve up, slowly and evenly.
"Well, we had some time after we rousted the riders out
for Speck and Tinker and before you were done with
Shadow. Until now I hadn't thought the information
was important, just social gossip, his way of passing
time."

"Yup."

Cary looked at her niece and laughed. "Well, he *is*
an attractive man."

"If you say so."

"I know. You go more for the tall, red-headed type."

Doreen flushed. "He's not red-headed, he's sandy
blond."

"Red, sandy, it doesn't matter. I *saw* how you looked
at him on the train, even if no one else did," Cary teased.
"Really, Doreen, what *would* your mother say?"

Just as Doreen opened her mouth to retort, a party
of horsemen rode into the yard. The women stepped out
into the sunshine to see who they were. They were the
tracking party. Doreen recognized the large black horse
in the lead at once. Its rider nudged it close to the porch
and removed his hat respectfully. There was no mischief
now in the gray eyes that looked down at them.

"Laramie Smith, ladies. Blue Mountain. We met
briefly at the train." He half-turned in his saddle. "Red
and Tony from Johnsons'." Two riders removed their
hats. "Fats from Blue Mountain, Tex and Ole from the
Lady R. Your men're with McTaggert bringin' in the
cattle from that piece of range." His eyes shifted to the
space between his horse's ears. "There weren't any
calves among 'em, ma'am. You've been cleaned out

43

there. My boss suggests you lay some of that newfangled bob-wire along the boundary with the Rolling W, and McTaggert agrees. He'll be talkin' to you about it when he gets in." Smith studied his hands, crossed on his saddle's horn, for a long moment, then looked Doreen in the eye. "We lost the trail, ma'am. They drove their cattle and your calves up a stream and onto a rock shelf. Sorry."

The men replaced their hats and rode away.

CHAPTER

3

DOREEN WATCHED the men ride away, feeling a strange, unpleasant emptiness. Two men had died in just a week's time. Her employees. Protecting her property. She put a hand to a suddenly queasy stomach. "Aunt Cary, I think I'll go lie down for a while," she said faintly.

Alone in her room, Doreen closed the curtains, lay down on the bed, and shut her eyes. Images of Shadow, bleeding in the office, replayed again and again inside her closed lids. Such savagery seemed to be normal out here. Nausea rose, burning, into her throat. She swallowed painfully and forced her mind to be still, to shut Shadow out. She could not have said how long she lay in that silent inner darkness, only that, at last, she forced herself to examine what had happened, what would likely happen again. Two men had died. Speck and Shadow had been shot and were unable to work. What kind of people were these, to take such unnatural death so calmly?

Despair and fear washed over her. What could she

do? Find work as a stranger's drudge, with no hope of ever being more? Try to scrape together enough money to be trained as a teacher or secretary? Ranch here, see men die, and hope she would get used to it? Stay at Three Rivers and devise some plan for protecting the men? How could the men be protected and still watch the cattle? Doreen rolled over and beat the pillow with her fists in frustration.

Some time later she rose, washed all traces of tears from her face, put her hair back in order, straightened her dress, and went out to find McTaggert. He was leaning on the corral fence, smoking a pipe and watching the last of the shoeing. The moment Doreen broached the subject of protecting the riders to him, she knew from his sudden stiffening that she would have to work hard to convince him to change anything. She also knew it would never do to argue with her foreman in public, and she was quite sure they were going to argue. She told McTaggert to come to her office. He stalked after Doreen through the kitchen and down the hall, the very snap of his boots on the floor hard and unyielding.

The moment they were inside, McTaggert presumed on the thirty-year gap between them. He shut the office door firmly, like a father about to discipline a child, removed his pipe a small distance from his lips, and pointed the stem at her. "You said out therrre you want to keep rrriders from injury. It canna be done, lass. If you keep them in the rrranch yard, they'll rrride broncs and fight and hurrrt themselves rrright before your eyes. If you dinna, what happens, happens." He sucked on his pipe and stared at her belligerently, as if daring her to contradict him.

46

Doreen's eyes slid away from his. "Including getting shot?"

"Guns and killin' arrre parrrt of life here," McTaggert said around the pipe clenched between his teeth. "You canna stop that. I'm here to make this rrranch a profit, not play nurrrsemaid to a bunch of wild—" McTaggert refrained from completing his thought.

"If keeping them nearby won't work, assign them to work in twos, to protect each other."

McTaggert snorted. "You're payin' them to watch cows, lass, not each other." He spun and left the room.

Doreen stared at the door, stunned. She was the owner, and he had not only told her he was going to do nothing, he had walked out on her. She snatched the nearest object on the desk and hurled it at the closing door. It was a porcelain inkwell. Empty, fortunately. She stood a long while looking at the shards of porcelain. She had not handled the confrontation well. She could have ordered him to assign the men to work in pairs, or to take other safety measures and fired him if he refused, but she had not been sure she knew what was a safety measure and what would merely put more men at risk and had been afraid to force her opinion on a man with decades of experience in the cattle business. Doreen dropped into the desk chair and just sat, shaking, for a while. Slowly she pulled a piece of writing paper toward her, dipped a pen in ink, and began to write.

Dear Amelia,

My only friend, what I would not give to see you now. I don't know how to run a ranch and I must learn very fast. The ranch itself is little like I thought it would be and thieves are stealing our cattle, so there is little hope of profit this year. One of our riders was killed just after we came (can you imagine what I feel, knowing that a human being died protecting *my property*?) and the foreman tells me there is no way to prevent the same from happening to others. The house itself is spare, by which I mean that it is not as we have known houses— the walls are horizontal timbers, painted; there is not even one plastered wall. There are only hooks for hanging our clothes, which means they are soon wrinkled. The water is outside and I can imagine what getting water for a bath or laundry will be like in winter!

We have been bathing in our wash basins, as there is no tub and no immediate hope of getting one. I fear we will soon lose the graces and conversation, even the cleanliness, of civilized places in this wild country. We cannot have an egg for breakfast (there are no chickens) or cream in our coffee (there are no milk cows). If we whiten our coffee, it is with tinned milk, which I doubt I shall ever like to taste. Even our vegetables are dried or from tins.

I feel so alone and so desperate that I do not know what to do. In such circumstances, memories of you are painful. Yet I miss you more than I can say. I will see you again, somehow. I *will*. If I could come back to Chicago to stay right now, I would.

Your loving friend,

Doreen lifted the paper to reread it, signed it, blew over it to dry the ink, and inserted the letter into an envelope. She held it in her hand, stared at it, sighed, then put it in the growing stack of letters to go out with the mail rider.

Doreen refused to let herself dwell on the bad news. The roundup party, where she would be meeting her neighbors for the first time, was only a day away. Doreen washed her hair, then sat in the sun for several hours to dry it and catch up on her mending. She checked for the fiftieth time the pale-lemon silk dress she had spruced up for the party. The sight of the dress, so unsuitable for ranch life generally, stirred excitement to life in her, temporarily blocking out her worry and fears for the future. She wrapped it in a sheet in preparation for carrying it to the Blue Mountain Ranch.

On the day of the party, Cary, Doreen, Luke, and Diego were up and on the road before dawn. The ranch's riders rode sedately behind the wagon or whooped and shouted and raced up and down beside and around the wagon. The noise and the dust set Doreen aback and made her glad she had decided against wearing her party dress on the drive over.

Doreen felt as excited as a child and had to keep a vigilant watch to prevent herself from fidgeting and wiggling like one. She glanced repeatedly over her shoulder into the wagon box at the sheet-wrapped party dress. The people at this party were the only people for several days' ride in any direction. She wanted to look her best.

Doreen turned her attention to the road. This was her first look at it in daylight. It was merely two ruts climbing through a low place between mountains and it was only inches wider than the wagon. On one side a gravelly slope slanted upward, not quite close enough to touch. On the other side, the mountain dropped a hundred feet or so. Doreen clutched the rough edge of the board seat and wondered how Bill Haycox had found the nerve to drive them over such a place in the gray uncertain light before dawn. Her breath sucked in involuntarily. Diego glanced at her sympathetically.

"Eet ees nothing, Mees Doreen. No one has ever gone over. Except once a prospector and hees mule. But that was long ago."

One is more than I needed to hear about just now, Doreen told Diego in her head.

After that, she resolutely kept her eyes somewhere other than the edge. She imagined what the ranch house, the party, the guests would be like, and that blunted the discomfort of jolting and bouncing over the rough road. Butterflies fluttered gently in her stomach. Doreen could see the ranch house in her mind's eye, its rooms brilliant with lamps, people circulating through, talking, laughing, and maybe dancing, perhaps in the parlor.

Then the Blue Mountain spread came into sight. The gray ranch buildings clustered around a spring. The house was far too small and plain for such an event as she had been imagining, and Doreen laughed ruefully at herself. White canvas tents spread across the meadow behind the house. Wagons, some tethered horses, and a buggy clustered in the open area in front of the house. Smoke rose from a large fire at the edge of the meadow. Small shapes that had to be children ran around and around the fire or chased and dodged in and out of tents. Children. Families. Other women. Doreen watched the approaching scene eagerly.

A blond freckled young cowboy met the wagon when it came into the yard. He talked exclusively to Diego, blushing deep red and stumbling over words every time he looked at Doreen. Doreen found his embarrassment irritating and scolded herself for her lack of charity. Such shyness was apparently a common malady of young men in the West. Even among her own men, only Diego could speak to her with any ease. The others were as tongue-tied and shy as this young cowboy.

You'd think they'd never seen women, Doreen told herself with some amusement. Then she sobered. They probably didn't see many.

The young cowboy directed the 3R party to a tent marked with their brand on a large paper label. "Make yourselves to home, ladies," he said, still not looking at them. "Dinner won't be for a couple of hours yet. The pump's over there." With a blush and a wave of his hand in the direction of the pump, the young man was gone.

Diego helped the ladies down from the wagon, then drove away to wherever wagons and horses were to be left. Doreen and Cary ducked through the tent's front flap. There were two cots, each with its own quilt and pillow, and a pitcher of water, sitting on a nail keg. The women removed their traveling bonnets and veils, brushed the road dust from their dresses, washed their hands and faces, and sailed out of the tent to meet their neighbors. Within minutes of the time they left the tent, Bill hailed them with a wave and a nod, excused himself to the stocky, bearded man he had been talking to, and hurried toward them. He grinned appreciatively at both of them, but his eyes rested on Cary. "Aren't you a sight for sore eyes! I was expectin' you an hour ago, but I guess I was thinkin' horse-time. I haven't driven that road in a wagon since Ann died. Come"—he extended an arm to each of them—"meet Asa Johnson." He led them to the bearded man he had just left. "Cary Williams, Doreen Anderson, this is Asa Johnson. His is the nearest friendly spread, after mine."

Asa Johnson thrust out a massive furred hand and

welcomed the women warmly. "Glad you stayed in Wyoming, Miss Doreen. I could've used the extra grazing on Three Rivers, but getting to and from it would've been awkward. Offer's still open, though, for a week or two if you change your mind." He shook his head. "After that, when I know how much I've lost to the rustlers . . ." His voice trailed off and he shook his head again.

Johnson was only the first of Bill's many introductions. The women were warmly welcomed, then their newness seemed forgotten in the bustle of getting ready for the party. They quickly learned that many of the guests had had to camp at least one night on the way and that there would be a barn dance almost every weekend while the roundup lasted. This dance, the first of the season, would be the biggest and most elaborate. After that, a larger and larger number of cowboys would have to be away, holding their spread's herd as the roundup progressed. There would be a break in the rounding-up in early July for haying, then the fall roundup would begin, with another round of parties and dances.

"Makes up for winters without any such-like," a wizened old lady confided to Cary.

When the rich, oily smell of roasting beef began to fill the air, Cary and Doreen followed a crude sign beside the back stoop that informed them the parlor had been set aside for "ladies' use." The women of the ranches were taking turns before the parlor mirror. Women were washing up or brushing and rebraiding their hair, or shaking out dusty party clothes, party clothes that were simple denim skirts and shirtwaists or ruffled calico dresses.

Wrong again, Doreen thought ruefully. The silk's far too elaborate for this. She shrugged. She'd been embarrassed by mistakes far worse than being overdressed. She would survive. She began unbuttoning her dusty traveling dress.

The excitement of the dance to come sang in that small parlor. Doreen slipped the silk dress over her head and smoothed it into place. She glanced around. No one appeared to be wearing gloves. Apparently, then, ladies did not *always* wear gloves when dressed up, as she had been taught. She slipped hers into the folds of her traveling dress, then turned around once before the cloudy mirror. She twisted around her finger the tendrils of red-brown hair that had so carefully escaped her chignon, then moved aside so someone else could see. Doreen looked around the room at the chattering, brightly dressed women brushing, bending, mending, tying, braiding, and lacing. In spite of her resolve not to let her dress embarrass her, she suddenly felt isolated, a stranger at a family reunion. For a moment, she missed Chicago badly. She had understood the social rules there.

A tall woman, bulging mightily in a shirtwaist and dove-gray skirt, examined herself in the mirror, smoothed her bun, straightened her lace collar, turned to Doreen, and thrust out a work-worn right hand. "Maggie Johnson. Circle X. You must be Doreen, from Three R. Glad to meet you. Bill's talked some about you and your aunt. You're just as pretty as he said. See you at dinner." The woman picked up her shawl and left the house.

Doreen followed her into the late-afternoon sunshine where the fragrance of crushed grass, coffee, onions, and boiling potatoes, plus a tang of sage from the range, joined the mouth-watering smell of roasting beef. The smell came from a young steer on a heavy spit, which occupied a place of honor in the center of the meadow/campground. Doreen walked closer to see how the roasting was done. The two cowboys turning the spit followed her with appreciative eyes and Doreen felt excitement spin to life inside. Fun. This day and night would be fun.

Blankets had been spread for seating and already families had begun to settle on them. Children in pinafores screeched and ran and giggled and squabbled all over the meadow. Near Doreen, a young woman in a split skirt cradled a baby on one hip. Farther off, two small boys fought over possession of a fuzzy orange pup. Doreen noticed that most of the women present wore their skirts shorter than was fashionable or modest, exposing considerable ankle and, sometimes, a bit of their lower limbs. One or two older women were actually wearing denims as if they were men! Doreen tried not to be shocked, telling herself life was different in the West. Her advice to herself did not work.

To Doreen's left, a young cowhand stood talking to several couples on blankets, his arm across the shoulders of his pretty, pregnant wife. Two of the young women sitting on the blankets were actually knitting instead of paying the speaker their entire attention. How rude, Doreen thought. Then she stood still, thinking about the differences she had already seen between her old way of life and life in the West. The woman with the baby, for instance, obviously rode astride. There was no other use for a divided skirt. In Chicago, she would have come to the party in a carriage or wagon or would have ridden sidesaddle, as a lady should. If she had not, she would have been condemned as a loose woman who invited men's improper attentions. Doreen herself had come to the party in the wagon partly for lack of a lady's saddle at Three Rivers.

In Chicago, the pregnant young woman would have stayed modestly at home and avoided indecently stimulating low thoughts in the young and the delicate-minded by displaying the obvious result of indulging her husband's animal instincts. Doreen mentally shook herself. Ladies never thought of such goings-on. They physically accommodated a husband only as necessary. Doreen lifted her head proudly and set her chin. She would refrain from condemning women for behaving with such indelicacy, but that did not mean she herself would adopt their behavior. Doreen's mouth tightened. She had worked for her living for eight years without becoming brazen or loose. She would not start behaving like a hoyden now.

Doreen glanced over the crowd and spotted Cary's moss-green dress. She headed toward the group around her aunt, then stopped abruptly when a beginning walker staggered into her and clung to her skirt, swaying. The pinafored baby threw its head back and grinned up at her in toothless triumph. A pair of boys perhaps twelve years old, trailing a girl of six or seven, politely relieved her of the baby, then stood a little way off, discussing among themselves the merits of a certain stallion as a stud. Doreen sucked in her breath, her ears burning. Children! With such knowledge! Boys of that age perhaps needed to know such things, but a little girl? When the little girl began bragging to one of the boys about the quality of foals the stallion produced,

Doreen moved away, slowed by shock and, she admitted to herself, by curiosity. These children knew more about reproduction than she did and had no qualms about discussing the most indelicate matters out loud and in public. Clearly she had much to learn, and some of that knowledge would be just as unpalatable as learning to watch men die.

"Excuse me? May I speak with you a moment?"

Absorbed in her thoughts, Doreen jumped with surprise. She spun. Sir Adrian stood at her elbow.

He smiled disarmingly. "Miss Anderson. It's good to see you again. I've been looking forward to getting better acquainted, and this party seemed a good chance."

Without asking her permission, Sir Adrian drew Doreen's hand through his arm and began walking toward the edge of the crowd. Wordlessly she withdrew her hand. Sir Adrian continued speaking in an even voice, as if nothing had happened.

"I would most like you to save a reel for me later. So many of the dances they do here are so rowdy, but the reel allows one to partake of some of the social intercourse in this place without lowering oneself to the common level. May I also have the pleasure of your company at dinner?"

Dinner with a spoiled and presumptuous aristocrat, discussing the cultural shortcomings of her new neighbors, was not what Doreen had had in mind for the evening. "Not tonight, Sir Adrian," she replied courteously with a small, polite smile. "I'm keeping my aunt company."

He bent his head in courteous acknowledgment. "May I join you?"

Doreen studied his narrow handsome face for a second. What made him so interested in her? Surely Chicago was not that impressive to a man who had probably seen much of Europe. Perhaps he thought she would stroke his ego better than the local women. Perhaps he thought to buy her land, and its water, with charm. He was most confident of the power of that charm. "I'm sorry, Mr. Granscomb-Whitly," she said firmly, "but I believe my aunt has made other arrangements." This was not exactly true, but it would do.

"Please, Sir Adrian, if you will, Miss Anderson." He paused a moment, then met her eyes with a sincere, direct look. "To be honest, Miss Anderson, I had hoped to discuss business with you over dinner. I've hesitated to send my men back to the Pinto because of the disagreement our people had last week." His voice faltered when Doreen stiffened at the word "disagreement," but he continued. "I need the water. What can I do to convince you?"

"Show me a written contract."

"But there *is* no written contract!" In his frustration his voice became almost a wail.

"Then you will have to be satisfied with the water rights, *which* I expect you to keep paying for." Doreen turned to go to her aunt.

Sir Adrian laid a restraining hand on her arm. "The season's short here. You can't let the matter drift."

"I need time."

"I don't think you realize how important—"

"Take your hand away, *Sir* Adrian."

"May I come and talk to you in the next few days?" His grip tightened and there was an almost desperate urgency in his voice.

"Take your hand away this instant!"

"Don't refuse me on all fronts, please."

"The lady told you somethin', Whitly. Do it."

Doreen and Sir Adrian both started at the sudden, cold interruption.

Sir Adrian looked over Doreen's shoulder and stiffened. "This is none of your concern, Smith."

Smith took a jingling step closer to the pair. "When a man forces his attention on a woman, it's any gentleman's concern, Englishman. And don't say what you're thinkin' or, tenderfoot or not, you're dead!"

Sir Adrian paled, released Doreen's arm, and backed away. "We were talking business—"

"Then talk business when the lady's willing to listen. Get!" He then turned to Doreen as if the Englishman did not exist. "It's time to be sittin' down to eat, Miss Anderson. Yore aunt sent me to get you, seein' I was handy at the moment."

Sir Adrian's pale face flushed red. "I'll see you at the dance, Miss Anderson." He spun on a toe and stalked off.

Doreen realized she had been clenching her hands into fists in distress. She looked up at Smith and slowly made her hands relax. "Thank you," she said softly. "Though I probably could eventually have gotten rid of him . . ." She took a steadying breath. "You now have an enemy there, sir, and on account of me."

Smith shrugged. "Probably. I'm not goin' to get too worried about it."

"Did Aunt Cary really send you?"

The tall rider smiled, a sudden, arresting smile. "Nope, but you looked a mite out of yore depth, ma'am." Smith's voice quivered with suppressed laughter. "Sir Adrian's used to the sophisticated ladies of

London and New York, who deliver a real classy brush-off."

"And you don't think I could've—"

"Now, now. Don't get yore feathers ruffled. I wasn't insultin' you at all."

The corner of Smith's mouth quirked in amusement and his gray eyes danced wickedly. In that moment Doreen decided she did not want to be rid of Sir Adrian with the help of this bold, impudent man. His mocking words and quicksilver personality changes kept her always off balance. She was not used to any man being able to do that, and she did not like the feeling. Smith seemed to know this and was laughing at her. He touched the brim of his hat, then strode away.

Moments later, the feast began. Everyone received a generous slice of steaming, dripping beef. The meal that went with it was plain, reflecting the all-male state of Blue Mountain's cookery, but it was also delicious and portable. People walked around the meadow with their plates, stopping to eat or talk as they felt inclined. By the time the dance was to begin, Doreen had met most of the neighbors, had learned about local peddlers and the best place to shop in Jamesville, had played a simple game of catch with three toddlers, and had snuggled a five-month-old baby. The fiddler was tuning up, the men crushing out their cigarettes or knocking out their pipes, the baby-watchers were making a cozy nap and play area in a hollow in straw placed in a corner of the barn for that purpose.

Doreen found a seat with several other women on a bench along the edge of the broom-clean dance floor. Bill already headed a square with a spry, bent little woman who must have been one of the oldest people present. Asa Johnson was partnering Cary. Maggie Johnson, baby on hip, shoved newcomers into correct positions for the first dance. Diego offered Doreen his hand and jerked his head toward a forming square.

Doreen shook her head. "I don't know how. I'll just watch."

Diego laughed and pulled her to her feet. "Eet's so easy, Mees Doreen. If you make a mistake, someone weell push you where you belong." He took a step closer and whispered confidentially, "Sometimes the caller even confuses a square on purpose."

Doreen chuckled and took her place beside him as fourth couple. For each of the following squares, Doreen had a different partner—a young cowhand, a grizzled veteran of the late War, a middle-aged man who was foreman at the Rolling W, several riders of uncertain age from various spreads. Doreen felt both exhilarated and embarrassed by her popularity; she had never in her life been so much in demand. Yet she noticed that the other unmarried young women and even small girls were being treated in much the same way. She also noticed that often two men paired off for lack of a female to partner. Perhaps Sir Adrian had not been out of line in his persistence. Perhaps women were actually sought after here because there were so few of them.

The caller announced a rest and left the box he had been standing on to get himself a beer, mopping his forehead with a red bandanna as he went. Doreen left the floor with relief and sank onto straw piled beside the dance floor as a cushion. Immediately three riders crowded close, clamoring to bring her lemonade or cool water or tea. They appeared to Doreen to be close to blows over who would have the honor. She had no idea how to stop the argument. Never had she run into or even seen such a situation. She glanced around the barn desperately, hoping to catch the eye of someone who could help. Sir Adrian dropped his conversation with three middle-aged men, crossed the barn floor, and somehow he insinuated a hand around the snarl of cowboys and drew Doreen to her feet.

"I'm taking the lady for the reel. If you gentlemen will excuse us?"

Without waiting for a reply, Sir Adrian gave Doreen's hand a discreet tug. A second fiddler was tuning up. Sir Adrian led her to the head of a forming set, as if that position were his by right, ignoring the hard looks of some of the other men. "This, at least, is a dance done in civilized parts of the world," he told her as he moved forward into the pattern of the dance.

Doreen flushed. She knew his comment had to have been heard by neighboring couples. Doreen touched his hand as the music required and stepped back.

"You look upset," Sir Adrian murmured as they stepped together again. "I beg pardon if I've offended you. It's the last thing I want to do. Please, forgive me."

"It's your neighbors in the reel who have a right to be offended, sir."

"What did I say? I only mentioned that—"

"Please, don't repeat it, sir."

"I don't understand you Americans at all. There have always been unbridgeable differences between classes and, for the most part, the denizens of this part of your country belong to the lowest strata even of *your* society."

"Enough, sir!" Doreen snapped.

"I hope you don't think I included you, Miss

Anderson! You are a lovely and charming young woman." Sir Adrian smiled, and suddenly Doreen had an almost overpowering urge to shove his brilliant white teeth down the back of his patrician throat.

Doreen's voice shook a little with her anger. "For a man who believes himself well-bred, you are remarkably rude."

"You have a sharp tongue, Miss Anderson."

"Not sharp, just honest, sir." The music ended and Doreen's words rang out in the sudden quiet. "I'm tired," she continued, ignoring curious and sympathetic eyes. "Please excuse me."

Sir Adrian's face tightened and his forehead creased in irritation, but he recovered his poise quickly and escorted her from the floor. "You Americans are so touchy!"

"'Touchy'!" Doreen, though furious, kept her voice at conversational level. "Sir, have you no feelings of decency at all? A man *died* in that 'disagreement.'"

Sir Adrian's face froze into stern and aloof lines. "Lots of men die out here, Miss Anderson, and sometimes women." With those words, Sir Adrian left Doreen at Cary's side.

"Was that a threat, Doreen?" Cary's worried voice defused the explosion building inside Doreen.

"Yes, I think so."

At that moment, a Circle X rider, introducing himself as Tony, asked Doreen to dance. They took position as head couple in a square and if he held her a little closer than strictly proper when they were swinging, or kept her hand a little too long at the head of the set, Doreen put it down to high spirits. After all, a lot of rules of etiquette were ignored here in the West. Thinking of those rules brought to mind Sir Adrian's casual rudeness to his neighbors and that led to Laramie Smith, who had never apologized for bumping into her on the train and had contradicted her in public. She glanced around the barn, looking for his reddish hair. He was leaning against a stall door, rolling a cigarette and watching her. He nodded slightly to acknowledge her look, licked, rolled, and lit his cigarette, shaped the words "the waltz is mine," and sauntered outside into the cool darkness. Perhaps he stopped just outside the door, for Doreen could see the red glow of a cigarette there.

Doreen refused partners for the next two sets so she could rest and watch. She thought, ruefully, that popularity was very wearing. But as her body rested, her inner tension increased. The not-quite-respectable waltz would soon begin. It was the last dance before the long break for refreshments. Smith would claim his dance. Thinking of his dancing eyes, teasing voice and impudent manner, and of her own confusing reactions to him, Doreen toyed with the ideas of disappearing or of acquiring another partner. She accused herself of cowardice and laughed, weakly, at her own reluctance. When the lilting strains of the waltz finally began, Doreen's stomach knotted and her palms began to sweat. She stood abruptly to escape into the darkness outside and, at that moment, a large, callused hand slid under her right elbow.

"Miss Doreen, may I have the pleasure?" Smith did not wait for her to respond, but swept her out onto the dance floor and into his arms.

The touch of his hands only increased her agitation.

She resisted the feeling. "You might have waited for an answer!"

"You might've refused, an' I've been lookin' forward to this all evenin'." He pulled her a little closer and led her through spins and turns that were a pleasure in their grace and easy execution.

"You dance very well, Mr. Smith."

He laughed down at her. "Better than you expected of a rustic?"

"That's not what I meant!" Already he was getting her off balance, teasing her.

"No? That's what your friend the Englishman thinks of us."

Doreen looked up into Smith's face, trying to see what he was getting at, but his face was bland and innocent. "He's not my friend. Not by a long shot. He's been threatening me, sir."

Smith was instantly serious. "What did he say?"

The change in him was chilling. "It—it wasn't clear, really. He claims Jacob agreed to sell him some land."

His hands tightened a little more. "What did he say?"

Doreen shook her head, no longer trusting her own interpretation. "He said men get shot often here, and women, too."

Smith looked thoughtful. "That's true, about *men* gettin' shot, at least, and nothin' anyone can hang him with, but if I was you, Miss Doreen, I'd be mighty careful not to ride out alone."

A shiver ran up Doreen's back. "Are you serious?"

"Completely." Then he smiled and held her a little closer. "But this isn't the place to be serious. You're safe as can be, especially from an oaf like that Englishman."

He looked down at her, his eyes sparkling with mischief again, his drawl soft and teasing. "Do you dare dance as the Viennese do?"

Doreen looked at him in surprise. "Viennese?"

He chuckled. "Shore. I spent a year in Europe as a marksman with a Wild West show. *Do* you dare?"

He was definitely offering a challenge. "What if I say no?"

Smith took them through a tight spin. "Then we'll both know what a little coward you are."

"And if I say yes?"

"Yore neighbors may think you're a little fast. More'n likely, they'll think I've had too much to drink and got carried away by yore lovely presence. I can live with that."

"Have you?"

"Have I what?"

"Had too much to drink."

"What do you think?"

He did not smell of liquor or beer, only cigarette smoke and soap.

"Do you dare, Miss Doreen?" His voice was a soft, tempting whisper.

She looked into his dancing gray eyes and his mischief caught her up. She felt reckless, and sure of herself for the first time since she had arrived at Blue Mountain Ranch. "You're on, Mr. Smith."

He pulled her so close a piece of paper could not have fit between them. Doreen had never been so close to a man before. She swallowed nervously and hoped he did not notice her apprehension.

"Hold up your skirt a little in one hand so you don't trip," he ordered softly.

Then they were whirling in spirals among the slower dancers, dancers with a proper air space between them. Doreen felt every muscle of Smith's long hard body as they danced and understood why the Viennese fashion was such a scandal. Her body responded to the music and to him, accommodating itself to his movements, trembling with a sweet longing she did not understand. His cheek rested against her hair, his hand burned through the silk of her dress, his heart beat against her cheek. The whirling, the music, the feel of him made her weak and dizzy. She leaned against him to steady herself and that disturbed her even more.

"I can't go on," she whispered. "I'm too dizzy to stand."

The spirals gentled, slowed, and stopped. When Doreen opened her eyes, they were beside Cary and Bill. Smith held her by the hand while she sank onto a bench, then stepped back to look at her.

"You'll survive," he said, gently teasing. He spun away and blended into the crowd.

But will I? Doreen knew if *he* decided to deepen their acquaintance, he would be far more difficult to handle than the smooth, arrogant Sir Adrian. Smith recognized none of the polite barriers that made city social life so predictable. And so safe.

CHAPTER

4

THE PARTY WENT on until late Sunday afternoon. All the people Doreen had ever known spent the Sabbath resting, according to the Fourth Commandment, even eating cold meals to avoid the work of cooking. Here there was hot food all day, business discussions among the ranchers in the morning, card games in the afternoon, loud chases and rounds of hide-and-seek among the children, a bronc-riding contest, and continuous packing and departures by visiting families. Clearly, this was the custom here, as Bible-reading and quiet conversation was in Chicago. Doreen felt the outsider again, and the hurt was worse for the fun and acceptance she had had the day before.

Doreen returned to Three Rivers with Cary that evening, still deeply troubled by the differences a thousand miles made in the way people lived. Codes of dress, conversation, work, even of religious observance—all would have to be relearned, if not adopted, if she were to live comfortably with her new neighbors. When 3R's turn came to host the roundup, for instance, she would be expected to put on a barn dance, at least, and offer entertainment and food on Sunday. Breaking the belief of decades would be hard, but she must do it. She could not alienate her neighbors, when her survival and the ranch's hung on their help and advice.

Immediately after that first dance, the cook and almost all of the cowboys left for the far side of Blue Mountain's range, the starting point of the district's roundup. The only two men left on the place were Luke, who was away rounding up the last of the horses for 3R's crew, and Diego, who had his hands full repairing tack and tools, cutting and bringing in logs for the woodpile, and taking care of the preparations necessary for 3R's turn as host. As a result, the women had to do their own cooking, pump their own water, carry their own firewood, sometimes even split it. They limited themselves to this essential work, in order to have time to study the accounts and stock books. After four days of struggling to understand the accounts, they saw that money looked very tight for the next four months at least, so Doreen decided to have Bill explain how a rancher paid for anything between one autumn sale and the next. She had Diego saddle Mona while she rigged a mounting block from a large, empty keg. When she went to mount, Diego insisted on riding the mare first. "She has been out to pasture for days," he said and, with no further explanation, swung into the saddle.

Doreen bristled at his presumption, but a moment later she was grateful for it, because Mona put on a spectacular display of jumps, twists, and turns. It was brief, but Doreen knew she could not have held on. She thanked Diego, mounted from the keg, crooked her knee around the saddle horn, arranged her skirt modestly, and set off for the Blue Mountain.

Several hours later, she cantered into the Blue Mountain ranch yard, rode past the corral, which was full of dust and horses and noise, and drew up at the front stoop. She saw with dismay there was no mounting block to help her out of her saddle and no hitch rail for her horse. She rode around to the back. There was a rail, but no block there, either. The noises from the corral fell to nothing. Doreen looked over her shoulder. Three cowboys leaned on the top rail, watching. She flushed, angry with them and with the lack of accommodations for a lady rider. She eyed the porch. Perhaps she could edge the horse alongside that, unhook her knee and slide off without exposing any of her limbs to the avid eyes of the men in the corral. She nudged the mare, but it did not understand the signal, or pretended not to. Apparently even the horses followed different rules in the West. She tugged at the mare's mouth. Mona shifted her feet and backed a little, but moved no nearer to the porch. Doreen resisted the urge to whack the horse from sheer frustration. Her only choices seemed to be to sit where she was and ask one of the men in the corral to get Bill for her, to shout for Bill (which would be most unladylike), or to grab the horse's mane and slide off, hoping her skirt did not catch on the saddle and make her fall. The skirt would ride way up her limbs and—

"Hey, Bill," one of the men in the corral shouted, "you've got a visitor. A pretty one for a change."

Doreen bit her lip in fury and tried again to get the horse to turn its side to the porch.

A second man vaulted over the corral fence and strode across the yard. Doreen knew the moment he came over the top rail who he was, and her stomach fluttered in panic. She unhooked her knee, then hesitated. It was a long way to the ground.

"Fool woman," Laramie Smith drawled, coming to a stop at Mona's side. He glanced contemptuously at her decorous skirt and graceful sidesaddle position. "Nobody can keep proper control of a horse thata way." He looked up at her speculatively. "You want to jump off? I'll catch you."

Doreen clutched the horse's mane.

"No?" Laramie shoved his hat back on his head and leaned against one of the porch's roof supports. He crossed his arms over his chest. "You want I should call Bill instead?" When she did not quickly reply, he turned his face toward the house. "Bill!" he bellowed. "Company!"

Doreen flushed with embarrassment.

"Looks like you've got a little problem," Laramie continued, his eyes glancing from her to the ground, making a point of the distance. "Women out here generally have more sense and ride astride, so they can get off their horses without help."

"If you're here just to torment me," Doreen snapped, "go away!"

"Actually, it was instruction I had in mind," Laramie said softly, "but you don't seem to be listenin'."

Before Doreen could draw breath to retort, Laramie had lifted her down and set her before him on a porch step. They were almost eye to eye. He smelled of dust and sage and tobacco and he was not teasing. Doreen swallowed and licked dry lips.

"It's none of my business if you kill yourself," Laramie said carefully, "but I'd hate to see this neighborhood lose a pretty face just from pure ignorance. This isn't the East and this isn't an Eastern horse. She's half-wild and always will be. With a 'limb'"—his tone was sarcastic—"on either side, you could hold on if she spooked or bucked. Sitting up there as if you were on one of those ridiculous kidney pads Easterners call saddles—" Laramie's hands tightened on Doreen's waist. "And you hold the reins *this* way"—he pressed both strips of leather ungently into her left hand—"and rein mostly against her neck or she won't know what you want. Luke gave you a good horse with a soft mouth. Don't go pullin' at it."

Boots clunked across the porch boards. Laramie looked up. "She was stuck, Bill, couldn't get off her horse without one of those Eastern mountin' blocks. See if you can talk some sense into her." Laramie dropped his hands and was gone.

Bill motioned Doreen into the house ahead of him and she went, her face still feeling hot, her hands shaking a little.

The upshot of her conference with Haycox was that ranchers lasted from one season to the next in bad years by very careful spending and by making-do a lot. Their discussion stirred up many new ideas, and Doreen continued to think about them on the ride home. Clearly, the ranch needed some other source of income, for emergencies.

Doreen wanted to work through the following Saturday, telling herself she had so much work she could not afford the play time, but a tiny voice inside accused her of avoiding another encounter with that

71

impertinent, sandy-haired cowboy. She firmly silenced that voice. Cary refused to leave her at the ranch unchaperoned, so they both missed the second barn dance.

In the middle of the second week, as Doreen tried to make flapjacks without eggs or fresh milk and without butter to put on them, the ideal source of extra income came to her: they could raise chickens, maybe get a cow, too, for milk and butter. She was so filled to bursting with the idea that she could not wait until the next day to tell Bill. She told Cary and then sat down to pour her excitement into a letter to Amelia.

Bill and McTaggert came by to be sure all was ready for the arrival of the roundup crews. After McTaggert had made his courtesy call on his boss, drunk the coffee offered, and gone out to inspect Diego's work, Bill lingered in the kitchen. He received Doreen's idea with a laugh and a glance toward the ranch yard, where McTaggert and Diego were setting out markers for the tents the neighbors would bring for the weekend. "McTaggert might wish you'd had that idea a month sooner, Miss Doreen. It would've made hiring a cinch. A man'll ride a long way for a promise of eggs for his breakfast and cream in his coffee. And butter—" He contemplated the grounds in the bottom of his cup for a few moments, swirling them slowly. "Cream."

He stood, set his coffee cup on the drainboard, then stopped halfway out the door. "Cookie said not to fret about the food for the party this time. He and McTaggert have taken care of everything."

Later the same afternoon Doreen laid out the dresses she would wear for the weekend. She lifted the lemon silk; it was just as inappropriate as before, but it was the most becoming thing she owned and she had nothing more suitable. Then she noticed its hem, gray-brown with dust for close to three inches from where it touched the ground. The blue serge had a similar stain. Reluctantly, Doreen unfolded the other two dresses she had worn during the past weeks. They were work dresses, used for several years at the boardinghouse, but they, too, were dirtier at the hems than they had ever been before. She looked at the rest of her wardrobe; a pale-blue silk with sleeves tight from wrist to elbow and tiers and tiers of ruffles, a dark-blue poplin with wide velvet bands, a white wool trimmed in black satin piping, a black serge skirt, and several lacy shirtwaists. She had been so proud of her selections in Chicago, and now the serges were the only practical items she owned. Even if she shortened the others . . . Doreen ground her teeth in frustration. Dust in the yard, in the garden, even in the house from boots and shoes. Dust and dirt like she had never had to deal with in the city. If she wore any more of her lovely new clothes here, they, too, would be ruined. If she didn't, then the money spent for them was gone, wasted, and she could not afford to waste money. She laid the white wool dress and two blue ones in the bottom of the trunk with the serge skirt and the shirtwaists on top. Perhaps she could remodel the skirt into something useful. Doreen thought of the shortened skirts she had seen at Blue Mountain. Did she really have to make a choice between cleanliness and decency? She thought of Maggie Johnson's comments and of Laramie's about her riding as a lady should. She took one more look at the stained silk, glanced out the window at the sun, and strode out to find Luke and Diego.

She had the two men set up the big copper laundry tubs in the yard, fill them with boiling water, and rig a clothesline from whatever rope they had at hand. Together the women began to struggle with hard yellow soap and alkaline water, stirring heavy tangles of clothes in long tubs, dragging them out, letting them cool enough to wring, rinsing, cooling them again, then draping them over the hastily rigged lines. The silk dresses had to be carefully sponged and dried. Around them, a 3R crew worked, marking camping spots, dragging in firewood, and sweeping out the barn.

The next day Doreen rose before dawn, knowing time would be short, and set irons on the stove to heat. She and Cary had only the few hours until the first roundup crews arrived to make their party clothes presentable. Three hours later they were only half done with the ironing. Doreen looked up from the seventh tier of ruffles on her second-best petticoat and met Cary's eye. Cary's petticoats lay over the back of the kitchen chair, the top three rows of ruffles on the top petticoat still wrinkled and stiff. Cary herself sagged against the long kitchen table, red-faced, sweating, weary.

"We didn't know what we had when we could send out the laundry, did we?" Cary asked, her mouth twisting wryly.

Doreen set her cooled iron on the stove and wiped the back of her hand across her forehead. "I'm going to take off the ruffles, most of them. I can't imagine ironing like this every week! There's so much that's more important to do."

Cary patted a stream of sweat from beneath her eyes with the corner of her apron. "You won't get any argument from me."

The women snipped and tore until each petticoat had just one row of ruffles around the bottom. Doreen collected her laundry, ironed and not-yet-ironed, over her arm. "Our first step on a long downward path," she commented bitterly, looking at the rows of puncture marks where ruffles had been.

"Don't be pessimistic, Doreen," Cary came back sharply. "This isn't Chicago. As you said, we have more important things to do."

"Perhaps Peggy did, too," Doreen muttered as she headed toward the hall.

"Perhaps she did, dear, but we paid her to do our laundry and do it she did."

Doreen was still in her room, smoothing hair that had been mussed by sliding on the clean dress, when someone knocked on the back door. She hurried to answer it, brushing away wrinkles around her waist as she went. Carson Brown of the Circle X, the roundup boss, had arrived to refresh his memory of the spread and was paying his courtesy call.

Several hours later, chuck wagons and cowboys from Blue Mountain, the Rolling W, Lazy R, Fishhook, and Circle X arrived. They rode through the barnyard and east toward the first camp. There were lean mustached men who, in street clothes, would not have been noticed on the streets of Chicago, but there were also small dark Mexicans, muscular black men, and even an Indian with braided hair and a dancing spotted horse. Of that parade, only the man in charge of each spread's roundup crew stopped at the house.

"Oh, think how exciting seeing a roundup will be!" Doreen breathed, her nose almost against the glass, her mind for the moment diverted from her own out-of-placeness.

Cary snorted derisively. "Dust and noise and swearing and—"

"And horses running and men throwing ropes to catch calves and—"

Cary chuckled. "McTaggert came by, gritted his teeth, and offered to take 'The Boss' out to watch. Why don't you take him up on it? *I* don't have to see calves branded to enter how many there are."

After two dull and work-filled weeks, McTaggert's offer of time off was irresistible. Doreen hurried to arrange a time.

The first of the neighbors' wagons arrived early Saturday morning. By noon everyone was set up in the meadow in front of the house. Children swarmed over the house and yard, whooping like Indians. Their fathers, gathered along the corral fence to watch various cowboys take on a local outlaw stud, were little quieter. The women gathered on blankets under the apple tree in the garden or sat in chairs on the porch, chatting, knitting, and sewing. Doreen checked the barn. The floor had been swept, a corner banked with straw prepared for the little children, and a crude platform of boxes set up for the fiddler and the caller. She waited on edge for the first sight of Laramie Smith's rangy body or the sound of his soft drawl. She considered skipping the dance; she might be too busy hostessing to risk another disturbing waltz in his arms.

He's only a cowboy, one of Bill's hands, she chided herself.

But that knowledge did nothing to take the edge off her apprehension. She had not been teased as Smith teased her since she was in pigtails, nor scolded so, for that matter, and she did not like it, not one bit.

Shortly before the meal, Doreen was talking with several young couples when she felt someone come up behind her. She turned, dreading and expecting to see the owner of a pair of dancing gray eyes.

Sir Adrian sketched a bow. "May I speak to you a moment, Miss Anderson?"

Doreen glanced at the others in the group. She did not want to leave, but something in Sir Adrian's tone told her he would insist, perhaps, probably, to the point of unpleasantness, if she refused. She had been well trained to avoid unpleasantness.

"There's the matter of my land along the Pinto, Miss Anderson."

Doreen made herself smile graciously. "*My* land, Sir Adrian. I'll let you know if I decide to sell any land after I talk to my uncle's executor." She turned again to join the young couples.

The Englishman laid a restraining hand on her arm. "I need land along the river now. I *need* that land."

Doreen rounded on him angrily, tearing herself free of his hand at the same time. "I don't believe there was a contract, sir! My uncle's land was more important to him than family. You wouldn't press so hard if you had a rightful claim. You'd sue." She spun away.

"But I must have the water—"

"You *have* the water, sir," Doreen said over her shoulder, "on lease."

She looked for the young couples she had been talking to, but they were gone.

"You're improvin'," drawled a voice at her elbow.

Doreen started, then looked up. Laramie Smith's

eyes were not laughing at her. He means it, she thought. Aloud, she said, "You move very quietly, sir."

Smith's eyes twinkled. "Got my dancin' shoes on." He lifted a foot, clad in a low-heeled black shoe, for her inspection. "Shore makes walking quieter, havin' no spurs. Feels a little strange, though." Then he sobered. "Miss Cary's been lookin' for you. Can I see you to the house?"

Without waiting for an answer, he turned her with an impersonal hand under her elbow and steered her toward the kitchen. He left her at the door. "See you at the dance. Sorry I had to miss the last one."

Doreen watched him stride away, feeling mingled disappointment and annoyance. She laughed at herself. She had been "too busy" to go to the last dance partly on Mr. Smith's account, and he had not gone, either.

"See" her was all Smith did at the dance. But by the end of the evening Doreen was sure he had danced two or three times with every other woman there.

Three days later, in the dark before dawn, Doreen rode with McTaggert and the recovered Speck to the roundup camp. Four chuck wagons formed a large square on the greening grass. In the open area between them, the cooks had dug fire trenches where they now poked among the coals, setting one Dutch oven more on the heat or moving another farther away. A few cowboys were still washing by the light of the cook's lantern, pouring water over each other's hands and splashing a little on their faces. Two men passed McTaggert and Doreen as they sat their horses at the edge of the circle. They dropped bedrolls onto a wagon already filled with them. Most of the cowboys were either eating or standing in line at their spread's chuck wagon, taking plate, cup, and eating tools, then spearing biscuits and a steak from a row of Dutch ovens and pouring coffee from a huge pot suspended over the fire. The rich, dark smell of the coffee perfumed the gray morning air. Pink and gold flared across the eastern horizon. McTaggert, who never spoke if he could avoid it, nodded Doreen toward the 3R wagon and told Speck, "You're not fit for rrroping orrr cuttin' yet, so stick to rrridin' herd, mon," and rode off to check the day's work with the roundup boss.

Doreen dismounted beside the wagon and let her horse's reins drag on the ground as she had been instructed by McTaggert always to do.

Cookie frowned at her. "This ain't no place for a lady."

Doreen put on her friendliest smile. "McTaggert invited me to come. I'll stay out of the way."

Cookie grumbled something under his breath, but slid a plate from the stack on the wagon's tailgate and forked steak and a biscuit onto it. "There's tallow for soppin' and coffee in the pot yonder," he said gruffly. "Don't burn yourself."

Doreen poured coffee into the tin cup offered, singed her lip on its edge, and looked for a place to sit. The cowboys were crouched on their haunches or sitting cross-legged on the ground, stuffing in their breakfast with silent concentration. It was not a position or an eating method for a lady. Doreen settled for sitting on the chuck wagon's tongue and watching the action around her.

A bunch of horses dashed up, tossing heads, snorting, bringing the smells of dust and horse with them. Most of the men got up, dropped their plates and utensils in a large dishpan, and tossed their coffee grounds on the grass. In moments, several of them had made a crude rope fence around the shoving, snorting horses. The thin, dark rider called California ducked under the hand-held fence and opened a loop in the rope he carried. Diego shouted a name to him. California glanced over the herd, picked out a horse, swung and tossed his loop. The horse plunged as it felt the rope fall over it, but stopped and stood still the moment the rope tightened. Diego left his place on the rope fence, bridled the horse, and led it away to saddle it.

The herd thinned rapidly. When only four men and California were left, some of the cowboys with saddled horses took places on the rope and the remaining men got their mounts. Then came the mounting contest, men against horses. All over the camp men were shouting, horses whinnying, snorting, plunging, bucking. Shadow's horse reached around to nip him as Shadow tightened the cinch and Shadow rapped it once, lightly, with the edge of his hand. The horse swung its head to the front and stared into the activity of the camp as if mischief had never occurred to it.

Across the square formed by the wagons, men suddenly began a wild whooping. Doreen's head flew up. A yellow-brown horse, its head almost to the ground, was bucking and twisting viciously, jolting and tossing its rider in the saddle, slamming its forefeet into the ground, kicking his hind feet so high it looked like it might flip over itself. The watching cowboys laughed and shouted advice. The horse charged stiff-legged across the open space between the wagons. Cookie dashed toward the coffeepot, rescuing it just before the horse jolted through the fire trench and out onto the flats beyond. Cookie, cursing, rushed to right over-turned ovens, and began choking on the ashes stirred up by the horse's passage.

Doreen moved to help with the mess. Cookie turned on her, snarling curses. When he realized he was not talking to one of the cowboys, his face turned beet red and he apologized profusely, but he also made quite clear he wanted no one else messing with his equip-ment. The cowboys, mounted now, passed in a column, laughing at Cookie's rage and at the shambles of his fire. Doreen mounted, but McTaggert, seeing her, shook his head sternly and pointed toward a ridge overlooking the camp. A rider on a Circle X horse paused and looked down at her.

"There won't be much to see until dinner anyway, miss. We'll be beating the brush in the hills and draws till then." He touched his hat and rejoined the column.

The sun was now fully up and the cowboys soon disappeared into draws and folds in the foothills. A hawk circled lazily high overhead. A yellow ground squirrel came out of its hole and reared up to look and sniff. Doreen smiled at the tiny forepaws held so tight against the white belly. The hawk's shadow passed the ground squirrel, making it vanish with a squeak into its hole. Doreen's horse shifted its feet and a skink, which had been invisible on its sunny rock, flicked out of sight. Doreen breathed deeply of the sharp, clean air and let her mind wander. A scent of cedar drifted from higher in the hills, where the ground was still white with snow under the trees.

The sound of moving cattle roused Doreen from her dreaming and she rode down to watch the activity. A few cowboys on quick, smart horses were cutting calves from the lowing, clacking herd. Doreen admired the dexterity with which men and horses avoided the sharp, tossing horns, but the pitiful bawling of the calves and the anxious calling of their mothers tore at her heart. She rode closer to see what happened next, but the smell, composed of sweat, horse, smoke, burning hide, and blood, quickly drove her farther away. She turned toward the ranch.

Diego crossed her course and held up his hand for her to stop. "Are you returning to the rancho, Mees Anderson?" When Doreen nodded, he continued. "McTaggert, he say we find too few calves in thees part of the range. He theeenks the rustlers are busy already theees season." Distress shadowed Diego's face. "We began the roundup early, mees, to try to get ahead of them, to get the calves branded first, you understand."

Doreen nodded and Diego went back to work. Doreen rode slowly, thinking of the profit that became slimmer and slimmer as the roundup went on.

CHAPTER

5

AFTER TEN DAYS, the roundup moved to the Rolling W. Reports from McTaggert did not improve much: calf numbers were down, seriously down. The four town boys McTaggert had hired, none of them more than fifteen, came to string barbed wire along the 3R's boundary with the Rolling W. They and Luke were the only employees left on the ranch. Doreen and Cary set to planting vegetable seeds and designing shelters for the projected new chicks and milk cow. They drove themselves and the boys hard. Then the sky fell in. California charged into the kitchen early one morning, asking for McTaggert.

Doreen's head snapped up at his shout and she spun from the recipe she had been reading. "We haven't seen McTaggert since the roundup left here. Is something wrong?"

California's entire body betrayed his anxiety. "He left the roundup three days ago, saying he had something important to tell you, but he's needed. When did he leave?"

Doreen felt a stirring of fear. "Like I said, he hasn't been here since the roundup left."

California had each of the women repeat every detail of the last time they had seen McTaggert, his lean young face getting grimmer by the word. When they finished, his mouth was a thin hard line, his face was stark and angry. He looked far older than his twenty years. "With your permission, Miss Doreen, I'll call some riders from the roundup to look for him. He was headed here. He may have had an accident on the way."

Luke was set to searching immediately. Five 3R men came and Bill and Asa Johnson sent two riders each. For three days the men scoured the hills and the lower slopes of the mountains. They followed every possible trail from the Rolling W to 3R and found no sign of McTaggert. Cary spent a large portion of those three days staring out at the mountains. Her conversation had one refrain. "What will you do if he's hurt too badly to work, Doreen? You don't know enough about the ranch to keep it going."

Doreen could not answer. She did not want even to think about it. Haycox had said California could handle the job, but the skinny, intense cowboy seemed so young to Doreen, too young to take on so much responsibility. Doreen flinched away from thinking that McTaggert might not be just hurt, that he might be dead. They could not afford to lose an experienced foreman in such a desperate time!

On the fourth morning, Cary's worrying rubbed right through Doreen's frazzled nerves to a raw spot. "I may not know enough about ranching now to keep us going, but I'm going to learn. I *won't* go back to cleaning up after other people and putting up with insults and crude propositions, just to keep eating. I won't! I'm going to help look for him." She spun toward the west wing.

Cary grabbed Doreen's arm. "What makes you think you can help, when men who know this country haven't found him? You'll risk your good name and what can you gain by it?"

Doreen lifted her chin stubbornly. "Respect, maybe. I *am* the owner. I *have* to do something. Maybe, just maybe, I'll see something they haven't. It's worth a try." She looked down at the fraying hem of her blue serge dress. It had been such a nice dress when she left Chicago. Shabbiness still hurt her, even after eight years of it. She took a deep breath. "I'm the owner. I'm responsible for my men. I have to *do* something!" Brave words! she scoffed inside.

Cary dropped her hold. "Her reputation is all a lady has in the end, Doreen. Nothing can fix it if it's stained. And your life may be at great risk out there. Please think again."

"I'll ride by myself, if you're so worried about what people will say."

Cary grimaced. "I don't know that that's any better, but I won't stop you. It *is* your ranch. Just be careful, all right?" She kissed Doreen on the cheek and walked briskly down the hall toward the public end of the house.

Doreen flung on one of Jacob's faded red flannel shirts, for warmth, and the black serge skirt, tucked her hair under a faded sunbonnet, drew on her riding gloves, and headed for the corral. She took Mona, climbed aboard from the porch, hooked her knee around the horn and rode out the mare's spiky morning

85

bucking, sidesaddle, without losing her seat. So much for *that* warning, Laramie Smith! she thought smugly. "Fool woman" indeed!

She rode northeast along the edge of the valley to the point where the Roaring River came tumbling out of the mountains, then turned into the hills. Searchers were supposedly working from the valley floor clear back to the roundup. Doreen looked carefully, hoping to see one of them, but she saw nobody. The grass underfoot was green, the poplars had dropped their red flowers to the ground, and the sticky-sweet pungency of new poplar leaves gave a tang to the air. Along the river, the aspen and willow had leafed out and bent gracefully in the breeze. A jay, somewhere in the cedars on the hill to Doreen's left, shouted harshly, and a magpie flapped away in a flash of black and white. The morning air was still, the sky above blue and cloudless. Doreen turned Mona toward the cedars to see what had disturbed the birds. Perhaps it was one of the searchers, she thought, though surely if it were, he would have hailed her. It was probably a coyote, or maybe a fox.

The cedars, high on the side of the hill, told her nothing, but she paused there a moment to glance back at the ranch. The low buildings with their cheery red roofs looked comfortable and safe. A tiny horseman turned from the road across the pass toward the Yellow, forded the south fork, and climbed the ridge on the other side. The long legs of the horse and the jodhpurs identified the rider.

"Sir Adrian's out early this morning. I wonder what for?" Doreen nudged Mona into the shadow of the cedars to make her red shirt harder to spot. She stroked the mare's neck to ease her impatience with standing still. "Don't want him to get any ideas about joining us, Mona." Mona stamped and blew.

The rider stood in his stirrups, outlining himself against the sky, and waved as if he saw her. Doreen ignored him. He waved again. She shook her head. He could not have seen her. He was waving at someone else. Perhaps he saw searchers from his vantage point. Doreen turned to look at the slopes behind her and saw no one. The rider in jodhpurs and his horse disappeared over the far side of the ridge. Doreen shrugged and led Mona into a fold of hills.

The climb from there was easy and comfortable. After an hour or so, the air warmed. Doreen loosened her bonnet strings and let the hat slide back to rest on her neck. She reveled in the wind, the clean mountain air, the smooth movements of the horse under her. For a time she forgot the grim reason for her ride and Chicago, with its smoke and grit and bustle, seemed part of another life. She was one with the sun and the bright clean air.

As she rode across a grassy flat with dark, cedar-clad benches on either side, a bevy of brown birds flushed in front of Mona's feet and scuttled away like determined old women. Mona stopped abruptly, snorting. Doreen leaned forward, patted the mare's neck, and spoke soothingly to her. "It's all right. It's just birds."

The mare's neck was warm and damp and silky. The birds had gone, but the mare still trembled and snorted nervously. Doreen felt a prickle of uneasiness. A movement caught her eye. A dark, heavy-bodied bird was lurching into flight nearby. Then Doreen saw McTaggert, or what was left of him. There was no need to go nearer. She could smell his death.

A slight movement on the bench to her right caught her eye. Two men on horseback were hiding behind a clump of cedars. The movement she had seen was one man pulling a bandanna up over his nose to hide his face. Doreen made her eyes glide past the cedars slowly, as if she were admiring the mountains beyond, but she did not turn so far that she could not still see the men out of the corner of her eye. One man edged his horse out of the trees a tiny distance, lifted his lasso silently from its strap, and began shaking out a loop. A dented and dusty hat hid those parts of his face his scarf did not cover. Fear surged through Doreen. She felt light-headed and weak.

Those are McTaggert's killers and that rope is for me! For a moment Doreen felt frozen in place.

The man with the loop rode slowly to the edge of the bench, his horse silent on the needle-covered rock, and started down the side toward the grassy flat and Doreen.

Anger surged to Doreen's rescue. The fool thinks he can just snare me!

Her eyes flicked from side to side. The strangers' hiding place was between her and the way she had come. Doreen swallowed and tightened shaking hands on the hard leather of her reins. She had ridden right past them! The man on the horse began to raise his loop. Doreen turned her head, slowly, innocently. There had to be other escape routes! She fought the panic that urged her to abandon reason and run. She heard small, brushing sounds. The stranger's companion was edging out of the cedars. Doreen wiped a clammy palm on her skirt and licked dry lips. There was so little time. Doreen heard the loop humming. Seconds. She had only

88

seconds to evade the loop and death. She hiked up her skirt, rose suddenly in her stirrup, flung the leg that had been hooked around the horn across the saddle and into the stirrup, and jammed both her heels into the mare. One of the men behind her let out a shrill whistle. Doreen laid the reins across Mona's neck and gave the horse a sharp crack with her quirt. Mona spun left and plunged down the slope, which dropped away sharply. The rope hissed close and rattled across the gravel beside the mare. Streams of the tiny stones trickled alongside as Mona gouged deep trenches in the slope. Doreen clutched her hat and clung to the horse with her knees.

"Get her!" a hoarse, muffled voice shouted.

Doreen glanced over her shoulder. Two men were whipping their horses as the beasts struggled to cross the wash that separated their path from hers. A third was already across. Doreen swallowed hard.

Dear Lord! A third one! She clung to Mona's back, riding low, urging her on with voice and knees.

A horse slithered and slid on the slope behind, coming closer, then another. Doreen crouched lower and hit Mona with the quirt. A gun barked. Doreen flinched and her teeth caught her lower lip. *Shot. Oh, dear God, I don't want to be shot!*

Something buzzed past her ear. She crouched lower. Close, so close! The gun barked again. Mona squealed, veered toward the valley and ranch, and ran faster. Another bullet zinged by Doreen's face, so close she felt the wind of its passing. Hot bile surged into her throat. She choked. Mona veered again, Doreen's hat flew off, and her hair streamed out in the wind.

"Stop!" a voice shouted. "You haven't got a chance!"

Panic clawed Doreen's stomach. Three horses, at least three horses pounded behind her. She thought she heard others, to the ranch side, the sounds coming closer, gaining, cutting her off from the safety of the house and yard. The back of Doreen's neck prickled, expecting a lasso to fall any moment. Ahead, scrub willow and aspen along the bank of the Pinto offered cover. The hooves behind thundered closer and a rope began to hum. Doreen licked dry lips and put all her skill into sticking with the flying mare. She felt with hands and legs the mare's faltering and her mouth dried with fear. The mare was not going to make it. Doreen shot a look over her shoulder. The lead rider was so close she could count his shirt buttons, and it was his rope she heard. Suddenly Doreen realized the rope would bring down the mare, not her. She touched the reins to the mare's neck and Mona swerved abruptly. The rope fell where she had been and its thrower cursed.

The mare plunged onto a narrow trail leading into the tangle of cottonwood, willow, and aspen along the riverbank. Low branches tore at Doreen's shirt and whipped her face and arms. Mud-brown water glistened through gaps in the undergrowth and muttered against rocks and debris. Pursuit crashed through the trees behind her. Ahead, mingled with the loud rush of meltwater, Doreen heard other horses.

They've circled, she thought in despair. I'm lost. Terror blacked out the world for a moment.

The mare burst out of the scrub and plunged into the river. Icy water shocked Doreen out of her panic. The river churned past, spinning clumps of grass and sticks and swirling them away; streaks of mud wound through the swirls, spreading, diffusing— Mud! Doreen looked upstream in wild hope. The sound she had heard ahead was not pursuit but the thrashing of cattle being driven across the river. The roundup! Men from the roundup were still along the Pinto! Behind her the first of her pursuers burst out of the scrub with a shout. The gallant Mona needed neither quirt nor spur but sprang toward the milling cattle with the last of her strength. Sand pulled at her feet, slowing her. The rush of the river drowned out the noises of the riders behind. Doreen concentrated her attention on the herders. Doreen waved and shouted. Did the clamor of the river drown her cries? Doreen risked a look over her shoulder. Her pursuers were coming up on both sides. They would have her in a moment. Doreen ducked her head close to the mare's neck, urging her on. The herders saw. Two of them broke from their work, jumping their mounts into a run.

Doreen glanced to the side. Her pursuers were pulling their horses up in showers of mud and water. They wheeled and rode away, whipping their weary animals viciously. The third drover whistled piercingly, then joined the other two in the chase. In moments, two more riders appeared on the riverbank. One of them took the cattle in hand, the other rode quickly to Doreen and slid from his horse.

"You're safe now, ma'am." He laid a sympathetic hand on Mona's streaming neck. "You're all heart, girl. Name's Preacher, Circle X," he added to Doreen, and held out hands to help her down. "You must be Miss Doreen of Three Rivers."

Doreen slid from her saddle and leaned against

Mona's heaving side, faint with shock, her legs too shaky to stand alone. Mona stood trembling, head hanging, breath heaving from her in gasps, legs braced wide apart. Doreen gave the mare a pat, staggered out of the water, and sank onto the wet sand with her legs straight out and her head drooping.

"Would you take off her saddle?" she whispered. "I can't just now and Mona has all she can do to carry her own weight. I hope I haven't killed her."

"Ma'am, if you'd killed her, she'd be dead on the ground." Preacher moved to Mona's side, talking softly, coaxingly, and took off the saddle and dripping saddle blanket. He set them both well up on the bank. He did not look at Doreen. "That was some kind of riding, ma'am. Most Eastern ladies would've fallen out of their silly one-stirrup, ride-in-the-park saddles a long way back." He cleared his throat. "I'm not meanin' to criticize your people, ma'am." He mounted his horse and looked down at her, his brown eyes sympathetic. "You rest here awhile. Save your story for the roundup boss. You ain't looking like you could tell it twice. I have to get someone to take my place here."

In only a short time Preacher was back. He carried Doreen ahead of him on his saddle, talking in a calm, matter-of-fact voice, calming her, easing her terror. Several hours later his horse picked its way among men clustered on their haunches near the chuck wagons, balancing plates on their knees and gulping hot coffee. It was noon and all the roundup riders had gathered for a meal and fresh horses. Horse wranglers, all of them youngsters, drove the tired morning horses to water and grass and brought fresh ones for the afternoon's work. Cattle, several hundred head, grazed beyond the camp, watched constantly by men on horseback. Preacher stopped at the Circle X chuck wagon, dismounted, and helped Doreen down, then he turned to Carson Brown.

"Boss, this lady has a story to tell ya. The horse she was riding is still down by the Pinto, recovering her strength." With that, Preacher ambled off to find himself a meal.

Doreen still felt badly shaken. She wondered what condition she would have been in if Preacher's instinct had not been to gentle her like a frightened horse. She stood facing Brown, trembling, unwilling to trust her legs for very long. Solicitous hands helped her to the side of the chuck wagon and provided a stool for her to sit on. She sagged onto it and let her head fall back against a wheel spoke.

Brown came to stand in front of her. "We met briefly over at your place, Miss Doreen. What happened?"

Doreen told him. As she talked, men who could hear what she was saying came closer—a man with a wild black beard, a very young wrangler whose cheeks bore a fine brown fuzz, a dark stocky man with narrow eyes and a tic in his cheek, a taller man with sandy hair and cool gray eyes. Doreen met Smith's look and for a moment his face, taut and grim like the others', softened in sympathy.

Brown looked critically at the gathered men. "I want six volunteers. Two of you get McTaggert's body. Take a tarp to wrap him in and get him to Three Rivers. Tell Miss Cary that Miss Doreen's all right. Four of you'll track McTaggert's killers if you can. I'm not dreamin' he died accidental, not anymore."

Six men silently left the group, saddled up, and

93

rode toward the river. Brown studied the remaining men. "We've a lot of work still to do here, boys, but I need someone to take Miss Doreen home." He looked over the group and his mouth twisted in thought. He looked speculatively at Laramie Smith. "How 'bout you, Smith, considerin' your outstandin' qualifications?" Brown let his eyes linger on the dark holster on Smith's hip. "No offense meant, of course."

"None taken," Smith responded in a cool, even voice. "I'll get her home."

"Just a minute." The dark man with the tic stepped forward. "Considering Mr. Smith's reputation—"

Smith's eyes narrowed, glittering dangerously. The man broke off without finishing his thought and an ominous silence fell. Doreen looked anxiously at the cowboys, puzzled by the sudden change of mood. Brown stepped casually in front of her, shielding her from Smith and the other man.

"I take offense, Bekkerson." Smith's drawling voice was hard and sharp-edged. "But why should I waste a good bullet on a no-'count gambler like you?"

Doreen heard a sharp crack, then Bekkerson sprawled on the ground. From behind Brown Doreen could see only Bekkerson's face and shoulders.

Bekkerson's fingers gingerly inspected his jaw. "You'll regret that, Smith."

"Not in yore lifetime." Smith spun away from the prostrate man and approached Brown, who stepped aside. Smith bowed to Doreen. "At yore service, Miss Anderson."

"Need any help?" Again Brown's eyes rested on the gun.

Smith's eyes narrowed again, then he visibly relaxed. "Unlikely," he drawled. "You're goin' to need all the hands you've got left to get the work done. I worked Blue Mountain years ago and I know my way around. Miss Anderson'll be safe with me."

Brown nodded and went back to his lunch. Smith came to Doreen's side and crouched beside her so their eyes were on a level. He spoke very quietly. "We'll be takin' a long-cut back, just in case you have any more 'friends' out there. Don't let on anythin' different from what I say. Can you last the trip?"

Doreen nodded wearily. All she wanted was to fall into bed, cry away her terror, and sleep, sleep, sleep. Smith stood.

"I'll get you a fresh horse, Miss Anderson," he said in a much louder voice. "The ride'll take about two hours."

Doreen nodded. The watching riders noted the end of the drama and returned to their food. Smith came back quickly and helped Doreen to mount a wiry pinto. She swayed in the saddle. Smith shot out an arm to steady her. The rider with the tic looked at her intently. Smith, too, studied her.

In a very low voice he asked, "Are you sure? We'll be ridin' near four hours."

"I have to," Doreen whispered. "I'm going to break down and I don't want to do it in public."

Doreen thought she caught a flash of admiration in Smith's eyes before he turned to his own horse and led the way out of camp. When they were well away, Smith stopped by a tangle of aspen and hawthorn and held up his hands to help her down.

"Do yore breakin' down here. You're goin' to need all yore nerve and concentration. I'll go have a smoke."

95

He dropped a jacket on the ground for her to sit on and walked around a boulder out of sight.

Doreen looked down at the jacket so gallantly left to protect her clothes, clothes that were wet and gritty with sand and weed seeds, and she giggled. Then the dam she had erected inside herself broke and tears flooded out. She cried and cried. When at long last the tears passed, she wiped the traces of them from her face as best she could and called Smith to resume their journey.

Perhaps an hour along the wagon trail, Smith stopped in the cover of a cedar grove. He held Doreen's eyes. "This is where the hard part starts. This way's rougher and steeper than the wagon road, but it's unexpected and so it's safer. Whoever tried to catch you will try again. Three R's got water enough for two spreads, and there's some who'll do anythin' for more water." Smith looked down at his saddle horn. "Someone's shore-nuff decided to try to get the ranch by gettin' you. You couldn't be in worse danger."

Against her will, Doreen remembered Sir Adrian's remarks about the notches in this man's gun. He was a danger, too. As if he read her thoughts, Smith's face softened, he met her eyes squarely, and his voice deepened with concern. "Do you think you can ride three hours in rough country? The wagon road's a lot easier."

Mentally Doreen kicked herself. Which should she trust, a conceited Englishman or her own instincts? "I'll make it," Doreen whispered.

They rode into the hills, Doreen holding onto her saddle horn for support whenever she was sure Smith was not watching. Their path led through stands of cottonwood, then aspen and cedar and jackpine. Time passed in a blur for Doreen as she concentrated on each step of her horse, watching the ground pass under its feet, thinking how wonderful sliding off and lying on pine needles would feel, forcing herself to stay upright in the saddle. Smith stopped at the mouth of a dry wash. He listened, then rode a short distance up the wash, then stopped to listen again. At last he seemed satisfied and motioned her to follow. "I thought I heard somethin' out of place, but I guess not. We'll chance it. Come on."

Doreen hung back. "Chance it? I've heard of flash floods—"

"You're not a complete tenderfoot, are you?" Smith's voice held a note of gentle teasing. "That was a smart thought. This wash, though, hasn't had water in it for longer than even the Indians remember. Long, long ago a rock slide closed it off. The water runs down the other side into the Roaring now. Flood's not the danger. Slides are. Or ambush."

Doreen's hands tightened on the reins. "I thought you said no one would know . . ." she whispered.

Smith looked grim. "Nothin's guaranteed, Miss Anderson. I'm playin' the odds. Are you comin'?"

Doreen touched her heels to the pinto and they began the slow climb up the wash. The footing was very rough. The horses had to pick their way over a jumble of sand, gravel, and large rocks, some the size of a human head. The cut deepened as they climbed. The sound of the horses' hooves bounced echoes off the yellow walls. Doreen let her horse follow Smith's, making no attempts to guide it. She rested her hands across the horn and let her head sag forward, too tired to conceal her weariness any longer. "I didn't know fear could be so exhausting," she whispered to herself.

Her horse stopped abruptly. She looked up.

Smith had stopped and was looking at her. "Did you say something?"

Doreen shook her head. "I was just talking to myself."

Smith nodded, taking advantage of the stop to pass her a canteen and to take a drink himself, then they rode on. In some places the ancient stream had cut away softer stone in the walls, leaving bowls and saucers in the rock. In other places the stone had been harder than the wall around it, and these places stood out from the walls as shelves and columns. Smith stopped frequently, listening. Once, during such a stop, they heard a sharp crack, followed by a slithering sound.

"Rock slide," Smith explained curtly. "Sounds like a small one."

They rode on. The riverbed became smoother and large rocks, except at the foot of a slide, became rare. The horses quickened their pace.

"There." Smith pointed ahead to an arched opening ahead of them where the trees that crowded the top of the rock wall opened up and the light was brighter. "That's the top, just beyond that open spot. We'll stop there and—"

He whirled, gun in hand so quickly that Doreen did not see him draw it. A hoof cracked on the stone at the top of the cut and a thin stream of rocks rattled down the wall. "Get off yore horse and under that rock shelf," Smith ordered without taking his eyes from a spot at the top of the wall. "Run!"

"Wh—"

"Run!"

A tremor shook the ground. Doreen slid from her mount and ran on wobbling legs toward the shelf. Smith fired twice. Another tremor shook the ground and a large chunk of wall peeled away. Doreen watched, frozen, as the large piece knocked loose other pieces. Smaller rocks, shaken free by the tremors, pelted the riverbed. Smith's horse dashed past, riderless. Doreen turned to look for Smith. He was leaping and dodging rocks. The sound of the slide escalated to a roar. Dust choked the air. Fist-sized stones rolled down the wall and bounced, raining bruising blows on Doreen's legs and shoulders. Doreen forced her legs to run and dodge. Large rocks bounded down, boulders big enough to crush a horse. Doreen stumbled and fell. A powerful arm wrenched her up and dragged her into the shelter of the rock shelf. Bitter dust swirled around them, the ground jumped under their feet, the roar of the slide shook the world. Smith crushed her against the wall, his body between her and the slide, his arms like a vise around her. Around Smith's shoulder Doreen saw the entire wall under which they had been standing disintegrate and fall into the riverbed with a crash that set the rocks already there bouncing and made Smith stagger. Doreen took a deep, shuddering breath and hid her face against his shoulder.

CHAPTER

6

THE GROUND STOPPED shivering, the dust settled, the last small rock rattled and was silent. Doreen did not move. She felt as if every remnant of strength had been torn from her. Smith's heart thudded under her ear, slowing gradually to something close to a normal rate. Slowly he loosened his crushing grip and let his arms drop to his sides. Doreen looked up at him.

Is my face as white as his? she wondered. Then she slid down the wall, sitting with a thud. "I don't think I can move," she whispered.

Smith sank down beside her and leaned his head back against the rock. He felt in his vest pocket for cigarette makings, looking down only when the pouch and papers lay in his hand. He spread a paper and opened the pouch. Tobacco sprinkled on the paper, his hand, his lap, Doreen's knee. He balled the paper with its shreds of tobacco and hurled them at the rock fall.

"Damn!" he said savagely. He wrapped his shaking hands around one upraised knee and stared into the distance.

They sat in silence for a long time. The light beyond their shelter faded. The insects and small animals that lived in the draw came out of hiding and went back to their businesses; their tiny noises and the whisper of the wind in the trees on top of the wall were the only sounds.

Doreen shut her eyes. This can't be real! she kept telling herself. I'm not the sort of person anybody wants to kill. I'm going to wake up soon. This isn't real! It can't be!

But the sound of Smith's breathing beside her and the rustle of another cigarette paper, the feel of dust between her fingertips, the deep ache in the arm Smith had grabbed, these were all real. Doreen rubbed her arm to ease the pain.

Smith looked down at her. "Did I hurt you?"

"Some. But I'd rather have a sore arm than be dead. I owe you my life."

"I was just doin' my job." He looked away, up the wash, and took a long drag on his cigarette. "I hope I got the bastard on top of the wall."

If he realized he had used a word not fit for a lady's ears, he gave no sign of it. They sat in silence until he had smoked the cigarette down to his fingers. He stood, crushed the cigarette under his boot, and offered her his hand.

"It's time to go." He pulled her to her feet, then turned and whistled through his fingers. "We'll have to ride double," he said over his shoulder. "Yore horse didn't make it." He jabbed his thumb toward the rockfall.

Smith's horse came down the wash to them snorting and hesitating, but it came. Smith mounted, then pulled Doreen up behind him. "Put yore arms tight around my waist," he ordered, and urged his horse back the way it had come.

His warm, solid back was comforting. His flannel shirt was soft and damp against Doreen's cheek. Its smell combined wool, wood smoke, lye soap, cigarettes, and the salt of fresh sweat. Doreen let the smell and feel of the shirt bound her awareness—nothing more, nothing less. It shut out remembering the terrors of the day and thinking about a future in which people tried to kill her.

They arrived at Three Rivers Ranch well after dark. Smith dismounted, lifted her off his drooping horse and onto the porch, then pounded on the door. A light came on in Cary's room and moved down the hall. Then Cary was at the door, lamp in one hand, the other hand holding her dressing gown closed at the throat.

"Doreen," she breathed. She set the lamp down and wrapped her arms around her niece. "I've been so worried about you! Three Rolling W riders came by to say outlaws of some sort had chased you and that they had been chasing them, but they didn't know what happened to you. Are you all right?"

Doreen nodded weakly.

Cary sighed in relief and released her. "Can I offer you coffee or something to eat, Mr.—?"

"Smith, ma'am. Laramie Smith."

"Ah, yes, I remember you now. We met at the train. You and Tennessee."

Smith managed a weary grin. "Yes, ma'am. The one and only. I appreciate yore offer, but I reckon the thing I want most just now is a bedroll and a place to throw it."

"We started home at noon, Aunt Cary, and on the

102

way someone tried to kill me. If it hadn't been for Mr. Smith—" Doreen's voice broke.

Cary put her arm around Doreen again and squeezed. She looked up at Smith questioningly.

"Someone tried to bury us in a rock slide. Miss Anderson's horse was killed. I know you're wonderin', but I'm all in and Miss Anderson's tireder than that. Ask what you like in the mornin', ma'am."

There was no arguing with the authority in his voice, tired as it was.

"There're only five beds occupied in the bunkhouse right now," Cary said. "Put your horse in the barn for the night and bed down with the other men."

Smith touched his hat and led his horse into the darkness.

Doreen slept late the next morning. When she wandered into the kitchen just before noon, Cary was sliding jelly out of a mold onto the jelly dish.

Cary looked up from her work and smiled at her niece. "Hello, honey. I hope you feel better this morning."

Doreen touched a brown and purple bruise. "My arm's real sore, but that's the worst of it. That and the nightmares."

"Those will pass. Laramie's already told me what happened yesterday, so you don't need to. I have a feeling that that young man knows a lot about danger."

Doreen poured herself a cup of coffee and sighed. She did not want to think of danger right now. "With McTaggert dead, how will we manage?"

Cary bustled over to the stove. "We'll think of something. Or Bill will. Laramie headed back to the roundup an hour or so ago. He suggested you see what

Bill has to say about foremen." Cary looked over at her niece. "You can't afford to give up now, honey."

Doreen sighed again. Instead of no-account boarders, she thought, I have a ranch, rustlers, a conceited neighbor who uses 3R land whenever he thinks he won't get caught, riders shot, a foreman murdered, and two attacks on me in the same day. Matters look worse and worse.

She paced slowly to the window and looked out at the mountains. Charcoal clouds wrapped the peaks and a gray mist of rain crept from them down the mountains toward the ranch. A streak of yellow light raced from one dark cloud to another and, moments later, thunder rumbled ominously.

It rained all day. The entire basin turned deep green as if by magic, the color more startling by contrast with the charcoal clouds. The rivers ran bank-full. Thunder shook the house and rattled the lamps. In the tiny ranch office, Cary sat at the desk, fussing, fidgeting, and snarling. Doreen ran her fingers distractedly through her hair and looked across her aunt to the cottonwood grove beyond the window and the track to the pass. Without a good foreman, a beginner could not run a ranch successfully. Yet they could not scrape together enough money for another rooming house. They were stranded in this wilderness.

Doreen could not let herself dwell on that. McTaggert was dead. The calf crop was way down. And she was ignorant. Helplessly, frustratingly ignorant. She slammed out of the office and roamed the house, feeling as if all her nerves were standing on end. Doreen looked out the nearest window at the rain.

Even if it weren't raining, I wouldn't dare go

outside. Someone tried to kill me. Twice! I can't protect my ranch. I can't protect myself. What do I *do?*

She paced. She wandered in and out of the office until Cary slammed her fist on the desk. "Will you get out of here! Find something to do. You're driving me crazy!"

Doreen got "out of here" as far as the parlor, where the contrast of charcoal gray and brilliant green outside again caught and held her attention. Luke in his slicker, driving in what remained of the remuda toward the ranch yard, made a bright-yellow splash against the rain-washed green flats.

A fast ride, until I'm too tired to think, that's what I need. But I can't risk it. Images of her last fast ride raced through her mind—the violent motion, the fear, the whiz of bullets, the mare trembling between her knees. She whirled from the window. *If I hadn't ridden astride, I'd be dead.*

Unbidden, Laramie Smith's comment weeks before about riding astride came back. She shivered. Maintaining her modesty was not worth losing her life. She took her black serge skirt, scissors, and her sewing kit into the office and spent the rest of that day and part of the next keeping her aunt company and constructing a divided skirt.

Early the next morning, the rain ceased. Doreen took a break from her sewing to walk around the yard, enjoying the fresh, clean smell of the air. The moment she stepped off the porch Luke was beside her. She prowled the ranch yard and the barn. Luke did not leave her side. She knelt in the garden to yank out weeds. Luke leaned against the apple tree and waited. Significant looks did not send him away. Finally Doreen sprang to her feet and glared at the young black rider. "Why are you following me?"

Luke scuffed the toe of one boot in the dirt. "Smith said to guard you, Miss Doreen." His hand shifted fleetingly to the butt of his revolver. "Someone tried to kill you. Smith said someone should always be around to protect you."

"Mr. Smith doesn't give orders here."

Luke looked even more embarrassed. "No, Miss Doreen, he doesn't."

"Then why are you following me?"

Luke's thin face took on a stubborn look. "Because he's right. You're a tenderfoot, Miss Doreen, and a woman. It's a man's job to protect such-like."

"And if I order you to stop?"

"I ain't goin' to, ma'am. Not even if you fire me. You don't know the danger. We do. Bill, now, he'll make you see when he comes. Till then, I'm stickin' close as long as you're outside."

And Luke did stick to her, like her shadow, both amusing her with his persistence and frightening her with his continual reminder that the men of this country thought she was in mortal danger. Finally she could take that reminder no longer and returned to her sewing inside.

Only a few hours later, Bill Haycox strode onto the porch and rapped loudly on the back door. "I'd like to talk to you for a few minutes, a matter of business," Bill told Doreen as he stepped through the door, his voice urgent.

Doreen nodded. Bill would not ride for close to two hours to "talk a few minutes" if what he had to say was not very important. She motioned Bill to a seat in the parlor.

Haycox did not wait until he was fully seated before he began. "Miss Doreen, I'm gonna be blunt, because you don't have much time. You *own* valuable land and a fortune in water, while most of the rest of us are operatin' on grazing rights only. Lord knows how Jacob talked the Indians out of it. Anyway, two attempts have been made on your life. I believe, and Asa and Carson Brown agree with me, that there'll probably be more. You're a tenderfoot, and a woman, and at risk on both counts. You haven't been willin' to go back East, so you're gonna need a bodyguard, someone who knows the territory and knows how those outlaws think." Doreen started to protest but Bill held up his hand. "Now, wait. Think about what's happened to you. Did you know about that back trail? Would you have heard the horse on top of the wall soon enough to save yourself? Do you know good hiding places on your own land? Can you defend yourself with a gun?"

Doreen swallowed and shook her head. She did not want to think about danger, she did not want to talk about it, she did not want to acknowledge it.

Bill leaned toward her and his urgent voice gentled. "I know it has to be hard for a lady like you to believe someone'd kill you. But there're men who'll do anythin' to get what they want, and someone wants your ranch, or at least its water. You haven't changed your mind about goin' back East?"

Doreen shook her head.

"Then you must protect yourself." Bill stood and circled the room once. He stopped and stared down at his boots; his mouth twisted. He turned to Doreen and took a deep breath. "Without a guard, you'll almost *have* to stay inside your house to be reasonably safe, but you have this ranch to run—"

"And how do I do that now, with McTaggert dead?" Doreen cringed at the rudeness of her interruption, but she did not want Bill to make her look more closely at her personal danger.

"California's a good man. He'd do well for you as foreman. But your *life*." Haycox caught and held Doreen's eyes. "What are you willin' to do to save your *life*?"

Doreen looked down at her hands, clenched in her lap. Her hands, despite her care, were lightly tanned and beginning to freckle. Fear washed over her in sickening waves. "What do you advise?" she whispered.

"Well, I say pick an absolutely trustworthy man to guard you, and there are damn—excuse me—few men around here that I'd stake my life aren't rustlers. Ten, maybe, and two of them work for you. Diego's no marksman, so he's out. California could guard you, and guard you well, but you do have that ranch to run. His skills are more valuable to you as foreman."

"Who, then?" Doreen's voice shook.

"Laramie Smith. He's a dead shot and knows this part of the territory like the back of his hand. He's also absolutely trustworthy."

Laramie Smith. Doreen swallowed hard. Laramie Smith. Not a safe half-day's ride away, but beside her all day long. His teasing voice, his dancing eyes, his reputation with a gun . . .

"I thought you hired him to do special work for

you." Her voice had gone husky. She cleared her throat discreetly.

Bill nodded. "I did, but I'm willin' to loan him to you, if you're willin' to stick close to your house when he has to do things for me."

Doreen looked down at her hands knotted in her lap. "Have you asked Mr. Smith about this?"

Bill grimaced. "Uh-huh. He wasn't too happy about the idea, but he sees the need."

"He was your foreman once. Would he take that job here and leave California to guard me?"

Bill shook his head. "That'd be a bad trade. Larry's one of the best shots in North America. Why would you want less? Besides, the foreman's job commits him to you for the whole season, and I can't spare Larry that long."

Doreen studied her clenched hands. She did not want Mr. Smith's constant company, but she did not want to die, either. She stood. "Do I officially hire him on?"

"Reckon that won't be necessary, Miss Doreen. Between the two of us, we'll call it a loan. To everyone else, it'll look like he changed spreads. All right?"

Doreen nodded and they shook hands. Haycox hesitantly rested a hand on Doreen's shoulder in comfort and encouragement. "Larry rode out this mornin' on business. He should be back early tomorrow and come here the next day. You take care of yourself till then."

Doreen nodded. Haycox gave her shoulder the slightest squeeze, then strode out of the house.

Doreen stuck close to the ranch house for the next

two days. The first day she offered California the foreman's job. Though California was not as shy as most of the other riders, it was an uncomfortable session and Doreen felt wilted when it was over. On the second day, it rained again. Doreen watched the storm from the parlor window, still fascinated by the rain-washed brightness of the colors. Two riders in yellow slickers broke from the trees and came toward the ranch house at a canter.

"Company's coming, Aunt Cary. I wonder if it's Mr. Smith." She looked closer. "There are two riders, though."

Seen closer, the horses were clearly long-legged Thoroughbreds.

Sir Adrian. For an instant Doreen's memory flashed back to the rider on the long-legged Thoroughbred who had waved, she had thought at her, the day she found McTaggert.

The two riders dismounted swiftly, wrapped their reins around the porch rail, and stepped up onto the porch. Sir Adrian draped his slicker over the porch rail beside his reins and rapped on the front door. The man with him tossed his slicker toward the rail, then stood, shifting impatiently from one foot to another. He was the dark, sharp-faced rider with the tic in his cheek who had watched Doreen at the roundup.

"Sir Adrian and a friend," Doreen announced.

Cary grimaced, smoothed her frizzing hair perfunctorily, and stood, brushing the wrinkles from her dress. "I'll let him in. He's persistent. You have to give him that." Cary stalked out of the office and up to the front door.

Sir Adrian must have heard her footstep, for he

110

pushed open the door and walked into the parlor. Doreen felt her aunt bristle, but Cary Williams was too well-bred to give the man the set-down he deserved for walking in uninvited. The dark rider followed Sir Adrian in and shut the door hard. The rider's face was set and Doreen felt a tiny shiver of apprehension.

The Englishman bowed to Cary. "Miss Williams." He turned to Doreen. "I've just learned about McTaggert's death. Too bad. He was a good man. However, as you've probably learned already, there's no time out here for mourning. You need another foreman as soon as possible." He motioned the dark rider forward. "Miss Anderson, this is my cousin, 'Tic' Bekkerson. We've been concerned about Three Rivers, what with the rustlers and that gunfighter Smith and all. Tic has offered to be foreman here until the end of the season (he's been managing the Rolling W) or until you see the value of getting this ranch's dead weight off your hands." He looked at Doreen with moving earnestness. "It *will* be a dead weight, Miss Anderson. It takes years to learn to run a spread like this. You'll lose the ranch to creditors long before that."

Cary, who had been getting pinker and pinker at the Englishman's busy-body impertinence, sounded for a moment like she was choking, but when she spoke her voice was calm and very sweet. "I understand you know a lot about the local creditors, sir."

Sir Adrian sniffed. "I imagine you picked up *that* bit of gossip from that Haycox person."

"Gossip can be an ugly thing—" Bekkerson began, only to be silenced by a look from his employer.

"I'm afraid my p— my cousin is a bit impatient sometimes with the necessities of courtesy. I do have several years' experience here in the territory, ladies, and I offer advice from what I've learned. I remember well what it was like being a tinhorn—"

"Greenhorn," Cary corrected dryly.

"As you say," Sir Adrian snapped. He took a deep, unsteady breath. "I'm willing to make a new agreement, with you, for the land I now lease along the Pinto. I understand Johnson and Haycox offered you installments for the whole ranch, after the roundup. I'm offering cash, now, for that property." Sir Adrian pulled a thick wad of greenbacks from an inside pocket of his elegant riding coat and extended it toward Doreen. "Here's the money, ten thousand dollars, and I have a receipt for it right here." Sir Adrian pulled a folded piece of heavy vellum out of another inside pocket. "If you will just sign here . . ." He laid the paper on a small lamp table. "I have a pen, Miss Anderson." He extracted a gold-plated pen and a slender traveler's inkwell from an inside pocket of his riding coat.

Doreen felt another warning prickle. "I've told you no, sir," she said, proud that her voice did not waver.

Sir Adrian shook his head as if that were nonsense. "Believe me, you will need cash before fall." He extended the pen.

Doreen kept her hands at her sides, willing them to stay quiet and appear relaxed. "No."

"I already lease the water rights—"

"Then pay your first quarter's rent. It's a month past due."

Sir Adrian waved his hand dismissively. "That is just a pittance compared to what I offer now."

Doreen stiffened. Men usually used such a condescending tone with women who needed to talk business,

but being used to it did not make her like it. "Pittance or not, you owe it!" She picked up Sir Adrian's paper and began reading it.

Bekkerson nudged his boss. Sir Adrian plucked the paper from her fingers. "There's no need for you to bother your pretty head with details, Miss Anderson. Perhaps I could contact your attorney to discuss this further?"

"Mr. Granscomb-Whitly," Doreen cut in, her anger almost beyond her power to control, "that paper isn't a receipt. It's a bill of sale, and you didn't allow me to read far enough to find out how much land you were buying with your ten thousand dollars. We may be women, Mr. Granscomb-Whitly, and tenderfeet, but we're not fools! Take your foreman and go home."

The manager shot Doreen a dark look, then looked at Sir Adrian. Doreen thought she saw the Englishman give the tiniest shake of his head.

Sir Adrian shrugged gracefully and smiled his charming smile. "Surely you don't blame me for trying? I thought—"

Doreen exploded, all thoughts of ladylike behavior forgotten. The gall of the man, so calmly admitting his attempt to cheat her! "You thought to steal this ranch, sir! Steal it! From two 'gently bred' women who have no man to protect their interests."

Sir Adrian backed away a step. "Surely that's a little harsh. I was not buying the *whole* ranch." Sir Adrian's voice was conciliating.

"You'll excuse me if I don't believe that, sir, since you snatched back your document before I could read it through. I *do* know how to read, sir!"

Sir Adrian backed another step away from her

anger, his face registering a well-bred distaste. "Really, Miss Anderson! That's nothing to enrage yourself about. I never said—"

"What's the matter, *Sir* Adrian? The other ladies of your acquaintance don't get angry?" Doreen closed the distance between them, fists now clenched, heart pounding. She refrained from shouting only with extreme effort. "Your men murdered Tinker. Murdered him, sir! You try to steal not just the land in question, but an unnamed larger amount. You—you—take your 'cousin' and get out!"

"Your approach obviously isn't working," Bekkerson snapped. "Give me a chance." His eyes brightened as he looked at Doreen and he flexed his hands.

Doreen went cold. The man meant to hurt her. She reached one trembling hand out and closed it over the steadiness of a chair back. What could she do? She had no means to protect herself. And she had thought Sir Adrian lived by the rules of polite society!

Bekkerson took the pen and the document from Sir Adrian, who now looked as pale as Doreen felt. "Really, Bekkerson, couldn't we . . ."

"You had your turn," Bekkerson snarled. "It didn't work."

"You'd better sign," Sir Adrian told Doreen. "My cousin has an unpredictable temper, unfortunately."

"You touch me, you snake, and I'll have the sheriff on you so fast—"

Bekkerson grinned nastily. "You try that, Miss Anderson. The sheriff's an old friend of ours."

"Sooner or later you'll get hurt holding onto this place," Sir Adrian added.

Doreen knew what he meant. Bekkerson would in

seconds slip his leash and then . . . She willed her voice to be steady. "I'll get hurt right now is what you mean. Get out, before I call my men!"

"Your men are off chasing 'rustlers.'" Bekkerson sneered. "We made sure of—"

"The lady told y'all to leave. Git!" The slow, dangerous drawl from the hallway froze everyone.

The women turned slowly. Laramie Smith stood, tall, lean, dripping, in the doorway from the kitchen end of the house. His slicker was still settling into a gleaming wet mound at his feet.

Bekkerson stiffened. "What're you doing here, Smith?"

"That's none of yore concern, Bekkerson. I heard the lady tell you two to leave."

"I'm here on business," Sir Adrian said haughtily.

"So am I, Sir Adrian." Smith's voice was slower and softer and sent a chill of fear up Doreen's back. "Miss Doreen's my boss now and I heard you and yore gambler friend threaten her."

"You lie, Smith! You've always worked for Haycox," Bekkerson snarled.

"Get into the hall, ladies," Smith barked.

Doreen and Cary quickly obeyed.

"Now, Bekkerson," Laramie continued, "I'm tellin' you to take back what you said. Right here, right now. I don't lie. *Don't* go for yore gun or you're daid, ladies' parlor or no. Say you lied, Bekkerson."

"No two-bit gunslinger—"

"Say you lied. Now!"

Bekkerson's face turned deep red. His hand jerked for his gun but before it could clear its holster Sir Adrian had wrenched Bekkerson's arm behind his back,

115

his speed, strength, and courage surprising in a man who appeared so soft and affected.

"Say it!" Smith thundered.

"I lied." But Bekkerson's poisonous look said that Smith had not heard the last of the matter.

Laramie's stance relaxed a hair. He looked a command at the two unwelcome guests.

The Englishman shoved a struggling Bekkerson toward the door and his horse. "Fool!" he snarled, just before he flung Bekkerson's slicker at him.

The two mounted and galloped away. The women came slowly back into the parlor.

"That's the last we'll see of them," Doreen said, relieved. "Thank you, Mr. Smith. I was so frightened!"

"Just doin' my job," Smith drawled. "And if that's the last you *see* of them, that damned Englishman's not finished. I'll bet he hasn't even got the ready cash to pay the water rent. That wad of bills had to come from his gambler-partner."

"Partner?" Doreen had thought she understood what had happened, but now she was not so sure.

"Didn't you know? Bekkerson is a gambler, lately of Jamesville, who won half the Rolling W about the time you came here. Sir Adrian's flat broke. Gambled it away. Bekkerson's foreman and the real boss over there to protect his own money. Though I don't imagine he'll stay longer than he has to. Workin' isn't a gambler's way."

"I could use a cup of coffee," Cary said in a shaking voice. "You, Laramie?"

Smith smiled, a slow lighting of his lean, tanned face. "Shore could, ma'am." He ducked out of his hat, exposing a white strip of untanned forehead.

Doreen followed them down the hall to the kitchen, trembling with reaction. Without Smith's intervention, she would have been hurt, perhaps a great deal. And if Sir Adrian had not stopped Bekkerson, a man might have died, in her parlor, before her eyes. This man, walking so calmly ahead of her, had been ready to kill. She found the change in him hard to believe. He was nothing like the teasing man on the train or the flirting cowboy of the dance or even like the man who had saved her from the rock slide. That man had been as frightened as she.

Smith stopped in the kitchen door and leaned against the door frame, watching Cary get down the cups and pour the coffee. Doreen could not pass into the kitchen without touching some part of him. Tall and lean and dangerous he was. She felt suddenly afraid of the power and the danger and the attractiveness of him. She resolved not even to try to pass him. Instead, she summoned all her courage and glared up at him. "Go back to Blue Mountain, Laramie Smith. I won't have a hired gun here!"

"Doreen!"

Cary's shocked voice brought Doreen to a sense of the proprieties, but it was too late. Smith's face had frozen into hard and angry lines. He came away from the door in one smooth motion and towered over Doreen. "I've never hired out my gun. Never! I came to Three Rivers because my friend said you needed my help. I'm a marksman, nothing else. I told you that and I told the truth. But Bekkerson and the Englishman believe otherwise, though I didn't tell 'em, and you're not to say different. Understood?"

Doreen nodded and guilt made her flush. She could

not understand where her sudden anger had come from. She *had* hired him to guard her. He *had* told her he was a marksman, when they were dancing, but she had lost the words in the feelings his arms had awakened in her. She forced herself to look him in the eyes. "I—I'm sorry. I was told—You—I'm sorry."

His face softened. "I'm forgettin' you're a tenderfoot still, and ignorant." He paused to see if she would react to his gentle barb. "I apologize for snarlin' like I did. You cain't know what that kind of talk means to a man. Friends?"

Another sudden change in him. It rattled her. Doreen turned away, clutching her hands as if they were cold. "I—I don't know." She heard his soft laugh and spun to face him. "You said that just to fluster me!"

"Did I? Tsk, tsk, tsk." His gray eyes were dancing with mischief.

Doreen spun and busied herself setting out saucers and plates for cookies. Her hands shook a little, the plates chittered against each other, and she knew, without looking, that Smith noticed and enjoyed her agitation.

He crossed the kitchen and stood behind her. "Turn around," he ordered gently, "I want you to look at me when I say this, so you know for sure I'm not teasin' you."

Doreen's hands clenched on the table edge. She did not turn.

"Please."

His quiet dignity compelled her. She turned and looked up at him.

"You do need protection, all the time. That'll be my

118

job. I'm a crack shot and I know the district pretty well."

That was probably an understatement, Doreen thought, taking a deep unsteady breath. She looked away and her hands tightened their hold on each other.

"You aren't goin' to like this next part." Smith's voice was low and oddly hesitant. "You'll go around the ranch buildings and yard with Diego or Luke, whichever isn't workin' the horses. If you want to ride farther, you'll have to go with me, or, if I'm away (and I will be sometimes, because Bill needs me, like he told you), with California. No one else. That's the list of completely trustworthy men here. NO ONE ELSE! Even if that means you have to stay at the house."

Doreen looked down at the floor. Her mouth felt dry. The danger was real. It was close. She scooted a tiny bread crumb around with the toe of her boot, giving herself a moment to be sure her voice would be steady. "How long do you think this will go on?"

"Until Sir Adrian gets caught with enough evidence to interest the U.S. marshal or until one of his gambler friends shoots him for cheatin' at cards."

Doreen studied Smith's face. He was deadly serious. "Sir Adrian? You're sure?"

"As sure as a man can be without seein' the b—the Englishman runnin' brands or palmin' an extra ace."

"How long before—before—?" Doreen could not bring herself to finish her thought.

"Before the ranchers catch him? They have an association that's tryin' to collect proof, but till they have it, they can't go to the marshal, and the sheriff is in Sir Adrian's pocket."

"It sounds like it'll take forever."

"Not that long." Smith smiled a little. "But it may take till fall. Sir Adrian plans to have Three Rivers Ranch, Miss Doreen. Don't ever doubt it. He tried charm first, hopin' to marry you and get the ranch that way without spending a cent. But you clearly weren't interested. So he'll have to buy the ranch, or kidnap you and take Three Rivers for your ransom, or kill you, but he means to have this ranch and its water."

Doreen shuddered. She stared at Smith's middle shirt button and forced herself to look coldly at what had already happened to her, what might happen to her. Smith was telling the truth. She was in real, personal danger. She could no longer hide from it, look away from it. She needed Smith's knowledge and his skill with guns if she were to live through the summer. She adjusted her image of the future to include this impudent, serious, teasing, deadly man. She had met many young men in Chicago in the years before her parents died. None of them had mocked her, held her, danced with her as this man had. None had had the skills necessary to save her life. With none of them had she felt this fluttery panic at the thought of seeing them, being near them for months. "I'm afraid," she whispered.

"I know," he replied. "So am I."

CHAPTER

7

THE MORNING AFTER Smith's arrival, Doreen helped serve her cowboys their usual hearty breakfast. Laramie Smith lingered in the kitchen after the others had gone. He leaned against the outside door with his arms crossed over his chest and watched the women help Cookie clean up. Cookie wore a savage frown and muttered violent things under his breath. Smith chuckled. "Ease up, Cookie. The ladies'll get used to bein' waited on and'll leave you alone soon enough. 'Sides, you're goin' back to the roundup this afternoon."

Cookie shot Smith a look that made him tremble in fake terror.

"Hey, now, *I'm* just doin' my job. If Miss Doreen wants to go out, I have to be around to take her out." Smith looked over at Doreen. "California recommends we spend the day lookin' over yore land. He thinks now I'm here, it's time you learned yore spread. The odds against you are heavy enough without you bein' ignorant. I agree with him, but what we do's up to you. You're the boss. I do have horses waitin' outside, an' I'll bet

121

Cookie'll quick make us a lunch, if only to get you out of his territory. Miss Cary, you want to come?"

Very neat, Mr. Smith, Doreen thought, a suggestion framed and arranged to make it hard for me to turn it down.

Cary glanced at Doreen, then chuckled. She hadn't missed Smith's technique, either. "I don't ride. Besides, I agreed to do the books and I have a lot of work there." Cary untied her apron and disappeared down the hall toward the office.

Traitor! Doreen thought at Cary's retreating back, with both apprehension and amusement. You're leaving me unchaperoned with this cowhand.

That was her out if she wanted it, that she was an unmarried woman without a chaperone. She stole a glance at Smith. He would be insulted if she said it. It was unthinkable out here for a man to make an improper advance to an unescorted woman. Besides, she told herself ruefully, you've been a spinster for years. But there had been that waltz. . . . She hesitated.

"Miss Doreen?"

Doreen looked up. Smith straightened and came closer. He spoke so quietly that Cookie couldn't overhear. "It's purely business between you an' me from now on. Any flirtin' I did with you was before I knew I'd be workin' here. Any cowhand's got a right to flirt with a pretty girl, but not with the boss. That teasin' yesterday—after Sir Adrian—you looked scared white and I thought I'd get yore mind off what might've happened." He turned. "I'll wait outside. Will fifteen minutes give you time to change?"

Doreen nodded, took off her apron, and went to her

room. She had nothing to wear riding but the altered black skirt, and she had not tried that out. Her mouth tightened. The men were right; she did need to know her land, and Smith was a gentleman. If the skirt rode up, he would not look at her exposed lower limbs. Her tall boots would also help preserve her modesty. Quickly Doreen put on an embroidered shirtwaist, slid on the newly divided skirt, tied on a bright scarf for dust. She walked back and forth across the room. The skirt pulled a little. She would have to get to Jamesville and get a dressmaker's help with making a better one. And get fabric for more practical dresses. She pulled on her tall English riding boots. They were old, and a mite too small now, but she would not be doing any walking in them. Last, she picked up a jaunty bonnet to keep her face from tanning.

Smith was waiting, as he had said he would be. His eyes flashed over her, but his expression revealed nothing of what he was thinking. He offered his cupped hand to boost her into the saddle of a tall roan, then swung onto Tennessee. They rode into the foothills.

At the crest of the first, Smith pulled up his horse and looked back over his shoulder. "One of the first tricks of findin' yore way back—look where you've been. Find some rock or tree or hollow as a mark and remember it." He took a thin pad of paper and the stub of a pencil from a pocket and handed them to Doreen. "Write down what you see. A cattleman's life depends on noticin' things: where he is, first; then what condition the waterholes and streams are in, how the grass looks, what varmints are out and how many, whether the cattle are healthy or thin or ailin'."

Smith touched his heels to Tennessee and they

began climbing again, through the hills and up the lower slopes of the mountains. Spring wildflowers covered grassy areas with splashes of yellow, white, purple, and pink. Smith pointed out small pools of water, streams that would dry up later in the summer, game trails, possible fords of the Pinto and which ones were unusable in spring, the cattle they passed and their brands. Most were 3R.

"Roundup always misses a few," he told her. "We hope to catch those in the fall."

But as they rode higher, they saw more and more 3R cattle.

"There're too many," Smith commented, almost to himself. He stopped a moment, thinking, then moved on.

They dismounted at midafternoon on the bank of a clear, narrow stream and ate their lunch. Doreen hoped she successfully concealed the discomfort her chafing corset caused when she moved. She told herself she would get used to it, just as her body would get used to riding a horse again. After lunch they began circling back toward the ranch. They saw an eagle, sailing high and motionless in the bright, cloudless sky, and watched it for a long moment. They saw a stag in velvet, a doe and her fawn. They saw a coyote den with fuzzy yellow pups wrestling and growling outside the door. Smith pulled the rifle from the sheath under his knee.

"No!"

Doreen's sudden shout scattered coyotes in all directions.

Smith's body went taut. His shot was gone. His mouth thinned. "You're the boss, but they're varmints. A pack of 'em can take down a calf easy."

Doreen stifled an angry retort and thought a moment. This was not the East. Here, humans and animals competed for survival and each animal had to earn its right to exist. She thought of the grace and power of the eagle, the doggish playfulness of the coyote pups, the 3R stock already severely depleted by rustlers. She nudged her horse closer to Tennessee, laid a hesitant hand on Smith's rigid arm, and looked up at him.

"I'm sorry. I acted from ignorance and sentiment. We don't have calves to spare, do we?"

He studied her face gravely. "Do you want them shot after all?"

"I don't *want* them shot, but if it's necessary, Mr. Smith . . ."

The muscles under her hand relaxed. The rifle slipped back into its sheath. The lean face turned toward Doreen. "It's necessary, but I reckon I don't have to make you watch. If we sit real quiet, maybe they'll come out in the open again and you can watch them awhile. Those pups are shore cute."

They sat quietly for some time. Eventually, the female coyote poked her head out of the den, sniffed, looked around, then emerged. She stretched luxuriously and yawned. The pups crowded up to her belly for a snack, then, just as quickly, resumed play as if nothing had happened. Smith and Doreen watched them play for some time in companionable silence. Then Tennessee shifted his feet and the coyote family vanished.

"Thank you, Mr. Smith. I've never seen anything like that."

He looked down at her and smiled a lazy smile. "'Mr. Smith' seems mighty formal," he drawled. "You're the only person I know calls me 'Mister.'" He looked down at his hands, resting lightly on his thighs. "Reckon you could call me Laramie?"

The "Mister" did sound odd, now that he mentioned it, yet it helped keep a distance between them. If she called him by his given name . . . "Is it safe?" she asked, very low, sure without knowing why that he would understand what she meant.

His gray eyes were serious. He studied her face. "I think so. A man like me doesn't even dream of ladies like you. Besides, I won't be at Three Rivers long and I reckon Bill's job will be my last."

Doreen looked at him sharply. "You're going into some other kind of work?"

"No, ma'am, I reckon I won't be doin' any work at all after that."

It took a moment for the meaning of his words to come clear. Dead. He expected to be killed. The thought chilled Doreen to the bone. These Westerners talked of killing and dying as if life meant nothing! Then fury swept her. How could Bill allow it?

Doreen was saddle sore the next day. She hobbled about the ranch house, going outside only to the necessary, trying to keep her disability from the sight of her riders as much as possible, because the sorest muscles were in the most indelicate of places and her gait made that fact most obvious. In the afternoon, she conferred with California in the office. The young rider had a sharp mind and a practical nature. After the conference, he returned to the roundup, leaving behind suggestions for managing the ranch that came very close to being orders. Doreen sat staring at the wall for some time after he had gone. She had so much to learn.

She sighed and went out to find Laramie to tell him she would be ready to see more of the ranch the next day.

Laramie was ready and waiting immediately after breakfast. It was a brilliant, warm morning. Doreen dropped the jacket she had planned to wear over one of the kitchen's benches, tied the strings of a snug, dark bonnet under her chin, slipped on riding gloves, and followed Laramie outside. Laramie glanced over her, his face disapproving, but he said nothing.

He only criticizes people he doesn't work for, Doreen thought, stifling a giggle.

He did not offer to help her up, so Doreen had to lead her horse to the porch to mount. It was an inauspicious beginning and the day ran downhill from there. The sun was hot, Doreen's gelding spooky, the air still, Doreen's corset stifling and rubbing spots still raw from the previous ride. Doreen resolved not to betray her discomfort, because she had no doubt Smith would find her condition amusing. But the effort impaired her concentration. Several times Laramie had to speak sharply to draw her attention to something he considered important for her, usually a landmark.

As the day advanced, the pages of Doreen's notepad sometimes swam before her eyes and her tongue felt cottony and thick. Lunch, in the shade of some cottonwoods along a tiny stream, was a brief respite too soon over. They went from the shade into the blazing sun of the open grassy flats at the mouth of the valley. Heat shimmered in the air. Laramie pulled up his horse and pointed to a bird's nest in the grass, hidden from all except an expert eye. A puff of breeze flapped the hems of Doreen's divided skirt. Her gelding flung his head up, then down, and began to buck. Doreen clung with all her skill, determined to show Smith she could stay on, but by the time the horse calmed to mere hops and sidles, Doreen's hair had pulled loose of its neat bun and trailed in damp strings around her face and down her neck. Her shirtwaist clung to her, sticky with sweat, and she felt as if her corset were suffocating her. She gasped for air, the entire world seemed to shimmer, then it spun and blurred.

When she came aware of her surroundings again, she was resting against something narrow and hard. A little breeze stirred her hair. Slowly she opened her eyes. Laramie was fanning her with his hat. The hard object under her head was his thigh. "Damn fool woman," he was muttering. When he noticed she was watching him, he did not even have the grace to be embarrassed. "A tight, black hat on such a day. And a corset! What *were* you thinkin' of?"

Doreen felt her face go hot with embarrassment. She hardly knew the man and he was talking to her of intimate underthings she was not sure even a husband would mention. Worse, resist as she would, her eyes kept flicking toward the bulge in his denims so near her cheek.

If Smith noticed her embarrassment, he gave no sign. "Dress for the work, woman! Stays are for dress-up. You cain't ride in 'em, especially on a day like this. You've got to be able to breathe." He thrust her black bonnet into her hand. "You have to let air in around yore head, too. Put that damn Eastern contraption in a drawer and leave it!" He boosted her ungently to her feet, jammed his Stetson on her head, and almost threw her onto her horse. "We're goin' back to the house. If you want to learn about this place by ridin' with me, dress for it!"

He said nothing more until they were in the kitchen, where Cary was stirring a pot on the stove. "Miss Cary, Miss Doreen passed out from the heat. Keep her inside, make her rest, and give her lots of water." He snatched his hat back and stalked out of the house.

Doreen sagged onto the bench and let her head rest on the table against her crossed arms. She still felt woozy and the humiliation of Smith's lecture still burned. She had been told how to dress, in blatantly improper terms, by a male employee. Not only that, but she would have to follow his orders or he would not ride with her, and if he refused to do that, she would never learn about her ranch, because he was her bodyguard and she could not, would not risk riding alone. And if she did not learn about the ranch . . . Her thoughts spun, trapping her between necessity and propriety.

In the end, necessity won. Just before dawn two days later, Doreen and Cary, with Laramie as guard and Diego driving, set out for Jamesville in the wagon to buy Doreen a suitable hat and practical fabrics for work clothes for both women.

Laramie at least has the grace not to look I-told-you-so, Doreen grumbled to herself.

The road was, if anything, worse than Doreen remembered it. The wagon rocked and complained. Before many hours, Doreen's sitting muscles were complaining, too. She began to envy Laramie his horse, though she knew she could not possibly have ridden such a long way. She tried to keep her mind off her discomfort by going over and over her shopping list. It helped only a little. Always, at the edge of her vision or riding ahead, was Smith, moving with his horse as if the two of them were one, his eyes examining the land for some distance along the road, his rifle resting easily in the crook of one arm. Even Diego had a shotgun lying on the seat beside him. Doreen eyed Laramie Smith resentfully. His presence reminded her constantly of her danger and her fear. And of her discomfort, because he looked so comfortable and relaxed.

Doreen's discomfort was approaching agony by the time they reached Jamesville. At Sarah James's, she permitted Smith to lift her from the wagon, which spared her hips and thighs movement. Doreen winced just from the effort of standing, then looked up at Laramie. "Thank you," she whispered, weary and sore beyond measure.

"Think nothin' of it, ma'am," he drawled, and for a moment his face was alive with mischief.

"Ma'am" was formality far beyond anything he usually offered, and Doreen knew he was waiting for some sign from her that she recognized his teasing. She smiled at him. "I'd curtsy, sir, but this wagon ride and two mornings on horseback prevent it." Then she dropped her eyes and blushed deeply, appalled at the unseemly frankness with which she had spoken to him. One did not talk about such things even to the men of one's own family!

The shopping and fittings went well, and in two days the small group was on its way home. About midway, thunderheads began piling up on the horizon. Doreen watched them, towering gray-black and magnificent on the horizon.

"Ooh. We have no clouds like *that* in the East," she said, to no one in particular.

Laramie gave her a sharp glance, but said nothing, just extracted slickers for everyone from the back of the wagon. The drenching rain slowed them, but the trip home was otherwise uneventful.

At the ranch, Doreen's ignorance became for her a nightmare about an impossible deadline. She had to learn as much as she could as fast as she could. On the first day home, Doreen rose extra early to try wearing the black skirt without a corset. It could not be fastened. Thinking of going without her protective armor made Doreen blush. However, Laramie had been most definite and her new skirts would comply with his order, but for this ride she could not oblige him. Cary helped lace her up. If Laramie Smith said anything, if he refused to take her with him until the new skirts came . . .

I'll fire him for his presumption! Who is he to tell me what *underclothes* to wear!

But common sense stopped her. She had to learn *now*. She had no time to wait, either for corsetless skirts or a new teacher. She quickly finished dressing. From the parlor she saw Laramie leaning against the corral, smoking. She brushed imaginary dirt from the crown of her new Stetson, swallowed, then went out to face him. But her worrying was for nothing. Laramie gave her little more than a cursory glance and swung into his saddle.

Doreen's split skirts arrived from Jamesville four days later. She was very surprised how much easier it was to mount, how much more comfortable she was without her stays, how enjoyable the gentle swing of her horse's gait was. She wondered briefly, heretically, if she could give up corsets altogether. The lessons, which had been a necessary agony, became enjoyable.

In the next two weeks, Laramie taught her as much about the West as about her ranch. He pointed out and named the wildflowers. He showed her likely hiding places in gulches, washes, and cedar groves for cattle or men. He showed her how to tell from the way a beef stood and walked and lay down, from the way it held its head and ears, whether the animal was sick or well. And he made her repeat and repeat what he said until she remembered it. Frequently he quizzed her on earlier lessons, too, in a gentle, friendly manner that took the sting from employee teaching boss. He talked to her about winter work, also, about breaking ice on water-holes, bringing hay by sledge to the cattle in deep snow, especially to the white-faced hybrid cattle that Laramie held in considerable contempt for their stupidity. He spoke of wolf and coyote hunts and of someone occa-sionally having to kill a grizzly that came out of the mountains to feast on winter beef. She watched him rope, tie, and milk cows whose nursing calves had died. Once he delivered a calf on the open range and Doreen watched, not even thinking until later how entirely improper of her that had been. True to his word, Laramie never teased her or flirted.

This is what I want, Doreen told herself repeatedly. I was afraid of him and his teasing, but there's no reason. He himself has set a proper distance between us.

But she missed his teasing, missed seeing mischief dance in his gray eyes, missed hearing his chuckle. She did not realize how much until the day they came upon a stretch of the new barbed-wire fence, cut and knocked over. "Damn piddling harassment," Laramie muttered, swinging down from Tennessee to repair it. Doreen helped him and, for that short time, she felt the warmth that comes when two people work well together. Laramie felt the warmth, too. It glowed in his eyes and his smile, but he said nothing.

Their long working days usually ended on the ranch house porch after supper. The air smelled of grass, apple blossoms, and summer. It was restful to sit and watch the stars come out. Bill often joined them, saying it was to hear 3R's coyotes sing. Doreen suspected it was Cary, not coyotes, that drew him. Laramie was on the porch, too, of course. He almost always sat on the bottom porch step, silent, separate, his long-barreled revolver within easy reach. But he could seldom be brought into the conversation and sometimes did not seem to hear it. Yet the smallest uncommon sound brought his head up, alert and ready for danger. When he spoke, in answer to a direct question, he was curt, almost as if he resented the intrusion into his private thoughts.

Doreen often watched him, studying his profile, sharp against the fading light beyond the porch. He sat quietly, studying the hands draped over his bent knees, or staring at the ground, or leaning his head back against the porch pillar and looking out over the mountains. Occasionally he smoked, and the red glow in the darkness reminded Doreen painfully of that first dance, when he had watched her from the darkness outside the barn until time for the waltz. He had been fun then, if a little frightening. Now the conversation on the porch seemed to flow over and around him. At times he looked so isolated that Doreen's heart ached and she longed to reach out to him somehow, to soothe the loneliness, but she could not. It would have been a violation of their silent agreement, a breaking of their contracted distance.

Midway in the second week back from Jamesville, Laramie took his first day on "Bill's business" and Doreen had to stay close to the house. She told herself this was a fine opportunity to catch up on weeding and letter writing, but she found herself most reluctant to do either and she wore her riding clothes, just in case Laramie came back in time for a lesson. He was gone overnight.

He returned in a thunderstorm. Doreen was watching the storm from the parlor window, entranced as always with the deep charcoal of the clouds and the brilliant greens after the rain started. She was only half-aware of the kitchen door slamming and the thud of boots in the hall.

"Time you learned how ranchers see this kind of storm."

She whirled, startled. Laramie stood in the hall, dripping, holding out a slicker to her. He frowned at her hesitation.

"Come on! You're still looking at thunder and lightning with city eyes."

Reluctantly Doreen took the slicker and in a few minutes she and Laramie were riding fast toward the hills on the Blue Mountain side of the ranch. Laramie pulled his horse in at the top of a high ridge. Doreen followed, her mind playing back to her all the warnings she had ever heard about being in high open places in a thunderstorm. She swallowed nervously. Out in the basin, lightning danced and thunder rolled. The display was awesome and frightening.

"Watch for fire," Laramie shouted above the roar of the wind. "Men are sent out to each ranch's highest points as soon as anyone sees clouds."

Thunder shook the ground. Rain whipped across the valley below in cold gray sheets. Lightning lashed the clouds and ground. Laramie turned to Doreen.

"Lightnin' can set the grass afire—even in all this rain. And in a wind like this, a fire can race through summer pasture or burn a winter's hay. A tree up in the hills, when it's struck, can smolder for hours or days, then burst into flame. We all watch, because a neighbor's fire can soon become ours. Later in the summer, when it's dry, the danger's far worse. Sometimes a storm'll come over with nothin' much in it but lightning and thunder."

Thunder crashed somewhere behind, so close that the ground shook and the sharp smell of burned air whirled around the pair on the ridge. Laramie turned and looked. Even Doreen's unskilled eyes could see wisps of smoke in the grass.

"Come on," Laramie ordered.

Doreen swung onto her horse and followed. They found flames licking outward from a scorched circle about four feet wide. Laramie slid from his horse before it came to a full stop, grabbing a shovel that Doreen had not even seen he was carrying.

"Stamp on it," he ordered, pointing at flames creeping through the grass on the other side of the charred place. He began beating at flames with the back of the shovel himself. Those that would not die he buried in swift shovelsful of dirt.

The danger was over in minutes. Laramie felt the ground at the perimeter of the fire with his bare hand, then stood, slipped his riding glove back on, and smiled. A smudge of gray ash crossed his cheek. "Good work, boss."

Doreen felt herself flushing, uncommonly pleased with the simple compliment. For a moment, the straggling hair dripping down her back, her squishing boots, and the miserable chill of being wet clear through were not important. She had done well when it mattered.

They returned to the ridge and, though they watched until the storm moved on, they saw no more smoke. When they returned to the ranch, Laramie gave Doreen a swift, hesitant pat on the back and a quick smile as they parted. Doreen surprised herself by being proud of having stayed out, although cold and wet, to protect the ranch from fire. She knew she would never look at a thunderstorm with city eyes again.

During the next day's lessons, Laramie seemed a little less formal and polite, a little quicker to joke and laugh. His more relaxed behavior warmed and pleased Doreen. They had worked well together yesterday. Maybe he was no longer seeing her as just an ignorant Easterner. Perhaps they could become friends. They were riding over familiar territory in companionable silence and Doreen let herself daydream what it would be like to have Laramie for a friend. All at once Laramie stiffened. His sudden stillness roused Doreen from her thoughts. She followed his look. A strange rider sat on the ridge just ahead, watching them. Laramie slid his rifle from its sheath under his leg and rode toward the rider, rifle ready, its butt resting on his thigh. The rider spun his horse and disappeared over the ridge at a gallop.

The next day they saw a strange rider again, again he disappeared when Laramie rode toward him. Then, two days later, along the lower reaches of the Yellow, they found a running iron in the black remnants of a fire. Laramie dismounted and felt the ashes, then remounted swiftly, gave Doreen's horse, then his, a whack with his quirt, and led the way back to the ranch at a run. He watched Doreen dismount at the ranch porch, his face grim. He did not dismount himself.

"Those ashes were still hot, Miss Dee. I'm goin' to start teachin' you to shoot. First lesson's before we go out tomorrow mawnin'."

Doreen blanched. "A gun? But I don't want to—"

Laramie cut her off with a sharp, impatient motion of his hand. "There're strangers on yore land now, strangers that run off when I go to meet them. I'm not goin' to be here forever. You need to protect yourself. If we'd run into those brand-burners today, we'd have been in real trouble. You're not in the East anymore, woman!" There was anxiety as well as anger in his voice.

Doreen's chin set stubbornly. "Laramie, I don't want to learn to shoot."

His eyes blazed. "You'll learn or you'll stay in the house for the rest of the season!" His voice softened a little. "Miss Dee, I want you to be prepared—to find your way, to live off the land, to defend your life." He scooped up the reins of her horse and rode off toward the barn.

The next day California ordered Diego to go learn to shoot, too. Diego vigorously protested.

Laramie watched the argument with amusement for a moment, then he broke into it. "Diego, you cain't hit the side of a barn with a shotgun. What kinda help'll you be to Miss Doreen if she needs it? As it is, Three R just keeps you on for use of that crack cuttin' horse of yores."

Diego grinned then, for his abominable marksmanship was well known. He slid a shotgun into his saddle sheath and mounted.

Laramie had already set up a practice area for himself at the edge of the foothills. A wooden target with many bullet holes in it and many tin cans lying around, shot through, showed Doreen he used the practice range a lot. The first lesson, for Doreen, was how to handle Laramie's unloaded revolver. He slid the gun from its holster, ejected the cartridges, checked the cylinder to be sure the gun was empty, and laid the gun across Doreen's hands, making obviously sure that the gun was pointing at no one.

"It's a special gun," Laramie said, stroking a forefinger down the long black barrel. "It's got a ten-inch barrel for accuracy and range. The long barrel doesn't kick as much as a short one, either." He looked at Doreen. "The gun I used in Europe had a sixteen-inch barrel, but that's mighty awkward for gettin' out of a holster to shoot a rattlesnake. It's possible to hit somethin' at two hundred yards with this one, but I gotta aim about eight feet over my target to even have a chance of hittin' it." He grinned. "Still, I hit the target a lot oftener than most men. At distances under ten yards, speed is real important, and draggin' that thing out of its holster isn't speedy, so I try to keep my targets farther out."

138

Though he spoke in a light tone, Doreen knew he was deadly serious. If a fast, human rattlesnake got close, Laramie was in grave danger.

Laramie took his hands away from the gun. "There. Feel it. Hold it in your right hand. Let it hang easy down at your side. Feel how heavy it is. Now lift it and aim it. No, no. You have to have it at eye level."

The lesson went on for about an hour and then they sent Diego home and continued the range lessons. The next day Doreen learned how to hold the gun, aim it, load it, unload it, clean it. After three days, she felt used to the feel of the long, dark weapon. Then she had to learn to fire it. Laramie slid his gun from its holster, unloaded it, and handed it to her.

"You saw me take out the cartridges. Even so, don't ever point a gun at me or anythin' livin' you'd mind killin'. Sometimes a body'll miss a chamber."

"There're some people I wouldn't mind—"

An iron hand on her chin wrenched her head around. "Don't ever think killin's easy. Even when it's necessary and right, killin' does somethin' bad to you inside." He spoke with pain as well as anger.

Doreen swallowed hard and licked suddenly dry lips. "I'm sorry, Laramie. I won't forget."

"Let's get back to the lesson, then."

Diego slid his shotgun out, loaded it, and began firing toward a cedar stump striped with bands of red barn paint. Laramie showed Doreen how to load, balance, and aim his revolver. It was heavy and, in spite of her practice, it dragged at her arm. Her shots went low and wide.

"Look," Laramie said at last, exasperated, "for

accuracy you brace yourself and steady it with both hands. Let me show you."

He stood, feet apart, cocked the gun, braced the forearm of his gun hand with the other hand, and fired. The tin can target tumbled from its rock. Laramie lowered the gun and nodded. Doreen set the can up again, fingered the ragged hole through its center, and tried again. And again. And again.

"I need a bigger target," she complained.

Diego grinned. "That's what I say always, too, mees. But Meester Smith, he say I need a barn and a barn ees too beeg a target."

"Try to hit that stump square, Diego," Laramie snapped. "Here," he said to Doreen, "I'll help you this time."

He stood behind her, extended his arms along her arms, cocked the gun, put his hands over her hands to aim it. The warm length of him pressed against her back, the hard muscles of his arms rested against hers, his long square hands positioned hers, his breath stirred the hair over her ear. Doreen suddenly found breathing difficult. Laramie dropped his arms and stepped away from her abruptly.

"That's enough for today." His voice sounded thick.

"But I haven't—we didn't—" Doreen stammered, still breathless, bewildered by that breathlessness and by Laramie's sudden decision to stop practice altogether.

But Laramie was busy examining Tennessee's cinch.

She carefully removed the cartridges, set them in a pile on a stone, set the hammer on an empty chamber, and came to stand beside Laramie. "Here's the gun."

He did not look up. "Just lay it on that rock with the cartridges. I'll be through here in a moment."

He did not turn around until she was on her horse. He would not meet her eyes at all, they did not take their ride that day, and, although the shooting lessons continued once or twice a week until Doreen became a good shot, he never touched her again.

CHAPTER

8

A T THE END of June, the roundup ended and the men came home for haying. California turned the tally over to Doreen the moment he returned. It could not have been much worse. Doreen stared at the smudged and wrinkled sheets of paper. They promised a bleak winter at best, bankruptcy at worst. She struggled to keep back tears; a lady cried only in private.

California shuffled his feet and stared at the floor. "Wish it was better, ma'am." He lifted his head and put on a more cheerful face. "Maybe it'll get better in the fall. Leastways you have the Fourth to get your mind off'n the tally for a while."

Doreen looked at him questioningly. "The Fourth?"

"The Fourth of July, ma'am. There's big doings in Jamesville on the Fourth. The ranchers always give their hands that day off, and traveling time."

Doreen looked at the cowboy skeptically. Ranchers were not ones to hand out days off easily. But California was perfectly serious, and it did seem possible that the birthday of the country was considered sufficient reason for a holiday. She smiled, a little crookedly, at the fidgeting rider. "Some men have to stay to guard what beef you brought back."

It was permission. California's face lit up like a little boy's at Christmas. He left the house sedately, if a little hurriedly, but he let out an ear-splitting whoop before he even left the porch. Other riders took it up, and the whoops rang out above the bawling and shuffling of the incoming cattle.

Seems there was some doubt that the new owner would let them off, Doreen thought dryly, watching the jubilation in the yard. She turned away from the window with a shrug. Her men were clearly enthusiastic, but she could see no reason to take the long, uncomfortable drive to Jamesville herself.

But Bill persuaded Cary to take time for a holiday, so Doreen decided to go, too. She did not want to be left alone with her disturbing bodyguard.

Jamesville was decked in party style. Bunting hung across store fronts and in loops above the main street. The sound of firecrackers, large and small, was everywhere. The 3R men announced their arrival by firing their revolvers in the air, shouting, whooping, and making their horses prance and rear. Doreen felt distinctly uncomfortable, sitting in the middle of such noisy exuberance.

Laramie, riding guard beside the wagon, leaned down from his saddle. "Embarrassed?" he asked softly, his voice teasing.

Doreen looked up. His light tone warmed her and

prompted her to reply in kind. "No," she lied. "I'm just a little miffed that I can't join in."

Laramie's eyes twinkled. "I think you're lyin' to me, but there's one shore way to find out." He shifted the rifle that lay on his knees enough to pull his revolver from its holster. He extended the long, dark gun to Doreen.

Doreen bit her lip, both aggravated and amused. She shook her head with mock regret. "I, uh—I really can't, Laramie. What would people think, me shooting up the town?"

Laramie chuckled and slid the gun back into its holster. "Coward," he murmured, with laughter in his voice. He paused a moment, shifted in the saddle, cleared his throat. "You may not like guns, Miss Dee, but you're buyin' yourself one this trip. Don't go white like that! A gun's not as dangerous in a holster as in yore hand." He leaned down again to be sure she could hear him over the racket going on around them. "Which is more important, Miss Dee, yore life or what 'people' think of you?"

Doreen sighed. "I know it must sound crazy to you, but it's hard to say, raised as I was." She looked up at him. It was important that he understand. "Reputation is everything, Laramie."

"Yeah, don't I know it!" His voice was suddenly hard and bitter.

Doreen stared at him in puzzlement. He had a very good reputation, as a man and as a marksman. Yet, clearly, something about his reputation, something she didn't know, caused him bitterness and pain. Was it the notches in his gun Sir Adrian had made so much of? But there were no notches; she had looked at the first opportunity. She would ask. But already Laramie's face had closed against her. She could feel the fun slipping away and she would not let that happen, not if she could prevent it. It had been so long . . .

She swallowed and spoke very softly so none of the others could hear. "Laramie, I've—I've missed having fun with you. Could we go back, just for tomorrow, to the way things were before you came to work for me? I thought—"

Her voice failed her and she could not make herself look up to see his reaction to her brazen admission. Yet she'd had to make it. The thought of spending the holiday in his stiff, professional company had been unbearable. She liked him so much and they would so soon be separated, either because she would have to find work in Denver or Salt Lake or Cheyenne, or because Bill would have taken Laramie back, to do a job Laramie believed would cause his death. When Laramie had first told her that, she'd been angry. She still felt angry, but she now realized that every time her own riders went out, she was expecting the same of them— that they would be ready to die to defend what was hers. Suddenly Doreen was close to tears, and she turned her head aside so no one would see.

Bill pulled the team up behind the livery stable, bringing Doreen back to the present and the silent man beside her. Bill helped Cary down from the wagon. Before he could come around for Doreen, Laramie swung from his saddle and lifted Doreen out. He did not let go as if she were scalding hot, the way he had ever since that moment at target practice. Instead, the hands at her waist felt heavy and tense.

When he spoke, his voice was harsh and had a raw

edge to it. "Don't ask me to go back to the way things were, Miss Dee. I have to be with you all day tomorrow. That's enough." He let his hands drop away from her waist. "That's more than enough," he added bitterly, under his breath, and turned to take his horse into the stable.

Doreen heard those last words and laid a restraining hand on his arm. This time Laramie did jerk away. "Don't!" he snapped.

Doreen let go at once, hurt and bewildered. "What's the matter?" she almost whispered. "These past weeks—I thought—I thought we'd become friends."

"Friends! Gawd!" He whirled and glared down at her. "You don't know, do you? You haven't the slightest idea." He spun away again and led his horse into the dim interior of the livery stable.

Doreen looked after him, bewildered and hurt. What was happening between them? First she'd found a hidden sore spot having to do somehow with his reputation. Now he was putting even friendship off limits, and that hurt more than she could ever have imagined. Was there a connection? Was there something about his reputation that made him want to keep her at arm's length? She shook her head. What was she to do? Prying into a man's business was something no one did in the West. Everyone started with a clean slate here, Bill had said. The past did not matter if the present was clean. She gave a futile swipe at the dust on the front of her skirt and turned toward the hotel where Cary stood waiting on the stoop. Laramie's present was more important then anything in his past, so, if she did not pry, perhaps their friendship could survive.

The next day, Laramie seemed to have reconsidered. If he was not as bold as he had been the first few times they met, he was less formal and distant than he had been for many weeks. Doreen even managed to forget for the day that he was guarding her life.

Morning began with a heavy, cannonlike explosion, which Doreen later learned had been gunpowder set off under the blacksmith's anvil. Then firecrackers, it sounded like thousands, began going off all over town. That racket went on all day. The festivities opened with a greased-pole contest. Doreen and Laramie watched one youth after another attempt to reach the five-dollar bill attached to the knob at the top of the pole. Contestants slithered up and slipped or tumbled down the pole and the spectators laughed. It felt good to laugh with Laramie again.

Footraces down Main Street followed. Then, according to Laramie, the next event was the horse races. Doreen knew that "next" was not strictly true, for Cary was dragging Bill off to see a quilting exhibit in the general store, but she was content to go where Laramie went. Today, today he's my friend, not my bodyguard, her heart sang.

And Laramie behaved like a friend. He stood beside her, pointing out the likely race winners according to their conformation and reputations. Diego's prize cutting horse was also a very fast horse. By the second race, Doreen found herself caught up in the excitement, shouting to Diego and cheering him on like the rest of 3R was. She turned to Laramie afterward, her blood pumping with the excitement of watching and shouting and seeing Diego win, wanting to share it. He was watching her with something like pain in his eyes. He turned his head quickly away.

They stayed beside the dirt track until Diego had won all three of the races he entered, then the two of them moved to a large meadow at the edge of town where the Methodist women's circle had prepared a low-priced box lunch. Doreen and Laramie waited in line, talking easily about what had happened and what was still to come. When their turn came, Doreen dug into her reticule to pay for her lunch. Laramie stopped her with a very light touch on her hand.

"My treat today," he drawled.

His unexpected offer made Doreen's heart beat a little faster. It felt almost as if they were stepping out together. They ate with Bill and Cary under a free-standing canopy Bill had had the foresight to bring along and listened as the Jamesville mayor began the obligatory Fourth of July political speech. The mayor droned on and on. Laramie licked the last crumbs of chicken crust from his fingers appreciatively and leaned over to whisper a scandalous criticism of the mayor's last point in Doreen's ear. Doreen giggled. A few minutes later Doreen mimicked the man's rapid mouth-pursing on pauses. "Like a fish," she said. Laramie chuckled. The speech went on and on, Laramie and Doreen exchanging whispered irreverent remarks until at last Laramie burst out in a loud guffaw, smothered too late. Cary turned her attention from the speaker, looking fierce.

"Shoo!" she ordered. "Go play someplace else. You're keeping the adults from listening."

Laramie grinned at the scolding and gave Doreen a hand up. They wandered through the picnicking families, past the displays of jams and preserves in the store windows, paused to watch a group of boys playing ball, and ended up on the bank of the little river that flowed north of the town. They sat on the bank in companionable silence, watching the ripples on the water and the fish under it, listening to the birds in the rushes along the water's edge and the whisper of the wind in the cottonwood leaves. Once in a while, one of them said something and the other answered, but, somehow, conversation did not seem necessary. After a time Laramie lay back on the grass, watching clouds and occasionally pointing out strange creatures in them. Gradually his eyes drifted shut and he slept. Doreen watched him for a long time. His face looked so much younger and softer when he was asleep. Doreen felt deeply at peace.

That golden holiday was too soon over. Everyone returned to their homes and the work. The first day back, Laramie did not show up for Doreen's daily lesson. The other riders reported he had ridden off before dawn. He was gone all day. Long after dark, a horse clopped past the ranch house and Doreen was sure the rhythm was Tennessee's. The next morning, Doreen was sitting alone at the kitchen table enjoying a slow cup of coffee when Laramie stalked in.

"I've got to talk to you," he said without preamble. He strode down the hall toward the office, not even looking to see if she followed.

His drawl was thicker and slower than usual, and that always meant he was either very angry or very upset. Doreen shut the office door behind them and leaned against its comforting solidness. Laramie hovered beside the desk. His face was pale and his entire body looked strung tight.

"I'm quittin' this job. I cain't stay here anymore."

Doreen shut her eyes and swallowed a sudden lump in her throat. It was a moment before she could speak. She opened her eyes slowly. "Why, Laramie?"

He would not look at her. "It's more'n I can handle. I'm goin' back to finish up for Bill."

Doreen felt the rush of heat that preceded fainting and willed it away. Bill's job would kill him. She had to stop him somehow. She threw her head back and challenged him, though it took all the courage she had. "That's not good enough. You've worked from here before. Why not now?"

Laramie would not look at her. "I just told you, I can't handle it anymore."

"I don't believe you! You can handle a job you believe will kill you but you can't handle working for me?" Doreen stepped closer to him and forced words through a throat tight with pain. "What are you doing for Bill that's easier but dangerous enough to kill you?"

"I can't say. I promised." He studied the pegged wood floor. "I agreed to work for Bill first, before I ever knew you existed." The last words came out harsh and bitter.

Doreen stepped closer, so close she could have lifted his head and made him look at her if she had dared. But she did not dare. "What's wrong here? It isn't the danger, obviously. Is it the friendship? Can the prospect of being friends with me—"

"Friends!" Laramie's head reared back and his eyes burned into her. His hands closed painfully on her shoulders, as if he wanted to shake her and was forcibly reminding himself she was his boss. "Friendship wasn't where we were goin' and I think you know that, inside, even though you may not be willin' to admit it yet."

150

He took a deep breath, released his hold, and turned to the desk. He gripped its edge until his knuckles whitened and stared down at its littered surface with bent head. When he spoke his voice was so low Doreen had to strain to hear it. "You're a lady, born, bred, and educated. I'm a poor cowhand who never finished eighth grade. Once this ranch begins to pay again, you'll be a wealthy woman and can go back East where you belong. I own my horse and saddle and a couple changes a clothes. But those things wouldn't have to matter, not between us. What does matter is that I'm a wanted man back in the States. You didn't know that, did you, Miss Dee? The Yankees put a thousand-dollar price on me durin' the war and I've spent most of the last fourteen years dodgin' bounty hunters." Laramie straightened and faced Doreen with a fragile dignity that tore at her heart. "Over the Fourth, I caught myself dreamin' of a future for you an' me; I played like it could be true. But there's no future because *I* have no future. Bounty hunters or rustlers, I'm goin' to get killed. And even if I weren't, I wouldn't ask you to share a life on the run. I— I have to leave." He spun away and strode out the door at a pace only slightly slower than a run.

The next morning he was gone.

CHAPTER

9

LARAMIE'S ABRUPT departure hurt, though knowing he had gone to protect himself from caring more about her made living with the hurt a little easier. Doreen kept telling herself that maybe, if he was worrying about bounty hunters, Laramie was no longer so sure Bill's job would kill him. She kept telling herself that he was wrong about that job, that he had misjudged the risk. She kept telling herself that in the fall, after roundup, he would come back. . . .

She appointed Diego and Tiny her guards and stayed close to the house. One week crawled by, then two. Doreen thought of Laramie often, especially when she and Cary sat on the porch in the long quiet evenings. In her mind's eye she saw him sitting at the edge of the porch, his long-fingered hands loose on his knees, the long-barreled gun on the porch floor beside him, the red glow of his cigarette a bright point in the shadows. Questions about Laramie's past and his dream for their future whirled round and round in her head. She sat and rocked and thought. And missed him.

What can the Federals want him for? He was only fourteen or fifteen when the war ended. As for a future for us—being poor would have made him entirely ineligible in Mother's eyes. To know that he's also a wanted man . . .

Doreen shook her head. She, too, might have turned her back on him if she'd known about the price before she knew the man. The thought led to remembering his last, moving revelation, and that memory always shook Doreen and made her resolutely turn her mind to other things.

High summer browned the landscape. Doreen rode out often to watch the haying or to check levels in the watering holes, usually with California as guard. Heat shimmered over the yellow-brown grasses and the air hung heavy and sweet with the scent of fresh-cut hay. The nestlings Laramie had shown Doreen in the spring had fledged and flown. The coyote den was empty. She missed Laramie with a deep, painful ache that never really went away.

The fall roundup began in August, right after the last of the hay had been cut and stacked. Over the next few weeks, word came of massive rustler raids around the district. The gang struck and moved on with amazing speed. Then Bill rode over just long enough to report that rustlers had made a daring attack on the herd being held at Fishhook and had killed two men. When she saw she could not convince him to stay long enough to eat something, Doreen saw him out to the porch. Bill swung onto his horse and then leaned down for one final word.

"You put more men to guarding your cattle, Doreen, and then you don't even walk out of the house without a guard checkin' first. No more ridin' around

153

like you've been doin'. In breeches and astride, you look enough like a man from a distance to be mistaken for one. Or to provide someone with the excuse that he mistook you for one." Bill eyes held Doreen's. "You know how badly that damned Englishman needs your water, Doreen. You mustn't provide him with an easy mark."

Shot. Killed. Her femaleness no longer any protection. Doreen swayed with shock and blackness rose before her eyes. She caught and held onto a porch column until the blackness went away again. She stared at Bill for a long moment, terror turning quickly to rage.

"Send him back, Bill. I can't run a ranch from inside the house. Send Laramie back now!"

"I can't."

"You and I had a bargain. He was to protect me. I want to be safe again. California and Luke are all I have left here, and California has to go back to the roundup tomorrow. Send Laramie back!"

Bill's mouth thinned and his whole face tightened. "Ain't no way I can let him go now, Doreen. You agreed I could use him when I had to."

"Use him? Use him? He's set to *die* for you. What kind of work do you give him, that he's sure to die doing it?"

"I can't tell you. He and I made a bargain, and not talking about it was part of it." Bill's hand lifted the reins and laid them against the horse's neck to turn its head away from the house.

Such anger swept through Doreen that she feared she might burst into flame with it. She sprang forward and grabbed the horse's bridle.

"Don't leave without telling me what's going on."

"It's private, Doreen. He felt he owed me somethin' from a long time ago."

"And you called in the debt. You'll send him to die for an old favor?"

Bill would not meet her eyes. "Larry agreed to the risks before he came up here. I expect you to stand by our agreement, like I know Larry will stand by his. A man can't hold up his head in the West if he doesn't keep his word, no matter what it costs. I reckon that's something an Easterner, and a woman, can't ever understand." Gently Bill pried Doreen's fingers from the bridle and rode away.

Reluctantly, Doreen sent Diego and Tiny to join the four riders California had already assigned to guard the cattle. That left Luke, the wrangler, with all the work around the ranch yard and Doreen with no guard until the roundup came to 3R. To stay in the house was not possible, however strongly Bill had urged it, so when Doreen moved around the ranch yard or worked in the garden, she carried the small derringer Laramie had had her buy in Jamesville.

Confinement and danger made her loneliness worse. Every time her hand slipped into her pocket and touched the derringer, she thought of Laramie. Every time she stepped off a porch into the yard, every time she looked out over the foothills they had ridden so often, she thought of him and longed for his company. She told herself she missed him so much because Cary and Luke were the only people she saw regularly.

It's no people and no riding that's making me miss

155

him, she insisted to herself. I want to run Mona across the flats and feel the wind in my face.

And have Laramie beside you, a small insidious voice added.

It was true. It was too, too true. Doreen imagined the mountain meadows crisp with frost, the sharp scent of cedar, the acrid smell of dried grass, the pungency of sage, the sounds of the wind in the cedars. And Laramie's drawling voice pointing out something new and interesting. There the pain began: she might never even see him again alive. The thought hurt more than she could ever have imagined. She threw herself into work to keep herself from thinking of Laramie dead. She cleaned, a job she hated, with furious abandon. She yanked weeds from the long rows of vegetables behind the house, plucked eggs from under indignant chickens, raced Mona around and around the home pasture. She fell into bed at night, exhausted, but her weariness did not keep her from dreaming about Laramie and the pleasure she had had in his company. She missed him deeply, painfully. She thought often of going to the Blue Mountain to see him, but she could not. He did not want to see her anymore.

One morning late in September, Doreen leaned against the corral fence watching Luke replace a cracked rail. Quite a comedown for the banker's daughter, she taunted herself. Watching the wrangler mend a fence is only slightly more broadening than watching the grass grow.

Doreen stared across the top of the fence, past Luke to the horizon beyond the mouth of the valley. Heat shimmered upward from the yellow-brown flats. A

156

vulture floated high, high, above, a black speck against the blue. The pounding of Luke's hammer was the only sound in the hot, bright silence. Doreen leaned her chin on her crossed hands and lost herself in thoughts about Chicago, where she could be walking freely, where cool breezes from the lake eased the heat of every summer she could remember, where people lived by a code she understood. Yet, even as the thought crossed her mind, Doreen knew it was not homesickness that was bothering her, because she was beginning to love the clear skies and mountain air. It was Laramie.

I'd forget about him after a while if I could go back to Chicago, she told herself. But she found herself imagining Laramie in a tweed suit in Amelia's parlor, or walking along the lakeshore, or . . .

A horse clopped into the yard. Doreen came back to the heat, the feel of warm, rough wood under her hands, the scents of the corral. She turned toward the sound. Luke stopped pounding and picked up the revolver that lay on the nearest fence post. Tic Bekkerson pulled up a rangy gray Thoroughbred beside the fence. He hooked one knee around the horn, rolled a cigarette, and lit it, his eyes taunting Doreen over the flame; then he leaned his head back and blew a cloud of smoke toward the sky.

"Found half a dozen Three R yearlings almost in sight of our main buildings," he said lazily. He jerked his head toward the home field. "Left 'em over there. I reckon Smith's trying to lay a trail to our place. It won't be long, miss, before someone catches him red-handed. Then we'll hang him."

Doreen bristled. "Laramie Smith is no thief!"

Bekkerson slid his free foot back into its stirrup,

tossed his cigarette to the ground, and looked down at Doreen. "Sir Adrian didn't think you knew, since you've been a lot in Smith's company lately. He'll be glad to know he was right about that."

Doreen bristled. "Laramie was working for me as a bodyguard."

Bekkerson laughed harshly. "Bodyguard! Guarding you against seeing his men at work, more likely." He leaned down toward her and spoke confidentially. "He's a dead man, Miss Doreen. Stay away from him." Bekkerson straightened and rode away.

His words echoed Laramie's uncomfortably. In spite of herself, Doreen remembered the afternoons Laramie had been away "on business," the nights when he had not come in at all, and shivered.

Bekkerson can't be telling the truth.

But Laramie's wanted by the Federals. He said so himself. How much do you really know about him?

He's honest. He wouldn't have told me about the Federals if he weren't. He's straight. I'd swear to it. I've trusted my *life* to it!

Doreen shook off her thoughts, but a cup of coffee and an hour with a book did nothing to quiet the wild restlessness the questions left behind. Only vigorous action would put an end to it, and there was nothing left in the house or yard for her to clean. What was worse, she had a terrible fear that the only reason Bekkerson had dared show his face at 3R was he knew Laramie was dead or otherwise out of the way. Dread over-whelmed her. What if Laramie was dead? Bill. Bill would know if Laramie was all right. She had to check with Bill.

Doreen flung on her riding clothes, grabbed her gloves, shouted, "I'm going out, Aunt Cary," and sprinted back to the corral.

"Luke, catch and saddle Mona for me."

Luke had finished the rail and was picking up the tools. He froze, then straightened slowly, horror written on his thin dark face. "You're not planning on leaving here, are you, Miss Doreen? You know what Smith and California said."

"Luke—" Doreen could not explain her fear. She knew it was irrational but was helpless to control it. She stood a little taller. "Get Mona, Luke."

Luke's dark-brown hands gripped the top fence rail. He examined the wood, obviously hesitating to argue with his boss. He finally looked at her. "It ain't no safer out there than it was, Miss Doreen. You shouldn't go."

"I'll be careful." Doreen could see Luke struggle with himself between the combined authority of Laramie and California and the ultimate authority of the boss's order, tenderfoot or not.

Luke shrugged bony shoulders. "You're the boss, but I think you're taking a crazy chance. Smith'll be mighty riled when he hears about this."

"Laramie Smith doesn't work here any more," Doreen snapped.

Luke hesitated, opened his mouth, then shut it, shrugged, set down his load of tools, and took a coil of rope from a post.

Perhaps half an hour later, Doreen had passed the narrow "waist" of the valley and was turning up the trail east to Blue Mountain. A light wind blew down the valley, soft with dust and the scent of sage. She looked north briefly, toward the flats where the cattle spent most of the summer. A vulture hung on the wind overhead. That dark hovering shape reminded Doreen of McTaggert and that made her feel uneasy. She was taking a great risk. She bit her lip and reconsidered. She was not that far from the ranch house yet. She could turn back and send Luke for Bill. It would be much safer. She even turned Mona's head toward the barn. But she could not go back. She had to know, today, that Laramie was all right. Or that he wasn't. The need drove her with unexpected urgency. She spurred Mona toward the shortcut.

White-faced cattle with stolid faces looked up from their grazing as she passed, their jaws chewing round and round. They were the result of Jacob's cross-breeding longhorns to an imported bull from England and did not spook as full-blood longhorns did. A meadowlark somewhere overhead burst into a golden shower of song. Doreen looked up for it and noticed what appeared to be a light fog clinging to the western side of the valley. The meadowlark let fall another beautiful shower. Doreen, still looking for the bird, saw a rider on a black horse disappearing over the top of a hill. Doreen pulled Mona to a stop and felt in her pocket for her gun. Was the rider one of the outlaws? He did not reappear.

A jackrabbit bounded by. Moments later, another leaped right across Mona's path. The mare threw back her head and danced nervously. Doreen soothed her, then looked after the rabbit. Rabbits didn't normally run under horses' feet.

The rabbit's behavior increased Doreen's uneasiness. She should not be out here. She should not be alone. She turned back and kicked Mona into a canter. But ahead, along the west side of the valley, the fog was thicker.

It's not possible for a fog to be there, Doreen told herself. I've never seen fog in Wyoming.

A small herd of antelope appeared at the edge of the fog, which was now quite yellowish, and bounded jerkily toward the woman and mare. A fox slunk by, ignoring the rabbits zigzagging in the same direction. More antelopes passed and Doreen now heard the rustle of unseen small animals in the long dry grass.

"There's something wrong," Doreen whispered to the horse, "there's something very wrong, girl." She smacked the quirt against the mare's rump twice.

Mona leaped forward. The "fog" was spreading across the valley, cutting them off from the ranch. An orange line flickered at its base, and the wind carried the acrid smell of smoke and burning grass. Doreen urged Mona into a gallop. The fire spread with unbelievable speed across the valley. Doreen swallowed a rush of fear. Death. Just ahead of her. She had to make the right decision the first time. She could race for the flats. She looked over her shoulder and knew the fire would race through that dry grass far too fast to outrun. Water then, she must ride Mona to water. Doreen glanced toward the Pinto, but the wind was blowing down the valley, blowing the fire toward her along the river. Smoke drifted thickly along the Pinto's bank. There, for just a moment, there seemed to be a rider, half-hidden by the billowing smoke, then the illusion was gone.

The fire roared now. Doreen glanced to the east. The

Yellow lay a mile or more away, but Doreen could still see its green strip of trees and scrub. It was a chance. She struck the mare harder. "Go, girl!"

The mare laid back her ears and ran. They passed a clump of white-faced cattle, lumbering away from the fire. Smoke billowed along the ground. They reached the midway point. Fire rose beside them. Doreen darted a look over her shoulder. Flames licked the grass behind, with shivers of heat in the air above. They were caught. The flames were forcing them north and the river was perhaps too far to reach in time. Doreen crouched until her face was almost on the mare's neck. "Run! Run!" she cried to the horse.

Small animals of all kinds ran with them, shadows in the smoke. Doreen felt their fear and Mona's. Hot air surged past, carrying an ominous crackling beside and behind them.

"It's spreading too fast, Mona." Doreen choked on smoke. "This is no wildfire. It was set and we're going to die!"

Acrid smoke now blurred the landscape and made the line of trees along the Yellow difficult to see. Doreen knew to die by fire was to die slowly and in great agony. Terror gripped her. The wind came up, fanning the flames higher and hotter. A fit of coughing seized Doreen and while she bent over the mare's neck, weak and gasping, Mona seized the bit and bolted, veering away from the river and its fringe of flame toward the flats and the mouth of the valley. Doreen struggled to regain control but could not. She clung to saddle and mane, no longer seeing, only hearing the fire roar through the dry grass, the terrified bawling of cattle, the screams of animals caught by the flames, and once, perhaps, the rapid beat of another horse's hooves. Mona stretched out, running for her life. She crossed into an area where the smoke was thinner and Doreen could see the ground. It was a prairie dog colony. Doreen tugged frantically, fruitlessly at the reins. She heard a sharp snap, then she was flying through the air. The ground rushed up to meet her, there was blinding pain, then nothing.

CHAPTER

10

"D EE! DEE! Wake up!"

Doreen struggled away from the demand in that hoarse shout, a demand that she face unbearable danger and fear. Sharp pain stung her cheeks. She cried out. Her head felt as if it were splitting. An urgent voice cut through that pain, shouting at her, demanding something. She tried to push the noise away and was savagely shaken for her trouble.

"Dee! For Gawd's sake, get up!"

She was yanked mercilessly to her feet. Pain cleared her head and she opened her eyes. Laramie's fear-twisted face was blurry. She whimpered. Laramie jerked her toward a horse's side. "Mona's dead. We both have to ride my horse." He shook her. "Do you hear me? Get up there or we're dead, too."

Doreen fumbled for the saddle horn. She could not seem to keep hold of it. Laramie made a short, impatient sound, flung her over the saddlebow, mounted, clamped an arm around her drooping body, and set the wiry mustang at a gallop. Heat, crackling, an ominous roar, choking smoke rising around them. Every jolting contact the horse made with the ground sent searing pain through Doreen's head. An antelope with smoldering hair and fear-glazed eyes bounded past them as if the flying horse were standing still. Laramie's body was rock-hard and intent, as if he could speed the horse with his own effort. Orange and yellow flames curled through the grass under the horse's hooves. Man and woman and horse moved through a yellow-gray cloud. The air grew thick and searingly hot. Every breath hurt. Doreen bent double, coughing. Laramie's arm tightened until her ribs creaked, but he said nothing. Smoke hid the ground, flames roared just behind, Laramie was coughing, too. The horse staggered and choked.

"The river," Laramie shouted above the roaring flames, "hear the river, boy!"

A wall of flame rose in front of them. The intense heat made Doreen's skin feel dried tight. Doreen closed her eyes. *We're going to die. There's no way through that. We're going to die!*

"GO!" Laramie shouted. The arm around Doreen tightened at the same moment.

The horse leaped. Doreen turned her face into Laramie's shirt, unable to look death in the eye. She felt both man and horse flinch, then hooves clicked on the gravel of the riverbank and water gurgled around the horse's trembling legs. Hesitantly, feeling strangely reluctant to look, Doreen opened her eyes. They stood in the water of the Yellow. The air was thick with smoke and the stench of burning grass, but they were safe.

"Hold on," Laramie ordered her, and slid from the saddle. He scooped water with his hat and poured it over the mustang's singed hide. The horse stood patiently, its muscles twitching where it had been burned. Laramie examined the horse, caressed it, then stepped back into the saddle. He patted the horse's neck. "The water won't help much, boy, but we're not far from Three R's barn. You'll be all right."

Except for an occasional encouraging murmur to the horse, Laramie said nothing all the way up the river to the ranch. He rode directly into the barn, set Doreen ungently on the ground, dismounted, and disappeared briefly into the dimness at the back of the building. He returned in a moment with a tin of thick yellow salve. He tenderly stripped the horse and began applying the salve to its burns. He did not seem to remember Doreen's presence. She turned away and started unsteadily toward the house.

"Don't take another step," Laramie barked, without as much as turning from his work.

"My head!"

"That'll wait. I'm gonna talk to you first."

Something told Doreen that to disobey would be dangerous. She leaned against the boards of a stall, quaking inside. Laramie could not have been more gentle with the horse, but the lines of his body, his every motion told of tightly controlled anger. Laramie led the mustang into a box stall, gave it water, set the salve carefully on the ledge beside the stall, shut the door, and stalked toward Doreen. His face was white and his eyes two glittering chunks of ice. Doreen shrank back against the wall. Laramie stopped very close to her, his hands clenched at his sides as if he were restraining himself from hitting her.

"I told you never to leave sight of the house alone.

Bill told you. California told you." His voice was very soft and slow.

Doreen was so frightened that her heart's pounding threatened to strangle her. Anger flared to her defense. "You make me sound irresponsible and stupid! You don't even know why I went out! Bekkerson came and I thought Bill should know what he said."

"So you went out alone!" Laramie seemed to loom larger. "Didn't it occur to you that you might be ridin' into a trap? Bekkerson comes with somethin' that sounds important, at a time when all the men are gone?" Laramie's voice became even slower and softer. "You little idiot! That fire was set, and you rode right into it! Someone oughta whale the tar outa you!"

"Are you volunteering?" The moment the words were out, Doreen knew they were a mistake.

Laramie gripped her shoulders with fingers like talons. His face—Doreen wanted to crawl away and hide from the rage in that face. "That fire was meant to get *you!* Where would you be now if I hadn't been out there and seen the smoke? Dead! Fried like Mona! You'll stay home if I have to tie you to the porch!"

"Whale me, order me, tie me up—you demand obedience as if you're my husband when you're not even—"

Laramie's fingers tightened, bruising, hurting. "You reckless—stubborn—mule-headed—little—devil!" Laramie punctuated each word with a head-snapping shake, each shake filling Doreen's pounding brain with stars and colored blotches. "I was—in that part—of the range—only—by—chance. You'd—be dead—if I—if I—"

Laramie stopped shaking her abruptly and stared

down at her. A look very like despair crossed his face. The hands on her shoulders trembled. Slowly he bent his head and his mouth touched hers gently, hesitantly. The kiss deepened quickly, his arms slid around her, he crushed her against him. A strange fire raced through Doreen's body and she melted against him, inflaming him more. He slid one hand down her back to press her hips against him, the other tangled itself in her hair and held her head still under his demanding mouth. Her lips opened involuntarily under his and she was lost, drowning in dizzying waves of a need she did not understand.

Laramie wrenched his mouth away and pushed Doreen's face into the hollow of his shoulder. The sound of his harsh, rapid breathing and the frantic pounding of his heart under her ear only added to Doreen's own turmoil. For a time those sounds were her only world. Slowly she came aware again—of the smells of smoke and burned flannel, of the soft nap of Laramie's shirt and its steamy wetness, of her own hair tickling her neck and cheeks where it had been pulled from its pins. She had behaved like a wanton and shame made her tremble. Laramie's arms tightened and he laid his cheek against her hair.

"What a tender scene." Tic Bekkerson stood just inside the door of the barn, a gun steady in his right hand.

Laramie's head snapped up and every muscle in his body tightened. "What're you doin' here, Bekkerson? You finished yore work here this mornin'."

Bekkerson examined Laramie insolently. "'Work' here? Why, what can you mean, Smith? I'm just being a

168

good neighbor. Saw smoke and figured you might need some help."

"More likely you came back to see how that 'wildfire' worked out."

Bekkerson's face assumed an expression of exaggerated puzzlement, but his eyes were hard and calculating. "Say what you mean, Smith." When no explanation from Laramie seemed to be forthcoming, Bekkerson shrugged. "It's too bad you have a fire. Sorry you don't want my help. I'll just offer you newlyweds my congratulations, then, and be on my way."

"What's that supposed to mean?" Laramie was very slowly loosening his hold on Doreen, though his arms did not change position.

"Well, I thought my meaning was obvious. I heard the lady say, 'you're my husband.'"

"How long were you listenin'?"

"Long enough."

Doreen, who had been too shamed by being caught in such a compromising situation to look at Bekkerson, turned her face toward him in horror. "You know what I said after that, too," she whispered.

Bekkerson tipped his hat back with his left hand. "Sorry, ma'am. That part must've slipped by me."

"You aren't tellin' anyone else that story, Bekkerson." Laramie's voice shook. His arms held Doreen only very loosely now.

"Now there you're wrong, Smith." Bekkerson grinned maliciously. "The whole district's going to hear about it."

In one lightning move, Laramie thrust Doreen behind him and leaped toward Bekkerson.

Bekkerson pointed the barrel of his revolver directly at Laramie's chest. "Hold it right there, Smith. You're not gonna get a chance to draw on me. Maybe the lady'd get hurt. *If* she *is* a lady."

Laramie's body tightened till it shook with the strain. He kept his eyes trained on Bekkerson's gun.

"Now that's a fair question, ain't it?" Bekkerson went on, visibly enjoying Laramie's helpless rage. "Anybody'd have a right to wonder about her after seeing that kiss." He fanned himself with his left hand. "Hooee! Only two kinds of women get kissed like that— wives, sometimes, and tarts. Which're you, 'Mrs.' Smith? *Don't* move, Smith. You don't want to make your bride a widow so soon after the wedding, do you?" Bekkerson laughed nastily and backed out of the barn, keeping his gun on Laramie. "You knocked me down, Smith. You made me say I lied. I think we're going to be even for those two little mistakes of yours real soon." He mounted his horse and backed it around the corner of the barn before holstering his gun and heading toward home.

Laramie listened to the fading beat of Bekkerson's horse. "Go fix your hair and pack your best dress," he said without turning. "We're makin' a visit to Jamesville."

Doreen did not move. She pressed her hands against the sides of her head, trying to lessen the pain. Laramie came quickly to her side. Doreen saw his brown boot-tips, the barn floor, dusty and pocked with hoofmarks, the smoke-blackened blue of Laramie's denims.

"Dee." His voice was a gentle breath of sound. His hand slowly, carefully, tipped her head up, then cradled it against his shoulder. "It hurts like hell, doesn't it? No, don't talk. Let me do the talkin' for now."

One of his arms held her lightly, the other hand massaged the back of her neck. Slowly Doreen's taut muscles relaxed, the blinding pain eased, and tears of fear and weariness finally came, wetting places on Laramie's shirt not already damp with sweat or river water. Laramie's slow massage continued until the tears had passed.

"Listen, Dee, and don't say anythin' till I'm done. We're goin' to the Methodist preacher in Jamesville and he's goin' to marry us." His arm tightened a little to subdue her feeble struggle of protest. "Now, I said not to say anythin' till I'm done. Give yore poor head time to quiet down." He resumed his gentle rubbing. "Bekkerson'll destroy yore reputation, to get back at me, without givin' you a thought. He'll tell his story to put us in the worst light, but word it so I can't call him a liar. He'll imply we're just pretendin' to be married. You'll need protection, then, 'cause every woman-hungry man in the district'll think you're fair game and what they'd do to you is beyond tellin' a lady."

Laramie's hand began to slowly stroke her hair, sending a shower of pins onto the floor. "You'll need protection and my name'll give you that. I'm not askin' anythin' else of you, just to take my name." He took a long, unsteady breath that shook Doreen as well. "I decided long ago never to marry, because of the bounty hunters and the dangerous work I do, so I've stayed away from good women all these years. Except for you, Gawd help me." He stood very still, so still that Doreen felt the tiny tremor that went through him. There was a

171

long silence, then Laramie spoke, slowly, haltingly. "I can do this much for you, save yore reputation, and soon you'll be free again. I'm not goin' to survive this job."

"Then why did you take it?" she whispered.

"Because someone had to do it."

"But why you?" Doreen's question was almost a wail.

"Because I owe Bill more'n I can ever pay back and because, of all the men who were willin', I was the only one who had no—ties. No"—he pressed his fingers gently against her protesting mouth—"don't. I'm in too far to back out without wreckin' everythin'. This marriage is for yore protection. Only that."

He was leaving something out. His voice was thick and raw with pain. Doreen wanted to comfort him, this lean, self-sufficient, lonely man, so she slid her arms around his waist and hugged him. She heard his sharply indrawn breath, then his arms crunched her bones and his face buried itself in her hair, which had tumbled down around her neck. They stood so a long time, drawing strength and comfort from each other.

At last Laramie straightened. "How's the head?"

"Better."

"Can you think of any other way out?"

Doreen shook her head gingerly. "I'd go back East if I could, but we haven't got the money. Oh, Laramie, I didn't want to be married this way!"

Laramie stroked her soothingly. "I know, darlin'. You can have a weddin' the way you wanted the next time."

"Don't say that!"

Laramie bent his head to look directly into her eyes.

His voice was stern. "Don't fool yourself into believin' anythin' else. I have no future, Dee. I haven't since I was fourteen." He put aside his bitterness almost visibly. "Let's get ready to go. Tell yore aunt and see if she'll come with us. Bill, too, if he's here."

Doreen cringed from revealing their predicament. Her eyes slid away from his. "Do we have to?"

Laramie gently brought her head around to look at him again. "We'll need witnesses, and you can't leave Cary out. You've said she's yore only family, so you can't leave her out." His grip on her chin tightened briefly. "Besides, her word, and Bill's, and the marriage paper— they're yore protection when I'm—when I'm gone."

Doreen was not prepared for the pain those last words caused. "Laramie!" she cried, tears gathering again.

"Hush," he whispered. He brushed damp strands of hair back from her face and held her head between his hands. "It's all right. I haven't—haven't got any reason to go on livin'."

He shut his eyes tightly for a second. Doreen turned her head and kissed the thumb beside her mouth. Laramie's eyes flew open and his hand jerked away as if burned. "Don't!" he snapped. "This can't work between us if you do things like that!"

Startled and hurt, Doreen felt the hovering tears well up and overflow. She turned her head quickly away so Laramie would not see them.

He turned her back to face him. His voice was low and intense. "We have to live together, Dee. To be convincin', we have to live together, and I've promised you to ask nothin' of you. That's goin' to be hard. Real hard. Don't make it harder for me to keep that promise. All right?"

Doreen smiled tremulously and nodded, carefully. "You'll have to tell me wh-when I'm doing it wrong." She felt the heat of a blush in her cheeks but did not let her eyes slide away from Laramie's in her embarrassment. He was being painfully honest with her. She could do no less. She swallowed, then plunged into the hard part. "I don't—I don't know much ab-about that—about—being married."

Laramie smiled. "I'll tell you when you're makin' it hard." He let his hand caress her cheek briefly, swiftly. "I never thought I'd find a woman I'd call 'friend,' but we are friends, aren't we?"

Doreen nodded.

"Good. We'll carry this off, Dee, you'll see. We'll tell Cary our narrow escape made us see how much we care about each other. She'll believe us. Go on, now. Get prettied up. Your first weddin' day should be somethin' you remember without regret—pretty dress, flowers, honeymoon, even." He gave her a little push toward the house. "I'll bet I'm ready before you are." But the teasing lilt was missing from Laramie's voice and his eyes were grave.

Cary accepted their story without appearing to doubt it. She sent Laramie out to find Bill, who was rounding up his team to go home. The moment he was gone, Cary turned to Doreen. "Are you sure, honey? You look so pale."

"We came very near dying, Aunt Cary. That would make anyone pale. Yes, I'm sure. We're sure. This is what we both want."

Cary hugged Doreen and kissed her. "Then I'm happy for you both. He's a good man. Now, let's get you ready. Shall we plan on leaving in the morning?"

"I—I think we're leaving as soon as we can. It's a long ride and we don't want to wait . . ."

Cary chuckled. "I'm beginning to understand myself what that kind of impatience feels like. Maybe with you safely married, Bill and I can—" Cary broke off, laughing. "You get together what you're going to need. I'll give the big bedroom a quick cleaning."

"Please, no, Aunt Cary. I'll clean it when we get back. Laramie's going to be gone a lot and that will give me something to do."

"As you wish. I'm sure Bill will give Laramie a few days off, even at roundup, so you two can be alone for a little while."

Doreen made herself smile brightly. "Thanks. That would be kind of him."

For the wedding, Doreen selected the powder-blue silk dress, with its tiers of delicate and useless ruffles, because she remembered the appreciative light in Laramie's eyes when she had worn that color before. She lifted the dress from the trunk and shook it out. Tiny lavender flowers fell to the floor. She looked at them ruefully. The dress had been so obviously unfit for Three Rivers that she had not even once unfolded it. She wrapped it carefully in a sheet and carried it to the wagon, the slightly bitter scent of lavender floating along with her.

The four of them drove to the church with horses for Laramie and Doreen tied to the tail gate of the spring wagon. They camped overnight at the road ranch—the women sleeping in a tent and the men in the wagon—arrived in Jamesville after dawn, rested and cleaned up in the hotel, and were at the church door by eleven. Laramie wore a new blue flannel shirt and clean denims. Doreen looked at the tanned face, sandy hair, and gray eyes and remembered the laughing, impudent man on the train.

What are we doing! she asked herself.

Laramie brought a bunch of daisies from behind his back and presented them with a flourish. "Your bouquet, wife."

Doreen smiled and curtsied and took the flowers. "You're most kind, sir." But she did not feel like joking.

Laramie's eyes told her he did not really feel like joking, either. He offered her his arm and they entered the dim, cool interior of the church. Shafts of golden light fell through the east windows, dancing with dust motes. The pews marched in straight-backed, rigid rows to the open floor in front of the altar. The thin, bald minister in his stiff, high collar and black frockcoat hurried to his place from a side door, ran his finger around his coat collar to flatten it, nodded to the plump organist, still not quite settled on her bench, and opened his black book. Doreen heard Cary and Bill come up behind and saw the minister acknowledge their presence with a curt nod. She held harder to the daisies and the pungency of the bruised stems stung her nose.

"Dearly Beloved, we are gathered together in the presence of God and these witnesses . . ."

The minister droned through the words from the book, words he must have read a thousand times and whose ancient beauty entirely escaped him. Doreen and

Laramie said their vows, without a ring, for there had been no time to get one, and knelt for the blessing. The ceremony was over. They were united until death. Laramie's death. The minister thrust the marriage certificate toward Doreen, with his signature and the organist's as witness already on it. Doreen noticed it had been backdated one day and wondered what Laramie had done to persuade a preacher to fudge the truth by even one day. She signed her name with trembling hand and handed the pen to Laramie. He dipped the pen in the well the minister extended, signed the paper, blew on the ink to dry it, folded the paper, and tucked it into his breast pocket. Doreen looked up him and he squeezed her hand reassuringly.

"It'll be all right," he whispered.

But Doreen wondered how it could possibly be all right. She forced herself to turn and smile at Cary and Bill as if she had just achieved her heart's desire. Laramie dropped a casual arm across her shoulders, squeezed, then accepted Bill and Cary's congratulations with an appearance of pride and pleasure. He looked down at Doreen with glowing eyes.

Doreen's heart skipped a beat. She mentally shook herself. It's a performance, Doreen, she reminded herself. He's just a better actor than you'll ever be.

"All this excitement's made me right hungry," Laramie drawled. "How 'bout we all go have an early dinner somewhere?"

The four of them ate a leisurely meal together at Sarah James's, then separated, Cary and Bill to get some sleep and then drive back, Doreen and Laramie to spend the rest of the day in town and the night at the hotel "to get better acquainted," as Bill dryly put it. They would be alone together, in a bedroom, for the first time. Doreen did not know what to expect and her apprehension hung over the day, spoiling it with a tension so great she was close to being sick. What set a man off? she wondered. What if she, in ignorance, did something that caused Laramie to break his promise of a marriage-for-his-name-only? Finally, shamefully, remembering the kiss in the barn, Doreen wondered if she truly wanted him to keep his promise.

You want him to keep it. Of course you do, she told herself fiercely. He doesn't want to be married. He married you for *your* sake, to save you from humiliation and worse. He's been truly your friend.

But a part of her wanted to be touched, held, kissed. Torn, confused, ignorant, Doreen jumped a little every time Laramie came close to her. But he did not touch her, not that day, nor that night, when he slept at the very edge of the bed with his face turned away from her. Perversely, watching him strictly keeping his word, Doreen wanted him close, to hold her and tell her again things would be all right. She dared not ask him to. She dared not even touch him, because she did not know what aroused a man's animal instincts and she could not risk pushing him, through ignorance, beyond his control. He did not want to be married.

The two of them had breakfast at Sarah James's the next morning. They were just finishing when Bill and Cary walked into the dining room.

Doreen stood abruptly and rushed to her aunt. "Aunt Cary! Is something wrong?"

Cary flushed rose-pink.

Bill, too, reddened. "We talked after you and Larry left last night. It's a long ride to the preacher."

"And you don't need a chaperone anymore." Cary flushed even pinker with the implication of her words.

"And we were plannin' to tie the knot at Christmas, anyway," Bill added.

"So we decided to save ourselves another long drive and get married today," Cary finished.

Doreen looked at the older couple, still flushed and smiling and fidgeting a little under the newlyweds' surprised eyes. Laramie strode over and thrust out his hand. "I'm mighty glad to hear that, Bill. You'll let us stand up for you, of course."

Bill gripped Laramie's hand and shook it wordlessly.

"We hoped you would," Cary said shyly.

"If you were up at a reasonable hour, that is," Bill added with a lascivious wink.

"I'd be hurt if you didn't let me," Doreen said, and hugged each of them.

Two hours later, Laramie and Doreen were on the road back to Three Rivers. They rode in easy stages, quieting the new wariness of each other with stops beside interesting rock formations, along a small mountain brook, at the edge of a colorful, narrow canyon. They had plenty of time. Bill had given Laramie three days off for a honeymoon. Cary would move into Bill's house immediately and the Smiths would be alone together at Three Rivers. On the way, as she swayed in rhythm with her horse's gait, Doreen mulled the idea of this strange marriage over and over. It had not been the wedding she had dreamed of, this quick, secret wedding

179

to a friend who expected to die soon. Mrs. Laramie Smith. The title felt unreal. Mrs. Laramie Smith. Widow-to-be.

They spent the night at the road ranch. Doreen surprised herself with lascivious wonderings about what Bill and Cary were doing that night that she and Laramie, by agreement, could not do. Her dreams, and guilt about them, troubled Doreen all night. When they rode on in the morning, Doreen was weary and cross and Laramie was in no better temper.

The sudden darkness of night in mountain country had fallen by the time they reached 3R's side of the low pass. The horses picked their way carefully toward the ranch buildings, their hooves clicking occasionally on stray rocks in the ranch road. A lone mourning dove cooed from somewhere in the cottonwoods.

"I sent for my mother's ring while we were in town," Laramie said, his voice distant and impersonal in the darkness. "I know Jen will mail it right away, but Lord knows how long it'll take to get here. Promises are what makes a marriage anyway, not rings." He turned his face toward Doreen, his voice closer, his tone intense. "I want you to wear *that* ring, not one some stranger makes up for you."

Doreen accepted that in silence. If it were important to him, she would wear his mother's ring. When they reached the ranch house, Laramie pushed open the front door, swept Doreen up in his arms, and stepped over the threshold. "Old customs must be satisfied," he whispered in her ear as he set her down inside, just for that moment the playful cowboy again.

As he fumbled in the dark for the kerosene lamp on

the parlor table, Doreen fought the teary weakness that brief moment in his arms had caused. She could not understand it. The lamp flickered, then burned steadily. Laramie picked it up and looked at Doreen questioningly. She led him down the hall to the big bedroom and opened the door. Laramie looked down at Doreen, his face tight and controlled.

"Where do I sleep?"

Doreen looked at him blankly.

"Oh, come on, Doreen! You can't be that innocent! You're my wife! Two nights in the same bed with you I can manage, but not many nights. Who'll know we don't sleep together?" He turned toward the door, his patience thinning visibly. "Will you show me another room or do I have to look myself?"

"I'll show you." Doreen forced the words out past a thick lump in her throat. "There's another bed next door."

The next room was narrow, with just enough space for a bed and a low bookcase. Its window looked out on the mountains. Laramie set the lamp on the bookcase and came back to shut the door. He stood with one hand on the edge of the frame and looked down at Doreen, still waiting in the hall. "It'll do," he said, his voice harsh. "I won't need it long."

"Don't say that!" Doreen whispered.

Laramie's hand shot out and tipped her chin up so she had to meet his eyes. "I have to say it. I'll say it often and you have to believe it! You'll hurt less if you don't get attached to me. I'm not goin' to live out the season." He let her chin go and walked to the window. He stared out the dark square. "We'll take Bill's three days and

181

then I go to work at Blue Mountain again. I'll come to you just enough to keep up appearances. It'll be easier on both of us that way."

She bit her lip to keep the tears from falling. "I'm going to bed, Laramie." Her voice was husky but pride kept it from wavering. Without looking at Laramie she stumbled blindly to her bedroom, tugged off her gloves, untied her bonnet, and lay down. Shock, anger, hurt, bitterness, and sadness swept over her in waves. Too much had happened. Her control broke. She rolled onto her stomach, stuffed the pillow into her mouth so Laramie could not hear her, and cried herself to sleep.

CHAPTER

11

A HEARTY "ROLL OUT!" jarred Doreen awake. She turned over and sat up, dismayed to remember that she had not bothered to undress. Her shirtwaist and riding skirt possessed more wrinkles and creases than any three decent outfits should and she was sure her eyes were still red and her face blotchy from crying. She knew she had made the worst mistake of her life, because she could not maintain a safe emotional distance from her husband. He was already very dear, and when he died—Doreen knew she would never do anything harder than face losing him.

"Are you decent?" Laramie asked from the other side of her door.

"No."

"Well, get that way. I'm bringin' you breakfast this mawnin'."

His cheery voice only made Doreen feel worse. Doreen Anderson Smith. Widow-to-be. Doreen listened to the sound of his boots going toward the kitchen, then sprang up, slipped out of her rumpled clothes, quickly washed her face in the icy water from the pitcher on her commode, splashed a little extra on her cheeks and eyes (hoping Laramie would mistake for cold any redness that was left), and put on the dressing gown of ruffles and lace Cary had insisted on giving her. She pulled the remaining pins out of her hair and sat down to brush it. Fragrant coffee and bacon smells drifted in from the kitchen. She heard her door open, but Laramie did not come in. Doreen turned, still brushing. Laramie was standing in the doorway with a tray in his hands, watching her. His mouth twisted wryly.

"I haven't seen a woman brushin' her hair since I left home. My sister Jen—" He came briskly into the room and set the tray on top of the dresser. "I didn't think you should have to cook the first day in yore new job."

His voice held the old teasing lilt and Doreen tried to meet it with lightness of her own. She could not. She looked at the sandy hair, the clear gray eyes, and felt tears coming. She turned away, fighting them, not wanting Laramie to see. He was doing his part to make this unnatural marriage feel natural, why couldn't she?

She couldn't because the words the minister had spoken echoed in her head: ". . . for better, for worse, in sickness and in health, until death do you part." Until death did them part. It was already September and he expected to be dead before winter. Less than four months. The tears came faster. Doreen covered her face with her hands. She heard Laramie's feet shift.

"Dee, what's the matter? What's happened?"

She shook her head. He had told her not to get attached to him. How could she tell him she already was, that the thought of losing him was too painful to bear? How could she talk to him about his own death?

She felt a light touch on her shoulder. "Dee, tell me what's wrong?" His voice was soft with concern.

That light touch was like a match to dry tinder. Doreen threw her head back and let all of her anger and grief fly free. "What's wrong? You can ask me what's *wrong?* You're planning to make me a widow soon and you ask me what's *wrong?* You're my best friend. I *care* about you. I don't want you to die and you're so calm and matter-of-fact about it."

He stiffened a little. "I have to be."

"Tell Bill you've changed your mind. Tell him you won't do his dirty work any more!"

Laramie shook his head.

"Then at least tell me what you're dying for!"

Laramie's mouth tightened, but his hands were gentle as they pulled her to her feet and held her still in front of him. "I gave my word not to tell anyone what I was doin', darlin'." His voice was gentle, as if explaining to a child. "A man's word is all he has out here. I have to keep my word." He shook her very gently. "I married you *because* it wasn't goin' to be for long. You know that. You knew that. And I told you before I left here I'd never take a woman into a life on the run. There's no hell on earth worse than life on the run, darlin'."

He hurt. Doreen could see in his eyes that he hurt. If he weren't there, if he would just stop touching her, her training would take over and she could regain control of her feelings. But he did not stop touching her and she could not regain control. The slow tears turned into a silent flood. Laramie hesitated a moment, then pulled

185

her against a solid, flannel-shirted chest. That tenderness broke what little control Doreen had left. Her arms wrapped tight around his waist, her body crowded as close to him as it could get, her tears became a storm that shook them both. Slowly, reluctantly, Laramie let his arms slide around her, let one hand stroke her tumbled hair in comfort. He murmured in her ear, a soft crooning that quieted her. The storm of tears passed. Still Laramie held her, still he stroked her hair.

Doreen lifted her face from his sodden shirt front and looked up at him. "Larry, please. I don't want you to die!"

He stared down at her for a long moment. "It never mattered before," he whispered. "Dyin' never mattered, until you."

He brushed a heavy strand of hair back from her face and let his hand rest where it stopped. His free hand lightly stroked ruffles away from her neck. It was a hesitant, almost fearful, caress. Still more hesitantly, his thumb wiped away a string of tears from her cheek. It touched the edge of Doreen's mouth, then slowly traced the shape of her lower lip. Doreen tasted the salt of her own tears. The roughness of his calluses made her lip tingle. A little pressure exposed some of the soft, damp inner skin.

"Dee, darlin'," Laramie breathed.

He bent and his tongue touched the soft inner surface he had exposed. He let his lips touch hers very gently. Doreen felt a delicious weakness. She stood on tiptoe to feel more, her breasts rubbing across the rough flannel of his shirt in the process. In an instant, every part of her tightened. Laramie took a harsh breath, then his hands slid between them and lifted the weight of her. One palm rubbed round and round, teasing, tempting. Doreen whimpered, on fire with that sudden need she had felt before with him, in the barn. Laramie's kiss became more urgent. He began freeing the tiny buttons of the dressing gown with fingers that shook.

Distantly, a part of Doreen urged embarrassment and retreat, but she did not listen, spellbound by the feel of his mouth and the light caress of his hands. Slowly Laramie broke the kiss. He spread the gown apart, as if exposing a treasure for the first time. His eyes devoured her. Doreen waited, trembling, burning.

Laramie let his fingers glide reverently over the skin above her chemise, then they slipped under the fine lace. Doreen gasped as fire raced from his fingers to her vitals. His lips brushed the skin above the lace, then his fingers untied the first few ties. His hands lifted, his tongue and lips explored. Doreen clutched blindly at his arms, lost in a whirling world of pleasure beyond understanding. Pleasure and a driving need. She felt for the buttons of his shirt. She had to feel his skin, to touch him as he was touching her.

Laramie moved fractions of an inch away, to help her, without stopping the devastating caresses of his mouth. Doreen spread his shirt open. Laramie pulled her against him and they both groaned as damp brushed against dry, smooth against rough. His kiss consumed her. Her hands stroked the wiry hair on his chest, slid across the smoothness of his back, held him as close as if she could become part of him. Her fingers ran round his back under the top edge of his belt. Laramie's hands cupped her hips and pressed them into him. Dizzy and burning, Doreen slid her fingers behind Laramie's belt buckle and down. Laramie caught her hand in steely fingers. He broke the kiss and stood, his breathing ragged, with his forehead against hers. Doreen felt him go rigid with the effort of regaining control.

"Dee. I promised you and I've almost broken it already. Help me." His voice was harsh and strained.

"I don't want to help you," she whispered. "I want you to touch me and kiss me and—"

Laramie groaned. "Gawd! Dee, what we were doin' leads to makin' babies."

Doreen let her hand lightly caress his neck. "I may be innocent, Larry, but I do know that."

Laramie crushed her close. His voice was low. "I promised you I wouldn't touch you. You married me on that promise."

The mad need was fading. Doreen gave a quiet, husky laugh. "It sounded more workable at the time than it does now." She stood on tiptoe and kissed his neck. "You really married me to protect me from the animals that would come round once Bekkerson told his story. I'll always be grateful."

"Grateful? I don't want—" His mouth snapped shut. He took a deep breath. "I'm not goin' to make a baby with you, Dee. You have no idea what it's like to have to raise a child alone. My mama had to raise two. I can't do that to you."

Doreen let the hand on his neck slide to caress his cheek. She framed his face in both hands and made him meet her eyes. "That's going to make life together very difficult, isn't it?" The next thing was going to be very hard to say. She took a deep breath. "You're my best friend, Laramie Smith. I want a child from you, a part of you to stay with me when you're—when you're gone."

Laramie groaned and kissed her hard, but without

passion. "I've seen how bad it is, Dee, alone. I won't leave you with a child." He hesitated. His look caressed the soft skin behind the chemise's lace. His hand moved to touch, then fell back to his side. "There's ways to protect you and still— When I was in Europe— Aw, hell! It'll be easier to show you than it is to say." He kissed her again, with a tenderness that made her want to cry. "Sleep on it. Be absolutely sure you want to lie with me. I'll never be able to resist—touching you—once we've lain together."

He spun and left the room. Doreen dressed slowly and thoughtfully, then ate her breakfast—bacon, eggs, and toast—cold. She recalled scraps of woman talk among her mother's friends about the pain and indignity of doing a wife's "duty" and could not connect that with the shivery excitement Laramie's touch awoke in her.

When she went into the main part of the house, Laramie was sitting in the parlor, reading an old *St. Nicholas'* magazine. He looked up when she came into the room, a thoughtful, assessing look. Doreen stopped beside his chair.

His mouth quirked up the tiniest bit. "What would you like to do this mawnin', wife?"

For the first time in her life, Doreen felt the power in the tiny word. "Wife," she would be truly his wife, for as long as the Lord allowed. She did not need another night to know what she wanted. But he might. She smiled back. "I want to go riding with you. Like we used to."

"We can ride more than half a day's from the house without settin' the gossips goin' now, and we've got three days. You ever been campin', Eastern woman?"

189

"Oh! Can we? How can I help?"

"Just sit. I'm used to packing quick. I have to be." Laramie pushed himself out of the chair and left the room.

His last sentence left a chill in the room. Mattheson. Others like him. Of course Laramie had to know how to pack and be gone.

In what seemed to Doreen to be a very short time, Laramie was at the front porch with two horses packed for a trip. He nodded to the roll of blankets behind her saddle.

"Yore bed. In case you change yore mind. You can tell me after supper. Until then, don't tempt me. All right?"

Doreen nodded. He boosted her into the saddle of a round pinto he called Bandit and they rode out of the ranch yard and down the valley. It was hot and dry and silent. Shimmers of heat created illusions of silvery ponds on the parched grass. There was not even a breeze. Doreen braced herself for what she knew she would see beyond the next rise.

The valley floor lay blackened and desolate. In several places along the Yellow, trees stood bare, branchless, and glistening. Bloating lumps told of cattle or antelope that had not escaped the fire. Doreen reined her horse to a stop, staring at the devastation. "It—it came so far!"

"Kerosene," Laramie said, his words rough, "in two separate fires. One of yore men brought in a couple cans this mornin'. Like I said, that fire was meant to get *you*." His voice shook and he took a long, slow breath. "The Englishman wants Three Rivers very badly, Dee. You've seen just a peek"—he nodded toward the blackened grass around them—"at how far he's willin' to go to get it. So far, you've been lucky." He kicked his horse into motion.

They rode along the Yellow for miles, then turned into the hills, following a narrow game trail that was very rough, thick with large rocks, deep cuts, and wide crevices. There was between them a long thoughtful silence, broken only by the thud of the horses' hooves, the sigh of the wind over grass and through trees, the lonely call of a bird. By midday Laramie had selected a campsite on the lower slope of a mountain. He laid a campfire, tossed their bedrolls under an old pine tree, and staked the horses. The newlyweds spent the rest of the day climbing rocks, wading in a stream like children, stopping to watch a butterfly on a flower. They listened to the busy noises of hard-working parent birds, watched eagles soar, talked and laughed. They had never really played together before and Doreen enjoyed herself immensely. With appalling regularity, she also found herself imagining the coming night, lying in Laramie's arms, the warm length of him against her, the touch of his long hard hands, his kisses. Her thoughts embarrassed and excited her.

It seemed as though only an hour or two had passed when Laramie looked regretfully at the sinking sun. "It's getting late. Let's head back to camp, wife."

"Wife." That small word, after an afternoon of freedom and joy, hit Doreen like a splash of icy water. She was a wife now, she would soon be a widow, and Laramie was coming closer to her, becoming more important to her by the hour, by the moment. He would leave a gaping hole when he was gone. She could not bear it. She sprang to her feet. "Last one to camp does the cooking."

She darted away. Laramie gave a startled gulp of laughter and then was right behind her, reaching out, trying to catch her. His hand touched her shoulder. Suddenly there was more at stake than having to cook dinner. Fear gave her speed. Even slipping on the pine needles she began to increase her lead. She felt Laramie's determination to catch her as if he had spoken it. Suddenly, at the top of a dip, Doreen lost her footing and went tumbling down the incline, Laramie close behind her. They rolled over and over, laughing like children, to the bottom, where they lay side by side, still laughing. Laramie rolled over and looked down at her, his lean face still bright with fun. In an instant the fun was gone, replaced with an intensity that made Doreen's heart beat faster. His hands gripped her shoulders, his breathing quickened, his face came close, so close. Involuntarily Doreen's lips parted a little to receive the kiss and her own breathing came faster. Laramie's hands tightened.

"No!" he said fiercely.

"Yes!" she said just as fiercely and lifted her head to touch her mouth to his.

He was lost. His weight crushed her, his mouth consumed her, his hands turned her to fire. Then he rolled to one side, kissing, touching, holding, and Doreen felt swept into a whirlwind; it seemed natural for clothing to disappear, natural for thought to disappear and feeling intensify. In what seemed mere moments, Laramie's lips were caressing her collarbone, then her breastbone, then her ribs, teasing both of them by avoiding the places both of them wanted most for him to kiss. Doreen fumbled with his buttons, frantic to be closer to him, to touch his skin, feel his heat. But in the madness and desperation that swept her, she could not seem to remember how the buttons worked. Worse, no matter how she writhed and twisted to place them in his path, he skimmed past the soft, sensitive places that ached for his mouth and touched and kissed and tormented other places until Doreen thought she would go out of her mind. Suddenly his mouth answered her need and his fingers sent her spinning out of control. She thought she heard Laramie whisper tenderly, "That's the way, darlin'," and then his weight was over her. A moment of pain and then he was in, smooth, rhythmic, a quiet pleasure to follow the whirlwind. But it was not enough, this quiet pleasure. Doreen clutched his hips, pressed him closer, faster, harder.

"Dear Gawd! Dee!" Laramie gasped.

He reared back convulsively. A moment later his head drooped forward and his wet forehead rested against hers. His breath rasped in his throat. Doreen rested her hand over his heart and felt it pounding against her palm. Laramie put his hand over hers for a moment, then rolled to one side and pulled her into his arms.

"Did I hurt you?" he whispered, his forehead creased with anxiety. "I meant to go slow, darlin', but I've wanted you so long and you were so . . ." He kissed her deeply, with the memory of recent passion in the kiss. "I don't have words for how good that was."

"Neither do I," Doreen murmured, snuggling into his side. She lay still, half drugged with wonder and pleasure. This was what that raw need had been, the need to be completely united with Laramie, to be part of him, if only for a few moments. "Is this what 'desire' means?" she asked sleepily.

Laramie's hand stroked her hair, now tangled and tumbling all around her. "That's what it is, darlin'. It's been killin' me for months."

Doreen tipped her head back to look at him. "Really?"

"Why do you think I quit dancin' with you, or steadyin' yore hand to shoot? Bashfulness?"

Doreen chuckled. "Bashful? You? Even a tenderfoot from the East wouldn't make *that* mistake." She propped herself up on her elbows and looked down at him, fascinated by the softness in his face, his vulnerability in the moments after loving. "Larry—" Drawn by gray eyes now dark with desire, Doreen forgot what she had meant to say. She let her mouth slowly, slowly descend to touch his and they were once again lost to everything but each other.

The next morning, Doreen lay quietly in the bedroll they had shared, watching the man who was now both lover and husband pick up camp. She felt sated and full of wonder and at peace. The desperation was gone, and the wild need, too. She had wanted him. From the first meeting, she had wanted him, though at first ignorance had hidden that from her and, later, friendship. And no one had ever told her of the ecstasy.

"Out, wife," Laramie commanded, and unceremoniously yanked the bedroll out from under her.

Doreen grinned and dressed and helped load the horses.

The day passed too swiftly, a lesson time for Doreen as their rides together had always been, but the lessons were like none from those other days. This was a time of learning the power of touches to tease, soft laughs to tantalize, and looks to suggest the joys of the night ahead. Doreen could not have found her way home after that day's ride if her life had depended on it.

Evening found them midway up a pine-covered mountain. Their trail led along the base of a rough red cliff, then bent away from the cliff into a meadow. Falling water roared off to their right, its source hidden by the trees at the base of the cliff. Long grasses swished against the horses' legs. Seed heads clittered softly against boots and leather saddle parts. A stream wound, gurgling, through the meadow and down the sharp slope at its edge. Laramie drew his horse up.

"Camping spot, wife," he said and dismounted.

In a short time, the horses had been unsaddled and staked and a fire laid. Then Laramie pulled Doreen up from her comfortable seat on a bedroll. "I want you to see somethin' special."

But though he held her hand tightly, he did not move. He studied her face for a long time, then lowered his head and kissed her. They were touching nowhere but lips and hands, yet Doreen felt as if her knees had turned to mush. She watched Laramie's eyes drift shut. His grip on her hand loosened and his free hand closed gently around her upper arm. He put a fraction more pressure into the kiss and Doreen reached for something solid to steady herself with. His arms.

"Mmmmm," Laramie murmured. He straightened slowly, ran a fingertip lightly over her mouth, then turned and led her away from the campsite toward the cliff.

Doreen followed him up a steep path across the

195

base of the waterfall she had heard and around the back of the cliff. They climbed steadily for perhaps a quarter of an hour. Doreen reached the top hot and breathless. The view at her feet took what breath she had left. On her right, far beyond the edge of the cliff, mountains pricked the sky. Row on row, they marched across the distance, solid, majestic, humbling. The sun was a brilliant orange-pink, sinking behind the mountains, gilding their tips, spreading pink and red along the horizon in strips and piles of clouds and deepening the color of the pines around the meadow below from green to black. The colors paled rapidly to pastels.

She turned to her husband. "Oh, Larry, I don't think I've ever seen anything so beautiful!"

He smiled, pulled her close, and kissed her until she clung to him. He held her tight for a moment, then moved a tiny distance away. "More later, darlin'." His voice was husky and a little ragged. "We have to get down to ground level before dark. And our protection's down in my war bag."

"Protection?"

Laramie chuckled. "You haven't noticed? I'm flattered." He nuzzled her neck a moment and murmured in her ear, "It's a barrier to nothin' but babies, darlin'. I'll show you how it works tonight."

Laramie led her down again to the campsite and pointed to a large flat rock off to one side. "You can go watch the stars come out. I'm the trail cook."

Doreen scrambled up to the top and while Laramie cooked, Doreen watched the last traces of pink and lavender fade from the sky. The stars that blinked on in the following darkness looked close enough to pull down. The wind had risen when the sun set. It carried

196

on it the scent of pine needles and wood burning. Lazily Doreen turned her head to look at the cooking fire. A Dutch oven sat on coals to one side and a coffeepot hung over the flames on a hook. Laramie was crouching beside the fire, staring into the flames. He had pushed his hat back, exposing his white forehead. Impatiently he brushed a dangling lock of hair out of his eyes. His eyes, though on the fire, were watching something far away.

I wonder what he's thinking about, Doreen thought. She felt a surge of tenderness. He was such a fascinating, puzzling man. He'd always been a loner, yet he'd allowed her to become his friend. He'd planned never to marry, but he had married to save her reputation. He'd wanted her very badly, yet he'd promised to deny that want for her sake.

Doreen smiled into the darkness. That resolve, praise the Lord, had not lasted long. She smiled wider, thinking of her own indecent haste to see that promise broken. To be held again, kissed, touched . . . Soon. Now. Doreen sat up. Perhaps there would still be time, before whatever was in the Dutch oven was ready. She swung her legs over the edge of the rock and pushed off.

But her feet never reached the ground. Two strong hands lifted her and pulled her against a flannel shirt. Surprised, she put her hands on Laramie's forearms to steady herself. Touching the hard muscles stirred her and, without further thought, she slid her arms up and around his neck and pulled his head to her. At the first touch of her lips, Laramie surged against her, her arms around his neck and his weight holding her both off the ground against the rock and mouth to mouth with him. His tongue slipped between her lips, teasing, tasting.

Both his hands were free and they wandered over Doreen's body with devastating effect. He lifted his hips against her while his hands continued stroking, tweaking, circling. It was spark to powder and Doreen's need exploded. She went wild, struggling to get closer, to get through the interfering clothes, to make him take her. Her fingers dug into his back, then slid lower and her nails dug into the skin of his hips, pressing them harder against her. He moaned. His tongue surged into her mouth and out, in and out. Her body answered the motion, her hands tore at his shirt. Laramie wrapped her tight against him, forcing her to be still, both of them panting, both trembling, until the wildness faded.

Laramie lifted her in his arms and carried her to his bedroll. He laid her down, then his hand darted into the war bag at the head of the roll. Doreen's hands flashed to buttons and ties. In seconds they were in each other's arms again, skin to skin. In seconds more, Doreen's need of him was as wild as it had been. Hands swept over smooth skin. Mouths nibbled, tasted, consumed. Breath mingled. Tongues stroked and plunged. Doreen's hands urged him, her body moved to entice him. Laramie whispered soft words of entreaty and demand. He retreated a little. Timidly Doreen touched him as he wished. Steel in velvet. She stroked him, in wonder at the softness, and he shuddered. He slid a roll of very thin leather and guided her hand a moment. Doreen stroked the leather downward, watching his face tighten with every touch of her fingers, feeling him writhe as she coaxed the soft tube lower and lower, seeing his hands reach to caress her and lose their way in his ecstasy. She burned with her new power. She could pleasure him as he had pleasured her. She slowed. She ran her fingers around and around. She stopped and he moaned. She touched him again and he surged into her hand. She teased him as he had teased her and his arousal kept her afire.

"Darlin', you're killin' me," he groaned.

"Isn't it a sweet way to die?" she whispered back, remembering his hands on her, and smoothed the last wrinkle from the tube. Her fingers wandered into the mysterious, furred territory below, tugged, pinched.

With a low moan, Laramie shoved her onto her back, entered, stopped, his eyes shut. Then he began to move, slowly. His mouth teased her breasts and lips. Doreen felt the tension rising, the edge of ecstasy approaching. The pines, the mountain, even the stars in the sky disappeared. All that remained was fire and whirling and lips and hands and soft wet mouth. Then she slid over the edge, gasping, clutching, crying with the power of what he was giving her, and he followed.

Doreen drifted back to the present slowly. She and Laramie lay entwined on the bedroll. She let her hand slide along his arm, reveling in the smooth along the inner side and the rough along the outer side. Laramie murmured something in his sleep and snuggled deeper into her neck. Doreen jerked the edge of the other bedroll, unmaking it, and tugged its blanket over them, too sated to do more.

Morning came too soon and their time for parting was far too near. Laramie had to go back to the roundup. And to Bill's work. Doreen helped pack with reluctance. Bill's work. Work Laramie could not or would not explain. Dangerous work. Joy such as they had shared would come seldom, when he could get time away, and would be cut off early with Laramie's death.

A cold, unwelcome thought after such ecstasy. Doreen tightened Bandit's cinch with a jerk. She rested her head against the saddle's fender.

I will not cry. I will not cry. He has given me his name and knowledge and life and joy. Tears will spoil the hours we have left. I will *not* cry.

And by biting her lip and thinking of happier things, Doreen forced the tears away. She swung into the saddle and watched Laramie while he checked the fire to be sure the ashes were stone cold. He then mounted with a casual grace that hurt her to see and nudged his horse into the lead. He moved with his horse, head high, rifle across his knees. His vitality and humor and tenderness, his quicksilver mood changes—realization made her clench her hands on her reins in sudden agony. He was not just her best friend. He was the love of her life. She squeezed her eyes tight shut.

I love him. I love him and I can't tell him! Our marriage is the result of a mistake he believed he had to correct. He would never have married otherwise. And he told me he didn't want his feeling for me to grow. Dear God, how can I live with this?

But Doreen knew she had to live with it. Somehow she had to share her bed and her body with him and not betray how much she loved him. Well, it was far too late for regrets. He valued their friendship highly. She would have to be content with that.

And Doreen knew, even as she thought it, that that would be impossible.

CHAPTER

12

LARAMIE AND DOREEN said a passionate farewell in the big bed at the ranch house, then Laramie returned to his work at Blue Mountain. It was nearly three weeks before she saw him again. On a crisp morning in mid-October Laramie came into the ranch yard riding a Blue Mountain horse and leading Tennessee. He found Doreen in the garden. She looked up from the browned flower stalks she was removing, held motionless for a moment by surprise. Then she was on her feet and in his arms the moment his feet hit the ground, hugging him as tightly as she could, feeling his arms close blessedly around her.

Laramie chuckled. "That's some welcome, wife. You have me at a disadvantage," he added, opening his arms again to show the set of reins he held in each hand.

"Ground-tie them," she ordered.

Laramie laughed and obeyed. Then he crushed her close and kissed her until she ached with desire and longed to drag him immediately to the bedroom. He leaned back a little and looked down at her. His eyes were dark and dreamy, his body hard.

"Just when I thought I was getting used to the idea of living alone . . ." Doreen began.

Laramie touched a finger to her lips. "Dee, I'd give anythin' to stay with you"—he kissed her again so there was no doubt what he meant—"but I got a mighty impatient bunch of men waiting for me in the pass. I'm askin' you a favor, Dee." His hand caressed her cheek, momentarily distracting both of them. "We're goin' down to Fishhook to finish up there. Tennessee's a travelin' horse, not a cow horse, and he's not gettin' enough exercise with me gone so much. Will you keep him and ride him for me?"

What could she say? Another argument about Bill's work would only mar the moments they had, because Laramie would not yield on a matter of honor.

"Yes, I'll take care of him," she whispered.

Another too-brief kiss and Laramie was gone.

Doreen watched until he was out of sight, then she led Tennessee to the in-pasture gate. As she unclipped the lead rope she saw, tightly tied to the cheekstrap on Tennessee's off side, a small package wrapped in brown paper. She took it off, gave Tennessee a swat to send him into the pasture, and hurried to her room to open the box.

It held a slender gold chain from which dangled a golden disk. The disk had been engraved "LS" in the center with her initials and his and the date of their wedding engraved around the edge. Doreen picked up the bracelet and a card fell out. It read: "My brand, on my wife, until the ring comes. Larry."

"Larry," she whispered. She clasped the bracelet

around her wrist, felt the cool metal caress her skin, put her head down on the bed, and cried.

Frost sparkled on the grass most mornings now. Ducks and geese flew south in long, loud wedges. 3R's herd came back from the roundup and was immediately sent to graze under heavy guard on the flats at the mouth of the valley, to wait for the district drive to the railhead. Doreen quickly developed an affection for Tennessee. She rode him a lot, and his smooth stride made more bearable the boredom of sticking within sight of the house and barn. On the day a reliable report came in that the rustlers were working far south of Fishhook, California told Doreen she could ride without a bodyguard if she did not go more than a mile or two from the house. For Doreen, the prospect of getting away from the monotony of the ranch yard filled her with joy, but when she went to the far pasture for Tennessee, he was gone. She had all her available cowboys search for him, but they only found a trail which soon lost itself on rock slabs in the hills on the Blue Mountain side.

Two weeks later, the horse bobbed into the ranch yard, appearing no worse for his long absence. Doreen pampered him with lumps of sugar and apples anyway, thinking to keep him from walking off to look for his owner a second time.

The morning after Tennessee's return, Doreen rose especially early to celebrate, dressed warmly, for the November air was nippy, and strode out onto the porch. She rejoiced in being up on a bright morning to see the sun rise over the mountains. During the night, the peaks had acquired a dusting of snow. Winter was coming. She imagined what life would be like at Three Rivers when the snow came. There would be a skeleton crew of riders to mend the new fence, break ice on the watering places, and do other necessary work, and she would stay in the house most of the time. It would be a lonely, quiet house. It already was, since Cary had gone to live with Bill. Doreen shook off winter thoughts. This was the first morning in weeks that she had not longed for Laramie first thing on getting up and she was not going to spoil it.

She walked to the in-pasture fence and whistled. Tennessee lifted his head and came bobbing to her. She saddled him, mounted him from the block Luke had made, and turned his head toward the flats. Tennessee snorted and sidled, as he often did early in the morning, but he did not buck. He never bucked.

"Miss! Wait, Miss."

Doreen turned, startled. A stranger on a bay horse waved from the road. Doreen called for Luke, who came to the barn door at once, his hand on his revolver. He watched the stranger ride into the yard. Luke looked alert and competent, but not hostile. Doreen nodded approval at him. His bearing would keep almost anyone from making threats.

The stranger rode to a polite talking distance and pulled up. He glanced at Luke and his face tightened for an instant, then he turned to Doreen and swept off his hat. "Pardon me, ma'am. Looks like you've been having troubles here." He nodded significantly toward Luke's gunhand. "I won't keep you long. My name's Mattheson. I'm looking for a man named James L. Smith. Your neighbor at the Rolling W said you had a Smith working here."

Doreen smiled and stalled. "Smith is a fairly common name, sir."

The man looked down at his hat, which he was turning round and round by its brim. "I can understand your hesitation, ma'am. I *am* a stranger to you. But this man Smith is dangerous, he'd killed two men by the time he was fifteen, in fact. And he's worth a lot of money."

Doreen let her eyes slide away from the man's steady gaze, praying her shock would not show and betray her. *It's Larry he wants! James L. Smith. He's lied about his name. And this has to be a bounty hunter, gentleman though he acts.* She felt cold with fear but tried to hide it, willing her voice to steadiness. "My husband's name is Smith. *Laramie* Smith. But he doesn't work here, he works for Bill Haycox at Blue Mountain."

"Bekkerson was quite positive about the man working here." The man's voice was both humble and insistent.

Doreen put on a coldly amused tone. "We aren't on the best of terms with the people at the Rolling W, sir. Mr. Bekkerson has made trouble for us before. Why are you looking for this man Smith?"

"Like I said, he killed two men, two Union soldiers, during the war, ma'am. He's been avoiding capture for nigh on fourteen years, but I'm right on his tail now. I'm sure of it."

Doreen gripped the saddle horn to hide the trembling of her hands. Her head felt light and empty but she forced herself to maintain the air of cold amusement. "You're barking up the wrong tree, sir. My husband's lived in this part of the country most of his life. I'm sure he's not the man you're looking for."

"That's funny." The man was still acting polite, but his look and posture broadcast danger like a coiled rattlesnake. "You're riding a Tennessee walker, if I'm not mistaken. Smith always rides a walker, brought one with him when he ran from Tennessee."

Doreen laughed. "If you'd ridden a walker, you'd know why, sir. This is my horse. I don't do cow work and I like to be comfortable when I ride." She made her tone a little patronizing. "He's certainly nowhere near sixteen or seventeen years old, but you can check his teeth if you'd like."

Matheson made a disgusted sound under his breath, tipped his hat in farewell, and rode away. Doreen looked at her guard. His face showed he had come to the same conclusion she had.

"Luke?"

"He won't learn nothin' from me, ma'am. A kid of fourteen has to have a mighty good reason to take on two soldiers."

"Thanks, Luke."

A smile flashed white across Luke's dark face.

The hunter was gone, for now, but he was still very dangerous. Doreen gazed blindly out over the grassland beyond the ranch yard. Laramie could be anywhere out there. "I have to warn Larry," Doreen said, her voice a husky whisper. "Bill will know where he is."

Luke nodded and reentered the barn. Doreen turned Tennessee toward the hills, moving fast, fear pursuing her. If Laramie's job didn't kill him, the bounty hunter would. He probably had a picture, and if he didn't someone would tell him Laramie was the one.

All Mattheson has to do is see Larry and it'll all be over!

She urged Tennessee to stride faster. The wind was sharp. A V of geese passed overhead, honking. The aspens along the river, shivering in the wind, had turned gold and were dropping their leaves. Doreen and Tennessee forded the Yellow and entered the rough, sage-covered hills between 3R and Blue Mountain.

As she rode deeper into the hills, Doreen began to see cattle, 3R cattle, far more than there should have been so soon after roundup. The farther she rode, the more there were. Soon she saw burned brands, on cattle that had been 3R, Lazy H, which was from far south, Circle X, Blue Mountain, and Fishhook cattle. Lazy H, which was south of Fishhook. Warnings jangled in Doreen's head. The rustlers were on her range again or maybe the Fishhook story had been just a rumor, planted in the cattlemen's association by one of its members. Doreen stopped and listened for some time. She heard no human sounds, she saw no one, yet she knew she could run into rustlers at any moment.

"We have to get out of here fast!" she told Tennessee. "God in Heaven, help me get to Bill's place safe. Please!"

Doreen took her bearings, then urged Tennessee along the edge of a dry ridge, carefully keeping below the skyline. They crossed barren hill after barren hill, staying low on the slope whenever possible and using what little cover nature provided. Despite her care, Doreen knew a large black horse would be disastrously visible most of the time. At last, after more than an hour, Doreen saw Blue Mountain's grassy basin and ranch buildings, tiny with distance. In a direct line, not half a mile away, water glittered among cedars.

Doreen patted Tennessee's neck. "For a flatland horse, you've done very well, boy. But I'll bet you need a drink; we've still got a ways to go."

The water was almost within reach, only twenty or thirty feet away through a grove of cedar and pine, before the sound of horses made both Tennessee and Doreen turn their heads.

Doreen gulped down panic. Rustlers! It had to be, out here, and there was no place to hide!

She looked for a spot big enough to hide herself and a large horse. Over the next ridge, men laughed. Doreen glanced at the dense group of cedars near the water. It was very risky, that clump of cedars, but it offered their only hope. Doreen pulled the unwilling Tennessee from the water and rode into the cedar clump, forcing the horse through the thick, prickly branches. Hidden, she hoped, Doreen flung herself from Tennessee and went to his head, one hand ready to muffle any protests he might make about being deprived of water and the company of other horses when both were so close. Tack creaked and jingled nearby. Doreen prayed not to be seen, reciting the prayer over and over like a litany. She did not want to die, but more than death she feared the worse-than-death that outlaws would force on a woman.

A group of masked men, one of them wearing jodhpurs and riding a Thoroughbred, rode to the edge of the water and let their horses drink. Doreen examined the man on the Thoroughbred. The build was not Sir Adrian's. The men all dismounted at some signal, shed their masks, and started a fire. The man in the jodhpurs was Bekkerson.

I'll bet he dresses that way any time there's the least likelihood he'll be seen, Doreen told herself. Maybe Sir Adrian isn't involved with the rustling. Maybe he doesn't know about Bekkerson, either, or maybe he just looks the other way.

That seemed more and more likely the more Doreen thought about it and for a moment rage blocked her fear. *Spineless Englishman! Too "well-bred" to dirty his hands with crime, but most willing to take the profits of it! I'll bet Bekkerson was the visitor I saw the day I found McTaggert!*

McTaggert's name reminded her she was looking at men responsible for murder. Her stomach clenched. Her hand stroked Tennessee to keep him quiet. Her mind raced.

They're going to or coming from a raid, she told herself. There's no reason for any men to be here, between Blue Mountain and Three Rivers so soon after roundup.

One of the men produced a black and battered coffeepot and set it on the crude hanger a second man had suspended over a young fire. Doreen's heart fell. They were going to stay. She swallowed with difficulty. The longer they stayed, the smaller her chance of ever speaking to anyone again; she did not know enough about keeping a horse quiet.

A trio of men on the far side of the fire burst into laughter. "After this morning's work the tenderfoot won't be able to eat over the winter, let alone keep any kind of crew," one of the men roared joyfully.

"She sure takes a lot of beating," a man nearer the cedars said with grudging admiration.

"She's tougher than she looks," Bekkerson snarled, "but no woman's going to beat me. This last raid oughta force her to sell out. If she won't—" He paused significantly. "It'll be Rolling W land, one way or another, by snowfall."

"Sure of yourself, ain't you?" one of the group of three sneered.

"I have to be," Bekkerson retorted. "If it were up to that lily-livered Englishman, we'd never make a profit."

A latecomer rode up and swung from his saddle. Although his back was to Doreen, his way of moving betrayed him. She stifled Tennessee's attempt to whinny recognition.

No, no, no, no, she moaned without sound. It isn't. Please, God, it isn't!

Bekkerson looked at the newcomer and his face twisted into a snarl. "You take time off to see your 'wife,' Smith? That time in the low pass and now today. Maybe your ethics is too nice to be around when we discuss where to drive all those cattle for sale. Maybe it's all right to steal your wife's cattle but not to watch them sold?" Bekkerson paused. "There are a *few* benefits to that sudden marriage, though, aren't there, Smith? Control at Three Rivers ranch, for one. And your 'wife' for another. Now, she's right handsome. I'll bet she's a heap of fun in b—"

Laramie's fist ended Bekkerson's taunt. "Keep remarks about my wife out of yore dirty mouth, Bekkerson!" he snarled.

Bekkerson put his hand to his mouth and swiped at

the blood trickling from a cut lip. "The gentleman rustler! Well, if these boys knew what I—"

Laramie knocked Bekkerson head over heels into the shallow water at the spring's edge. He was at Bekkerson's side with his gun in his hand before Bekkerson's hand more than touched his holster. "I wouldn't try that," Laramie warned softly. "I'm not as fast as you, but I'm a much better shot. Remember that, next time you try to draw on me."

"I'll remember." Bekkerson stood slowly, dripping mud, hands well away from his sides. "That's twice you've nailed me, Smith. A mistake both times."

"You countin' yore visit to Three Rivers with that damned Englishman in that number?" Laramie gave a snort of disgust. "Wasn't me queered that deal, Bekkerson. You threatened the lady. I'd just been hired on to protect her—and get at her riders—and you threatened the lady. Wasn't anythin' else I could do just then *but* protect her. Anythin' else woulda blown my cover clean away. Then what good would I have been to you?"

Bekkerson glared. His hands opened and closed convulsively. Laramie backed away until he reached a tree not far from Doreen's hiding place. Doreen had lived in the West long enough to see the insult: Laramie had shown everyone present he thought Bekkerson would shoot him in the back, given a chance. Laramie rolled a cigarette and lit a match. The light gleamed briefly on his brown face. Doreen whimpered before she could help it. The sound had been very small, but Laramie came quickly away from the tree and looked toward the cedar clump. Doreen bit a knuckle to keep any other noise from escaping and her bracelet jingled.

211

He can't see me, she prayed. Dear God above, don't let him see me!

Laramie settled his back against the tree again and finished his cigarette. Doreen sagged against Tennessee with relief. He had not seen her. Or he was not going to betray her. Laramie tossed the last of his cigarette into the water and walked over to the men crouched around the steaming coffeepot. He kicked a glowing stick away from the coals. "Company's comin', boys, better kill the fire."

Muttering oaths and growling complaints, the rustlers scrambled to their feet. With the speed of long practice, they doused the fire, tossed out the coffee, packed up, and rode away.

Doreen crumpled to the ground, so deeply hurt she wanted to curl up and die. "He's a rustler, he's helping ruin me, and I love him," she whispered. "God help me, I love him and he's crooked!" She rocked back and forth with pain.

All the nights he was gone, all the days—he was stealing my cattle, running my brand . . .

Doreen curled into a tight ball with her arms wrapped hard around her knees and one cheek on the sharp cedar needles. Her pain went far too deep for tears. The cattle thief had married her to save her name. The rustler had touched her and turned her to fire. His laugh warmed her life, his smile was joy, his drawling voice . . .

Oh, God, God, God!

212

CHAPTER

13

DOREEN DID NOT remember how she got home. Perhaps she had just let Tennessee have his head. Nothing she saw registered in her memory and all she felt was the agony of being betrayed. She went to bed immediately and stayed there. She saw no one, ate nothing for two days. On the third day, Cary appeared, set a bowl of soup on the bedside table, and sat on the bed where Doreen lay huddled with her face to the wall. Bill hovered in the doorway.

"Luke sent for me. He told us there was something very wrong with you. Are you sick?"

Doreen shook her head.

"Are you pregnant?"

"Oh, God!"

"Are you in pain, then?"

"I hurt so much I want to die!"

Cary ran a gentling hand across Doreen's shoulders. "Is it something to do with Laramie?"

At his name, the dam inside broke and tears flooded out. Wrenching sobs tore at Doreen, shaking her and the bed. She cried wildly, hysterically for a long time. Cary could do nothing to ease her. When the crying was done, Doreen fell asleep, the first unbroken sleep since she had seen Laramie's treachery. She awoke in early afternoon, swung her feet over the edge of the bed, and sat up. She stood slowly and walked toward the wardrobe. She felt bulky and old. She put on clean clothes mechanically and went out. Cary and Bill were sitting in the porch swing, his arm around her. Doreen remembered the feel of Laramie's arm and bit her lip to keep from crying with the pain of "what if." Laramie Smith was a thief. What she had seen and heard would hang him. He was driving all the ranchers toward ruin. She must tell Bill.

But they'll hang him, she reminded herself in anguish, and she could not make herself step onto the porch. She spun away from the lovers and reentered the house.

I know what's right and I love the man so much I can't make myself say the words!

She sank into the nearest parlor chair and stared blindly at the wall, forcing herself to look at the facts again and again. Laramie was with rustlers. They talked about what they're doing. Rustlers were criminals who were hanged without trial. Executed.

But I love him. He's crooked and I love him.

Doreen stared at the pale autumn sunlight on the polished wood floor and grieved, for her ignorance, for what might have been. "It's like a nightmare," she whispered to the silent room. "Can I turn Laramie in and still live with myself?" Yet she had to choose. She could not hide from this decision. She stood like an old woman and walked slowly out onto the porch. Bill and

Cary were still sitting in the swing, watching the clouds and mountains. "Aunt Cary?"

Cary and Bill turned.

"You look like hell warmed over, girl, but I'm sure glad to see you up and out," Bill said.

Cary gave him a reproachful look.

"She knows what she looks and feels like, Cary." Bill looked at Doreen. "I don't know what happened the other day, honey, but I do know Larry's feelin' awful, too. He didn't tell me much, just that you'd probably hate him forever. Don't hate him, honey. No matter what the fight was about—"

"It wasn't a fight, Bill! He's a rustler! I saw him! He's betraying us all! He's ruining us!"

Bill studied her, his face unreadable. Was he surprised, or did he already know? Doreen wondered. Was *he* in with the rustlers, too? It was hard to believe, but then she never would have believed Laramie was crooked, either. Doreen spun away. She'd given her fatal information to the wrong man! Now what could she do? How many ranchers were in on this? The sheriff was the Englishman's for sure.

Bill cleared his throat. "I'm not gonna believe that, honey. I've known Larry twelve years and he's always been straight. There has to be some other explanation. I'll send some men out to look for him in the morning, but I can't believe he's gone bad."

"You're not going to do anything? The rustlers have wiped me out! I heard them say so. From what I saw, only Bekkerson's higher up in the gang."

"I said I'd send men out in the morning, Doreen. I couldn't get home early enough to send a search party out before dark, even if I left right now."

"Are you one of them? Is that why you're in no hurry to stop them?"

"Doreen!" Cary's face was as shocked as her voice.

"I'll let that remark go, Doreen, seein' as how you're a tenderfoot and overwrought besides." Bill's voice was icy. "You stumbled onto somethin' you weren't supposed to see and if you say a word to anyone else, Larry will be dead before morning."

Doreen swayed and reached for the porch posts. Maybe this is what Larry meant by the importance of reputation: his reputation here is so good no one will believe he's a thief. Pain rose, choking her. I should be glad the thieving traitor's gone! Glad! Why can't I be glad!

"Doreen! Are you all right?"

"No, Aunt Cary," she whispered. "I'm not all right and I don't think I'll ever be all right again." Doreen turned, then, and ran. She ran into the flower garden and flung herself down under the ancient crabapple tree, hating herself for the weakness that could not keep Laramie out of her mind and heart for even a short time.

It seemed an age before she got her grief under control. The ranch lay thick with long blue shadows when she opened her eyes again. She rolled onto her back and looked up through the bare black branches. At stake was 3R's survival and the survival of some of the other ranches, too. She could not allow herself to think what would happen to Laramie, what would happen to her. She stood, brushed dirt and bits of twig and grass from her cheek and her shirtwaist, pinned her hair into rough order, and turned toward the house. There was a big herd of stolen cattle out there. The roundup crews weren't all home yet, but surely Three Rivers and Blue Mountain had enough riders to bring those cattle in. She and the other ranchers could still salvage something of this disastrous summer.

The barn's owl cried softly, like a man in pain. A flight of bats poured silently out of the barn loft and separated to search for meals. They made her aware of time. "I'm too late! It's almost dark and they've gone back to Blue Mountain!"

She ran to the house. The porch was empty, but Cary was sitting with a cup of coffee in the kitchen, a lamp turned very low beside her. She turned up the lamp and looked at Doreen with concern.

"We couldn't leave you alone, feeling like you do, but Bill had to get back."

"I have to make him believe me!"

"You talked to him. You're too late for more. Only a fool crosses that path with anything less than a half-moon. Sit down. Have some coffee."

"I *saw* stolen cattle. I *saw* Laramie with the rustlers. We have to stop him before he helps Bekkerson drive those cattle out of the district!"

"Honey, sit down. Bill didn't seem to be awfully worried."

"Maybe because Bill's rustling, too. Maybe that's why he wants me to keep quiet. The stolen cattle are on *his* range."

"Doreen! You know Bill better than that!"

Doreen caught back a sob. "I thought I knew Laramie better than that!"

Cary stroked Doreen's limp hand. "Maybe you do. If you love him, and I think you do, have faith in him.

217

Things aren't always as they seem. Talk to Bill again if you must, but no one else. You must be sure you're right before you talk to other ranchers. Rustlers get hanged out here, you know. On the spot."

"I know," Doreen whispered. She shut her eyes against a fresh wave of pain and saw on her lids the image of Laramie jerking and twisting at the end of a rope. All that life and humor and tenderness— She cried out and bit her knuckle to prevent another outburst. "He knows what he's doing and he knows the price."

"You don't mean that," Cary said softly.

"I don't know what I mean, Aunt Cary," Doreen wailed, feeling lost and bewildered and entirely alone. "I do know where the cattle are. Were. Laramie saw me. The herd may already be moving somewhere else."

"Even if that's so, you aren't fool enough to try that pass tonight, are you? Get some sleep and get up at dawn."

Doreen nodded and walked slowly through the kitchen toward the hall. The disk on her bracelet clinked against the edge of the table as she passed. She looked at it a moment as if she did not recognize it, then she opened the clasp and lifted one of the lids on the stove. The disk spun in the updraft, "LS," "LS," "LS." Doreen could not make herself drop it in. She bit her lip and shoved the bracelet into a pocket. She had begun with an attempt to protect her husband from a bounty hunter. She had ended with an attempt to give evidence that would hang him. It was beyond coping with. She paused outside her bedroom door a moment, feeling again the wrenching agony of love betrayed. She went into the room, closed the door behind her, and leaned against it in the dark. Grief surged through her. Then she smelled smoke. Something was wrong. She sniffed cautiously. Cigarette smoke. Then she saw the red glow above the bed.

"I hoped you might come soon. If not, I was ready to come lookin' for you."

The soft, cool drawl stopped her heart. The shock of his presence, so soon after her attempt to turn him in, made her light-headed. "Larr—Laramie!"

"The same. I've come to say good-bye."

"Good-bye?"

"You're actin' like an echo, wife."

This was the end, then. He was going. Doreen shut her eyes and fought down the pain. *Mattheson. Rustlers. Betrayal. Death. A slow, shameful death.* "Cary knows what you're doing," she finally choked out. "And a man came three days ago, looking for you, a Mattheson." Doreen took a step closer to the red glow. Unable to stop herself, she blurted, "Leave Wyoming, Laramie. Save yourself, before you're caught and—and—"

"And hung?"

"Don't say that," Doreen whispered.

"Why not? That's what happens to rustlers, isn't it? If you tell other ranchers what you saw . . ." Laramie snapped his fingers. "Hangman or Bekkerson, I'll be just as dead. And my job not finished."

Doreen heard the bedsprings creak, saw the glow of the cigarette fall to the floor, heard Laramie's boot grind the glow out. Then Laramie lit the lamp. He looked at the black smear of ashes on the floor for a long time. When he looked up, his face was the cold, set face of a stranger. Yet his eyes devoured her, as if he were memorizing her. "Good-bye, wife."

219

He strode past her to the door without looking at her. He was going, forever, walking out, to whatever kind of death waited for him out there. Fear and rage gave Doreen courage.

"So! I've served my purpose! You don't need to hide behind me anymore! You're leaving me to deal with the consequences of your thievery!"

Laramie froze, one hand on the doorknob. "Don't prod me, woman! I wanted to see my wife just once more before I died. Just that. *See* her. Can't you understand that?"

"No!" Doreen heard her voice rising and she could not stop it. "I don't understand anything! We were friends, once. You've betrayed me. And Bill, who you said you owed so much to!" Doreen took a ragged breath. She clenched and unclenched her hands. "God help me, I wanted you with me," she whispered. "I'm your wife and I wanted you with me. You haven't wanted to be near *me* in ages!"

"Gawd! Are you so blind!" Laramie strode across the room and glared down at her, even then not touching her. "I didn't want to pull you down with me. We had somethin' powerful between us. You know that. I couldn't let you get in any deeper." He made a little shrug of resignation. "But it's better if you hate me. It'll make the pain less and the hurt'll heal quicker, after."

Doreen leaped at him, her arms raised to hit or—or she was not sure what. "Hurt?" she cried at him. "What do *you* know about hurt?"

His fingers gripped her upper arms so tightly that she gasped with pain. "Hurt? I've been in hell because of you. Hell! You're my wife. Before Gawd and man, you're my *wife*, and I've stayed away to protect you! When I saw you there among the cedars, knowin' yore danger, knowin' what you had to be thinkin', and honor-bound to explain nothin'—"

"Honor? *You* talk about honor? You've betrayed the people who loved you and you say 'honor'—"

"Stop! You go too far!"

"Too far?" Doreen loved him, hated him; she wanted him to hold her; she wanted him to be gone forever. But she did not want him dead, God help her, not dead. Her hand flashed toward his face. He caught it in iron fingers before it ever touched him. Doreen struggled wildly, frantic to escape the contact.

"Traitor!" she snarled. "Where can I go when the last of my cattle are stolen? Jamesville? Denver? Chicago? We'll be beggars, Cary and I, wherever we are, boarding grifters or—or living off the street—"

The look on his face stopped her. His grip tightened, if that were possible. "You've condemned me outa hand! Where's yore faith?" His voice was low and harsh and shook a little. "We were friends, once, and lovers, and you *are* my wife. A friend believes, a wife trusts."

Pain ripped through Doreen, pain enough to rip her apart. "You didn't trust *me*. You didn't even trust me with your real name! You're a thief, maybe a murderer!" She yanked the bracelet from her pocket and hurled it at him. "There's your brand back!"

A tremor ran through him. "So, all my restraint's been wasted. Then I'll take what I've been doin' without all these weeks!" He pulled her hard against him. For an instant she felt the wild pounding of his heart, then his mouth came down on hers, grinding her lips against her teeth. He kissed her cheeks, her throat, her mouth with bruising lips. One of his hands tore at the buttons at her neck.

Doreen struggled to escape. "Not like this! No, please, Laramie, not like this!"

He silenced her with another brutal kiss and carried her to the bed. He set her on her feet beside it. "Do you take yore clothes off or do I?"

Doreen stood immobile with horror. With a deliberation that was frightening, Laramie put his hands to the neck of the dress and ripped the bodice open. He looked down with eyes that froze her soul. She felt like a harlot.

"Shall I finish or will you?" He caught her look and added, "Don't scream. It'll hurt Cary and she can't do anythin'. You *are* my wife."

"I'll do it."

"Every stitch."

Doreen shut her eyes against the hardness in his face and undressed with trembling hands. She heard Laramie blowing out the lamp, his boots hitting the floor, then the rustle of his denims, the clunk of the heavy belt buckle, the whisper of his shirt.

"Larry—"

For answer he wrapped her in a crushing embrace and kissed her with burning, hungry lips, lips that devoured her mouth, her eyes, her throat, her shoulders, her mouth again. His hands roamed over her body, wild, hungry hands that could not touch enough of her. Then, suddenly, they were no longer hurting her but were stroking, holding, caressing, exciting. One hand slid up her side to her breast, cupping it, touching the soft pink tip with incredible gentleness. Laramie groaned against her mouth and bore her back onto the bed. His mouth followed his hand, his lips soft, his tongue licking, teasing. Doreen's hands closed convulsively on his shoulders. The short, stiff hairs there tickled her palms, stoking a fire that was building inside her. The need she had been feeling for weeks exploded inside her, spreading from her belly to all parts of her body. She whimpered with longing. Laramie raised his head in surprise, then kissed her mouth, gently, lingeringly, tasting her lips with the tip of his tongue, slowly moving his mouth back and forth across hers. His hands caressed her intimately, relearning every part of her, and the need inside her grew. His gentleness was far more devastating than his violent passion had been. He lifted his head and Doreen felt alone, bereft.

"No," she whispered, and pulled his head down again.

They were both panting, their caresses hurried and more urgent. Doreen writhed and moaned under his mouth, his hands. She felt as if she would burst out of her skin if the tension were not released somehow. And yet his hands and mouth continued to torment and pleasure her unbearably.

"Larry, please, please. Please help me."

He silenced her husky, pleading whisper with his mouth and his hand did something wonderful. Waves of pleasure washed over Doreen. Then Laramie raised his body over hers and the pleasure continued.

The two of them came slowly down to earth again. Doreen clung to Laramie in wonder. Laramie looked down at her with a soft face and sleepy eyes. He kissed her tenderly, then pulled slowly away and rolled onto his side, taking her over with him. He held her close and kissed the hair above her temple. After a few quiet moments, he tugged the blankets up over them, turned her over so they fit together like two spoons, pulled her back against his warm, wet body, kissed her shoulder, and went to sleep. Doreen slid into sleep more slowly, every nerve of her still alive to the touch of him against her bare skin, the smell of him, the sound of his breathing. Gradually the wonder and the pleasure faded, slowly, slowly, and Doreen, too, slept.

Sometime in the night, Doreen heard the thump of boot heels on the floor, the faint jingle of spurs. She thought she felt a hand lightly caress her cheek.

Laramie's voice whispered, "I'm sorry, Dee, darlin'. I didn't plan to do anythin' more than say good-bye."

The bedroom door opened and shut quietly. That woke Doreen completely.

"Larry!"

But he was gone.

Doreen flung the blanket from the bed around herself and ran out onto the porch. Clouds, white near the bright sliver of moon, scudded across the midnight-blue sky. The wind already had the bite of winter. Laramie was gone. Not even the sounds of his horse lingered in the stinging cold air. Doreen clutched the blanket tighter, but it could not warm the cold inside her.

"God forgive me," she whispered into the darkness. "I don't want to be free of him, no matter what he is!"

She had hurt him, called him terrible things, thought terrible things. Maybe if she told him she was his no matter what, that she'd follow him anywhere, she could stop him from throwing his life away. She dressed quickly, snatched her new sheepskin jacket from its hook beside the kitchen door, and went out to whistle up a bay named Rex. Doreen remembered what Cary had said about crossing the pass at night, but it did not matter. Laramie would die in the morning if she did not stop him.

14

THE PASS was difficult, but with the sliver of a moon, a lantern, and the patience to walk some stretches, Doreen crossed it without accident. Then she rode hard. She pulled the sweating Rex up at the Blue Mountain ranch house at sunrise. The ranch yard was very quiet. Frost whitened grass, rocks, fence posts, and the top of the black iron dinner bell. A thin stream of smoke rose from the far end of the house and the smell of bacon rose with it. Doreen ground-tied Rex and sprinted to the kitchen door. Bill and three of his riders, dressed for winter riding, were just leaving the house.

Bill looked at Doreen in amazement. "Doreen! What's happened? Cary—"

Doreen shook her head. "I have to talk to you, Bill, please. Privately. Now."

He nodded curtly. "Coffee?"

"Yes."

Bill picked up a steaming cup for her as they passed through the kitchen, then led the way to his cluttered office. He brushed a pile of newspapers off a chair and waved Doreen into it. He shut the door, sat in his desk chair, and tipped it back into a worn spot on the wall with the smoothness of long habit. But he was not relaxed. His face was hard and cold. "You're too late. He's not here."

The harshness in Bill's voice struck Doreen silent. How did he know she had come for Laramie? Why was he angry with *her*? She shook herself mentally. What mattered now was saving Laramie's life. Doreen steeled herself against Bill's anger and willed her voice to a steadiness she did not feel. "Where is he, Bill? He's going to get himself shot!"

Bill's eyes were colder than his voice, if that were possible. "Like I said, you're too late. He thought you were at least his friend, but you didn't trust him enough to wait until he could explain what you saw, and that cut him to the soul."

"No!"

The word was little more than a breath, but Bill heard it.

"Yes!" Bill's chair legs came back down on the floor with a sharp crack. He pointed a rigid, accusing finger at Doreen. "You'd become his life, his reason for hope. You made him dream of a future for the first time in fourteen years! He was plannin' on applyin' for a pardon again, if he lived through this. Then he could come to you a free man and he could ask you to stay with him. But you turned your back. He loves you, more deeply than it's given most men ever to love, and you turned your back on him!"

"No!" Doreen's cry was a sob of anguish. "He betrayed *me*! I *saw* him!"

227

"Listen to me, Doreen." Bill's voice softened a little. "I'm gonna tell you what only few people here know. I asked Laramie up from Arizona to get in with the rustlers and help us catch them. It was a suicide mission. He knew that when he took it on. Before you, he would've taken crazy risks that might have saved his life, because he didn't care if he lived or died. You made him care. The rustlers are gonna get caught today, Doreen, driving their herd to the railhead. But only Asa and California and I know Larry's our man, because we didn't know who else to trust. So if, by some bit of luck, the rustlers don't figure out what he's doing and kill him, the ranchers will. Larry left here like the devil was after him and I don't know where he went. I only know where he's supposed be later this afternoon. The moment the rustlers see us, Larry's dead. He knew that a long time ago. He hasn't got a chance, Doreen, when, for the first time since he started wearing a gun, he desperately wants a chance—Doreen!"

Bill sprang from his chair and pushed Doreen's head down almost to her lap. He crouched beside her. "Breathe slowly. Relax. You're not gonna faint now." He patted her shoulder. "I'm sorry I was so hard on you. That boy's been like a son to me, closer than my blood son ever was, and he came in here last night hurtin' so bad, so sure you despised him. But he was wrong, wasn't he?"

Doreen thought her heart would break. She turned into Bill's shoulder and clung to him. "Oh, Bill, what do I do? I love him so much and—and he's going to die thinking I hate him!" Doreen choked on tears.

Bill stood, pulling Doreen up with him, and patted her back comfortingly. "Honey, we know the rustlers have to go through Three R's hills to get to the railhead, but we don't know where the herd's bein' held. A lot of riders, fresh from the roundup, are strung through your hills now, waitin' . . ." Bill stared at the wall at a portrait of President Lincoln for a long time. He took a deep breath. "Doreen honey, we're not likely to even find his body."

Doreen gasped and the room went dark.

She came to on the floor with Bill patting her cheek and one of his cowboys holding a forkful of ripe barn cleanings near her nose.

"Finally!" Bill exclaimed. "I thought you'd never wake up." He nodded to the rider holding the fork, who carried it and its contents back outside. "Sorry for the quality of our ammonia."

Everything Bill had said coalesced out of the spinning in Doreen's mind, and she curled around herself with a little moan. Laramie couldn't be found until the stolen cattle crossed onto 3R land. He couldn't be found. He was sure to die.

She sat up quickly, then, remembering. The room whirled sickenly. She reached out a hand to Haycox to steady herself. "Bill, that's what I came to tell you yesterday but couldn't. The stolen cattle are on your range. If we get to them first, surround the herd, maybe, or set a trap, maybe Larry—"

Bill's eyes brightened, his head snapped up. "Cookie, ring the bell," he roared toward the kitchen. "I want the boys back in!"

In moments, the cowboys came pelting in. Doreen described the landmarks near where she had last seen the herd. One of the men went out immediately to get horses ready. Bill spoke urgently to the other two.

229

"Tex, you get over to Three Rivers. Tell Miss Cary to get Three R's riders across the Yellow quick. Dan, you hightail it over to the rendezvous. Tell the roundup boss we know where the herd is and to bring his men through the high pass. On the double! Stringbean, get fresh horses for you and me."

"Yes, boss!" The cowboy's eyes lit up. "We're gonna get those bas—" the cowboy flushed and glanced at Doreen, "Those outlaws!"

"We'll be too late if you don't get your—outa here!" Bill snapped.

The rider grinned and ran out.

Bill turned to Doreen. "The spare room's toward the back. Get some sleep and I'll send word as soon—"

Doreen stood and gripped a chair arm for balance. "You're not leaving me here!"

"A man who's been shot isn't a pretty sight, Doreen, and if it's your man—"

"I'm going with you. I'm going with you or I'm going alone, but I have to find him!"

"Then I guess you'll have to come along." Bill's wry grin belied the reluctance of his words. "There's only us and Stringbean, though." He nodded toward the round-bellied cowboy who had gone for horses. "We won't be able to stop those outlaws until the others come, Doreen, no matter what they're doin'."

Doreen tried not to think of what he meant and led the way out of the house.

The mountains wore their first dusting of snow and the wind nipped ears, fingertips, and noses. The sun was high when the three riders came to the top of the cut where Doreen had seen the cattle. They stopped, partly hidden from anyone below by scrub. The cut was churned up, but empty. Bill sent Stringbean to scout ahead, then slid from his saddle.

"You wait here. I'm goin' down to see what happened, and how long ago."

Doreen did not argue, though she longed to go with him. If the cattle were gone, Laramie had been here. Was he somewhere below, dead? Doreen clenched trembling hands around the saddle horn and prayed for her husband's life as she had never prayed for anything before. Huge, wet snowflakes began falling slowly, silently. After perhaps half an hour, rocks clittered down the side of the cut and brittle sticks and branches cracked. Someone was coming up. Bill. It had to be Bill. But Doreen slipped her gun out of her pocket and pointed the gun at the sounds. A few moments later and Haycox, snow-sprinkled and pink with effort, came around a clump of stunted cedar.

He froze, seeing the gun pointing steadily in his direction, then nodded approval. He mounted his horse and turned it in the direction the cattle had gone. "The cattle are movin' toward Bear Pass and they're not driftin', they're bein' driven."

Doreen slid the gun back into her pocket and followed him.

They cautiously followed the track up the draws and folds in the hills. They made as little noise as possible and stuck close to cover, for though the herd itself would be easy to detect by its lowing, clacking, and thudding, the rustlers would have guards trailing behind. A drier snow began to sift silently down. Doreen's knuckles ached from clenching her reins. Then they found a small cluster of Circle X stock.

231

"Maybe the outlaw's trail boss thought these weren't up to the trip," Bill speculated, studying them. "They are kinda young and skinny. Late calves, likely."

They rode on. Doreen's sleepless night and the suspense of not knowing what was happening to Laramie dragged at her. They were almost into the pass, but of the rustlers or the main herd they had seen no more than hoofprints. Doreen's attention drifted from weariness and her eyes sometimes refused to focus. She stayed awake only by castigating herself. *The one person in the world who should've believed in him and I didn't.*

She looked across the rocky landscape, broken here and there by solitary upright cedars. The trail led over the next ridge. Another ridge and then another one, and then another, she thought. It's like a bad dream. We ride and ride and never see another human being. We chase and chase and never catch up.

A rising wind whistled through the dry grasses. Doreen shivered, though not from cold. Guns barked. Doreen's head jerked up, listening, all weariness gone. She saw Bill whirl toward the sound. He held up a hand for her to stop. He listened for several minutes, while every part of Doreen strained toward the sounds, the danger, the man she searched for. The wind brought whoops and shouting and the sounds of more guns firing.

"There's fighting! Dear God! We're too late," Doreen whispered, almost to herself, wretched with guilt and despair.

Bill's entire body was taut with listening. He swung toward her, his face eager and fierce. "They've caught them. Doreen, stay here."

"But, Bill—"

"You could get killed, girl! Losin' Larry will be bad enough. To lose you both . . ." Bill swallowed. "You stay here."

"Bill—"

"No." He squeezed her shoulder. "Pray for him, honey." He spurred his horse and the horse sprang toward the sounds of fighting. Doreen watched Bill's figure disappear over the next ridge. Snow was falling faster now, powdering everything with fluffy crystals. *God in Heaven, don't let him be dead! Please, don't let him be dead!* But Doreen knew such a prayer was useless. It did not even comfort her. She knew that if Laramie were already dead, God would not make magic to ease one woman's guilt.

Doreen dismounted and ground-tied the horse. She pulled the collar of her sheepskin coat up around her ears and paced back and forth along the side of the ridge, too cold and anxious to stand still, too afraid of what she would see to walk to the top of the ridge and look beyond it. Then the shooting stopped. Doreen froze in midstep, listening. Shouting continued, but there was no more gunfire. She climbed swiftly into the saddle and spurred her horse over the ridge and the next one. She paused on the downward slope. Below her, two men were cutting cattle from a large herd. Other men were rounding up beef frightened off by the fighting. Still others were just vanishing over the crest of the next ridge, in hot pursuit of something or someone. Here and there, men lay motionless on the snowy ground or sat or stood, swaying or moaning. A cluster of men, some on horseback, some on foot, stood near the base of a long-dead pine. As Doreen watched, someone whacked the rump of a horse standing right under the tree and the

233

man on that horse's back swung into the air, kicking and jerking horribly.

Doreen gasped and felt the blood leave her head in a rush, making her sway and clutch the saddle. "Oh, no," she moaned. The last thing she wanted to do was ride closer to that savage justice, but she had no choice. If Laramie still lived but had been caught among the criminals . . . If Bill were not there to vouch for him . . . Hot bile burned in her throat. Doreen swallowed and urged her horse down the slope as fast as was safely possible.

She rode to the group under the tree. Their attention was so powerfully on the man at the end of the rope that they did not notice her approach. About a dozen men, hands bound behind them, sat their horses, waiting their turn to do that horrible dance, but neither Bekkerson nor the Englishman were among them. At the head of that row, with Asa Johnson just cutting his hands free, sat Laramie. Bill Haycox waited on Laramie's far side, his face taut and angry.

Doreen stopped, stunned. Laramie's hat was gone and his face was so white beneath its tan that it looked gray. Blood trickled from Laramie's hair down his cheek. The entire right side of his shirt was soaked dark red and steaming slightly in the cold. He swayed in his saddle. Doreen opened her mouth, but no words came. She urged her horse around the intent circle toward him. Laramie saw her coming and his eyes, which had been dull and glazed with shock, blazed for a moment with an emotion Doreen would have labeled hate, if she had had the courage. Then Laramie turned to Bill, his body drooping, hurt, like a lost and bewildered child.

"Larry!" she cried, feeling wounded and bleeding herself.

He flinched when she called him by name, but he would not turn or even look at her. He bent his head and rested it against Bill's shoulder. Bill put his arm around Laramie, looked over him at Doreen, and shook his head. His mouth shaped the word "later." Doreen put her fist to her mouth and bit the knuckles to keep herself from blacking out with shock and fear.

He hates me! Dear God above, he hates me! I love him so, but I believed the worst of him, and he hates me for it!

In spite of herself, Doreen came near to fainting and would have fallen but for Asa Johnson's hand, set firmly over hers on the horn. Doreen looked at him in surprise, for she had not, in her shock, seen him move.

"Mrs. Smith," Johnson said gently, "men from Fishhook saw Tennessee with the rustlers. They've been roaring all over the district, lookin' for the owner of that queer black horse ever since. They got a description of Laramie from someone and they got here first."

Doreen bent and rested her head on her hands and his. Her fingers clutched the horn so tightly they hurt. Johnson's free hand tentatively brushed back her hair.

"They had the rope around his neck by the time I came ridin' in here, Mrs. Smith. Bill was right on my tail, but Larry'd already had one narrow squeak to-day—Bekkerson shot him, before that varmint cut and run—and that rope around his neck was too much. It would've been too much for any man. It's the worst death a man can die, at the end of a rope held by his neighbors. And to know you're goin' to die when you're innocent—"

Doreen closed her eyes and bit her lip until she tasted blood. She would not, could not, display more of her feelings in front of strangers. "He hates me now," she whispered. "I didn't believe in him when he needed me to and he hates me for it!"

"That's not the reason, Doreen honey."

At Bill's voice, Doreen straightened.

Bill rested one hand on her shoulder. His fingers tightened as if to strengthen her. "He thinks you told the ranchers where to find him, Doreen. He thinks you're the cause of that rope around his neck. He would've had Asa and me to vouch for him if we'd caught the rustlers where we originally planned to."

"But you know I didn't tell them!" she whispered. "You know we're here to try to *save* his life!"

Bill nodded. "Yeah, I know it, but Larry's in no condition to listen. He's had some awful shocks in just a few minutes' time, honey—gettin' shot, then almost gettin' hung, and, worst of all, believin' you told the Fishhook men he was a rustler—and he's not feelin' too reasonable right now. Give him time, honey. In a few hours, when he's bandaged up and—"

"Bill, I need to tell him now."

"Later, honey. He won't see you. Let me talk to you a little while." He nudged his horse away from the crowd of men and drew Doreen's after him by its cheek strap. "You know about the bounty hunters, Doreen?"

"I've met Mattheson."

"Well, Mattheson didn't help Larry's case with the Fishhook men. Mattheson's been down there, too, lookin' for Larry. Generally, a man's troubles elsewhere don't follow him in the West, long as he stays straight, but when a man who's already wanted in the States is

found with rustlers—" Bill paused, mopped his forehead with an end of his bandanna, and cleared his
throat. "The federal government's had a reward poster
out on Laramie since the War. Fourteen years is a long
time to be runnin', Dee, but Larry thought runnin' was
better than killin' the hunters or bein' locked up in a
federal prison. Or hanged. Right after the war, the
federal government would've executed even a boy of
fourteen without thinkin' anythin' of it, long as that boy
was a Reb. Anyhow, Larry's smart and after a few years
of chasin' him, most of the hunters gave up. But
Mattheson's persistent. It's more than the money for
him now. He'll be back soon as he finds out the story we
fed him about Larry headin' for Montana is just that, a
story. Then Larry'll have to run again, or kill Mattheson,
or let Mattheson take him in."

Doreen licked dry lips. "Then he wouldn't stay, even
if I hadn't—even if he—"

"Honey, don't look so tragic. He loves you. But he's
got more pain than he can handle right now. Give him
time."

But, hours later, back at Blue Mountain Ranch,
Laramie was no nearer to speaking to Doreen. In fact,
when she went to his room to see how his wound was, he
refused to see her. Doreen went to bed that night in Blue
Mountain's guest room without as much as one word
with her injured husband.

The next morning she woke extra early and went to
the kitchen for a cup of coffee. Her eyes were red and
puffy from crying, so she felt grateful the kitchen was
empty, because she wanted no one to see her misery. A
steaming cup in her hand, Doreen wandered to the
kitchen windows. Snow had covered the ground over-

night. Laramie, one arm in a sling, was tying his war bag behind Tennessee's saddle with his good hand. He shook Bill's hand, listened to something Bill said and shook his head no, then pulled himself into his saddle. Doreen's heart stopped. He was leaving. Without a word to her, he was leaving. She stood a moment longer, frozen, then dashed for the door. When she burst onto the stoop, Laramie was still there, gray-faced, swaying and clutching the horn. Bill raised a hand to steady him and said something quiet and urgent. Laramie shook his head and lifted the reins.

Doreen took a deep breath, for courage. "Larry, stop!" she cried.

Laramie froze, and in that moment Doreen jumped from the stoop and grabbed Tennessee's bridle.

"I have to talk to you, Larry. Please."

Laramie turned his head slowly to look at her. "You said all you needed to when you told the ranchers where to find me," he answered, his voice rough. "They were goin' to *hang* me! They had the rope around my neck when Asa stopped them!"

"Larry!" Bill's voice was sharp with warning.

Laramie turned darkened, haunted eyes on his friend. "This is between me and my 'wife,' Bill," he said gently. "Leave us."

"Larry, Fishhook—" Bill began.

Laramie shook his head. "Please leave, old friend."

Doreen watched Bill walk slowly away. Her head whirled and her arms felt numb. Laramie was leaving, not just because of the bounty hunter but because of what he believed she had done. Fear locked her throat and for several moments she could not speak. She was going to lose him.

"Well," Laramie snarled, "you wanted to talk, 'wife.' So say somethin'."

Doreen trembled at the fury in his tone. She forced words past the choking lump in her throat. "Larry, I didn't tell anyone but Bill what I saw. Please, believe me! If you remember, that—that night you—you came to me, I pleaded with you to leave the Territory to save your life. I love you, Larry. I couldn't turn you in."

He shook his head, rejecting her words, and winced in the doing.

Doreen moved close to Tennessee and looked up at Laramie, pleading. "Larry, please, listen to me. Remember when Tennessee disappeared and I thought he'd gone after you? Well, he was on Fishhook range, with the rustlers. Fishhook's been looking for the owner of that odd horse ever since. *That's* why they planned to hang you, not for anything I said."

"Try again, wife. If I didn't believe that from Bill, I'm shore 'nuff not goin' to believe it from you." Laramie's voice was bitter.

"Larry, please, don't shut me out." She put out a hand to touch his leg, to make some physical contact with him, but one look from those haunted eyes stopped her and she dared not complete the gesture. Tears thickened her throat, blurring her words. "I love you. I couldn't turn you over to men who'd kill you!"

Laramie looked over Tennessee's ears into the distance. "You believed I'd kill and steal. You said so."

"God help me, I did. What else could I do? I *saw* you—"

He looked down at her, his eyes blazing. "You coulda come up with excuses for me or waited to judge me, knowin' I wasn't like that!"

Doreen threw her head back and glared up at him, anger coming at last to her defense. "*You* could've had faith enough in me to trust me with the truth, Laramie Smith! I didn't even know your real name until Mattheson came looking for 'James Smith' and the description fit you. You didn't even trust *me* with your *name*!"

Laramie's shoulders sagged. "There's a lot of things you didn't know about me, aren't there?" He lifted his reins again and his legs tightened against the horse.

In desperation Doreen grabbed a stirrup. Her heart pounded with fear and her mouth was dry with it. She had hurt him too much. He meant to leave for good. It was all she could do to force words out and her voice was a husky whisper. "Larry, please, I'll do anything to make up to you for the way I've hurt you. Anything! Don't leave. Please, don't leave! We'll apply for a pardon. We'll get rid of Mattheson, somehow. We'll have a real marriage, children—" She broke off suddenly. "Laramie" was not his name.

Laramie looked down quickly and read the look that flashed across her face. "My Gawd!" he breathed. "You're wonderin' if we're truly married, aren't you? You think I married you under a false name and used yore body without any right!" He shut his eyes for a moment, as if he felt pain too great to be endured with eyes open, then he reached under his sling and pulled a folded, worn piece of paper out of his breast pocket. "Here."

Slowly she unfolded the paper and smoothed it flat. It was a certificate of marriage, their certificate of marriage. Doreen let her eyes drift to the bottom of the paper, dreading what she might find there. The signatures at the bottom were Doreen Marie Anderson and

James Lawrence Smith. She looked slowly, reluctantly, up at Laramie's face. The bitterness and pain there made her cry out. He bent forward, pried her fingers from his stirrup, and straightened. He swayed and again caught at the horn for a moment.

Bill came to him quickly and looked up in deep concern. "Stay a couple more days, son. Let that shoulder begin to heal before you hit the road."

"I can't, Bill." His voice caught. "You know I can't. I'll write you when I get where I'm goin'." He touched Tennessee with his heels and the horse moved forward.

Doreen stood stunned, clutching the marriage paper in her hand. She felt as if she were not breathing, could not be breathing. Time stretched out as in a dream. He was going, angry, bitter, wounded, without even saying good-bye. Laramie rode toward the mouth of the valley without looking back. Doreen knew if she moved, she would break. She watched until glare from the snow hid him. It was several minutes more before she could move. She sank to the ground, the pain too great for tears.

RIEF MADE Doreen numb. She had had a great treasure, the powerful love of a very special man, and she had lost it, by her own actions she had lost it. She did not know how to begin coping with that. When Bill spoke to her, his voice seemed far away and she did not understand his words. He sat her up gently and lifted her chin so she had to look at him. He spoke slowly and clearly.

"What happened? Doreen! Are you all right?"

Doreen looked at him mutely. Tears began sliding slowly down her cheeks. Bill looked around in despair.

"Damn!" He turned his face toward the house. "Cary!" he shouted. Then he studied Doreen's face, pulled her to her feet, and held her against his shoulder. "It won't be forever, honey. Larry has to get Bekkerson. Only reason Larry didn't call Bekkerson out after he'd spread that story about you two was we weren't sure at the time if he was the leader of the rustlers or if Sir Adrian was. Larry put aside his pride and his honor until we knew. An' we found out yesterday. Bekkerson shot Larry and killed Sir Adrian. The Englishman lived just long enough to tell one of his riders how his gamblin' gave Bekkerson control of the Rollin' W and how Bekkerson was usin' his control to get Three R's water." Bill patted Doreen's shoulder awkwardly. "Honey, you're Larry's *wife* and Bekkerson named you the worst sort of woman. Larry *has* to kill him. The law's lookin' for Bekkerson, too, though. If the law gets him first, Larry can come home. If Mattheson's not still around."

Doreen shook her head, sobbing wildly. "Larry's never coming back, Bill. It's not Bekkerson and it's not Mattheson. It's me. Oh, Bill, I hurt him so badly!"

Bill stopped patting, stepped back, and gripped Doreen's shoulders. "He said he was going after Bekkerson, no matter how long it took. A pardon can take care of Mattheson. Larry has to take care of Bekkerson alone. He didn't say he wasn't coming back. Doreen honey, he *loves* you."

Doreen struggled to speak through great, gulping sobs. "Not anymore, Bill. He hates me now. He believes I turned him in to the ranchers. And then, if that weren't already enough, I doubted we were truly married. I only wondered for a second, but he *saw* it. He *saw* I doubted him. It was too much. He gave me our marriage paper and left. He's gone for good, Bill. I can feel it!"

Bill bent his head to hear the last, whispered words. He held Doreen tighter. A long while later, when the racking sobs had subsided to occasional shudders and the tears dried up, Bill set Doreen a little away.

"He may have hated you right then, but love like his doesn't die easy, honey. Give him time. The West is big, with a lot of holes for a rat like Bekkerson to hide in, but he's a professional gambler, Bekkerson is, and he'll have to surface somewhere to get himself a new stake. That's how Larry'll find him. He *will* find Bekkerson, he *will* find a way around Mattheson, and he *will* be back. Make yourself believe that, Doreen. Trust his love, and yours. Teach yourself to have more faith."

A wagon drove up, bringing their attention back to the present and to Cary, standing silently on the porch. Bill helped Doreen up the steps and Cary led her to a chair inside and sat down quietly with her arms around Doreen. Doreen stared at the worn and dusty pine floor. The boards blurred and ran together and Doreen saw again the look in Laramie's face, the horror that flashed across it, the hurt, and the anger. Even in their last moments together, she had not had faith in him.

The numb misery persisted for days. Even after the final tally was in, showing a tiny profit for Three Rivers, Doreen did not cheer up. Then, on a quiet Sunday afternoon, Asa Johnson and Bill paid her a visit. Doreen ushered the two men into her office with some trepidation, for their faces were tense.

"Mrs. Smith, you've had a rough year," Johnson blurted before he had even sat down. "You've done amazingly well for a tenderfoot, but we've been thinking you might want to go back to your folks in the East."

Doreen stiffened. The delicately unspoken reason was that her husband was gone, perhaps for good. She looked at Bill. He would not meet her eyes.

Johnson cleared his throat. "We're prepared to buy you out, a third each year for three years, cash." And he named a figure.

Doreen drew a sharp breath. With that much money, she *could* go East, live well if she were careful, get teacher's training, be within reach of her old friends, have pretty clothes, escape forever from the constant dirt and work of ranch life. A train ticket home. Blooded horses, parties, dancing—Doreen checked herself, remembering poignantly the pleasure of dancing in Laramie's arms. She pictured Laramie at one of Amelia's parties. Tall, courteous, polite, dressed in a city suit, he would charm them all. For a time. But his conversation and interests, his novelty, would quickly bore them and Laramie himself would chafe at such a useless life. She could not imagine him playing bridge night after night, or spending days at the races or on a sailboat. He would be utterly out of place. So would she, she realized suddenly. It had been a child's dream, returning to her parents' way of life. The luxury, the chasing after pleasure would bore her now. Her life was here, in the country Laramie had taught her to love. Whether he came back or not, she belonged to Wyoming. Chicago and its moneyed life were forever behind her.

Weren't they?

She came out of her reverie stunned and unsure. She looked at the tanned, weathered faces of her neighbors, then down at the brown tips of her boots. She cleared her throat. "I'm—I'm touched that you would make such an offer after such a hard year. I'll always be grateful." She looked down again, gathering her thoughts. "I need time to think. A lot has happened since I first planned to go back East. I've put down roots, I think, and I'm not sure I want to pull them up again."

She looked at the two men. Asa Johnson was nodding thoughtfully and Bill was smiling. A little of Doreen's discomfort eased. "You've been true friends to me, both of you," she continued softly. "Is a month too long to wait for a decision?"

Bill shook his head. Johnson extended his hand, man-fashion. Doreen shook it gratefully.

"I'd be just as happy if you decided to stay, Mrs. Smith," Johnson said, his voice gruff. "You've turned out to be a right good neighbor. Take till the end of February if you need to. Can't do much outside till after that anyhow."

Doreen nodded and stood. "I guess I'll go back to my room to think a bit. See you at supper, Bill. Will you stay, too, Asa?"

"Sure, anytime."

"Good." She smiled. "Thanks again for the offer." She headed toward the kitchen swiftly, feeling more like herself than she had since Laramie left.

Doreen began to ride her land again the next day. She quickly learned how hard it was going to be to separate her feelings for the ranch from her feelings for her husband. Just the act of mounting a horse—the squeak of leather, the chink of tack, the acrid smell of the animal—brought memories back. Everything she knew about her land she had learned from Laramie and memories of him lingered everywhere. Here was a fence she had helped him mend. Here was where she had watched as he helped deliver a late calf. Here was the wash where they had come onto the ranch after the rock slide, there burned-over land, now covered with snow. Every yard of Three Rivers Ranch held pain beyond her previous understanding. But the ranch also held remembrance of great joy. There was the target range, where Laramie had first betrayed his attraction to her, the barn stall where he had first kissed her, the slope where they had first lain together. Even the threshold of the house was precious because he had carried her over it. And the big bed, with its memories of ecstasy and loss . . .

In early December Doreen was sure. She sat her horse on a ridge in the sharp clear air and looked across Three Rivers. The horse's breath came up in regular puffs, like thin, white smoke. Rabbit tracks criss-crossed the snow under the horse and zigzagged across the open places between bushes. The horse snorted and shifted his feet, the only noise in the silent whiteness. So quiet. So white and clean and open. So different from Chicago with its hovering yellow-brown coal smoke and its crowds and its noise. Overhead a hawk circled and, for a moment, Laramie was beside Doreen again, telling her about the bird.

"How could I think of leaving?" she asked the icy wind. "How could I separate myself from all I may ever have of him?" She looked over her shoulder at the whitened mountains. "This is *my* land now. I couldn't be a Chicago 'lady' anymore. I've changed too much. I've fought for this land. I love it and, Lord knows, I've paid enough for it in pain and sorrow. This is where I belong now. Whether or not Larry comes back."

After that, Doreen forced herself to face her memories squarely, even the memory of the bitterness and pain in Laramie's face the last time she saw him. She told herself again and again that Bill was right, that Laramie would come back, but the words were just words, repeated without faith in them. To manage the pain, she made herself suppress the bad and remember the good times—the long rides in sunshine and in wind, his courage, his laughing eyes, his impudent grin, their honeymoon. But that memory brought back memories of Laramie's hands, his mouth, his urgent lovemaking, leaving her ready to scream with frustration, for she knew no relief for the feelings those memories brought but Laramie's hands, Laramie's mouth, Laramie's body, and Laramie was gone.

When December weather turned stormy, Cary and Bill insisted Doreen come spend the winter at Blue Mountain with them, arguing that it wouldn't be good for her to be alone with her memories at Christmas. Doreen reluctantly gave in. She did need to get away from the memories for a while.

In the following days, during moments of solitude in her Blue Mountain room, Doreen discovered a tiny hope that Laramie would come back. She turned that hope round and round in her mind, checking all its angles and secret places. It grew, but Doreen did not dare let it grow too much, because she knew Laramie's pain had been deep and terrible.

Then Bill came to supper asking her what she'd heard from Laramie. How could she say she'd heard nothing? He must have read her feelings on her face, because he flushed and cleared his throat.

"I—uh— Lord, I'm sorry, honey. I'd figured that if I had a letter—" His face was both embarrassed and sad. "Do you want to read it?"

Doreen shook her head.

"He said he was laid up in Cheyenne with infection and fever for a while. That delayed his trailin' Bekkerson, of course, and now he's afraid he's going to get caught by snow in some minin' camp in the mountains." Bill looked down at the floor. "Seems you were right, Dee. He says he's not comin' back until you've gone East."

Doreen stared blindly at Bill and Cary. "But I'm not going back East," she whispered. "I was waiting here for him."

Doreen struggled to accept what she had heard: Laramie was sick, in pain, and so bitter that he refused to face her at all. She bit her lip and shut her eyes for a moment, forbidding tears to come. She had been a fool to even dream of him coming back. There was no hope. Laramie himself said they were finished.

Bill gingerly touched her shoulder. "I know that letter sounds bad, honey, but consider how things looked to him. I've told him the truth. You tried to. This is why I went along when Asa talked about going East. But you didn't take the offer and I'm glad. Larry's pain will get less. Then he'll begin to remember the good you two had together and he'll believe what we've told him."

Doreen's control broke. Tears slid down her cheeks, heedless of her attempts to prevent them. Bill stepped closer to her chair and set his hands on her shoulders, rubbing them gently, comfortingly. Doreen buried her face in his stomach.

Bill stroked her bent head. "Remember what I said, honey. Have faith. Believe that he'll come back to you. He loved you very, very much."

"Once. Maybe once he did. All I see now is the look on his face just before he left. Bill, it's with me day and night." Doreen choked on a sob. "He didn't even write to me!"

Bill sighed, his hand stilled, he held Doreen a little

249

away from him and looked down at her. "I still think I'm givin' you good advice, honey. I can't make you change your mind."

"No," Doreen whispered, "only I can do that."

Cary and Doreen decorated the Blue Mountain ranch house for Christmas with cut pine branches and a small spruce tree, which they trimmed with ribbon bows and strings of popcorn. And, contrary to the expectations Cary had had when she talked Doreen into staying at Blue Mountain, Doreen missed Laramie more because Bill and Cary's obvious love for each other reminded Doreen sharply of what she had thrown away. Laramie was with her like a ghost. When the three of them decorated the tree, Doreen thought how useful Laramie's extra nine inches would be. When snow sifted quietly down and lay bright and glittering in the sun, Doreen wished Laramie were around to slide with her and throw snowballs and go for sleigh rides. When she or Cary baked cookies and fruitcakes, Doreen imagined Laramie sneaking a pinch of dough and laughing at her with his eyes as he licked his fingers clean. When they sat around the stove at night, making gifts, Doreen wondered what it would be like if Laramie were there— what materials would he use? what kind of gifts would he make? what stories would he tell?

But there were only the three of them to spend evenings sitting companionably around the stove, talking, laughing, and telling stories while they worked— Cary sewing, Doreen knitting, Bill whittling wood or embossing leather. Doreen was making a head scarf for Amelia and, against her better judgment, heavy warm gloves for Laramie.

In the last week before Christmas, Bill and two of the riders hauled a pump organ that had belonged to Bill's first wife out of the barn loft. Cary and Doreen cleaned and polished it, and they, Bill, and the cowboys still at the ranch gathered around the organ in the following nights, singing carols and hymns. Cary played well and sang in a clear, sweet soprano. Bill had a rough bass voice, Doreen sang alto. Most of the riders sang somewhere in the cracks. One night Doreen imagined Laramie was one of the group, his eyes bright, his arm around her, his voice an uneven baritone. She wanted fiercely to be with him, or to have him with her, and the power of her wanting left her trembling. Bill noticed and looked over at her.

"Doreen, are you all right?" he asked softly.

"As all right as I'll ever be," she whispered, her voice breaking in spite of her intention to keep it steady.

Bill searched her face, then, reaching over Cary's shoulder, slowly closed the hymn book, and said firmly, "That's all for tonight, boys."

The cowboys obediently said good night. There was a bustle of shoving arms into jackets, wrapping mufflers, pulling on gloves, then the riders left. When the last one had gone, Bill put his arm around Doreen and pulled her against his side.

"Missin' him a lot tonight?"

Doreen nodded, wordless with the effort of keeping back tears.

"You go sit down. A package came for James Smith in the mail today. It's from Tennessee and my bet is it's from Jen. There was a letter from Larry, too. No," he added as Doreen looked up eagerly, "it was for me, but you can read it if you want."

251

"Nothing for me?" Doreen's voice was husky and she had to shut her eyes against the pain.

"No, honey, and I'm sorry, but I did say it'd take some time." Bill tousled her hair lightly and affectionately. "Go sit down and work on those gloves you're makin'. I'll be back in a minute."

Doreen flushed. She had told herself many times the gloves were effort wasted, but something inside made her hope. They were as close as she could get to Laramie and they had become a kind of charm to bring him back. She walked slowly to her chair, picked up the tangle of needles, knitted work, and yarn, and sat down.

Bill came back from his office and laid the letter and a small brown package in her lap. "I don't know which to suggest you do first. The letter is bad news, from your point of view, the package probably good."

Doreen looked at her lap and, with shaking hand, picked up the letter. It was postmarked Cheyenne. That, in itself, was bad news. She opened the envelope slowly and pulled out a single sheet of cheap paper. She unfolded the letter.

November 25

Dear Bill,

The doc here said the shoulder needed at least two weeks more without being jiggled around. I will be leaving in the morning. Bekkerson is working the mining camps in Colorado.

I expect to catch up with him along the Gunnison or, worst case, in Silverton. As I already wrote you, I do not want to be trapped for the winter in the mountains. I am calling myself James Grimm now. I hope this will help

252

me catch up to Bekkerson. I also hope it will throw Mattheson off my trail for a while.

Because of Mattheson, though, I am telling you that Tennessee's papers, except the bill of sale, are under the mattress of my bunk in your bunkhouse. The marriage license is already with my wife, so she can use it to prove she has a right to what I owned.

If I'm killed, Bill, I want to be buried on your place, even if you have to burn my body to bring it back. Your place has been the only home I've had in fourteen years and you have been like a dad to me. I cannot ever repay you. I am sure you will tell my wife what she needs to know and give her the papers if such is needful.

Write me, James Grimm, at General Delivery, Silverton. I'll be by there in a month or two.

> Yours obediently,
> Larry

Doreen's hands clenched over the letter. *Not even one question about me, not one question. No request to take me a message, either. He wouldn't even use my name!* She stared unseeing across the room as the pain of that rejection consumed her. He had wiped her out of his mind except for his legal responsibilities. Doreen pressed her fist against her mouth and bit her knuckles. *I will not cry for him again, I will not!*

Bill gently pressed the little box into her hands. "Doreen," he ordered quietly, "open the box. Open it now, Doreen."

Numbly she tore away the brown paper. Inside was a small, old, wood jewel box. She lifted the lid and took out the folded paper on the top. Under it lay a wide gold wedding band. Slowly, reluctantly, Doreen took the ring out of the box. Inside the ring on one side, engraved in letters almost erased by years of wear, were the words: "Allen J. to Nancy, Jan. 17, 1850." On the other side, in bright, new letters, were the words: "James L. to Doreen, Sept. 21, 1878."

"His mother's ring," she murmured.

It was hers to wear, legally, but Laramie did not want her anymore. She should send it on to him at Silverton. Doreen twisted the gold band and the lamplight glowed from the mellow surface. Her fingertips caressed the warm, polished metal. She looked again at the words inside. They had not had long to love each other, Allen Smith and his Nancy, just thirteen years, but they had loved happily and well, that she knew from hours of riding with their son. Laramie and she could be happy, too, if he gave them the chance. Doreen's shoulders straightened and she lifted her head.

If Laramie Smith wants this ring back, he'll have to come after it! she promised herself. Doreen slid the ring onto her finger, then picked up the folded paper. The word "jim" had been printed in a childish hand on the underside. She held the paper out to Bill, who shook his head.

"Larry's *your* husband. The letter's yours to read."

"Please, Bill, you read it first. I can't handle any more bad news today." Doreen licked dry lips and looked away from the folded paper.

Bill unfolded the letter, scanned it, and handed it back. "It's from Jen. Read it. It might do you good."

Doreen took the note and turned it over.

dearest jim, I'll be so glad when you do not have to use that other name. Mama would be happy you have finally found a wife she sounds wonderful. does it matter to her that you have to run from that awful man? I should like to see if she is as beautiful as you say and I wish you could come back to Tenn. to show her to us but I know this is too close to sheriffs and such-like. Tell her I shall love her and that she has two nephews. already they look like you and daddy, jim. I am sad they cannot know their grandpa but maybe someday their uncle can come home. The ring I send with joy because you say she is very special.

> your loving sister, jen

Doreen let the note fall to her lap. He had told his sister she was special and that she was beautiful. She was not beautiful, but he had thought so. In September, at least, he had thought so. Her hands clenched, crumpling the note.

Larry, Larry, her heart cried, where are you! I need you. I want you. Come home!

That note was the last mail before snow closed the pass. Doreen moved numbly through the rest of the Christmas preparations and, for the first time in her life, felt nothing of the joy and excitement of the season. The fragrance of pine and spruce and cookies and mulled cider, the sound of Cary humming a carol or of all the cowboys singing around the organ, the gay ribbons on the tree and the small pile of presents under it, the flat package that would not be opened—Laramie's absence drained everything of meaning. On Christmas Day, seeing Cary's and Bill's devotion to each other was especially hard somehow: Cary resting her hand on Bill's arm with possessive ease as she talked to him; Bill's arm around Cary as she read parts of the Christmas serial from *St. Nicholas'* magazine; Cary sneaking a kiss when she thought no one was looking; Bill handing

Cary his present to her and waiting with pleased expectation for her to open it.

I could have had that, she thought. I could have had that and I threw it away!

She stood, took one last look at her gift to Laramie, alone now under the tree, and went to the office. Laramie planned to stay away from her, but Mattheson had driven him away from Blue Mountain and Wyoming and Mattheson might prevent him from coming back, even if he changed his mind about her. Doreen sat at the desk and pulled a blank sheet of paper toward herself. Maybe I can do something about Mattheson, she thought. Bill said a pardon would stop Mattheson and others like him. Then Larry could stop running. And if he could stop running . . . She turned her thoughts resolutely away. The best she could hope was that a pardon would make up in part for what she had done to him. She dipped a pen in the inkwell and began to write.

The new year arrived, clear and very cold. Doreen had planned to return to Three Rivers, but she could not face the days and weeks ahead with only memories for company. She busied herself with drafts of letters to Wyoming's Territorial representative, the governor, her father's political friends. At Bill's suggestion she added Chicago friends of her father's who might have influence in Washington, President Hayes, and Colorado representative Belford, who was a friend of Bill's and a real fighter for underdogs. But they could not be mailed until the thaw and the waiting became unbearable.

One evening in mid-February, Bill caught her looking out at the night and the blowing snow, twisting her ring round and round her finger. He put his arm around her and pulled her against his side. "He'll be all right, Doreen honey," he said gently. "You have to believe that or you'll go crazy before spring. See him whole in your mind. Tell yourself he's smarter than Bekkerson and a better shot than either him or Mattheson and that he's been hunted a lot of years. He knows the rules of the game, honey. He'll be all right."

Bill's sympathy strained the tight control Doreen had kept on her grief. Her face contorted with the effort of keeping back tears. There had been too many tears.

Bill tightened his arm for a moment, then took Doreen's hand and guided her to the settee. "Sit down. Let me talk about him for a minute, honey." Bill sat down, too. "Larry came here nigh ten years ago, hard, bitter, eighteen years old. He didn't stay long then, but he came back the next year, shot by some bushwhackin' bounty hunter. Lord alone knows why he came here. Ann and I took care of him and he stayed on two years, most of that as my foreman. Then Mattheson showed up. Larry didn't want to kill him, so he vamoosed. He kept in touch, though. He kicked around a lot after that, a season here, a season there, two somewhere else, and a year in Europe with a Wild West show. He told you that, didn't he? I thought so. And sometimes he'd drop by to visit for a week or two. In all those years, he's never done a dishonest or dishonorable thing. I've often thought his mother must have been somethin' truly special, to raise a boy that straight without a man to help her and without havin' him till he was full grown. He told you why he's on the run?"

"Some."

"He was workin' the family farm in Tennessee, him

257

and his sisters. His father was in some Union prison, died there. Anyway, Larry came home to find two blue-coats rapin' his mother. He killed them. He tried to get a pardon while he was here, but the—unmentionable names—in Washington didn't figure any Reb was justified any time. He's been runnin' ever since, without hope. Until you came." Bill's hold on Doreen's hand tightened and he looked at her intently, as if willing her to believe. "Doreen, he's as straight and true a man as I've ever met. That's why I believe he'll come back to you in time. Believe it!"

"Oh, Bill," Doreen wailed, "what will I do if he doesn't?"

Bill took her other hand firmly and squeezed them both until pain stopped Doreen's slide into despair and she paid attention again. "Don't think about 'doesn't'! If he lives, he'll come back."

Doreen had to be satisfied with that.

The first thaw came, bright, glittering with melt-water and fragrant with the special smell of spring. Doreen returned to Three Rivers Ranch to begin preparations for the spring roundup and to wait for the first mail rider. The snow in the ranch yard turned soggy and gray. Water dripped monotonously from the eaves. Spring chores began. Out on the range, calves were being born. The first robin arrived and spent its days in the ancient apple tree, singing its spring song. Laramie had been gone almost five months. Doreen realized that, in all that time, she had not thought of Chicago at all, except as a source of help for Laramie. Staying with her land had been the right decision.

The sharp pain of missing Laramie had faded to a dull ache over the winter, but that ache never went

258

away. Daily Doreen stood at the parlor window, looking toward the pass, fretting, wishing the drifts of snow away so the mail could be brought in, and hoping, against all common sense, to see Tennessee's long, smooth stride coming down the pass. Come the first of March, she was fidgeting, snapping at her employees, and generally being hard to live with. She haunted the parlor's front window with its view of the pass. When the mail rider finally arrived, late of an evening and grizzled with ice, Doreen was waiting on the stoop. The man looked down into her anxious face and silently handed her the ranch's bag of mail. She motioned him toward the barn.

"Take care of your horse and then tell Cookie to warm you up. There's a bed in the bunkhouse tonight."

She waited on the stoop in the cold until he had entered the barn then, having done her duty, she opened the bag with shaking hands. There were six or seven letters from various sources, including one from Amelia and one from Congressman Belford, and at the bottom lay two letters addressed to her in Laramie's bold, sprawling hand. She hurried into the parlor and tore the end from the oldest envelope, postmarked December 16, 1878.

CHAPTER

16

OREEN SHUT her eyes and held the letter tightly for a moment, then she lifted it and began to read.

> Colorado, along the Gunnison
> December 12, 1878

Dear Doreen,

I find I cannot leave you ignorant about your inheritance, which is Tennessee. Bill has Tennessee's papers and breeding record. Perhaps you could make some money by putting him to stud.

If I kill Bekkerson, I will disappear so thoroughly that you should have no trouble getting me declared dead after seven years. Maybe Bekkerson will spare you that wait. An annulment would have been easier, though not quicker, and I am sorry for your sake that one is no longer possible. Unless you can bring yourself to lie to a judge and say you are still untouched.

> Your obedient servant,
> Laramie Smith

Doreen crossed her arms over her chest, holding tight to keep from crying aloud her pain. "Untouched," she moaned. "Dear Lord! Untouched! I'm not the person I was because he touched me and I can never go back, not to what I was, nor where I was, nor to what I thought I wanted to do with my life when I came here." Doreen stared blindly at the wall in front of her. "He says 'annulment,' 'disappear,' 'killed.' Not even a mention of where he'll be next." She felt nauseous. She clenched her hands and heard, distantly, the letters in them crumple. "Did he know how much this letter would hurt me?"

Ice pellets rattled against the window beside her and Doreen looked out. It was a gray evening, whipped with sleet, and darkening rapidly into night. The ice pellets made the wind visible and the grayness streaming past was hypnotic. Doreen did not remember how long she stared out, only that the light had completely gone when she turned again to the room. She moved toward a lamp and paper crackled under her feet. She crouched and felt for and found the paper—Laramie's letters. She had not realized they had slipped from her fingers. She lit the lamp and opened the second letter reluctantly.

Silverton, Colorado
Jan. 28, 1879

Dear Doreen,

I was in the camps north of here over Christmas. Some of the saloons tried to dress up for it, but I reckon men alone don't have much heart for celebrating a family holiday. I know I haven't really had but one

Christmas since I was fourteen, at Blue Mountain the year before Bill's Ann died.

I write this by the window of a tiny hotel room. Bekkerson was here in Silverton before Christmas, won a pile, and moved on. I got trapped here by heavy snow that closed all the trails. Outside is the muddy main street and the miners slogging from saloon to saloon. I did not intend to write to you again. I wanted to start forgetting I ever knew you. It was not hard in the past months, living where a man has to be alert all the time just to stay alive. As I sit here, I sometimes wonder what Christmas might have been like in Wyoming with a tree all decorated up and special cookies and presents and singing. I hope you all had a happy season.

Your obedient servant,
Laramie Smith

He was bored and stuck, Doreen told herself, but writing for those reasons is better than not writing at all. What if it hadn't snowed? Lord, I feel so helpless. I've hurt him so very badly and I can't tell him how much I regret doubting him, how much I'd give to be able to take back those words.

Grief at her loss surged through her. She jammed the letters into a pocket and turned toward her room, where it would be easier to keep her resolve to cry no more for Laramie. But the resolution could not be kept.

Much later, eyes swollen, face splotched with red and still damp with tears, Doreen lit the office desk lamp and sat down to write Laramie a letter of explanation and contrition. Letters from Laramie, even such brief, curt letters, let her know he was alive and willing to keep at least a tenuous connection between them. As long as he was willing to do that, there was still a chance for them. Hours later, surrounded by small, crumpled balls of paper, Doreen had not yet found the right words. And if she did find the words, Laramie would be gone from Silverton before her letter could reach him and she did not know where next to write. Doreen crossed her arms on the desk top and let her head droop onto them.

But by the next time the mail rider came, Doreen had a letter to send, to Laramie and to Washington. The rider left a letter from Laramie, rumpled from its travels in saddlebags, waterstained, precious.

Silverton
Feb. 20, 1879

Dear Doreen,

They say the trails should be safe to travel later this week. Some miners headed south yesterday. I will wait to see if they turn back. I would not want to be caught and killed by an avalanche.

There's not much to do here but drink and play cards. I used to be a fair hand at poker and the knack is coming back. I will need it when I catch up to Bekkerson. And I *will* catch him, if I have to search every mining camp and army post in the West. Until Bekkerson is dead, I have not kept my word to Bill and the other ranchers. Besides, I could not hold up my head anywhere if I let Bekkerson live after the ugly stories he spread about you. After that, I'll lose myself, and Mattheson, perhaps in Europe. They're always fighting somebody over there and a marksman would be welcome. Of course, there's always the chance that a war would free you of me.

In God's name, why couldn't you have believed in me!

His pain was so deep, so close, that Doreen almost
cried out with it. Why, indeed, had she not believed in
him? She paced the office, trying to wear off the pain,
but pacing did not work. She looked outside. A light
drizzle was falling. She threw on her slicker and went
out for a ride. Soft rain, stinging cold air, a horse with
the morning jumps still in her, then a long hard run—
Doreen had discomforts and risks to take her mind off
the pain. She did not need California to show her how to
handle the horse or the outdoor work anymore. She did
not need a bodyguard anymore. But she wanted him.
Oh, how she wanted him!

The next two letters arrived together.

Silverton
February 25

Dear Doreen,

I am still here. They say there is eighty inches of
snow on level ground here now, and more coming down.
It is deeper in bowls and gulches. That party of miners I
was going to follow hasn't been heard from, but a party
behind them was turned back by drifts. People here say
the snow often lasts, in the mountains at least, until
May. I wish I had known that sooner. Maybe I would
have tried to catch Bekkerson by coming up from the
south.

Outside my window a mule train is hauling shoring
timbers through the mud to some mine. The slopes and
hollows here are filled with diggings of one kind or
another. I think mining must be one of the most
dangerous trades there is. In the weeks I have been here,
at least one miner has been killed or badly hurt every
day. But the work pays well, if you work for a big
company.

I think saloons, gamblers, and gambling houses are what the camps have most of, more gamblers than miners sometimes. Just two blocks from here, on Blau Street, there are better than thirty saloons, sporting houses, and dance halls.

I don't see families much. Even the store and saloon keepers seem to leave their wives and kids, if they have any, in safer places. Those few women that are here are not such as you'd want to know. And they have to walk across the street with their skirts held high to keep them out of the mud and manure.

Feb. 26

I thought I had taken this to the freight office already to go out with the mail. I talked to a gambler just up from the south last night. The trail along the Animas is finally open, barely. I will be leaving in the morning.

Yours obediently,
Larry

Silver City
Mar. 9

Dear Doreen,

This is my first real stop since Silverton and I am enjoying it. The Animas trail was slippery, and cold, and beautiful. The river was bank-full with meltwater and sang to me the whole way to its end. The trees have begun to green a little, the willows are yellow, and some of the bushes at the river's edge had bright red stems. I saw a bank swallow on the way down, like the ones that live along the Pinto.

I came down the mountains, skirted Apache territory, and headed for Albuquerque. Along the rivers, the cottonwoods were flowering and gray dippers were dashing into the water and out again. There are a lot of pueblos on that road south, Dee. Pueblos are large cities built by the local Indians, one row of houses on top of another for four or five levels. Hundreds and hundreds of Indians can live in a very small space that way. Between Taos and Albuquerque, along the Rio Grande, I saw at least five pueblos. I do not understand how these Indians have survived so long in this dry, dry land. And there are many, many more such cities that lay away from my path.

I am getting sick of mining towns. I have been to seven of some size since last I wrote you and passed through too many camps and claims to count them. Here and there I catch a rumor of Bekkerson, a hint that he might have passed through some time last season. His trail seems to go on forever.

I have spent most of my time alone the past five months, Dee. A man thinks about many things when he has a lot of time alone. I have thought about the way I left you. The bitter words I said leave a bad taste in my mouth. I am sorry I was so harsh with you. You are a tenderfoot still, and ignorant of Western rules and Western ways. I should have allowed for that. Perhaps I would have done the same as you did, in your place.

Larry

Doreen read and reread the last letter. He had left Silverton before her letter arrived, apparently. He did not mention it. But he was beginning to forgive her. His spirits were up and he was beginning to forgive her. He had apologized. For Doreen, hope burst open, bright and sudden as a desert flower.

He's not determined to stay away anymore, she told herself. I must *make* the men in Washington see the injustice of that bounty! I must *make* them see Larry deserves a pardon. Then he can choose to come back.

So Doreen busied herself writing more follow-up letters to state representatives, congressmen, senators, the president, the governor—prodding, pleading, arguing that Laramie had been justified in killing those soldiers, whatever the color of their uniform. And the letters from the south kept coming.

on the trail to Tuscon
Mar. 18

Dear Dee,

You should visit this part of the country some time. It is far drier than Wyoming. The land is bare in many places, or carries nothing but cactus and other plants too small or dry to feed stock. It takes many, many acres to keep even one cow alive. But it is very beautiful, too. The buttes are red and orange or black or almost purple. The sands are yellow, or white, or brown, and sometimes red. The cactus, when it blooms, has flowers that are brilliant beyond my power to tell you. You would have to see the flowers to understand what I mean. I wish I could send you one.

My shoulder has been completely healed some time now. It is not stiff, as I was half afraid it would be. Tennessee is taking the trip well. He does not like mountains, but he is good humored about it. I do not know what I would do without him. I need a laugh now and then and Tennessee's grumbling when he faces another steep trail provides it. We ride four days and rest one, ride three and rest one if the going is rough.

I reckon you are starting spring chores up there. It feels odd not to be doing the outdoor work on a ranch this year.

I have been to Lordsburg since last I wrote. They are mining copper, gold, silver, and lead around there. Bekkerson went through a month ago. Men who played him say he looked flush and talked of going to Mexico till the cattle drives start moving north. I've been casting back and forth like a bloodhound for the last week and that is the only clue I have found. He is gone, vanished like smoke. That shows he knows I am behind him, because the trail is not just gone, it is hidden.

I had a brush with a bounty hunter yesterday, one of the old-timers. That, and Bekkerson vanishing, tell me it's time to lay low for awhile, earn some money to eat on and to buy new shoes for my horse. I've spent my life ducking out of sight, packing up, leaving family and friends, all to avoid the bounty hunters. It is a hell I would never have put you through.

I have a friend from the old days in Texas who has a small ranch outside Tucson. I am on my way to hit him for a job.

Larry

General delivery, Tucson
Mar. 25

Dear Dee,

Just a card to tell you I arrived safely at my friend's place. Tom has a ranch here, a cute little wife, Amy, and four kids already. It makes a man feel old. They're all towheads and the youngest, a girl, Lord, she smiles and I want to pick her up and hug her. I will be working for Tom as a horse-catcher, probably until early May. Tom is giving me a stake and the pick of my catch.

Did you come through the winter in good health? I think of you often.

Larry

General delivery, Tucson
Apr. 20

Dearest Dee,

Amy handed me your letter first thing when I got back (we have been out after horses). Reading your letter was like hearing your voice and I missed you. I needed that, to have you say you are sorry. I am sorry, too. I should have trusted you with what I was doing.

When I look out the bunkhouse window, I see a carpet of yellow, orange, and purple flowers and I think of Wyoming, with its gray skies and March snow. The winter rains are over here, the creeks are running full and the skies are blue and clear. I wish I could make a picture of the desert for you with more than words.

The children are a wonder. I have not been close to children since I left Tennessee. Tom's oldest, a boy, is seven and full of questions about horses and tack and the gun I wear and what I have seen and where I will be going next. The two middle ones are twins. They have already learned (they are four) that they can both get into trouble and only one get caught if they split up the moment Amy sees they are into mischief. Sometimes I have to leave quickly when they pull this stunt so I do not laugh and spoil what Amy is trying to teach them. Lorna, the youngest, is two and a half and already full of feminine charm and coy smiles. Maybe it is because she is the only girl.

We have a good catch. There is a bay colt among them that will make a great cutting horse one day. I will leave him with Tom for awhile. I am very near thirty now and my bones are not as break-proof as they used to seem, so I let younger men break the horses. Tom still rides the likeliest wild ones and that drives Amy crazy. She says she does not want to be a widow with four kids and a ranch to support. Had you been in Amy's place, would you have objected to *me* breaking the likely ones?

Yours, always,
Larry

Doreen looked up from the travel-spotted paper. "Idiot!" she muttered. "Of course I'd object. Your bones are in enough trouble with Mattheson without offering them to a wild horse!"

Then she smiled, thinking of Laramie and little ones, and for a moment regretted having no result growing out of their last, unprotected, meeting. "Ah, what a daughter would be able to do with you, my love," she whispered.

But Mattheson was still hunting Laramie and Bekkerson was a treacherous snake who could not be expected to follow the rules of the West if they were not to his advantage. Laramie had been right. To have made a child with the future so uncertain would have been the utmost foolishness. And then Laramie had left, he thought forever. But the letters were changing; the last two or three were tender and caring. And the last one started, "Dearest Dee" . . .

General delivery, Tucson
April 24

Dearest Dee,

We hit a run of luck and trapped a large band of mustangs not far from the ranch. There were many fine horses. Tom will be able to run his place for a year on the money these will bring once they are gelded and halter-broke.

Lorna, Tom's youngest, has adopted me. She's as

hard to shake as a begger-tick. She serves me at mealtime and insists on tying my neckerchief of a morning. She has big blue eyes and they shine so when she is happy. And she feels so good to hold. I'm beginning to envy Tom, Dee. I wish you could see Lorna and her brothers. And then I think of a child of yours and mine and pretend I see it. I wish there were no bounty hunters, no dead Yankees in my past.

I miss you. I love you.
Larry

General delivery, Tucson
Apr. 30

Dee,

That last bunch of horses ends Tom's needs for a horse-catcher for awhile, the drives are starting north from Texas again, and I need to get out after Bekkerson. Tennessee has new shoes and is fat and sleek from his long rest. He and I are going to hit the forts between Tucson and the trails north. I should be able to find out at Fort Concho if Bekkerson is following Goodnight's trail. If he is I may be back in Wyoming Territory by the end of summer. If he is not headed that way I will go to Fort Worth and Chisolm's trail. I will be hitting El Paso, Fort Stockton, Fort Concho, Fort Worth, and Dallas. I will let you know when I reach Concho which way I am going.

I miss you more each day. I had not known one person could miss another so much. It was like opening that magic box (do you remember that story from school about the girl who opened a box full of good and evil things and could not shut it again?) because once I let myself know I missed you, I could not shut the feeling away like I had before.

271

I am writing a new petition for a pardon, which I will mail in El Paso. I do not let myself hope too much, though. Many people in power still hate Southerners too much to help them at all.

Would you write to me at Fort Concho? Then, no matter what trail I follow, I will know how you are doing.

Yours,
Larry

Doreen leaned her forehead against the window and looked down at the dusty boards of the porch. *I miss you, too. I can't let myself think about you too long or I'm no good for anything and there is so much to do here in the spring. If only you could really be back here by the end of summer!*

A letter. At last she had an address and could send a letter. She smiled wryly. *If only you know how many letters have left this house* for *you, you'd know a little of my joy at being able to send a letter* to *you.*

Doreen hurried to the office and started the letter to send to Fort Concho.

El Paso
May 10

Dee,

Our last night together still haunts me. I came to you that night just to say good-bye, like I told you. I was very sure I would not live another day and you were very precious to me. You *are* very precious to me. Darling love, you were so beautiful and so angry and so out of reach, and then you taunted me. I was angry because of what you thought and because I was losing you. I had been keeping myself away from you for so long that I

272

had stretched my control to its limit. It snapped that
night and I do not regret it for myself, but because you
were unwilling and because I did not protect you from
getting pregnant. I have worried that I might have
gotten you in the family way. I wish I had that night to
do over. I cannot say I would resist any better, because I
love and want you so much, but I would be far gentler
about it. There is much I would change if I could.
Perhaps the good Lord will give me time to make up to
you for what I've done.

I love you,
Larry

Doreen read this letter over and over, and then the
others, until the letters blurred and ran together. She
lifted her eyes and stared blindly at the far parlor wall.
Lamplight softened the edges of the room and its
furniture, yet made the room seem emptier and lonelier
than it ever did in daylight. In the daytime she had work
to do and riders to supervise. After dark, work was over
and the men retreated to the bunkhouse. She was alone
with her thoughts and memories and regrets.

*Please, God, keep him alive for me. He is more
precious than I could ever have dreamed another human
being could be. I have so much to make up to him. Let him
come home!*

The next two letters came in the same mailbag.

Fort Stockton
May 17

Dee,

    The herds are starting north. I have learned that
Bekkerson went through here only two weeks ago. He

did not do well, so he will have to stop for a stake somewhere soon. I hope to catch up with him then. I will send a letter from Fort Concho. For today, this card will have to do. I cannot sign my name. You know why.

L.

Fort Concho
May 23

Dee,

I received your letter today. Thank you for remembering to address it to James Grimm.

I have been afraid that I killed your love. Your forgiveness is more than I deserve. I thought I hated you those first few months, but it was pain I was feeling. I want you to know I love you and have never stopped. If the President grants me pardon, I will come back to you on wings, because missing you is tearing me apart. I want to kiss you, hold you, make you my wife for ever and always. But I will not come without a pardon. I will not, cannot put you into the danger that follows me. I once knew a man on the run who took his wife and child with him. The child was killed in a shootout with bounty hunters and the woman, she turned bitter and old. She died of a broken heart not a year after the child.

I am near the end of this trail. Bekkerson is only a week ahead of me now, headed for Dallas.

Tom writes that Mattheson came by his place, looking for me. He says Mattheson intends to get me dead or alive. Dead, I am worth no money to him, but perhaps that doesn't matter to him after all these years. He has to get me for pride's sake. Pray for me, love.

Larry

For days Doreen read and reread the letters until the paper was soft and furry with handling. She felt strung tight with waiting—waiting for another letter from Laramie, waiting for word about the pardon from Washington, waiting to learn if Laramie would be coming home. She watched the road from the pass daily, dreaming that Laramie would come riding down it and missing him as she had never before missed anyone, even her much-loved parents. The long, lean shape of him, his smell—of sage and dust and sweat and tobacco—the touch of his hands . . . Each time she thought of him, the pain of remembering and the loneliness forced her away from her watchpost and into a flurry of work.

Then the letters stopped.

CHAPTER

17

FOR MORE THAN a month, Doreen told herself that getting no letters meant nothing, that she did not need to worry, that Laramie was far from postal services, or so close to catching Bekkerson that he did not remember to write, or that his letters had been delayed in the mail. When her own good advice failed, she scolded herself for worrying, reminding herself that there had been month-long gaps between letters before.

July came, and haying began. New owners moved in at the Rolling W. The silence continued. To make matters worse, the petition for pardon moved at a glacial pace through the many channels and byways of Congress and there was nothing Doreen or the petition's supporters could do to hurry it. From the President she heard nothing at all. Doreen worried and grieved. Her agitation finally disturbed Cary enough to make her interfere.

It was a hot afternoon in August and Cary had come for conversation. When Cary arrived, Doreen was scurrying around the house with a mop and a damp rag.

Then, instead of sitting quietly in the parlor and talking with her guest, Doreen flitted from parlor chair to the window to the kitchen for a cool drink to the parlor chair to the window again to look up the road. Cary rose suddenly from her chair, grabbed her niece, and held her still. "Doreen, you're going to make yourself sick with this rushing around. What's the matter with you? You've been behaving like a crazy person for weeks."

Doreen's face crumpled. "Maybe I am a little crazy, Aunt Cary. I haven't heard from Larry since the end of May. I don't know where he is or how he is. I'm frightened. He was planning to come home, to give me another chance. Something's happened to him, Aunt Cary. He was so sure he was almost at the end of his hunt. He wouldn't go so long without writing if he were all right."

Cary stroked Doreen's damp hair back from her face. "Maybe he's so caught up in the chase that he's forgotten," she said soothingly. "Or maybe he's too far from a post office. Chisolm's trail runs through Indian Territory, I've been told. I don't imagine there are many post offices there."

Doreen shook her head and pulled free to pace the room from window to window. "I've told myself that, but I know he'd find a way to let me know he was still all right. He was coming back. He said he was applying for a pardon again and would come back when he was free." Doreen stopped and faced her aunt, her hands clutching each other. "He's been hurt, Aunt Cary. Maybe he's even dead and I don't know where he is!"

Cary put a hand on her niece's shoulder near the edge of her neck and began massaging the area gently. "Take it easier, honey," she urged, her voice low and urgent. "Word will come. The mail rider's due in today. Maybe there'll be something from Laramie then."

But when the mail came, no envelope bore Laramie's dark scrawl. There was no personal mail at all, only business letters.

On his visit the next week, however, the mail rider brought a heavy vellum envelope with the crest of the White House in the upper left corner. Doreen tore into the envelope on the spot, too impatient to extend her usual invitation to the rider to take coffee in the kitchen. She unfolded the heavy paper and flattened it with trembling hands.

July 1, 1878

My dear Mrs. Smith:

James Belford of Colorado has recently presented me with a copy of your petition for pardon for your husband. On the surface, the circumstances seem to indicate that James L. Smith was justified in killing the two men, but it was wartime, Mrs. Smith. That changes matters. It might interest you to know (you had said your husband was away, looking for the last of the rustlers) that I have also received a petition for pardon from Mr. Smith, mailed from Dallas some weeks ago. I assure you I will look into this immediately and let you know as soon as I come to a decision on the matter.

Sincerely,
Rutherford B. Hayes

Doreen spun toward her aunt, who had come to Three Rivers solely to be present when the mail arrived. Hope lifted Doreen's heart and made her feel light and ready to take on the world again. "Aunt Cary, the

278

President himself sent me a letter! Larry sent him a petition, too, from Dallas, so I know he at least got that far. President Hayes is going to look into the pardon himself!"

Cary smiled and hugged her niece. "It's so *good* to see you smile again. But, honey, don't get your hopes up too far. President Hayes could decide against Larry."

"He won't. He can't! He just can't!" Doreen spun round and round with gladness, feeling as if the pardon were as good as granted. "The President himself wrote me!"

"Doreen!" Cary said sharply. "Stop that!" She forcibly stopped her niece's joyful dance. "Doreen! You got a letter, just a letter. The pardon's not promised. Keep your feet on the ground. You must keep the pressure on. Keep people petitioning Congress and the President both." She gave Doreen a little shake. "You can't go giddy just because President Hayes wrote to you!"

Doreen sobered slowly. Cary was giving good advice. Doreen folded the letter carefully, reinserted it in its envelope, and carried it into the office, where she sat down to write to Belford to thank him and to Wyoming's territorial representative to catch him up on what had happened.

When another week passed without word from Laramie, Doreen could bear the waiting no longer. She resolved to go to Dallas and follow Laramie's trail until she found him. She sent a note to Bill by the mail rider, asking him to watch the ranch for her, and began packing the necessities for the trip. Bill and Cary drove up to the house early the next morning.

Cary bounced from the wagon and sprang up on the porch with unusual alacrity. "Doreen," she began, before she was even through the parlor door, "what do you mean, you're going to look for Laramie?" Cary waved the note at Doreen in agitation. "That's no job for a lady, unchaperoned, unprotected, for hundreds of miles. Thousands. How do you think you'll find him? You'd have to carry a lot of money with you. What about outlaws and robbers? What—"

Doreen laid a gentle but determined hand over her aunt's mouth. Cary shut up from the sheer impertinence of the gesture. "I *have* to find him. He's as important to me as my own life. Don't you understand that? Who else could go? Bill? Two ranches need him. Larry's mine, and something awful's happened to him."

"He may be dead and buried." Bill's voice was heavy and slow.

"I have to *know*, Bill." Doreen looked from Bill to her aunt earnestly. "I need help, not hindrance. I'm taking the coach or the train to Dallas, whichever's quicker. I'll buy a horse there and start looking. To do all that, I have to get a loan and letters of credit, and that means a trip to Jamesville. And I'll need you to run this ranch until I, or we, get back, Bill. Will you? Will you go to Jamesville with me and see me off?"

Eventually, reluctantly, Bill and Cary went with her. The moment they arrived in town, Doreen went to the bank and got a letter of credit. She then swept out of the bank and down the street to the railroad station. There was no direct train to Dallas. She would have to go hundreds of miles around by way of Omaha. The delay was unthinkable. Doreen spun and headed for the

280

coach office. On the way, the energy that had driven her for the past two days evaporated. All at once, Doreen felt the lack of sleep and the effect of twenty-four hours without food. She stopped, suddenly dizzy and very tired. She was outside the post office. She stared at the gilt letters on the window. There might be mail.

The ranch's small brass-doored box contained only one letter. Doreen spun the combination, flipped open the door, and slid the letter out. It had come from Abilene, Kansas, and was addressed to "Doreen Smith, General Delivery, Jamesville, Wyoming Territory" in a curly, feminine hand. She knew no one in Kansas. Dread swept her. She did not even shut the box's door but slit the letter open at once.

July 29

Dear Doreen Smith,

I found this address on a letter in the warbag of a man calling himself James Grimm. Come to Abilene at once, if this man is important to you. He was badly shot up a month ago and he is dying. He was getting better and then a week ago he got the lung fever. The money he had with him is almost gone and with the season peaking I can't afford to keep him much longer. He calls for you often in his fever. Mother, sister, lover, whoever you are, if you care for him at all, come at once.

Caroline Evans
The Palace, Abilene

Doreen felt her knees collapsing and put her hand out to the wall for support. She shut her eyes and took several deep breaths. Laramie was badly hurt, delirious, dying. Quickly. She had to get to him quickly.

281

God, help me get to him while he's still alive! She sped out of the post office and down the wooden sidewalk toward the coach station.

Bill, who had taken the horses to the livery, caught up to her at the coach office door and stopped her with a hand. "Lordy, Doreen, what's got into you? You're movin' like the devil himself's after you."

Doreen took a deep shaky breath, unsure she could speak about the letter at all. She swallowed hard. "Larry's in Abilene, Bill, at a place called The Palace. He's hurt bad. She says he's dying." Doreen thrust the letter at Bill. Behind her she heard a sharp gasp. Cary, too, had caught up.

Bill's eyes flicked over the words. His tanned face went gray and his mouth tightened into a grim line. When he looked up, his eyes were dark with grief. "I'll drive you to Cheyenne. The train there goes direct and you'll be a lot more comfortable in my wagon than jammed into a coach with who knows what kind of people. No, don't shake your head," he said fiercely. "I'd go with you if I could, but one of us has to stay here to run things. If Larry's dead, I couldn't do him any good, anyway. If he's not yet, you're the best hope he's got." Bill put his arm around Doreen's shoulders and squeezed.

Doreen let her head rest against Bill's for a moment. When she straightened, she smiled tremulously. "Thanks, Bill," she whispered. "I've needed an uncle all these years and didn't know it."

Bill squeezed her again. "I'm just learnin' what I've been missing, too, honey. Get some rest. I'll have the wagon stocked and ready to go tomorrow."

"Tomorrow!"

"Lord, Dee, we can't just take off unprepared! We'll have to camp out three, maybe four nights on the way to Cheyenne, so we have to have bedding and cooking tools and stuff." Bill looked over at Cary. "You going along, Mrs. Haycox?"

"Of course I am." Cary turned to Doreen and hugged her. "It breaks my heart to hear Larry's so badly off and that you're going to have to face that alone. But at least we know he was alive the end of July and where he is and we'll help pay for the trip." Cary looked at Bill to be sure she had not spoken out of turn. He nodded. She looked back at Doreen. "Don't be afraid, honey. If he hung on this long, he's not likely to suddenly quit."

The offer to help pay brought immense relief. Laramie was worth the world, but Three Rivers Ranch was not yet on firm footing. "Oh, God," Doreen whispered under her breath. "Let him still be alive!"

Bill turned immediately toward the bank to get a loan. Cary and Doreen went shopping for things Doreen would need on the trip: a linen duster (necessary on the train), a small portmanteau, several changes of clothing, soap, some dried fruit to be eaten on the train, rolls of bandage, and some medicines. Bill bought supplies for the drive to Cheyenne. He even lavished money on telegrams to check on the progress of the presidential pardon.

"Get to Washington and think they don't have to be polite anymore," he grumbled, after reading the government clerk's reply.

Doreen had hoped to carry news of a pardon with her, but the clerk implied she could not even be sure

Laramie would get one. Wyoming's representative was a little more hopeful—after all, Laramie had been protecting his mother from illegal acts and he had risked his life to break up a large rustler gang—but he could promise nothing. By the time the three of them left Jamesville in the wagon, a premonition that she would be too late hung over Doreen.

The wagon ride was rough, the nights in the wagonbed cold, the delays, caused by a rockfall and a creek in flood, almost unbearable. Five endless days it took them to reach Cheyenne, only to learn there would be another day's wait for the train east. None of them could afford a useless night in a hotel, so Bill and Cary did not wait for the train. Before Bill climbed into the wagon for the return trip, he pressed five twenty-dollar gold pieces into Doreen's hand.

"We can get more to you if you ask. We'll find it, somehow. Take good care of him for me." Bill swallowed hard and looked away. "Good luck, Dee."

That was Laramie's name for her. Doreen choked on a rush of tears.

After she had waved them out of sight, Doreen paced the streets of Cheyenne, blind to its vigor and its people. She did not want to see the sights, shop at the stores, eat. She wanted the train to come, immediately. When driven to her room by darkness and the proprieties, she tried to sleep and could not, hounded by nightmares. She paced the floor of her tiny room, rumpling the limp rug, her hem sweeping a clear path through the dust on the floor. She tore several handkerchiefs to shreds in her anxiety and impatience.

With dawn, the train came. Its bell stirred Doreen

from her grim thoughts and sped her to the depot, where a cluster of passengers already waited on the platform. The train slid slowly into the station and stopped, hissing and steaming. The conductor swung down onto the platform and began collecting tickets. Doreen was a day-coach passenger and, therefore, had to wait for the few first-class ticket holders to get on board. Then she, too, handed the conductor her ticket to punch and mounted the iron steps into the car.

Passengers sprawled and slumped in the seats, most of them sleeping in spite of the bustle of people coming and going. Some had brought their own pillows and blankets, others used coats for covers. A few, their faces grimy with the dust and soot that always blew about inside a train, looked at the newcomers with early-morning surliness. A hawker came slowly up the aisle from the other end, offering rolls and coffee.

Doreen found a seat on the aisle. That, too, reminded her of Laramie. She tossed her bag into the overhead rack, collapsed into the seat, and laid her head back, right against a metal edge. She sighed. This did not bode well for the rest of the trip. The seat itself was one of the hardest she had ever encountered, and that included pews in churches famous for their belief that comfort in church was a sin. She twisted and wriggled until she found a bearable position. The conductor shouted "All aboard!" and the train jerked into motion moments later.

The train lurched out of Wyoming Territory and into Colorado. It stopped for two hours in Denver to take on passengers and freight. Many of the passengers left the train to wash in the depot and try to find something to eat. Doreen was too weary to follow their example. She bought a cup of tepid coffee and a stale roll from a young girl who walked along the platform from car to car. The grumbling of the passengers returning with soggy sandwiches and gluey pieces of pie convinced her she had done no worse by staying on the train.

The train resumed its journey. It rocked and shuddered across the high plains, throwing sparks and clouds of choking smoke. It stopped here and there for passengers or freight, coal or water. In late afternoon, a spatter of rain laid the dust and freshened the air coming into the car. Evening came, and a man went through lighting the oil lamps. The thick smell of kerosene soon filled the air. Passengers who had gotten on at Denver or who had packed their own food got out dried apples, bread, slices of cheese. Doreen's throat closed just thinking about swallowing that food dry. Afterward, row by row, as passengers decided to sleep, someone got up and turned that row's lamp down or off. Darkness closed in, and quiet, except for some snoring and thrashing about, and the occasional whine of a sleepy child. The train rocked along, its wheels seeming to say, "Don't let him die, don't let him die, don't let him die." The rhythm lulled Doreen at last into an uneasy rest.

The train rattled and clicked through the night and crossed into Kansas just after dawn. The land stretched flat and yellow in all directions. The only visible life outside was antelope, a few buffalo, and, once in a while, an eagle or hawk. Occasionally, through windows on the opposite side of the car, Doreen caught a glimpse of a river. The train seemed to crawl for hours and hours over flat, featureless land.

"Ellsworth! Everybody for Ellsworth!" The conductor passed through the car and on to the one behind.

Two farm families rose and stood swaying in the aisle, collecting their parcels and bundles from the racks above and the crevices under the seats. The train slowed, then stopped, hissing and puffing. The passengers filed out. From the front of the train came the grating squeak of the water spout swinging over the track.

"Next stops, Salina and Abilene," the conductor shouted as he passed back through the car.

The train arrived in Abilene at 9 P.M. by Doreen's watch, though what the time was in Abilene was anyone's guess. She stepped down onto the platform, dusty, exhausted, and faint with hunger. The platform lay in shadow, although the town was lighted for night. Gunfire sounded off to the west. Doreen tucked a straying lock of hair back under her bonnet and strode purposefully to the depot. Surely the ticket agent could tell her the quickest way to find the establishment called The Palace. But the rumpled and balding little man behind the ticket window ignored Doreen's "Would you direct me to the Palace, please?" Doreen repeated her question twice more, her tone sharper each time. The man looked up in irritation. His paper eye shade half hid his eyes.

"Madam, I'm a busy man and you're making a nuisance of yourself."

Doreen straightened to her full height and looked at the plump, rumpled little man with a feeling bordering

287

rage. The person she loved most in all the world was dying, perhaps already dead, and this underling was keeping her from going to him. She held her rage in, but her voice shook with it. "Your job is to serve the customers of this railroad, sir. You can be sure if you do not at once provide the information I requested, I will telegraph the head of your division immediately and tell him of your pointless rudeness."

The ticket agent tipped back his head to look at Doreen fully. "Madam, the Palace is, to be blunt, a sporting house, and you looked like a respectable woman. However—" He paused significantly, waiting for his meaning to penetrate.

Doreen stiffened. "I *am* a respectable woman, sir! Gratuitous insults—" She stopped, amazed to hear her own voice take on the slow, dangerous tone Laramie's did when he was very angry. "Gratuitous insults only make certain that I'll write a strong letter to the railroad. *Where is the Palace?* My husband's being cared for there."

"I'll bet he is!" the ticket agent leered and spun his chair halfway round so he was again facing his desk.

Weariness and anxiety making her reckless, Doreen leaned through the ticket window, shoved the man's chair-back so he spun around to face her, and fastened her hand in his high, stiff collar. "You don't treat me like a lady, I don't act like one. My husband's badly hurt. Tell me now!"

The man's eyes bulged like a goldfish's. His mouth worked without sound. Finally he found his voice. "Turn right, first street on the right. Middle of the row. You can't miss it."

Doreen stared at him coldly for a moment, then dropped him. He sagged into his chair like wet laundry. She spun away and almost ran to the door and out onto the wooden sidewalk. She paused to let her eyes get used to bright light again. Gray false-fronted buildings lined the dusty street. Signs proclaimed "saloon," "blacksmith," "pool hall," "saloon," "general merchandise," "baths," and "wagon yard." For the first time Doreen noticed the pungent smell of cattle and the heavy film of dust that lay on sidewalk, hitching rails, and windows. For the first time she felt the dry heat of that August dusk.

Right on the first street on the right. Middle of the row. Her portmanteau dragged at her arm.

The house in the middle of the row was a modest frame building that looked like any respectable house in any small town. Only the discreet sign over the paneled front door—"Caroline's Palace of Pleasure"—lighted by a gas lamp, betrayed the building's purpose. Doreen hesitated a moment in the darkness, twisting her hands. It was, according to all her training, an evil place, but someone here was taking care of Laramie. Doreen schooled herself to an appearance of calmness and mounted the three steps to the wooden stoop. She rapped on the door.

The sound was thin. Doreen had raised her hand to knock again when the door opened and a very young woman in a navy dress and white pinafore looked questioningly out at her.

"May I help you?" the young woman asked hesitantly.

"I wish to see Miss Caroline. Is she in?"

"Miss Caroline? Oh. Of course. Miss Caroline. I'll get her. Do you wish to come in?" This was asked rather doubtfully.

"My husband is here."

The young woman blushed and mumbled something about men and their ways.

"You don't understand. He's hurt. Miss Caroline said she was taking care of him here."

"Oh, that one! I'll take you to him and bring Miss Caroline up when she can come. This way, please, ma'am."

The young woman led the way up a graceful stair with oak treads and a gleaming banister. Doreen hurried after, trembling with nervous anticipation. She swallowed with difficulty. So close, so soon. He must still be alive. Surely the maid would have told her if he was already dead. He must still be alive.

Please, God, let him be still alive! Doreen licked her lips and wrapped one arm around her suddenly queasy stomach. What do I do when I see him? What do I say to him? It's been so long!

Her guide stopped outside a door at the end of the narrow second floor hall. "This is the room, ma'am. Can I get anything for you? You look quite ill."

"I could use a glass of water." Doreen's voice cracked.

The young woman sped away down the stairs and Doreen slowly opened the door. The room itself was very small, with space enough only for a washstand, a tiny wardrobe, a chair, and a single bed with a night table beside it. Doreen froze in the doorway. In the yellow light of the oil lamp on the night table, the man lying so still on the bed looked like a stranger. Most of his face was hidden by a full, red beard, and the parts that were not hidden were so white and the bones so prominent that he looked like a skeleton. Doreen put out her hand blindly and gripped the doorframe for support. It was Laramie. He was shockingly changed, but this length of bone and papery skin that breathed so shallowly that he seemed not to breathe at all was Laramie. The lean strong rider who had ridden away so many months ago had vanished.

"God in Heaven!" Doreen whispered.

CHAPTER

18

DOREEN SHUT her eyes a moment and took several deep breaths. Then she approached the bed. She touched Laramie hesitantly, still afraid that someone so white and fragile could not be alive. His chest rose and fell slightly under her hand. His breath wheezed in and out. Doreen took Laramie's hot dry hand between hers.

"Larry, I'm here. I'll take care of you. Oh, Larry, please don't die!" She kissed the papery skin and wet it with her tears.

She sank to her knees, still holding his hand, sick with fear and wondering frantically what she could do to help him. He was burning with fever. She closed her eyes and prayed for his recovery, then rose, stripped off her duster, washed her face and hands at the washstand, and dipped the dry cloth from his forehead in clean water. She was just wringing out the cloth when a petite blond woman of middle age entered the room.

"What are you doing in here?" the woman demanded sharply. "This man is very sick."

Doreen spun from the wash basin and examined the woman from her fluffy, mounded hair and painted mouth and cheeks to her snug satin dress and dainty feet in satin slippers. This had to be Caroline Evans. "You sent for me," Doreen answered, her voice sharper than she intended.

The woman relaxed a little, though she still watched Doreen with narrowed eyes. "It took you long enough."

"I left the day after I received your letter. No one could've made better time without wings." She went to the bed and laid the wet cloth on Laramie's forehead.

Caroline was not mollified. "He's a good man. Whoever you are, you're very, very important. Why did you let him come here alone?" She glanced at the wedding ring on Doreen's hand. "Or did your husband object to your 'friendship' with Grimm?"

The question took Doreen aback for a moment. Then she remembered. Caroline Evans did not know Laramie Smith, just James Grimm. Doreen eyed the woman speculatively. She would not recognize polite society's rules any more than Laramie had. She would not believe the discreet evasions a lady would use in such embarrassing circumstances. Nothing but the truth would do. "I'm his wife and he left me," Doreen said bluntly. She met the woman's eyes. "Grimm's not his real name. 'Laramie Smith' isn't, either, though that's the name I carry." Doreen looked down at the floor. She had to swallow a lump of tears before she could go on. "He's wanted by the Federals and he didn't want me to have to run from the bounty hunters, too. The Lord knows I would have come to him if I'd known where he was." Doreen's voice ended in a husky whis-

293

per. She looked at Laramie and tears began sliding silently down her cheeks. "We've had so little time together." She looked again at the blond woman. "How did this happen?"

The woman's face softened. "You do love him, don't you? Good. He's going to need it." Caroline came a little closer. "Bounty hunters, eh? Well, he's 'Grimm' to everyone here and he can stay that way." She paused and examined Doreen's face as if judging her. She nodded to herself. "I'll tell you how he came to be in a place like this. You know he came to town looking for a man called Tic Bekkerson?"

"Yes," Doreen whispered.

"Well, he found Bekkerson, all right. The bastard was forcing himself on me." The woman glared at Doreen, daring her to comment. When Doreen said nothing, she continued. "He'd already broken my finger and given me a black eye. All the other customers just watched. Your husband'd been in the back room, playing cards. He came out to see what the noise was about and said, 'Take your hands off her. The lady's mine for the night.'"

Doreen stiffened. Caroline shrugged.

"You asked how it happened. Anyway, the gambler, Bekkerson, called him a liar. Your husband looked him in the eye, called him a rustler and murderer, then turned his back on him. You should have seen Bekkerson's face! We was in the Bull's Head, which is a good place, and Bekkerson didn't dare try anything there, not with your husband's back turned. Well, your husband took me with him back to the game, finished the hand, and came up with me to my usual room." Caroline looked apologetic. "The season was on here, but I'd had

294

some delays with the carpenters I'd hired to fix up this place, so Joe was letting me and my girls use his upstairs. Anyway, Grimm, as we called him, went upstairs with me and he paid me for a *whole night*, but he didn't touch me. Honest. He sat in the corner of the room, smoking, until dawn. Then he grinned at me. 'Not even the most unreasonable man downstairs could expect me to keep up past dawn,' he says. 'I'm going down for some breakfast at the hotel.'"

Doreen looked down at the unconscious man and brushed her knuckles along his cheek. She felt a powerful surge of love for him. Caroline leaned back against the wall and continued.

"I come down a few minutes later to settle with Joe. Bekkerson's down there, with a couple of shots of whiskey in him already, and he's holding his gut and swearing a blue streak. Couple of his buddies are standing around, looking like they'd like to kill your husband right there, but everyone knows about the double-barrel Joe keeps behind the bar and they know he'll use it, too, if anyone tries playing dirty with a customer. Wants everything fair and square, Joe does. Anyway, Joe tells me, kinda on the side, that Bekkerson's been saying some real low things about you. They musta been pretty rare things, because I know I've never seen a man look as deadly as your husband did then. His eyes . . . Anyway, he looks like a firecracker about to explode. He'd already let Bekkerson have a fist in the belly, looked like. 'I'll see you in the street, Bekkerson. Six shots at ten yards,' he says. Bekkerson snarls at him, but he doesn't have much choice. 'That's too far,' he says to him. 'Too bad,' your husband says. 'It's that or I'll kill you right here with my bare hands.

295

No one talks about my wife like that. A low-down cattle-rustlin' snake like you— Your friends here'll stay strictly out of it.' He looks at Joe to see what he thinks of that. Joe nods and lays the double-barrel on the bar. Bekkerson's friends stand a little looser after that. Bekkerson hems and haws. You could see he'd been hoping he could get something started so his friends could help him, but now his friends are out of the game."

Caroline straightened and stood away from the wall. She looked at Doreen assessingly for a long moment, nodded, and continued the story. "The long and short of it is, the two of them go out into the street and Joe stands at the door with his double-barrel over his arm and his eye on the friends. Bekkerson stands right outside the Bull and your husband paces off the distance. He's cool, cool, cool. Bekkerson looks kinda pale and his fingers are twitching. He woulda liked to shoot Grimm right then, before he turns around. But he can't, not with Joe standing there. Well, Grimm turns. 'Ready,' he says. 'Nobody can get in a good shot at this distance,' Bekkerson says. 'You opened your mouth on the wrong words,' Grimm says, 'and now you pay for it. No one like that Englishman to hide behind here. You're out here alone and your yellow's showing.' When he says that, Bekkerson grabs for his gun. He gets off one or two shots before Grimm's gun clears. Your husband stands there in the street and takes a shot in the left shoulder while he aims real cool and collected. Then he shoots Bekkerson dead, just like that." Caroline snapped her fingers to illustrate. "One shot, Mrs. S— Grimm. Just one shot, and that skunk's dead. Unfortunately, there was friends around that Joe hadn't seen and they got your husband twice more before Bekkerson finishes hitting the ground. There they are, Bekkerson and Grimm, lying there in the street. Bekkerson's shot right through the heart. Your husband has a bullet in his shoulder and two in his upper leg. Plus that crease on his cheek.

"Anyway, your man had nobody in town and Doc had no room at his house to take care of him, so I had him brought here. I owed him. He was bad hurt, but he surprised us by getting better for about two weeks. Then he got the lung fever. It looked like he'd even fight *that* off for a while. Then he took this downturn. That's when I searched his clothes and war bag for some notion of who he belonged to, to let them know. Couldn't do that when it looked like he was recovering. Can't have customers thinking we're thieves. He's been bad sick, worse than when I wrote you. Don't know what's kept him alive this long, I really don't." Caroline shook her head in amazement. "Puzzles Doc some, too. He says folks usually die of it or start getting better within a week and your man's been lying here, slipping away for a lot longer than that."

Dying, and he'll never know I've come. Doreen sank to the floor beside the bed, took Laramie's hand and laid her head on the blanket. "Oh, God, be merciful. I need him," she whispered.

Caroline walked across the room and laid a comforting hand on Doreen's shoulder. "It's good you're here. Maybe it'll help. Get some sleep. You can't do nothing for him right now and you look mighty washed out. Doc'll be by in the morning, like I said. Keep the door locked and you won't be bothered by the customers. I'll tell the girl what was coming to watch him that she don't need to. You and I, we'll talk more later." She patted Doreen's shoulder and quietly left the room.

Doreen thought of examining Laramie's wounds, of cold compresses and clean bandages, of finding the doctor right away, but she was so tired, so very tired, and it was so good to be near Laramie again, to touch him and know he was, for now, still alive. She laid her cheek on his hot, dry hand, telling herself it would only be for a moment.

The sun shining in her eyes woke her. Laramie's hand still lay under hers, hot and dry and motionless. His breathing was harsh, labored, loud. Doreen raised her head and looked around. She guessed from the angle of the sun that it was midmorning. A shaft of sunlight lay low across Laramie's body. Doreen breathed a quick prayer of gratitude for being allowed to see him alive, gently kissed Laramie's hot, rough lips, and stood stiffly.

The pitcher on the washstand held no water. There was also no chamber pot, not in the commode, nor under the bed, nor in the small wardrobe in the back corner of the room. Doreen needed water for washing, she needed relief for herself after a night indoors, and she was a decent woman, alone and unprotected in a sporting house. She glanced around the room. There was no bell, bell-pull, or speaking horn to call someone up.

It's not likely the clients in this room feel any need to call for help, Doreen reminded herself grimly. Most of them don't stay long enough to need a pot, and Larry's been in no condition to use one. You're going to have to do for yourself, Doreen Anderson Smith.

Doreen took the pitcher, opened the door of the

room cautiously, and peeked out. If worst came to worst, she could use the pitcher as a weapon. No one was about. She listened for a long moment. No one seemed to be stirring on her floor. There was a murmur of voices from the floor below, however, and the click of dishes and the bang of pots from the back of the house. Her need was great. She would have to risk a trip downstairs. She left the room, closing the door quietly behind her, and went quickly, carefully, down and toward the back of the house. She found the kitchen, where a fat woman and Caroline Evans were just finishing coffee and bowls of mush.

Caroline nodded toward a narrow door at the side of the room. "Out back, Mrs. Grimm, as you might expect."

On her return, Doreen pumped the pitcher full at the kitchen sink. "Can I get hot water?" she asked.

Caroline nodded toward the giant teakettle steaming gently at the back of the cookstove.

"Will you also tell me where the doctor lives?"

Caroline shook her head. "I can understand your hurry about the doctor, but he had a real busy night last night and he comes by every day. Let him sleep. Your man's no emergency case anymore."

Doreen lifted the dripping pitcher from the sink and turned to go back to her room.

"Mrs. Grimm."

Doreen stopped, remembering to answer to the name only just in time, and waited.

"Remember what I said about staying in that room with the door locked," Caroline said.

Doreen bristled. "How can I do that?" she asked, rather sharply, her anxiety getting the better of her. "I

299

have—needs—which must be taken care of. There's no food up there, no water until now, no—pot—and no way to call for them. I have to have help if I am to stay in that room." Doreen straightened and lifted her chin proudly. "I don't ask for charity. I can pay."

Caroline's face hardened. "Don't talk about paying. I told you, I owe him. But you won't get any help, not from 'decent'"—she said the word like it tasted bad— "women like yourself, not while you're in this place."

She's offended, Doreen told herself, surprised. She thinks I meant to insult her. Doreen drew a deep, unsteady breath and met Caroline's eyes. "I'm sorry I snapped at you just now. It's just that I'm—I'm so afraid. L—Jim's so sick. . . ."

Caroline's face softened a little. "He hasn't been eating much since he took that turn for the worse, that's true," she admitted. "The girls have been getting water in him, and that's about all."

"Would you have the cook make some beef tea and lace it with brandy?" Doreen looked hesitantly from Caroline to the cook.

Caroline smiled. "We don't bite. Ask her yourself. Name's Mrs. Bradley."

Doreen turned her eyes to the cook. "Mrs. Bradley, would you? Please? I don't know what else to give him. He can't live on just water."

"No trouble, dearie." Mrs. Bradley lumbered to her feet and flicked a chunk of dried beef from an overhead rack. "It'll be brought up to you soon's it's ready." She dropped the meat into a handy pot and pumped water on top of the meat.

"Thank you," Doreen whispered. She turned again to the door.

Caroline patted her mouth delicately with a spotted napkin and stood. "When Doc comes by, ask about finding someplace else to stay."

"Someplace else?" Doreen felt as if her stomach had just squeezed itself into a tiny ball. "You want us to leave? With L—Jim so sick? I thought—"

Caroline put a steadying hand on Doreen's shoulder. "I'm not throwing you out. Dammit, woman, your husband saved me from getting beaten up!" She clucked in exasperation. "Like you said, you're gonna need help nursing him, but I can't spare a girl for you very often and no decent woman will come in here." Caroline laughed shortly. "I didn't hear no 'decent' woman offering to take him in after he was hurt, and after he'd rid this town of a skunk like Bekkerson, too. But that's done. My girls'll help when they can. If you want them to." Caroline paused, watching Doreen's face intently.

Doreen understood the unspoken question. There had been a time in her life when she would not have contaminated herself by *looking* at a woman like Caroline Evans, let alone by standing in the same room with her for even a moment. She swallowed the remnants of that old pride. "I want the help, Miss Evans."

Caroline squeezed Doreen's shoulder. "You're quality, Mrs. Grimm. And it's 'Caroline.' Nobody's called me anything else for years." She gave Doreen's shoulder a comforting pat and left the kitchen.

Doreen took two steps toward the stairs and hesitated, reluctant to leave the safety of the kitchen.

The cook leaned back in her chair. "Ye go on back to yer room, dearie, before one of the customers sees yer loose. I'll see to hot water and that tea for ye."

Doreen nodded and scurried up the stairs, nervous

301

as a mouse at the sound of any footstep. She slipped quietly back into the room and stood leaning against the door, breathing fast. Laramie had thrown off his blanket and now lay with one arm flung over his head, the other clutching the sheet spasmodically. His mouth had a sad cast, his face was shadowed, and lines she had never seen before ran from his nose to his lips. The sound of his labored breathing filled the room. Doreen went to the bed and laid a hand on his chest. Unnatural raspings vibrated her fingers. Doreen knew the sound and the feel. Every Chicago winter brought this vibration and this struggle to breathe to neighbors and friends; every winter more than half of those who got the fever did not live till spring.

"Lord, not Larry," Doreen whispered. "Help me save him. We've had so little time!"

Laramie moaned, just a breath of sound. It hurt her, that little painful noise. She went to the washstand, poured water from the pitcher into the basin, and carried the basin and the cloth from the stand to the bed. She lifted away the now-dry headcloth and sponged his forehead, then pulled back the sheet to begin washing his body. She felt a flash of the old injunctions, the shock that she would even think of looking at a man's bare body, let alone plan to touch it, and then the feeling was gone. This was her beloved husband, she already knew his body intimately, and he needed to be clean and cool.

The first thing she exposed when she opened his nightshirt was the little gold disk. It hung on a thin chain, lying slack against prominent bones. It rose and fell with each shallow, ragged breath. Doreen bit her lip and touched it with a quick, hesitant finger. His "brand"

and she had thrown it away, thrown it at him, and he had looked for and kept it. Resolutely she pushed that thought away. She could not see to wash him if she were crying. She began dipping the towel methodically in the basin and smoothing the cool water over Laramie's chest and arms, talking to him quietly while she worked on one side, then the other, shutting her ears to his thick, labored breathing, closing herself away from the sound of his dying.

She ran fingers lightly over the protruding bones of his near shoulder and tears filled her eyes. She bit down hard on her lip to stop them and began slowly washing down his body. The projecting bones at his hips, his knees, his ankles, the long sharp ridges of his shins, tore at her heart, telling her better than words how long he had been sick.

He's so thin, her heart cried. He's starving!

He had quieted while she worked, but when she stopped, defeated by the lack of clean linen to change the bed, he soon began tossing and turning, muttering, and sometimes crying out in pain or fear, sometimes choking on the liquid in his lungs. Doreen tried to soothe him by talking to him, by holding his hands still, but nothing seemed to help. She was at her wit's end when Caroline entered with a stooped, gray-haired man in a doctor's black frock coat.

The doctor bent over Laramie, listening to his chest and his heart, feeling his forehead and his pulse, examining the ugly wounds, then changing the bandages. At last he straightened. "I'm glad you're here, Mrs. Grimm. You are *Mrs*. Grimm?"

Doreen nodded.

"He's gonna need all the caring you have in you to

keep this fever from taking him, ma'am. He's coming back some when he gets restless like he is, but he slides into a stupor and you're like to lose him. He'll just slip away." The doctor dug in his black case and pulled out a dark-brown bottle with a glass stopper. "You keep wetting him down like you have been and give him this every five or six hours. Maybe it'll help bring down his fever. And this," he handed her a bottle with a thin, sticky streak down one side, "is for his lungs. It may help. I'll show you next time how to change his bandages yourself."

Doreen touched the streak with a finger and licked off the residue. Cherry bark syrup. For coughs. She opened her mouth to protest, then caught the drawn grayness of the doctor's face and said nothing. There was no medicine for the lung fever. One survived it or one did not. The doctor was leaving the syrup on a chance. Perhaps, since coughs came from lungs, the cherry bark might do something. She suspected the bottle had been left more to help her than to do anything effective for Laramie.

After the doctor left, one of Caroline's "girls" brought a chamber pot, a largish handbell for emergencies, clean sheets, a shirt, and the beef tea. She stayed long enough to help Doreen change the bed. Then Doreen was alone with Laramie again.

The room grew hotter and hotter as the August day advanced. Doreen pulled up the sleeves of her shirtwaist and folded down her high collar but it cooled her only a little. She pulled down the flimsy window shade to block out the glaring sun. Sweat dampened her shirtwaist and her long lisle stockings, but Laramie, for whom sweat would indicate the breaking of his fever, lay dry and hot, so very hot. Doreen kept bathing his head and chest and arms with cool water and, at regular intervals, forced down him the willow-bark infusion and the cherry syrup the doctor had left. It was difficult to rouse Laramie enough to take the medicines without choking. Doreen got the beef tea into him only fractions of a spoonful at a time. One of the Palace girls brought up lunch, and then dinner, but Doreen only pushed the food around with a fork. She had no stomach for food.

Doreen left Laramie's side only as necessity required. Once she left to open the room's window, hoping for a cooling breeze, but the sluggish air that entered was as scorching as the August evening. Grimly Doreen shut the window again. When night came, Laramie's fever rose. Doreen stayed awake as long as she could, sponging him and soothing his nightmares, but at last she sank to the floor beside the bed, exhausted, and fell asleep again with her head beside his hot, dry hand. In the night, Laramie tossed and moaned and cried, his pain and fear waking Doreen. She watched him, numb with weariness and without the skill to help him. She touched his forehead. It was burning. She could not believe anyone could be so hot and live. Fear wrenched her, making her feel empty and sick inside. In desperation, she wet his shirt and the sheet that covered him. After a time, he seemed to cool a little and Doreen collapsed in sleep again.

But the next morning Laramie was quiet, too quiet. The doctor at his morning visit looked at Laramie and shook his head. "Doesn't look good, ma'am," he said sympathetically. "Keep sponging him like you are. It's all you can do now." He left the room abruptly.

He doesn't think there's any use, Doreen thought in

305

despair. Larry's dying and he hasn't the courage to tell me! She looked down at the thin white face of the man who had haunted her day and night for months. *I won't let him go. I won't!*

Through a long day and longer night Doreen bathed Laramie's head and chest, force-fed him beef tea, and talked. She talked until she was hoarse and then whispered in his ear, hoping that somehow, some way, Laramie would hear her voice and know she had come. If she could hold him in this world with her voice, she would. If he were really going to die, she wanted him to know he was not alone. In despair Doreen realized that if he died, all color and laughter would go from her life.

Long after dark, she could no longer bear the helpless watching. She took off her boots and skirt, slipped into bed beside Laramie, put her arms around him, and cradled his burning head against her shoulder. Love for this man who lay so near death was a pain she could hardly bear. She tightened her arms and her tears fell unnoticed on his face. After a time he quieted and they both slept.

Sometime near dawn, Laramie began tossing and turning again. He flung out his arms and cried out in terror, he pleaded for help, his eyes stared unseeing at the walls. Doreen roused herself, hope stirring. At least the frightening silence was over. She seized Laramie's hands and talked soothingly to him, but the words did not penetrate the mists in his mind. He tore his hands free and struggled to get out of bed to fight whatever it was he saw. Doreen wrestled with him, forcing him with great effort to lie down, holding him with the weight of her body. By the time he subsided, Doreen was panting and trembling and bright-red blood again stained Laramie's bandages. Although lying on Laramie was like lying on a hot stove, Doreen dared not move because she was sure she would not wake up again, no matter how much noise Laramie made, and he could throw himself off the bed in his delirium. With the last of her strength, she pulled the bed's light blanket over both of them. She fell asleep with her arms around him and her head on his chest.

She awoke, a little after sunup, burrowed into the heat beside her, and drifted back to sleep. She awakened completely hours later, curled against Laramie's side. His side? She had been holding him down. She lifted her head with a snap and moved to sit up, only to find herself held down by the weight of Laramie's left arm. She slid carefully out from under it, sat on the edge of the bed, and tested his forehead with her hand. It was cooler and damp with his own sweat.

"Thank God," she whispered.

She leaned over his still face and kissed him gently. When she straightened, a pair of tired gray eyes was watching her.

"I've died and gone to heaven, 'cause I see an angel who looks like my angel." Laramie's voice was just a thread.

"You're not dead and I'm no angel, Larry."

His chuckle was a mere ghost. "I know, but I like to see you blush." He closed his left hand around one of hers and fell asleep.

He was not coherent again for days.

During those days, the fever did not "break" as much as slide, ever so slowly, lower. Laramie was half wakeful, aware enough to swallow gruel and egg soup or to use the bedpan, aware enough to help when he needed to be turned, but not aware of where he was or who was with him. Caring for him was strenuous and when Doreen slid into the bed to sleep at night, she was exhausted in mind and body. Yet Laramie was restless and fretful at night, the Palace was at its noisiest, and the dreadful August heat did not ease even after the sun went down.

She had waited in the room most of a day for water to be brought up, but none was. She stood at the window, looking out at the hot street, now tinted pink and orange with sunset, at the drovers and town women in the stores and on the walks, at the fringe of dark earth around the horse trough below where a small amount of water had leaked out. The Palace itself was alive with shouting, screeches of laughter, the clash of glass, and the heavy tread of patrons up and down the stairs. The night, now so close, would be louder, brighter, and hot, hot, hot. The bell would never be heard.

"It's like being in prison," she muttered to herself. "A week. I've been in here a week, alone, and Lord knows when I'll get out. Doctor says Laramie can't be moved until he's better and he's not getting better. So I can't go out, either. For my own safety, Caroline says."

Suddenly it was very important to get outside, to breathe air untainted by the smells of whiskey and beer and cigarette smoke. Doreen looked at Laramie. He was quiet, for the moment. She brushed a damp tendril of hair out of her eyes with a weary wrist and looked at the empty pitcher and bowl. Just a little water, for her thirst and to pat onto her face and wrists. Just a little water to make the heat more bearable. Just a few moments in the fresh, open air out back.

She picked up the pitcher, listened at the door a moment, heard no one, and slipped out. In moments she was standing on the brown-gray grass behind the Palace and breathing deep of the dry, dusty air, air that did not stink of whiskey and cigarettes. The slight breeze felt good against her skin. The old cottonwood beyond the outhouse rustled dry leaves. The dirt beneath the lip of the pump spout was dark and damp. She pumped cool water onto her hands, splashed her face, rubbed water on the back of her neck, filled the pitcher. Such simple actions, yet, in this place, they were dangerous. Caroline had said just leaving the room would be, for her, dangerous. Doreen watched the last light fade from the sky. She needed help with the nursing. She needed time away. Much more of this constant worry and wakefulness and confinement and she would be sick herself. They would have to find somewhere else to live.

CHAPTER

19

OREEN THOUGHT back to what the doctor had
said shortly after she arrived, that moving Laramie in his condition was too precarious to take
the risk. *He's not much better now and we have to go.
Somewhere. I can't keep on taking care of him alone.* She
walked slowly back to the room, closed the door quietly,
shot the bolt, and stood staring down at the knob for a
moment, her mind struggling with the problem of
moving a seriously ill man into new quarters when she
could not leave that man's side long enough to look for
new quarters.

"Who are you?"

The low voice startled her and Doreen whirled at
the sound. Although she could not see clearly, she could
see Laramie's head swinging from side to side and she
knew without asking that he was looking for his gun.

"Who are you?" he demanded again, sharply, struggling to sit up.

Doreen realized that in the dim evening light, he
did not recognize her, perhaps he did not even remem-

ber she had come. "Larry," she cried, "don't get up!" She crossed the room quickly and gently pressed him back into the bed. "You'll open your wounds again if you get up." She sat beside him and pressed down again, firmly, as he tried again to sit up. "It's me, Larry. Don't you remember? I've been with you a week."

He subsided, too weak to fight her, his face gray from pain, fear fading slowly from confused eyes. "Dee? Is that really you?" He touched her cheek to confirm it. "Where am I? What happened?"

The effect of that light touch shook Doreen and made her voice husky. "You shot Bekkerson, Larry, and some of his friends shot you. You're in the Palace. Caroline Evans brought you here—after."

"Bekkerson's dead?"

"Yes."

"And I'm in the Palace? Why?"

"You were badly hurt. Someone had to take care of you."

There was a long silence. Then Laramie turned his head toward the darkening window. "Yes. I remember that part now."

There was another long silence. Doreen ached for him. His voice was so thin and desolate. She felt a surge of raw desire that startled her. She suppressed it ruthlessly and made herself be satisfied with resting her palm against his unhurt cheek. Gingerly Laramie brought his left hand up to cover hers. He turned his head back toward her.

"Dee, darlin'," he whispered, "I love you so much."

Seconds later, his hand slipped back to the blanket and he was asleep. Doreen lit the lamp and looked down at his quiet face. Was it her imagination, or was he

311

breathing easier? Tenderly she brushed his forelock off his forehead.

In the morning, Doreen put a gold piece in her reticule and went looking for Caroline, who was in her parlor, picking up small mounds of underclothing. "C-Caroline, may I speak to you for a moment?"

Caroline looked up, nodded, then went back to her work.

"I must get Lar—Jim out of here. I'm at the end of my rope. I need help with him. No," she held up a hand to stop an angry outburst from Caroline, "I'm not complaining. You and your girls have done a lot for us. But I need a long break, several hours, and your girls can't afford to give me that." She looked down at her handkerchief, which she was twisting between her hands. "If one of your girls will stay with him while I look for another place, I'll pay her well." Doreen held out the precious gold piece.

Caroline took the coin, studied it, looked at Doreen. "I'll send Eva. She needs the money. She can stay with your husband all day and all night, too, for this price. You go looking. I'll send her up right away."

What was available in town was a room on the second floor of the Frazer Hotel, three blocks away. It was expensive, but none of the boardinghouses had any space and, once people learned they would be coming from the Palace, none of the private homes that might have been open to a "respectable" couple would take them in. Doreen worried about the cost of a hotel room for the months it might take Laramie to recover, *if* he recovered, but it was the hotel or a train trip home. She did not have to ask the doctor what a train trip would do to Laramie.

Once the room was engaged, Dr. Harker arranged to have Laramie carried to the hotel on a litter and stayed to supervise the move. The moment the carriers picked the litter up, Laramie's hands clutched its sides until his knuckles stood out like knobs. Each step down to the first floor and then to the street forced groans or stifled cries of pain from him. He had bitten his lip through before the litter reached the street. The doctor insisted on accompanying them to the hotel in order to "smooth Mrs. Frazer's feathers."

The room at the hotel meant a second set of stairs for the litter-bearers and a hefty tip when they had at last laid Laramie upon the bed in the new room. The room contained the bed, a comfortable-looking rocking chair, a small coal stove, a table and two chairs, a tall wardrobe, a commode beside the bed, and a washstand. Mrs. Frazer was a small, gray, birdlike woman who fluttered about the bed and then about Doreen, twittering about the meals, coal for the stove, the monthly rent, the schedule for the bath down the hall. Dr. Harker put an arm firmly around her shoulders and forced her to hold still and talk more slowly. Doreen was in no position to argue about the rent, but heard with relief that cooking in the room was permitted. That would save a little of the precious funds she had brought with her. The doctor explained Doreen's predicament and although Mrs. Frazer pulled a face at the mention of the Palace, she did not seem to hold the stay there against Doreen. She did insist on a month's rent in advance, however.

Doreen paid her, mentioning how exhausting the day had been, and watched with relief as the doctor took the hint and drew Mrs. Frazer out of the room with

313

him. He turned at the door and winked at Doreen, then shut it quietly behind him. Several minutes later, one of the litter-bearers returned with Laramie's war bag and saddle and the other items the Smiths had left behind at the Palace and collected another, smaller, tip.

Doreen set Laramie's Stetson on the shelf in the wardrobe and stood his boots beside the bed, a small sign of hope that he would eventually sit up and put them on again. She laid his holster in the commode's drawer and carefully cleaned his gun before putting it there, too. She sat in the rocker and looked at her husband's still face, at the scuffed and wrinkled boots that were so strongly his, at the dusty gray hat, the same hat he had jammed on her head to replace her useless bonnet that day so long ago. Even the long black gun . . . But the sight of it stirred the feeling that had whirled through her that day on the target range, a feeling she now recognized as desire, and she resolutely turned her thoughts to managing their lives until Laramie was well again.

The move brought a relapse for Laramie. His fever climbed and he was again restless and only half-aware of what went on around him. On the third day at the hotel, a Mrs. Sutton came by. Mrs. Frazer had invited the ladies of the local church to help Doreen with the nursing. Mrs. Sutton said she would stay for two hours.

The first thing Doreen did was to check with the livery stable about Tennessee. Doreen paid what was owed, extracted a promise that the horse would be brushed and let loose in the small pasture behind the stable, and promised herself to exercise the horse as soon as possible. She stopped next at the post office to see if there were any letters and to rent a postbox. A small stack of letters addressed either to her or to James Grimm was waiting (and one for Laramie Smith, on White House stationery, which she claimed by producing her marriage paper) in the general delivery mail. She scribbled a postcard, giving Bill and Cary the hotel's address, and headed back to the tiny second-floor room.

Mrs. Sutton declined both payment and thanks for her help and said that a Mrs. Penworthy would be coming tomorrow from one to three o'clock. Doreen must have showed her relief and gratitude, for as she went out the door Mrs. Sutton patted Doreen's hand in a motherly fashion and said, "What else is the church for but to help them as needs it?"

Doreen shut the door after her and breathed a brief prayer of thanks for help given and, after checking to see if Laramie needed anything, sat down in the rocker with the letters. She weighed them in her hands a moment, enjoying the size and texture of them. She leafed through them. There was a letter from Blue Mountain, one postmarked Tucson, one from Amelia, and two on White House stationery, both of them forwarded.

She opened the two White House letters first. They were identical on the inside, both from President Hayes's secretary, saying the pardon investigation was almost complete and that the President had received close to twenty letters speaking in Laramie's favor. "This must, of course, have bearing on the pardon consideration," the secretary had concluded. "I have little doubt a pardon will be granted." Doreen let the hands that held the letter fall to her lap, bit her lip, and repressed the urge to cry. Almost. They were almost free. She looked over at her sleeping husband and felt a shattering tenderness. Free. In a few weeks he would be free after all those years of running. If only she could tell him! But he was only vaguely aware of what was happening around him. There was no telling what his nightmares could make of such news if it were only partly understood. The pardon itself had to come. They were not protected from Mattheson or others like him until the pardon was in their hands.

The letter from Cary and Bill asked for news. Only then did Doreen realize that the day's postcard was the first word she had offered them; they did not even know she had arrived safely or, more important to all of them, that Laramie was still alive. Doreen hesitated before opening the letter from Tucson, for it was not her letter, yet it could contain important news and it was, from the postmark, already a month old. Slowly she tore off the end and pulled out the letter. It was from Laramie's friend Tom and the gist of it was that Mattheson had quickly figured out he had been sent on a fool's errand and had come by Tom's place on his way to Texas to tell him in clear and profane terms what he thought of such "obstruction of justice." The letter ended by warning Laramie to be careful.

Doreen looked out the window at the weathered false-front across the street. Sunlight silvered the wood and glinted from clean spots on the dusty windows. A tumbleweed rolled down the street, moving in fits and starts as the wind rose, died, then rose again. Doreen wondered how long it would take Mattheson to track Laramie down. If they were unlucky, if Mattheson caught up before Laramie was well or before the pardon was granted. . . . Her mouth thinned and she touched the gun in her pocket. She would have to defeat

Mattheson somehow. She was not going to let Laramie walk out of her life another time, no matter how noble or reasonable his motives were. Setting the letters on the sill, she rose, dipped a fresh cloth in water, and kissed her husband's cheek before laying the cool cloth on his face.

The next day, after Mrs. Penworthy had settled herself into the rocker and cheerily told Doreen to be off, Doreen took Tennessee out as she had promised herself, riding him on an easy stroll around the outskirts of town, painfully aware of how long he had been neglected and not knowing how much exercise would be too much for him. Afterward, she brushed him down herself, which scandalized the hostler, and returned to the hotel glowing and relaxed. She thanked Mrs. Penworthy as the woman went out the door, glanced quickly at Laramie, who was sleeping quietly, and shed her dusty, smelly clothes. A quick spit bath out of the wash basin, a fresh dress, and she felt energetic and happy. She glanced at Laramie again. He was watching her. She flushed. How long had he been awake?

He slowly held out a hand to her. Doreen went to him and sat gingerly on the bed. Hesitantly, as if he did not quite believe in her presence, Laramie's fingers brushed over her face. He traced her brows, brushed her eyelids closed, caressed her cheeks, rubbed a callused thumb along her lips, held her face between his hands. Then he began the exploration again. Every touch of his roughened fingertips lit in Doreen a tiny flame of joy and desire. He was back. He knew who she was. He wanted her. When he stopped a second time, a hand on either cheek, Doreen was trembling. She wanted him. He was so sick he could hardly move his hands and she

317

wanted him, passionately, desperately, with a wild, consuming joy.

Laramie was watching her face closely. His shaking arms fell to his sides. His eyes dropped to her lips. "Kiss me, Dee," he whispered.

She bent slowly, afraid of what such a kiss would do to her, to him. She held his face between her hands and kissed him, lightly at first, intending only a loving touch, but joy, tenderness, desire, and the feel of his mouth, warm and responsive after so very long, led her deeper and deeper into that kiss, until she at last had to pull away, breathless, her heart fluttering madly. Laramie laughed softly as she straightened, his arms falling away from her.

"Yore eyes! They're so big and dark! Oh, my darlin', how I'd like to love you now." He raised his left hand and tenderly lifted her loosened hair away from her face. "But I hurt too much. Did yore mother tell you how pain or sickness can undo a man?"

Doreen shook her head, too embarrassed to meet his eyes.

"Don't be shy about it, darlin'. We're married people. Out East, maybe, people don't talk about what they want, but that's stupid. Here we do. And I want you. In my head, I want you. My body's not up to it." He chuckled. "Though with another kiss like that, my body might try." He wrapped his left arm around her and she let herself rest blissfully against his chest.

"Darlin', the dreams I've had of you," he murmured after a long, contented silence. He kissed the top of her head, his eyes closed, and drifted back to sleep.

Laramie improved steadily after that. He was able to sit up in bed for short periods, then longer ones. After a week of steady improvement, Doreen could again handle the nursing herself. She thanked the ladies of the church and ended their visits. Laramie only needed help still with the bedpan (which galled him terribly) and with bandage-changing, so Doreen spent much of her mornings reading, either to herself or to Laramie, and afternoons exercising Tennessee. Evenings, after the dinner dishes had been carried down to the hotel kitchen, she mended or knitted, rocking slowly back and forth in the rocking chair. The even rhythm on the wooden floor was very peaceful and domestic. The nights, however, were bad. They had to sleep in the same bed, but Doreen made herself lie apart for fear her desire for him would push Laramie past a safe level of activity. She knew he could not make love to her, with bad wounds in his shoulder and thigh just healing, but she wanted him to. With every breath she drew as she lay beside him she wanted him to.

Soon after he could sit up by himself, Laramie wanted to get up and move around, but Dr. Harker laughed in his face. "You feel real spry, eh, Grimm? You were hurt badly, man. We thought you were gonna die. You're so weak you'll fall over like a cut tree and your wife here won't be able to do a thing about it."

Harker had not been gone an hour when Laramie levered himself into a sitting position and swung his legs carefully over the edge of the bed.

"Larry—" Doreen began, but he shot her a look that silenced her protest.

He sat on the edge of the bed, swaying, for several minutes. Doreen saw the muscles of his back tense and his left fist push into the bed. He managed to lift himself only a few inches off the mattress before he fell flat on his back, his face twisted with pain. He pounded his fist into the bed and swore savagely. "'Cut tree'!" he snarled at last. "I didn't even get *that* far!"

Though the effort made his wounds hurt terribly, he persisted, day after day, in sitting and trying to stand, refusing Doreen's help. "I feel like a cripple," he snapped. "I've never been laid up so long in my life!" His anger was not just injured manly pride; hanging like a ghost in the background was Mattheson.

September was almost gone when Dr. Harker okayed Laramie's attempts to walk. "Just from the bed to that chair—" He nodded toward a side chair Mrs. Frazer was setting beside the window. "You may make the trip as often as you like, but no farther than that this week. You understand me?" His sharp look demanded obedience.

Laramie nodded.

"And only leaning on your wife at first," Harker added. "You've been leaning on her a lot already, so to speak, so don't let pride get in your way."

"Yessir," Laramie said meekly.

The doctor suspected Laramie's innocent expression. "Don't go too fast, Grimm, or you'll be flat on your back again. You can't risk opening either your shoulder wound or the holes in your thigh. And don't look at me like that, Amanda Frazer! These are married people and they know more about each other than most people twice their age. She's been dressing that wound for near a month now!"

Amanda Frazer left the room in a huff. Dr. Harker turned to Doreen. "I didn't embarrass you, did I, ma'am?"

Doreen looked at the tip of her shoe, just peeking

320

out from under her dress, and shook her head. He could not know that her thoughts might have embarrassed him, had he known them. She wanted to touch Laramie, to caress him intimately, to make him want her, and he was still too weak to get out of bed alone.

Over the next two weeks, Laramie's walking progressed slowly, hindered by pain, even after the doctor left a bottle of laudanum to ease it. October brought shorter days and sharper winds. Mail from Wyoming appeared irregularly, and it bore no news of a pardon.

During those weeks of living and sleeping with Laramie, the longing to touch and be touched in love became a driving need Doreen could neither quell nor give in to. Some nights it was so bad she slept in the rocking chair because her hands itched to awaken his desire for her and she was too embarrassed and too afraid of setting his recovery back to tell him how much she wanted him. Her experience with loving had taught her that shoulders and thighs were essential to the process, and Laramie had the use of only half of his.

Conversation began to flag between them. Doreen's suppressed desire often made her cross and she suspected Laramie was experiencing similar frustration, for he pulled away from physical contact and snapped at her when she touched him too personally or too often. But despite his brave words earlier about frankness, he would not talk about it, even though she finally, timidly, edged around the subject several times. Tension hung between them, taut and humming as a telegraph line and it grew worse as Laramie grew stronger. Soon he was walking around the room without pain, though with a pronounced limp. He then tried the stairs, but blacked out from the pain. Only Doreen's sudden grab kept him from falling. Grim-faced, he continued to try the stairs every day, only to be driven back by the agony of putting all his weight, even briefly, on the wounded leg. After each defeat, he retreated to their room and spent most of the remaining daylight hours sitting or standing by the window looking down at the street. Doreen feared he was watching for Mattheson. Deep inside, she knew he was.

On a gray, overcast day, Laramie turned abruptly from his station by the window. "Get Tennessee for me, Dee, and bring him around to the front. I'll get downstairs while you're gone."

Doreen sprang from her chair in alarm, the book and mending in her lap spilling onto the floor unnoticed. "Larry, please, it's too soon."

He would not face her. She stood close beside him, her hand gripping his arm so hard he had to look at her.

"Your leg—you haven't even been able to go downstairs yet. Wait until it's better. That's your *mounting* leg, Larry!"

Laramie tore himself free of her hand and limped over to the door. He jerked it open. "Dammit, woman, don't you think I know that? I'm a rider. I've been a rider all my adult life. I have to get back to it."

Doreen watched him in despair. A wall was up, separating them as surely as if he were in another country. "It's Mattheson, isn't it?" she asked, her voice low and trembling.

Laramie's eyes blazed, hot with anger and something else, something Doreen could not name. "Yes!" The word hissed out. "He's coming here, Dee. Tom's letter said he was coming. I have to be ready."

Doreen stiffened. "Larry, don't even think of leaving

me behind. Not again. The President's secretary says a pardon is almost sure. Don't leave!"

Laramie shut his eyes as if in pain and took a deep, slow breath. "Darlin', I'm not safe until that pardon is in my hands. You're not safe if I'm with you. I can't put yore life on the line. Can't you see that? Don't you know how precious yore life is to me?"

"No," she said stubbornly, "I don't know. You talk to me about nothing but commonplaces. We sleep together and I might as well be sleeping with my sister! Dammit yourself, Laramie Smith! You're my husband. Larry, please—"

"Gawd, Dee, don't look at me like that!" His voice was anguished. "You make me want you so badly." His unsteady hand caressed her face, then he turned resolutely away. "Get me my horse, Dee."

She stood where she was.

"Dee, please." His voice was muffled and hard to hear. One hand clung hard to the door edge. "If you don't get him, I'll have to."

Doreen hesitated only a moment more, then, with a sob, she whirled and ran out of the room.

CHAPTER

20

W HEN DOREEN RETURNED to the hotel with Tennessee, Laramie was standing beside one of the porch supports, his hands clenched around the wood post, his face white and beaded with sweat, his teeth set.

"Larry!" Doreen whispered. She dropped Tennessee's reins and took a quick step toward her husband before she remembered herself and stopped. She would not shame him in front of passersby. "Jim," she said aloud, "shall I take him back?"

Laramie shook his head. "Bring him closer," he said hoarsely.

Tennessee whuffled and pawed the street, but he did not move from his spot, though he kept his eyes on his master, until Doreen picked up the reins. Slowly Laramie took one hand from the post and caressed the horse's muzzle.

"It's been a long time, boy." He let his hand linger, then nodded to Doreen. She could take him back.

"L—Jim," she said urgently, for his ears only. "Wait. Let me help you back to the room."

"I—can't, darlin'. I have to get back on my own. It's a matter of pride, darlin'." He looked from Tennessee to Doreen, and she knew that if they had been in private, he would have touched her. He smiled faintly. "You're more than I deserve. Take him back, darlin'."

She returned Tennessee, then walked back to the hotel slowly, to give Laramie time to get back to the room and recover himself. But he had gotten only as far as the foot of the stairs. He stiffened when she came up behind him. She touched him lightly, encouragingly, until the tension in his shoulders lessened and his breathing became less harsh.

"Let me help you?" she asked softly. "There *are* people in the lobby, but everyone here knows what happened to you. It's a wonder you're still alive. Everyone knows that, too. It's no shame to take my help—Jim."

Laramie nodded grimly and put his left arm over her shoulders. Doreen half assisted, half carried him back to their room. Laramie let himself carefully down onto the bed and lay flat. "You're the reason I'm still alive," he said, as if to himself. "I waited for you," he said, a little louder. "I think I would've waited until the Devil himself came for me, and he'd've had to drag me away. I love you more than I can ever tell you, darlin'." He looked up at her and the love he had no words for was in his eyes.

"Jim," Doreen whispered.

Laramie grinned crookedly. "'Jim.' I always thought that was what I wanted most to have you call me and now, when you have to, I learn 'Larry' is what I want to be to you. It's the name you used when we were riding together and that night I came to you . . ." His voice died away.

"Larry, I love you." She kissed him, quickly, and walked away from the bed again, before temptation could destroy their delicate balance.

Doreen haunted the post office, checking their box for mail two or three times a day, knowing her fear of the hunter was making her behave irrationally but unable to stop herself. On such a trip, late in the afternoon with the sun red on the horizon and the wind off the prairies sharp and cold, Doreen was almost to the post office door when she saw a familiar face coming toward her down the sidewalk. She spun away so her back was to him and slipped immediately into the nearest store.

"Mattheson!" she whispered, standing among the dry goods and flour sacks. "If he sees me, he'll know Larry's here."

She edged toward the dusty display window and looked out. Mattheson disappeared into the post office. She stood for a moment, debating whether to go immediately to the hotel, to take the letter from President Hayes's secretary to the town marshal, or to stay hidden in the shadowy store until Mattheson moved on.

If I say nothing, I won't draw the marshal's attention to Laramie, Doreen told herself. He can't protect Laramie from Mattheson without a pardon, anyway. Doreen looked blindly out at the sunlit street for a moment, struggling with fear that threatened to stop her ability to think altogether. She clenched her teeth and forced the fear to retreat deep inside her. She took a deep, unsteady breath and took up her train of thought.

If I don't talk to the marshal, all Mattheson has to do is ask him about Laramie. That won't protect us much, because everyone in town knows about the shooting, but the marshal is a powerful man. Maybe . . . Doreen took another deep breath. I have to talk to him. Maybe I can at least persuade him not to help Mattheson.

Doreen watched the street surreptitiously through the dusty window. Mattheson came out of the post office and walked briskly toward Texas Street. Doreen felt some of the tension drain from her muscles. He's going to the saloons, she thought in relief. The post office, then Texas Street. He must just have hit town.

Then she remembered the jail, where she was likely to find the marshal, was also on Texas Street. She shut her eyes for a moment, overwhelmed by terror. Texas Street. The most infamous street in a town full of infamous streets. Lessons from years past, lessons on how a lady suppresses any public display of emotion, eventually helped Doreen pull herself together and go to the marshal.

The sun had set and Texas Street was coming to life. Pianos tinkled. Raucous male laughter and the shrill giggles of females came out one saloon door. A lurching, vomiting drunk came out of another, right across Doreen's path. Five cowboys on dusty horses came charging down the street, whooping, and snapping their quirts against their leather chaps. Doreen shrank back against the nearest building. It was too much. She could not do it. Then she thought of Laramie, unable to ride, unable even to climb stairs normally, and still weak from his long illness. He would have no chance against a healthy and vengeful Mattheson.

I'm his only hope, she told herself tartly.

The cowboys passed in a cloud of dust and slid to a halt at the hitching rail of a saloon down the street. One of them spotted her and shouted. Doreen kept walking, always with an eye for Mattheson. A middle-aged drover wavered on the edge of the walk, watching her. Doreen felt like a mouse in a street full of cats. Then the marshal loomed ahead of her. He stopped, blocking the way.

"Lost your way, ma'am?"

Doreen looked up at him, suddenly speechless. Safety. For her. Maybe for Laramie.

"No, sir," she managed to get out, "I came looking for you."

The marshal lifted one eyebrow questioningly.

"I—I have a problem. That is, my husband and I have a problem."

The marshal continued to watch her with polite and wary interest.

"I'm Doreen Smith. My husband was shot here some months ago. He—" Doreen looked down at the tips of her boots and swallowed, then looked up at the marshal again. "He's calling himself James Grimm, Marshal, because he's got a bounty hunter on his trail and the hunter's in town and J—Larry's still too weak to protect himself." Doreen could see the man's face closing against her. In desperation, she put a hand on his arm to bring his attention back. "Larry's wanted in the States for something he did during the war, something that was a crime only because he was on the wrong side. And he's being pardoned for it, only the pardon hasn't arrived yet and the bounty hunter has. Here." Doreen dug into her purse and pulled out the White House letter. She handed it to the marshal, who read it quickly.

"Kansas is 'the States,' you know, Mrs. Smith," he remarked.

Doreen reached out a hand, but there was nothing to hold onto. The rustle of the letter falling was the last thing Doreen heard before the world disappeared.

When she became aware of her surroundings again, she was being held upright, rather stiffly, by the marshal. She still felt nauseous and consciousness flickered.

I've betrayed him, she thought. I try to save him and instead— In spite of herself, she began to cry.

The marshal held her away from him but kept a strong grip on her arms. He turned so that his back was against the wall of the nearest building. "Take it easy. I didn't mean to frighten you. You haven't betrayed him," he said urgently.

His tone penetrated the fog in Doreen's mind. She had not realized she had spoken her thought aloud. She looked mutely up at him, her tears blurring the expression on his face.

"I didn't mean to give you such a shock, Mrs. Smith," he said in a milder voice. "I only meant to bring the fact that Kansas is a state to your attention. I'm no federal officer. Your man's safe from me as long as he stays out of trouble. If you can stand now, I can look at that letter again." He nodded with his head toward the folded paper lying on the dusty sidewalk.

"I—I can stand."

The marshal picked up the letter, shook the dust off,

unfolded it, and read through it slowly. "Twenty letters of support, huh?" His mouth twisted thoughtfully. "What do you want me to do, Mrs. Smith?"

Doreen's hands clenched. Hope rose. "The bounty hunter's name's Mattheson. I saw him just a little while ago. He's been following my husband for years."

"Shot, you say," the marshal interrupted. "Here?"

"Yes, sir. He followed a man named Bekkerson down here, a cattle thief and gambler and the leader of a rustler gang back in Wyoming. Larry promised to get him and he did, but he almost died doing it."

The marshal's mouth twisted in thought. He was quiet for a time. "I remember now," he finally said, slowly. "Back in July. At the Bull. Caroline Evans was involved, too, somehow."

"She kept Larry alive."

"I can't do anything to Mattheson unless he makes trouble here. You know that, don't you?"

Doreen nodded. "I wasn't going to ask you to. I only ask you not to tell him Larry's still in town."

"He can find out elsewhere."

"I know. But he may come to you first."

The marshal nodded. "All right. That's easy enough."

Doreen went limp with relief. "Thank you, sir," she murmured. "Thank you more than I can ever say."

The marshal smiled a little. "When you get that pardon, ma'am, you bring it straight to me, you hear? Even before you take it to that husband of yours."

Doreen nodded, wordless with the effort of keeping her fear from showing. She and Laramie were on their own until the pardon arrived. If it arrived.

The marshal escorted Doreen out of the red-light

district and watched her until she reached the corner where she turned to go to the hotel. Doreen did not mention the incident to Laramie, but after he had dropped off to sleep that night, she got out his gun and hers, cleaning them and checking their loads.

Doreen stayed in the hotel most of the next day, afraid Mattheson might come looking for Laramie while she was gone, afraid she might meet him on the street if she left. But she had to go out. If she did not, they would be two days without mail. She fretted. She snarled at Laramie when he asked what was the matter. She paced. She took up her knitting and put it down for a book, then put that aside to go downstairs to look for a magazine or newspaper, then came upstairs and began pacing again.

Laramie, who was sitting beside the window alternately looking out and reading, watched her for several minutes. "Somethin's eatin' you. Out with it."

"It's the pardon. It hasn't come."

"You haven't been out today to look. Go. Look."

The sharp impatience in Laramie's voice set Doreen's back up. She opened her mouth to tell him why she had not been out, then shut it. If he knew Mattheson was in town, he would be on his way out of town, probably without her, as soon as he could throw his possessions in his war bag and hobble down the stairs. "I'll just do that," she snapped, and marched out of the room.

She paused in the hall, nerving herself for the risk of the walk. It does no good to stand and worry, silly, she scolded herself. You just be very careful not to be seen.

Doreen followed her own advice. She looked carefully at the street before she stepped out onto the hotel porch. It was the quiet time in late afternoon, when the new drovers had already arrived and settled wherever they were going to settle for the day and evening and the nightlife, which started up after supper, had not yet begun. She walked carefully, her eyes constantly watching passersby on both sides of the street, alert for Mattheson's face and broad body. She looked around each corner before she turned it. She reached the post office safely and there were letters in the box. Doreen spun the combination, pulled out the envelopes, and fanned them in her hands. The center one bore the White House seal and frank. Her hands began to tremble. She ripped the end from the envelope and pulled out the heavy sheet inside.

She read the paper, then read it again. She touched the presidential seal with a hesitant finger. The whole world seemed to light up.

"He's free," she whispered. "He's free!" she said louder. She wanted to shout the good news. But there was still Mattheson. She had to show the pardon to the marshal immediately.

She came close to running to the jail. The wait until the marshal finished his beat and returned seemed interminable. Then it was done. The marshal knew Laramie was pardoned. Doreen felt light with joy. They were free. They could go home now and manage the ranch and raise a family without the specter of pursuit always lurking in the background.

Giddy with happiness, Doreen swerved into the local dressmaker's shop to see if the proprietress had, perhaps, a tempting nightgown in her stock. Half an hour later Doreen emerged again with a nightgown of the palest pink trimmed in ruffles and gathers, all wrapped securely in a brown paper parcel. She would have the luxury of supper sent up, early, then— Her cheeks grew hot thinking of what she would do then. If the nightgown itself was not enough to persuade Laramie to do his husbandly duty—

She looked toward their hotel window. Was Laramie sitting there, watching the street? Doreen waved to attract his attention, then bounced up and down in a most unladylike fashion, waving, pointing to the paper she carried unfolded in her hand, then hurried toward the hotel. If he had been watching, if he had been watching he would be waiting, or perhaps standing at the top of the stairs, guessing the news, hoping, at the least, that the pardon had come. Home and loving and children were now possible for them. Lost in joy, Doreen did not hear the heavy thump of boots behind her until she was crossing the hotel porch. By then it was too late. A large hand grasped her arm and turned her around right at the door.

"Unhand me—" she began, twisting and tugging to get free, and then she looked up. She froze. "You!" she breathed.

"Me." Mattheson grinned maliciously. "And you're just the person I'm looking for." He twisted her arm behind her back and clamped his other hand over her mouth. "I wouldn't want you to scream and warn him," he told her conversationally. "Can't have him getting the drop on me after all these years. You're my key to your room, Mrs. Smith. Your husband *is* James Lawrence Smith, by the way, no matter what he told you. Or did you know all along?" Mattheson shoved Doreen through the door and into the thinly populated lobby. "Your husband has run the last time, Mrs. Smith." To

333

the handful of residents reading or conversing in the lobby he said curtly, "Out. I'm taking James Lawrence Smith, alias James Grimm, alias Laramie Smith, out of here and there may be gunplay."

In moments, Doreen and Mattheson and the trembling desk clerk were the only people left in the room. Doreen stared at the clerk, her mind numb with shock, her vision a narrow tunnel focused on the clerk's white, sweating face and terrified eyes. The young man ran a finger under his high starched collar and his Adam's apple bobbed convulsively. His eyes flicked from Mattheson to the cashbox to Mattheson again, torn between duty and danger.

Doreen's heart pounded as if to choke her and she went hot and cold by turns. *Laramie. I'm to be bait in a trap for Laramie, just as he feared. Think, Doreen! Don't let this killer scare you witless. You don't have to be afraid anymore. Larry doesn't. You're acting on reflex. He's pardoned!*

Doreen twisted her head from side to side and back again, trying to escape the stifling hand. When that did not work, she bit the imprisoning fingers hard. Mattheson jerked upward on the arm he held, making her gasp with pain.

"Try that again and I'll break your arm," he snarled.

"Take yore paws off my wife!" The low, intense drawl was accompanied by the *snick* of a hammer drawn back.

Mattheson tensed and spun toward the stair, forcing Doreen to turn with him. Laramie was coming slowly, painfully down, the long black barrel of his revolver pointed at Mattheson's head.

"Let her go, Mattheson. It's me you want. Leave my wife out of this."

"How do I know you won't shoot me the moment I let her go?"

"You know me better than that, Mattheson. I don't shoot people, as a general rule. But I'll shoot you if you so much as make her whimper again. Let her go and I'll put my gun down and go with you quietly."

Doreen struggled against the imprisoning hands and shook her head, but the two men were so intent on each other that Laramie did not notice her denial. He kept descending, his slowness suggesting caution to anyone who did not know it was caused by lancing pain.

"Why should I believe you?" Mattheson's hands seemed to be loosening a fraction.

"Because yore brains'll be spread all over this room if you don't." Laramie's voice was hard. Mattheson's hands tightened again. Laramie went on, "She has no part in what's between you an' me. I don't want her to see what happens when a bullet goes through a head."

"Hand me the gun and I'll let her go."

"Not a chance, mister. The gun stays here, on the stair."

Mattheson chuckled dryly. "I'll agree to that. You won't be needing guns where you're going."

Laramie bent to set his gun on the stair but did not move away from it. "Set her free, Mattheson." He looked at Doreen. "When he does, darlin', run!" Laramie stepped away from his gun, his hands out, open and away from his sides. Vulnerable. Defenseless. And he was doing it to protect her.

Mattheson chuckled again and Doreen knew, as surely as if he had said it, that Laramie would not live for more than a few seconds after she was released. She looked at Laramie. He knew it, too. Mattheson had hunted him too long. Perhaps the hotel clerk had the same impression, for there was a flurry of movement and the terrified man bolted. He was out the door in a flash, yelling, "Marshal! Marshal!" at the top of his lungs. Mattheson's attention wavered for a moment; Doreen could feel part of him following the screaming clerk, weighing the danger from the attention and the marshal, and she took advantage. She bit down hard on Mattheson's hand, rammed her free elbow into his belly, and stamped viciously at his arch. He released her, swearing, and jerked for his gun.

"No!" she cried. "He's pardoned!" shaking the pardon so the stiff parchment rattled.

Laramie threw himself sideways, grabbed his gun, and rolled. Mattheson fired. Doreen yanked her gun from her pocket, aimed carefully, took a deep, steadying breath, and shot a hole in Mattheson's gun hand. His gun fell from nerveless fingers. He turned and stared at Doreen with hate in his eyes.

"I told you he was pardoned," Doreen said coldly, forcing her mind away from the blood dripping onto the carpet. "I told you he'd been pardoned and you tried to kill him anyway." She looked toward the stairway. Laramie still lay on the floor, rigid, pale, sweating, his eyes dilated with pain, his gun trained on Mattheson's belly. "Larry! Are you all right?"

"No," he grated, "but I'll feel a lot better soon as this skunk's taken care of."

They waited several minutes for the marshal, both guns steady on Mattheson. When the marshal leaped onto the porch, gun drawn, Doreen turned away from the hunter and gripped the edge of the hotel desk as if her sanity depended on it. She looked at the little gun. It rattled against the battered oak with the shaking of her hand. She released it and pressed her hands flat against the wood to make them be still. Dimly she heard the marshal question Laramie and the clerk, then she heard two sets of booted feet leave the hotel. All that happened in another place, another time. No, that was not true. She had done the unthinkable. She had shot a man.

What has this country done to me? she moaned to the invisible censors in her mind.

This country taught you how to save your husband's life, was the answer. Your husband taught you. And he's truly yours now. He won't be going away again.

Laramie. Home. Laramie would never have to run again. She looked toward Laramie. He was hauling himself to his feet with the aid of the newel post. He stood at last, wavering on unsteady legs, shiny with sweat.

"It's true, darlin'? What you said is true?" His voice was little more than a whisper.

Doreen crossed the small space between them. "You're pardoned, Larry. You're free. Truly." She held the parchment toward him. "Signed by the President himself."

Laramie took the extended paper unbelievingly. He read it. He read it again. "After all these years," he breathed. "Free."

"In a way," Doreen said softly. She stepped close enough to put her hands on his arms. "You're not free of me. Never of me."

Laramie released the newel post with one hand, which he placed over one of hers. "Never. Help me upstairs, darlin'."

Once upstairs with the door closed and bolted, Laramie stripped off his gunbelt, eased himself to a seat on the bed, then pulled Doreen in his arms, wrapped her crushingly close, and buried his face in her hair.

"Darlin'," he breathed. "You're safe. I saw you wavin' and dancin' and was comin' to see what had happened and I looked down on the worst of my nightmares. He had you."

"Hush," Doreen whispered. She smoothed the wayward lock of hair off his forehead. "It's over. It's over forever. You can come manage Three Rivers for me and help me raise a bunch of kids—"

"Dee, I can't ride. I can't walk right. Maybe I never will—"

Doreen pressed closer and lifted her face to him. "Are you trying to talk me out of keeping you? It won't work. I want you. For always. In whatever shape you happen to be in. Your eyes that crinkle up when you laugh, and your laugh, and your drawl and the way you make me feel when I'm near you. It doesn't matter if you can't make a living on a horse anymore and you don't know yet that you can't. A ranch manager doesn't have to. If the awful things I said before, the awful things I believed about you are holding you back, forgive me, please. I'll make it up to you."

Laramie stretched out a trembling hand and gingerly touched Doreen's hair. His voice was rough with feeling. "You have nothing to make up. I'm alive because of you. I'm pardoned. We're even." The hand on her hair slid to the back of her neck and brought her to

338

his mouth. His kiss was fire and pain and joy all at once. He pulled her closer and lay down, taking her with him, and the kiss went on, searing her, branding her his. His mouth slid to her cheek, the hollow behind her ear. He crushed her closer still and buried his face in her hair.

"Dee," he groaned, "Dee, darlin'. I thought I had to give you up, go with Mattheson, for your safety, and it was like tearing out my heart."

Then his mouth was on hers again, moving against her lips, exciting her almost beyond bearing. His hand slid along her side and cupped her breast. She made a little sound of pleasure. It had been so long, so long! His kiss deepened and he began unbuttoning her shirtwaist.

Much later, Laramie rolled away long enough to light the lamp, then pulled Doreen back against his damp, bare chest. He rubbed his cheek against the top of her head. "Love of my life, you fit in my arms so well! I dreamed of holding you, loving you, until I nearly went loco. I want to marry you again, a real marriage this time, that second marriage I talked to you about once, remember?"

Doreen nodded, her hair brushing against his chest.

"Are you sure you want to tie yourself to me?"

Doreen thought she heard anxiety in his tone, or disbelief. "I'm roped, tied, and branded," she whispered against his shoulder. "I'd want you if you couldn't walk at all. Or talk, either." She propped herself up on one elbow and looked down at him. He was grinning at her last remark. She traced one of his brows with a gentle, possessive finger.

Laramie kissed her tenderly, his face softened with loving, then he kissed her again, passion stirring for a moment. He laughed softly. "You've turned my life

339

upside down, you know that? I'm alive, which wasn't in my plans, and married, which wasn't, either, and wondering how I ever could've made such plans." He hugged her suddenly, with rib-snapping force. "Dee, darlin', you don't know the hell I went through, lovin' you, wantin' you, wantin' to live, and knowin' I was goin' to die."

Doreen shuddered, remembering how close to dying he had been. "Don't think of that. Remember the good times—the barn dance, our rides together, the shooting lesson"—she looked at him and laughed at the wicked glint in his eye—"and the last night we made love."

Laramie looked at her intently. "You *want* to remember that?"

Doreen blushed and hid her face against his chest. "It could have been so awful. I'd thrown my accusations in your face, you wanted to hurt me, and yet you were gentle with me. You tied me to you forever with that."

"Darlin'," he whispered.

They lay tangled with each other for a long time, absorbing the pleasures of touching and the wonder of being loved. Doreen stirred sleepily.

"Turn out the light, Larry."

"I want to see you there, darlin'. It's still hard for me to believe I don't have to leave you to keep you safe."

"You're safe. I can show you the pardon again if you want."

Laramie gave a sigh of pure happiness. "Lord, but it'll be good to go where I please without lookin' over my shoulder all the time."

Doreen pulled away to look at him, mock severely.

"Going where you please? Don't you think you're taking a bit for granted? I own the place, remember."

Laramie chuckled. "You're reading me wrong, darlin'. I meant, I'm goin' to have a home for the first time in a lot of years and it's good I won't have to be watching my back trail all the time. As for goin' where I please, well, if I can live on my wife's money on her ranch, my wife can live with an uppity, sometimes, manager." Laramie nuzzled behind Doreen's ear. "I did hear you say I could manage Three Rivers Ranch if I wanted to, didn't I?"

Doreen wriggled away. "Well, I don't know . . ."

Laramie caught her, pulled her close, and kissed her until they were both flushed and panting. "Manager?"

"Manager," she sighed, and began to touch her husband in a thoroughly wanton manner.